# Return to Faith

Otis Farmer
Copyright © 2020

All rights reserved.

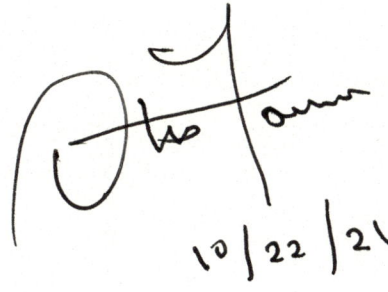

10/22/21

ALSO AUTHOR OF
MERLYN AND THE MORTAL'S CURSE
DEFIANT VICTIM

# DEDICATION

To Nancy Blair, Nita Blair, and Bob Blair who believed in the story and me. May the Lord bless you accordingly. In addition, thank you Nita and Bob for your valuable cover suggestions.

COPYRIGHT © 2020 OTIS FARMER ALL RIGHTS RESERVED

ISBN: 9798640318340
ASIN: B087LWB5TK

THE CHARACTERS AND EVENTS PORTRAYED IN THIS BOOK ARE FICTITIOUS. ANY SIMILARITY TO REAL PERSONS, LIVING OR DEAD, IS COINCIDENTAL AND NOT INTENDED BY THE AUTHOR.

NO PART OF THIS BOOK MAY BE REPRODUCED, OR STORED IN A RETRIEVAL SYSTEM, OR TRANSMITTED IN ANY FORM OR BY ANY MEANS, ELECTRONIC, MECHANICAL, PHOTOCOPYING, RECORDING, OR OTHERWISE, WITHOUT EXPRESS WRITTEN PERMISSION OF THE PUBLISHER.

COVER DESIGN BY: OTIS FARMER

# CONTENTS

| | | |
|---|---|---|
| 1 | Haunted By The Past | Pg # 1 |
| 2 | The Day Of Reckoning | Pg # 5 |
| 3 | The Final Sermon | Pg # 9 |
| 4 | The Not So Great Escape | Pg # 14 |
| 5 | When Even Having No Plan Fails | Pg # 26 |
| 6 | Forced To Leave The Past Behind | Pg # 35 |
| 7 | When Past Becomes Both Present And Future | Pg # 42 |
| 8 | The Mystery Deepens | Pg # 51 |
| 9 | No Answers In The Light Of Day | Pg # 57 |
| 10 | Is Truth Absolute? | Pg # 66 |
| 11 | By Accident, Or Divine Intervention? | Pg # 75 |
| 12 | When The Time Is Right | Pg # 82 |
| 13 | One Step Closer To Nowhere | Pg # 92 |
| 14 | When Reality Collides With Duality | Pg # 99 |
| 15 | The Best Step Back Might Be To Walk Farther Away | Pg # 108 |
| 16 | The First Steps Back Can Be The Worst Steps Forward | Pg # 118 |
| 17 | When The Tide Rolls in Be Ready To Put To Sea | Pg # 130 |

| | | |
|---|---|---|
| 18 | Life Is Precious But Oh So Fragile | Pg # 141 |
| 19 | When God Moves It's Not Fate, It's His Will | Pg # 150 |
| 20 | The Time Was Right To Learn The Whole Truth | Pg # 164 |
| 21 | When The Path Ahead Is Divine, Not Random | Pg # 172 |
| 22 | When God Communicates, It's Often Without Words | Pg # 184 |
| 23 | Do The Right Thing, Even If It Feels Wrong | Pg # 196 |
| 24 | It's Hard To Do The Right Thing, When It Feels So Wrong | Pg # 203 |
| 25 | The First Step Of True Faith Must Be Taken Blindly | Pg # 212 |
| 26 | Let The Payback Begin | Pg # 217 |
| 27 | That Feeling When A Plan Starts Coming Together | Pg # 228 |
| 28 | A Change Of Directions Doesn't Mean A Change Of Plans | Pg # 241 |
| 29 | When The Time Is Right, The Right Things Will Happen | Pg # 249 |
| 30 | Sometimes God Works In Very Overt Ways | Pg # 261 |
| 31 | When The End Is Only The Beginning | Pg # 274 |

# ACKNOWLEDGMENTS

Once again, two usual suspects lingered in the shadows and played vital roles in the development and fine tuning of "Return to Faith."

Thank you so much to my father, Jack Farmer, who once again loaned his "eagle ears" and patiently listened to me read important passages over the phone. There were a few times he said, "Son, I'm not sure exactly what you mean." In all honesty, once I heard the words out loud, I wasn't sure either.

Then there's Marge Blair, my friend and editor, who would read chapters and do some work ahead. Then we would spend hours on the phone reading every word, every line and every paragraph of every page so I could hear the story unfold. We will never agree 100% of the time on every word, mark of punctuation, or sentence structure. Yet when we reached the end, we agreed 100% that was the best we could do on that pass.

Even though "Return to Faith" is a fictitious story, the Charlie Webster character is based on a real person who has remained a close and dear friend since high school. The "real guy" is Charles Riehs, who owns the real Sunshine Racing & Auto Repair in High Point, North Carolina. Sometimes you have to give a shout out to a person who has made a tremendous difference in the lives of so many people.

# Prologue

The will to continue was long gone. It didn't happen overnight. Life had a cruel progression that was often wickedly subtle. Seconds ticked. Far too easily seconds equaled minutes that added up into hours of self-loathing. Compounded with remorse, the grueling hours labored into debilitating days that became endless weeks that rolled into mind-numbing months. It was hard to believe that afternoon was the tenth anniversary of the most horrific day of his life. The day he became a killer.

The hollow eyes and hard face of the man who stared back at Cal was decades older than they should've been. The years hadn't been kind to the man who loathed the haggard man who stood on the other side of the steamy mirror.

The thought crossed his mind again. If only the space-age, five-bladed razor in his hand were an old-fashioned straight razor. On that morning, Cal just might have the courage to slit his own throat. The only problem, he wasn't ready to stand face-to-face with the mysterious entity he used to consider his Maker.

He wasn't worried what God would say to him, but what he would say to God.

# 1
# Haunted By The Past

Cal placed the razor into the pool of warm water in the sink. There was no way to predict when or why the unnerving flashbacks would occur. The intensity was always unbearable. Cruelest of all, they were very real. The flashback would begin the last few moments Cal and Annie were in their home together with their infant daughter, Taylor.

It didn't matter how good Annie felt, or out of sorts she might be on any given day, at any second Cal could make her giggle like a little school girl.

"The problem is you're actually serious." Annie shook her head because as much as she didn't want to go out in public on such short notice, she knew she would soon walk out the door.

Cal was mid-30's, ruggedly handsome, average height and build. He flashed his famously disarming "boyish" grin, then tilted his head as if to innocently beg.

Annie had been the only girl for Cal since they met in kindergarten. His father always said, "Annie's cute as a speckled pup." That never mattered to Cal as they grew up. It was just natural that Annie blossomed into a gorgeous woman, whom many encouraged to become a model. That never happened because Annie had no desire to look good for anyone but Cal.

However, at that moment, Annie's hair was mussed and lovingly cradled in her arms was their eight-month-old daughter, Taylor.

"But Taylor and I just woke from a nap."

Cal held up a baseball hat and raised his eyebrows.

"But I don't have on any makeup."

"Don't need any."

"Not for you because you're foolishly blinded by love."

"And?"

## OTIS FARMER

Annie struggled for a second, then presented her best counter offer, "I have a great idea. You pick'm up, and when you get back, your two favorite girls'll be dolled up and ready for their milkshakes."

Cal was relentless, "I have a better idea. It's a beautiful day, and I want to share it with my two favorite girls." He playfully placed the hat backward on Annie's head and kissed her on the forehead.

"But what if we run into members of the church?"

"They don't give the death penalty to preachers' wives caught in public wearing a baseball hat." Annie's eyes turned up. "Even backward." He clarified.

Annie shook her head as she reached up and turned the bill forward. She and Cal shared a warm, loving look. That was the moment they knew that deep down they both really wanted to go out and enjoy the afternoon together with their baby girl.

It was an unusually warm spring day, given how cold early April could be in North Carolina. The windows were down. Annie smiled broadly in the back seat, her hand resting on Taylor's car seat.

Annie's hair blew whimsically as she enjoyed the drive. She watched adoringly as Cal focused on the road ahead. She turned to check on Taylor, who was wide awake and appeared to eagerly absorb the new sights and sounds of the adventure. Annie was the luckiest woman in the world.

Ever since Cal got his license at sixteen, he had been the safest, most conscientious driver Annie had ever known. She had comfortably slept on many long drives they'd made over the years. On that day they would be out for two or three hours at most. Then they would be back home where Cal would settle into the parsonage's cozy office to continue work on Sunday's message.

Annie's late afternoon and evening would be dedicated to living her dream. Taylor was comfortable in the swing that was strategically positioned in the middle of the kitchen, which had an impressive laundry room attached. It was a carefully choreographed routine where Annie would carry out the chores she genuinely relished as a mother, wife, housekeeper, head chef, and "laundry maven extraordinaire." Sometimes Taylor was very interested and watched her mother intently. Most often she either slept or kept herself entertained with the colorful attachments on the swing that turned, clicked, squeaked or rattled.

As long as Annie and Cal could comfortably manage financially, they were determined she would remain a full-time Mom and Pastor's Wife, which was a full-time job. Cal was always eager to help, but most often Annie "shooed" him away. "You go do that preacher man stuff you do so well."

On that fateful afternoon, Cal and Annie had decided to drink their milkshakes as they casually walked and pushed Taylor in her stroller along on the path in the little park near the library. On the way back home, Cal glanced at the digital clock on the dash of the Toyota Avalon. It was exactly 4:15 PM, Eastern Standard Time. They approached the same intersection they'd crossed countless times. It was on a winding road that swung out into the country before it lazily meandered back toward the parsonage. It was perfect for a short, scenic distraction. The light ahead was green for the Baxter's lane.

In a relaxed split second, Cal innocently yielded to the temptation to take one more adoring glance in the rearview mirror, where he saw his two favorite girls smiling. Taylor seemed to follow her mother's lead and she waved at the twinkling eyes looking back at them on the rearview mirror.

In that split second two drivers were innocently distracted. The other driver was behind the wheel of a fully loaded tractor trailer. The driver was lost and looked down at the map on his phone at the worst possible second. Already behind schedule, he traveled well above the posted speed limit on the unfamiliar road when he barreled around the gradual blind curve, fifty yards from the red light ahead. By the time he looked up it was too late to even stomp on the brake pedal.

The impact was brutal. Mercy completely abandoned Cal as he remained alert and heard the thunderous shredding and ripping of metal. The force of the impact severed the back half of the car from behind the driver's seat. After three complete and violent revolutions, Cal had a clear view of smoke rolling off most of the eighteen wheels on the semi-truck and trailer. The back half of his Toyota Avalon had been crushed and wedged under the truck between the front and rear tires. He would never be able to forget the hellish sound of metal scraping against the pavement.

Cal's precious Annie, and Taylor died instantly. In reality, three souls left Earth at that accident scene. Two were blasted from lifeless bodies, but the third soul abandoned the guilty husband and father who insisted his wife and daughter go out for a casual drive and a milkshake. Even though Cal wasn't at fault, he would never forgive himself.

The remorseful truck driver walked away without a scratch. The prosecutor made the decision to charge him with negligent vehicular homicide, but the judge reduced the charge to negligent vehicular manslaughter. The man would never drive another commercial vehicle. But he still had his wife and three children.

Then the unholy flashback mercifully ended, but not without inflicting additional damage. Cal had even more contempt for the man who stared back at him in the mirror.

It was a struggle to finish shaving, then shower and put on his neatly pressed black suit for the last time. During the long shower he accepted the inevitable. It was time to put an end to the slow death he had endured the last ten years.

······

# 2
# The Day Of Reckoning

Cal's fingers trembled as he lifted the ten-year-old photo from its place of honor on the dresser. That photo was taken on Annie's and Taylor's last day on Earth. Annie beamed as she snuggled with Taylor.

For multiple weeks at a time the photo would lay face down. Especially for the last three weeks. More times than not he beat himself up for the lost years he'd endured without them. Survivor's Guilt was a very real and evil master.

The photo was respectfully placed face down, even though he loved to fondly gaze at the image and relish the amazing memories. Now it was to protect his favorite girls from being witness to the unthinkable acts he must carry out over the next couple of hours.

There was no need to delay. He'd spent the last week packing up and moving his belongings to the temporary storage unit. The fully furnished Tabernacle Baptist Church parsonage was ready for its next occupants.

The keys to the storage unit would soon be in the hands of the one person he trusted to handle everything, once he was gone. For a man who had raced at light-speed well beyond the point of no return, he found comfort in the one decision he was certain he had gotten right. Gabby was the perfect person, the only person he could trust to tie up the loose ends.

Traffic was unusually light that mid-Sunday morning. Cal's sad eyes were laser-focused on the road. He was on autopilot as he navigated the moderate traffic. He would be early, more than likely the first car in the lot. Over the ten-year, slow-motion downfall of their pastor, membership dropped dramatically. The decision was made about this time last year to discontinue Sunday School classes.

The three-year-old Toyota Avalon's tires crackled even louder on the empty, crumbling asphalt lot. He pressed the brake pedal once he was safely off the street.

The aqua sky was crystal clear. The quiet street was lined with green trees and rows of average, well-maintained houses. He'd driven up and down that street countless times.

In the beginning, as an eager new pastor with his charming wife by his side, Cal and Annie knocked on every door in a three-block radius of the church property. That successful campaign fueled both doublings of the congregation. Young couples with elementary school-aged children were drawn to the enthusiastic and dedicated pastor, who had a great sense of humor. New programs for all ages were quickly started, flourished and rapidly grew.

The first two years after Annie's and Taylor's deaths, and due to several families moving away, the congregation only experienced a slight decrease in average of each service. The overwhelming majority of the church members went out of their way to remain compassionate, understanding and supportive. It was the Christian way. Until quite unexpectedly, one day the dam burst. What appeared to have been a bottomless reservoir of support, understanding, and compassion dried up overnight.

Cal became so consumed with battling his own demons that he never realized he no longer grasped his congregation's needs. Their shepherd had remained in the midst of his flock, but was deaf, dumb and blind to the evil forces determined to rip the lives of the once tight-knit church family apart on a daily basis. Too many calls were never returned, and Cal was mostly disconnected during most face-to-face counseling sessions.

At first, the entire church rallied around Cal. He couldn't have asked for more love and support.

The last few years were brutal, and all that remained of the once thriving multi-generational church body were the surviving members of the hardcore, determined pulpit committee. Once or twice a month a few infrequent retired members would attend a service when they felt guilty enough to get dressed and venture out on a late Sunday morning.

The surviving members of the Pulpit Committee refused to even consider looking for another pastor, even as they endured the church's painful decline into worse shape than when they first hired Cal.

# RETURN TO FAITH

A light Spring breeze rustled new green leaves. Scattered through the limbs, birds chirped happily with their gabby neighbors. A small plane droned overhead. It was a perfect Spring day to be his last day.

The aged brick church sat silent on the corner lot. A century of services to its credit. Thousands upon thousands of souls had absorbed spiritual nourishment while seated on the padded oak pews.

It was the spiritual weakness and lack of determination from the humans entrusted with the building's care and purpose that had slowly rendered the structure useless. There was plenty of blame to pass around, but on that morning one man would shoulder the ultimate responsibility. It was the right thing, the responsible thing to do. That truth didn't make it any easier, but it did make it justified.

Cal's white sedan could've easily been on autopilot as it pulled into the familiar parking space in front of the side door. A sign hung on a post, "Reverend Baxter." That sign would soon be removed.

There was no sense of urgency. Preaching wasn't scheduled to begin until 11:00 AM. Since there were no Sunday School classes, the building was still locked and empty.

The Avalon's wide door swung open. Cal was preoccupied as he exited the car. He closed the door out of habit, then clicked the door lock as he stepped away. Seconds later he remembered something important and spun around. "Click." He unlocked the doors. Cal reached across the console to retrieve a black Bible. The decision had been made and there was no turning back.

The hall was cool and dim, but the building would warm up by preaching. The temperature was to be above 70 degrees. The heels of his shoes clicked on the tile floor as he meandered to the middle of the hall where his office was located. The only reason he went in was to make sure all of his belongings had been removed. The coolness reinforced the lifelessness that hung in the air.

Up until a few years ago, an overabundance of Annie and Taylor photos had transformed the office into an obsessive shrine. This overcompensation Cal finally came to realize made matters only worse. Visitors soon became uneasy, surrounded by the unnerving mass of eyes, especially when it was the same two pairs of eyes that surrounded them.

Once all of Annie's and Taylor's photos had been removed, Cal refused to personalize the office. He banished himself at the same time he abandoned his congregation.

After a quick look around Cal was satisfied there were no remnants of him in the room. He locked the door and closed it. He decided to spend his last hour in the sanctuary, in the chair he sat when not at the pulpit.

On such a sunny day, that time of morning the angle of the brilliant rays painted the pews with soft, colorful, comforting hues from the stained glass windows. It was the perfect time and place for quiet reflection. Over the years he'd spent many hours in that chair as he waited for the first of his flock to arrive.

......

## 3
## The Final Sermon

Ralph and Sadie Jenkins arrived much earlier than Cal expected and requested a private meeting in the pastor's office. The conversation was light. They just wanted to spend a little time for idle chit-chat. Cal really liked the Jenkins. They were in their eighties and very sincere. They had an odd dynamic between them that could be quite entertaining.

Eventually, Pastor Baxter looked at his watch, which was the signal that it was time to end the conversation. Sadie took the hint and slowly rose.

"Well, we need to go and let you get ready," Sadie said as she reached over and tapped her drowsy husband's shoulder.

Slightly startled, Ralph snorted, "Yeah. Sadie, we've taken up enough of Pastor Baxter's time. Let's mosey in and take our seats."

Moments later Cal entered the hallway and closed the office door for the second last time. He heard an unexpected yet familiar distant memory. The sounds from a full sanctuary. At first he wondered if he imagined it, but as he took a few steps closer toward the door the Jenkins didn't completely close, there was no doubt. On the other side was the low murmur of people chatting and shuffling on the crackling oak pews.

Cal paused before his body could be seen through the crack. He had prepared his final sermon for the fifteen to twenty faces he'd become accustomed to each Sunday. There was no time to change it, or thoughtfully adapt the message to a large crowd. He had no choice but to deliver it, then bring a merciful end to what had become a disastrous, unfulfilling career. Especially a meaningless waste of ten long, grueling, unproductive years. Worst of all, he was only in his mid-forties and had no idea what he wanted to do, or even if he really wanted to remain on the planet. He hadn't intentionally indicated to anyone that he had entertained ending it all. He doubted he had the courage to take such a drastic step.

Cal lifted his arm and his iWatch lit up as the time changed to 11:00 AM. One thing he was known for, he rarely started even one minute late. He drew in a long breath and pushed the door open.

The murmur silenced immediately. All eyes turned to him. Obviously, word had gotten around. There wasn't an empty seat in the pews, and they had even added a chair at the end of both sides of the pews. It had been a long time since he'd faced this many awaiting ears. It was odd that he realized he just had a shiver of the same jitters he experienced the first time he preached to a large crowd. It was an unwelcome first for his last.

After a long, noticeably pensive breath, Cal made his way up the steps and crossed to the pulpit. He faced the congregation filled with many familiar faces. It wasn't judgmental, but it was a question that rushed to mind. "Where had these people been the last ten years?"

The answer came swifter and more powerfully than the point-blank blast from a shotgun. And the impact devastated the remaining tatters of his soul. As the Bible had commanded, all pastors were shepherds responsible for their flocks. Those familiar faces wandered away because he no longer provided any guidance, or had the capacity to even show genuine empathy for the trials and troubles in their lives. They deserved better, so they sought it and found it elsewhere.

What began as an uncomfortable few seconds of silence had become an uneasy standoff with apparently neither side sure what would happen next. Cal wondered how many had shown up to make him feel better about stepping away from preaching, and how many intended to show genuine respect at the end of the service. Were they there to encourage him and wish him well on whatever path he had chosen for the rest of his life?

Then an all too familiar light snore interrupted the dead silence. It emanated from its usual spot in the fourth row on the left side of the moderately sized sanctuary.

Sadie reacted with her usual and swiftly inflicted righteous indignation. A sharp jab with her bony elbow landed digging into her husband's tender ribs. Ralph was jolted awake, squinted his eyes, and pretended he'd been intently listening. Sadie glared at Ralph. A few innocent chuckles and giggles wafted across the sanctuary.

Meanwhile, Cal and the slightly amused congregation carefully studied each other. It was the preacher man's move, so he drew in a contemplative breath then opened his mouth to deliver his final sermon.

"Ten years ago, on this very day, my faith was strong. But at precisely four-forty-five PM, God turned his back on me."

Cal closed his eyes and paused. He knew he was about to relive at least a brief moment of the accident. Fortunately, in his mind he heard only the Hellish impact that took the lives of his precious wife and daughter. His fingers turned white as he gripped the edges of the Bible stand mounted to the top of the pulpit.

Everyone in the congregation sat prayerfully silent. Many held their breath. They knew he just endured another horrific memory. Most eyes teared up.

After the tense beat Cal drew in a shaky breath, then his eyes slowly opened. Instead of raw emotion, his voice was cold and stern, straight from a man whose heart had turned to stone.

"God took my reasons for living. And as a result I lost my passion, the very purpose for standing here. I could no longer represent an entity who could be so heartless and cruel."

There were a few involuntary gasps and sighs from shocked witnesses. None of whom dreamed they would actually hear such a dramatic confession. The entire congregation sat in stunned silence.

Four weeks ago Cal announced the day he would preach his last sermon at Tabernacle Baptist Church. That very afternoon phones rang in homes of the former members who still lived in the surrounding neighborhood. The original plan was to amass as many former members as possible for a show of support. They intended to encourage Cal with heartfelt wishes for a brand new start. But at that moment nearly every adult in the packed sanctuary realized their mission had tragically evolved into an intervention. Most worried what he actually intended to do once he left the church. Cal's next ominous statements only made matters worse. Each bitter word was charged with raw emotion.

Cal lifted his right hand and slowly clenched it into a tight fist, "My joy vanished." His voice was stern. "My heart twisted into knots until it choked my spirit and crushed my faith."

Cal paused to study the church members as they shared disbelieving glances.

"It hasn't been fair to all of you. I did a lousy job failing to live a lie I no longer believed. For the last ten years I've done all of you a grave injustice, and I humbly beg your forgiveness. Your mass exodus was proof of the obvious spiritual harm I've caused many of you." His eyes turned down to the opened black Bible he'd placed on top of the large, white pulpit Bible. Cal read, "Luke 9: 62 'And Jesus said unto him, No man having put his hand to the plough, and looking back, is fit for the kingdom of God.'" Then he deliberately surveyed the disbelieving congregation. "As of today, I resign from Tabernacle Baptist Church. But more importantly, I resign from the ministry, effective immediately."

With that said, Cal reached over and closed the black Bible, but he purposefully left it on top of the white pulpit Bible. Then he stepped around the pulpit and descended the steps. He strode with purpose down the center of the aisle, toward the back. He never turned his eyes to the left or right, and opted not to shake a single extended hand that protruded from either aisle. However, he did open the swinging doors to the small vestibule where he respectfully paused and turned. He would shake every willing hand of those who had been kind enough, and caring enough to attend his final sermon.

Cal wasn't prepared to stay long. Sincere folks had a great deal to say and appeared in no hurry to move on.

Twenty minutes later, those further back in the line decided to shorten their carefully thought out messages of encouragement for the retiring pastor.

Eventually all that remained were the fifteen surviving members of Tabernacle Baptist. They had deemed themselves "the survivor's club" and wanted to be the last to speak to Rev. Baxter.

Billy Thompson, a short, round fellow who at sixty-eight

years of age was the junior member of "the survivors" club. He stepped in the vestibule and pulled the doors closed. It was obvious he held something behind his back as he turned to Cal, "The lights are out and she's all locked up. Do you need to go back inside for anything?"

Cal shook his head. He'd said his piece and he was ready to walk away.

Sadie and Ralph Jenkins opted to flank Cal as he headed down the steps and held up his key ring, "Billy, I'll hang my keys on the hook beside the kitchen door after I drop the car off at the parsonage."

"Thank you," Billy was reluctant but he knew there was no need to press any further. Former Pastor Baxter was no longer an employee of Tabernacle Baptist Church. "That works. I'm supposed to meet the realtor around ten in the morning. I'll pick'm up then." As the Buildings and Grounds Trustee, the responsibility of managing the sale of the property and assets had fallen on him.

Cal paused at the bottom of the steps in hopes they would say their goodbyes so he could have a quiet, unattended walk over to his soon-to-be former car. But "the survivors' club" had no intentions to let him off the hook that easily.

On the slow walk to the car, Billy quickly caught up with Ralph and slipped something in his right hand. Ralph never looked down. He knew exactly what he held and casually slipped it behind his back as they arrived at the car. They formed a semi-circle around Cal. There was an uneasy, very awkward silence. It was the classic dog that chased a car, then caught it, but didn't know what to do next. Finally Cal spoke up, "There's no way I can ever thank you and apologize to you enough. Over the...."

Sadie spoke up, "We're way beyond that now. We just want you to know that as long as the Lord leaves us on this planet, we'll always be here for you."

"As long as it takes," Ralph said as he brought the black Bible from around his back and extended it to Cal.

Cal immediately shook his head and held up both hands, "I'm done. Give that to someone willing to believe in fairy tales."

Every member of "the survivor's club" was stunned and speechless as Ralph lowered the Bible.

## OTIS FARMER

"Sorry, my friends," Cal was sincere, "I will always consider you dear friends. But I wasted too many years of my life studying and believing in the ridiculous passages between those covers. It's time I finally faced reality."

......

# 4
# The Not So Great Escape

Cal carried the 8"x10" framed photo of Annie and Taylor as he exited the master bedroom and walked down the hall. He wanted to wait and take them with him as he left the parsonage for the final time. He knew it wasn't rational and he would never tell anyone why he'd made that odd decision.

A brief pause and glance around the den was all he could stomach. Then he strode with purpose through the kitchen and instinctively hung the car keys on their hook by the door. Seconds later he locked, closed the door and stepped into the carport. That was it. The last time he and his favorite girls would ever step out of that house.

Once again, most people would question his sanity had he shared his reason for thinking that way. Sometimes sane people had to find ways to cope with a tremendous tragedy, even many years later.

Since he had taken on the position as pastor of Tabernacle Baptist Church, Cal had really appreciated the use of the very nice car they would trade out every two years. It was great not to have to make monthly car and insurance payments, or pay his sizable gas bill. He briefly touched the Toyota as he made his way to his pride and joy. The one vehicle he had willingly paid monthly insurance payments to cover.

Cal's eyes were drawn to his reflection in the deep glossy black paint on the meticulously restored 1957 Chevy pickup truck. He lovingly patted the hood, "Well, Annie, it's just you and me, Old Girl." Cal opened the driver's door and lovingly placed the 8"x10" photo of Annie and Taylor on top of his overnight bag in the passenger seat. He made sure the bottom of the frame was tucked between the bag and seat, with the image facing out, so Annie and Taylor could watch.

There was a special reason the truck was named "Annie."

## OTIS FARMER

Those unfamiliar with the truck's history would assume it was named after his dead wife. They would be right, but for the wrong reason.

Cal's father had found the abandoned truck on the edge of the woods at a friend's family farm. Trees and various vegetation had grown through the cab and bed. It was in bad shape. It took three days to cut the truck out of the forest's stubborn death grip. They used a backhoe to lift it and set the heap of rusted metal on a trailer. It rested on shreds of rotten rubber wrapped around bent wheels.

"Boy, she's a mess," Annie stepped back and declared. "But this old girl's gonna be a stunner when we get her back in shape and on new rubber," Cal's newlywed wife promised.

Cal always considered Annie the most beautiful "tomboy" to ever grace planet Earth. Even Cal's dad couldn't have been happier or more proud of his new daughter-in-law. She was every bit the amazing woman his son deserved, while at the same time she was both the only daughter and second son he would ever have. Most folks would've had to think about that, and several would've never grasp the significance of his meaning.

A good family friend set aside a section of his garage for the proud trio to meticulously and lovingly disassemble the entire truck. From the Chassis up to the engine they had to use all possible methods to loosen dirty, corroded, or rusted bolts, screws and pulleys. They also had to remove other worn or broken pieces that they either replaced, or scrubbed, scraped, sanded, repaired, primed, and painted. Eventually the chassis and engine looked as if they had just rolled off the assembly line.

The transformation of the classic truck from a rusty hulk into an immaculate show vehicle was a labor of love. The rescued heap was Mr. Baxter's dream project, so it was his to name. Since Annie had been just as involved and gotten just as greasy and grimy crawling under, over and inside the truck, it was apropos to dub their newly-minted masterpiece, Annie.

Exactly twelve months to the day they liberated the tattered truck from its forest grave, Cal's dad proudly surprised Annie when he asked her to attach the special tag to the freshly chromed rear bumper. The tag was custom-stamped. It was an exact replica of an authentic black 1957 North Carolina tag. The yellow letters spelled, "Annie."

Mr. Baxter was a serious amateur photographer and put together a scrapbook of photos that chronicled their miraculous restoration project.

Unfortunately, three years later the photo journal and truck came to live with Annie and Cal when his Dad passed after a brief battle with cancer. Cal was his father's only living blood kin that they knew. His mother had abandoned Cal and his father when he was young, and they had no clue where she was or even if she were still alive.

Both Cal and his father were in dire need of a stable female figure in their lives, and Annie was the perfect match for that unique role. Cal and Annie joked when they got married that they adopted his father as their son. The truck project provided them more reasons to spend quality time together.

After a bitter-sweet journey down Memory Lane, Cal backed the truck to the end of the driveway. He paused. Reality set in. He had reached the end of his tortured life. At least the end of the wasted time he had aimlessly wandered around as Tabernacle Baptist Church's hapless, useless pastor.

From that moment forward his life would no longer be structured, ruled by schedules and responsibilities. It would take a very long time to get tired of that welcomed freedom.

When the whitewall replica tires rolled off the concrete driveway at Tabernacle Baptist parsonage, Cal became a man without a mission, or purpose in life. A lost soul with no clear direction.

On second thought, he did have one more unpleasant stop to make on his way out of town. There was no way this would end well for either one of them.

......

Granny's Doughnuts was an overnight success in Archdale, North Carolina. It was the "go to place" for those with a sweet tooth or "hankering" for a delicious, fluffy pastry.

Since childhood, Annie's Mom and Aunt Glenda, her older sister, dreamed of opening a pastry shop. Then one day, when they were both in their late sixties and retired, they found the perfect location. From that day forward, they did everything perfectly. They sat down and put pencil to paper to lay out their floor pan and crunch the numbers on their detailed business plan.

The next step was the most important. They activated their grapevine of chatty friends who saturated the surrounding neighborhoods with constant reminders, months before the grand opening. "Granny's Doughnuts will be the place to go for the best pastries and cakes in the state of North Carolina."

The much-hyped grand opening was packed and even made the evening news on the local TV station. From the time they opened the doors in the small kitchen of the "Little Shop of Pastries," they out performed their promise. Three times in twelve years they outgrew the perfect location. They had the traffic and order logs to make a fourth move or open a second location; but not in their early eighties, they decided to hire more help and spend less time in their current location. Future expansion would fall on the shoulders of the soon-to-be new owners. They were thrilled that their eager daughters and granddaughters stepped up to the plate. By the end of the year, if Gabby and Glenda were brave enough to actually follow through on their plan, their daughters and granddaughters would be ready to step into their shoes. Had Annie lived, she would've been one of the proud new owners.

However, Gabby and Glenda still hadn't informed the new owners of their intentions to retire at the end of the year. The main reason was that they weren't sure they had the guts to actually follow through on such a drastic commitment. Perhaps they could wet the tips of their toes with a semi-retirement. Better yet, the best possible plan would be an open-ended semi-semi-retirement.

At that moment, Gabby and Glenda sat on opposite sides of a small table in the back of the kitchen where they sipped on well-deserved cups of freshly brewed coffee. As usual their white aprons bore the chocolate streaks and sprinkle specks from the lunch battle. They had made it through another lunch crush, and it was time to relax and enjoy the mid-afternoon lull before the evening rush.

It was common for one of the bells on the opposing entry doors to "dingle" during their break, but they were never too tired or unwilling to warmly greet one of their regulars, or meet a first-time customer. It was especially gratifying when a "first-timer" would wander in during the lull. There was more time to chat and make new friends with locals who would more than likely become regulars.

The "dingle" sounded.

Glenda sat her cup down on the table first and beat Gabby to her feet, "I'll get this one."

Gabby held up her steamy cup in support, "Go get'm tiger." But her cup lowered and her smile instantly faded when Glenda paused between the swinging doors.

"What is it?" Gabby was concerned.

"It's not a what; it's a who," Glenda turned a sour scowl to her little sister.

Gabby became concerned as she lowered her cup to the table and started to rise.

Glenda held up her hand, "Sit tight. I'll handle this one." She said as she drew in a determined breath and let the swinging doors flop as she exited the kitchen.

Gabby's curiosity got the better of her and she slipped off her chair and made her way to the still clicking doors. At a diminutive five foot, two inches, Gabby couldn't see through the higher than normal windows in the stainless steel doors. They had talked about replacing the doors with a set that had lower windows, but they eventually adapted.

Glenda stepped up to the glass display case filled with a variety of colorful fresh pastries. Her brown eyes narrowed in contempt, "Well, Didn't think you'd have the guts to show your face in here again."

Cal paused. There was a 50/50 chance he would face Glenda's hate-filled eyes first, but he had to take that chance. It had been four years since he last visited Granny's, which was his first visit on their first day in the current location. He wanted to show his support and Gabby appeared to genuinely appreciate his effort. Even as busy as they were, she took a few minutes to personally serve him his favorite, a hot Apple Fritter. It was so sad Cal stood in a place that smelled like Heaven, but felt like Hell.

Glenda made no effort to sugar coat her contempt. She was brutally honest, "So you finally killed Tabernacle Baptist Church. We heard earlier that you've retired from preaching. So you really don't have any reasons to hang around town any longer."

Gabby pushed the swinging doors open. This was her battle and she would fight it, "No need to make a scene."

Glenda glared at Gabby, "You really want to see him?"

Gabby nodded and couldn't hold back her genuine, loving smile. It was so good to see Cal again. She wished he would come by more often, but she understood why. Glenda would never forgive him. "Of course, I want to see him. The love of my daughter's life is always welcome here."

Cal missed Gabby, but it was a close race between Glenda and himself as to who had the most contempt for him. He wished he had the courage to more frequently visit his ex.... Actually, Gabby wasn't his ex-mother-in-law because there was no way he and Annie would've ever divorced, which made it too painful to be around Gabby. He couldn't help but heap guilt on himself for causing both of them unending heartache. Yet on that day he had to stop in because this was his last day in Archdale, and at Gabby's age he may never see her again, even though he had a special favor to ask. His eyes cut to Glenda, who leered at him from behind the counter like a protective momma bear ready to leap into action. To rip into shreds the unwelcome intruder who intended to harm her little cub.

"At ease, Momma bear," Gabby gently touched Glenda on the arm. "Baby Bear's gonna be just fine." She looked up at her big sister who at six foot, one inch towered over her. "Be a dear and pour our special guest a fresh cup of coffee. I know exactly what he stopped by for and the last batch is still warm."

That was all Gabby needed to say. It brought the first genuine smile Cal dared to show on that difficult Sunday afternoon. In fact, he couldn't remember the last time his face so willingly yielded up a smile that felt so right. More than likely it was the las time he stepped into Granny's.

Gabby smiled, "Have a seat, my dear." She turned to Glenda, "You know what he wants, and I'll have one too. Try not to embarrass yourself anymore."

Glenda was satisfied she said her piece and she could manage to be civil for the remainder of Cal's visit, provided he didn't stay too long. It would be unfair to put her little sister through the fresh upheaval of missing her dear Annie, and the granddaughter she barely knew. It would be best if Cal were gone when Annie's older sister, Terri, got there for the afternoon and evening shift.

Gabby stepped around the long glass display case and gently took Cal by the arm. She led him to the far corner booth. Neither of them would dare offer to hug until Cal was ready to leave.

Glenda had adjusted her attitude by the time she showed up at the table with a tray that contained two steamy styrofoam cups and two warm, plump Apple Fritters.

Cal managed to keep from licking his lips like a goofy dog who could barely contain himself before he nearly swallowed the delectable treat whole, "Only have a few minutes. Got a long drive ahead."

"You can take those few minutes to enjoy your little treat," Gabby's eyes glistened with tears. It was so difficult to be with Cal. He was the only living connection to her precious Annie.

Cal's eyes closed. the amazing aroma wafted up from the golden brown hunk of Heaven and carried him away from the painful present. There was a light crunch as his teeth cut through the thin sugar glaze and sank into the cinnamon rich dough. His teeth sliced off a small chunk of sweet apple in the delectable bite. It was a delightful sensory overload. He dared to allow the sweet memory to recall Annie's girlish giggle. Now that was a life worth living. While Annie was pregnant, she ate at least one Apple Fritter a day. Cal went on numerous emergency runs to fetch her a hot, fresh one. They went on many little dates where they huddled in that very same booth to relish her favorite snack.

"Boy or girl," Annie announced at that very booth two weeks before Taylor was born, "Our angel's nickname is going to be Little Fritter."

It wasn't an accident that Gabby sat them at this booth. She often joined them for a few minutes when she had time.

Cal's eyes opened. He dare not stay in the past too long. It only made trying to exist in the present more unbearable. He found Gabby's eyes adoringly focused on him. She had also taken a brief respite from her torturous battle to overcome relentless grief.

Something wasn't right. His eyes tracked to the source at

the counter where Glenda disapprovingly leered at him. He stopped chewing and laid the plump pastry on the paper plate.

Gabby followed Cal's eyes and her tender smile vanished. Her eyes narrowed into a harsh glare at Glenda, who finally turned and pushed her way into the kitchen. She did so with enough force to cause the doors to click back and forth for a few annoying seconds.

The heartbroken mother-in-law turned compassionate eyes back to the man in dire need of reinforcement, but more importantly some straightforward advice. "She'll probably never forgive you. But, Honey, at some point, you're gonna have to forgive yourself." Her eyes became misty and her voice comfortingly nostalgic, "I remember the day my little Annie burst into the kitchen and boldly announced she'd met her husband."

Cal felt his lips widen into a smile the width he hadn't felt in many years. He knew that story well. Gabby loved to tell it and it never got old, "It was only the second day of Kindergarten. At that point, I wasn't too fond of girls."

Gabby giggled, "Bless her little heart. She wasn't about to be denied."

Cal chuckled, "The little pest. Darn near drove me crazy."

"From that day on, she insisted God made you just for her."

"She showed up at the most inopportune times. The oddest places. In the hallways. On the playground. In the cafeteria. She stalked me like a hungry lioness would a skinny gazelle."

"You mean a shy gazelle."

"No. An utterly terrified gazelle."

The laughter was perfectly timed. It was desperately needed medicine for two souls who suffered from the same incurable disease.

"My buddies called her Psycho Annie." Cal nodded, "Then one day, halfway through that year, we turned the same corner from opposite directions. We innocently collided, this time quite by accident."

Gabby shook her head, "No. By Divine appointment."

"She dropped the book she was looking at instead of watching where she was going. She was so embarrassed, so vulnerable. I'll never forget it. That's when I saw her differently. She wasn't on a mission. She was the real Annie." Cal chuckled, "Still didn't think much of girls."

"But you sure took a liking to my little girl."

Cal nodded reassuringly, "Yes, Ma'am. I sure did."

"You were the best things that could've ever happened to each other."

Cal nodded, though he was very conflicted between joy and pain.

Gabby spoke impulsively and realized she'd gone down the wrong path, but she couldn't stop in time, "I still haven't gotten an answer. I've asked the Lord a million times to give me some semblance of understanding. But He's kept a deaf ear turned to me. He took Annie and Taylor, but left you to suffer." Gabby reached over and laid her hand on Cal's shoulder, "Don't get me wrong. I'm so glad you're still here, but why did He leave you alone?"

At that point, Cal didn't have the energy or the desire to rip into God in front of Gabby. He opted to nod understandingly. She already knew why he'd lost his faith. It would serve no purpose to begin that conversation. He wasn't willing to let himself off the hook.

"She wanted to stay at home that day." Cal began, but Gabby cut him off as she gently took hold of his hand.

"All she ever wanted to be was the perfect wife and mother for you and Taylor."

"And she was... until...."

Gabby shook her head, "You gotta stop this."

Cal checked his watch, then rose, "I gotta get on the road, but I want to give you something before I leave."

Gabby pointed to the unfinished fritter, "I'll fix that for you to go." She said as she rose and walked behind Cal. She didn't have a clue what Cal wanted to give her, but she didn't have a good feeling.

While Cal was outside, Gabby tossed the half-eaten fritter into the trash and placed a fresh fritter into a bag. Then she quickly folded a flat dozen-sized box and loaded it with an assortment of his favorite doughnuts and pastries. She had it on the counter with the fritter bag on top of the box. Beside the box was a freshly poured to-go cup capped with a travel lid. Cal smiled when he returned.

Gabby focused on the thick black binder in Cal's hands. She assumed it was some type of scrapbook.

"Trade ya," Gabby grinned like a mischievous child as she pointed to her treasures.

Cal smiled, "That ought to be enough coffee and sugar to keep me up for an hour or so."

"What'cha got in that book?" Gabby pointed back to the same table.

This time Cal pulled his chair beside Gabby and opened his father's photo journal of the truck rebuild. Gabby shook her head.

"I can't accept this. It belongs to one who helped rescue her from a slow, unfair death in the woods. The one who helped give her a new lease on life."

Cal turned a few more pages until he uncovered an adorable 8x10 photo of a grease smeared Annie beside the rusty, raised hood. With gritted teeth, she flexed her muscles with a wrench in one hand and a screwdriver in the other. At the bottom was a handwritten notation. Gabby recognized the unique penmanship. She read the inscription aloud.

"When the boys can't handle it... Call in the girls." Gabby laughed and cried, "That was our Annie."

"Oh yeah. If you ever wanted her to take on a challenge, tell her she couldn't do it," Cal nodded as he teared up.

"And she would prove you wrong," Gabby said, then her head snapped to the left, where she faced Cal eye-to-eye. "This is goodbye. You're never coming back. Are you?"

Cal was silent, but there was something in his eyes that troubled Gabby. A possible cry for help from a tortured man who knew his end was near. More disturbing, he had every intention to be in control of that ending.

"I still have Annie. I'll get to drive her every day. I have no intentions of ever selling her," Cal promised as he continued to flip pages.

The next ten minutes were lost in time. In Gabby's and Cal's minds, on every page, Annie was very much alive and well. Every photo captured a piece of her unique personality and endearing character. Gabby firmly gripped Cal's hand.

"You sure you want me to have this?"

"Do you want it?"

Gabby nodded most affirmatively, "This captures the very

essence of all that was good about her. Oh yeah, I most definitely want it."

Cal derived tremendous satisfaction as he rose, "Then it's yours." He said as he reached to pick it up, "I'll carry it over to the counter for you."

Gabby quickly scooped up the bulky binder, "Oh no, you don't. If you get your grubby paws on it again, you might change your mind." She smiled broadly, then struggled to maintain a firm grip on the oversized binder as she followed Cal to the counter where his cold coffee and pastries awaited. She visibly strained to hoist the binder up on the counter.

"Let me fix you a fresh cup of coffee," Gabby offered.

Cal nodded, "Really appreciate that."

Even though he knew Glenda would give him a hard time, he was very reluctant to stop in. His and Gabby's venture down memory lane was strangely worth the hassle and heartache. More than likely his last visit to Granny's was very worthwhile. He was further comforted that Annie's photo album would be in the right hands. The hands of someone who could really appreciate its true value.

Glenda eased through the swinging doors with a freshly poured and capped cup of coffee-to-go. Her lips even parted in a weak, but genuine smile, "One for the road."

Cal reached over and offered his hand and Glenda didn't hesitate. They both exchanged firm and thankfully not in the least bit challenging handshakes.

"Good luck, Cal." Glenda turned the corner of her mouth up in a genuine attempted smile, "And I really mean it."

Cal nodded, "Thank you, Glenda. I wish you the very best in the future. And I really mean it." Cal flashed her a quick wink.

It would be the closest the two would ever come to signing a peace treaty, and they were both ready to end on at least a hint of respect for the other.

Glenda turned and eased back through the swinging doors. This time she was careful to prevent them from flopping. Her little sister deserved undisturbed time to bid her son-in-law a final farewell. She seriously doubted they would ever see Cal again, but for drastically different reasons than her little sister.

Gabby carried Cal's fresh cup of coffee out to the old truck and gently patted the hood, "Take care of our girl."

"Yes, Ma'am," Cal smiled. "Promise."

Gabby patiently waited as Cal lifted the photo of Annie and Taylor and placed the doughnut box on top of his overnight bag. Then he rested the photo on top of the box. Gabby's eyes immediately teared up as she focused on the photo. She was moved that the photo was in such a prominent position as if they were physically in the truck with him. That was cause for concern because there could be much deeper issues Cal had kept hidden. At this point, she opted to keep mum as she handed him the hot cup of coffee.

As if it were normal for the photo to be there, Cal placed the cup in the closest aftermarket cup holder mounted on the driver's side of the dash.

Without another word, Gabby reached up like an eager child in dire need of one more hug. It lasted longer than they both anticipated, but not nearly as long as they would've preferred.

"Put you a little note in the box. But don't read it until you stop for the evening."

Cal climbed up in the cab and Gabby closed the door.

"Never forget, there's a little old lady in Archdale who will always love you like a son."

Cal would've been surprised if Gabby had said anything different. He was certain she believed he was equally sincere.

"I want you to always remember that somewhere out there is the man who married your daughter and, as an unexpected bonus, got the mother he never had, or deserved." They joined hands. "Love you, too."

As Cal pulled out of the parking lot, he felt better that he didn't ask Gabby to hold on to the rental agreement and key to his storage unit. That would be a matter he would address later. He could always send her the key and contract from on the road.

Just like that, Calvin Baxter's life in Archdale, North Carolina, came to an end. He drove past the welcome sign on the Northbound lane, as he headed Southwest on Highway 62, on the ten minute drive that would take him to Highway 109, in Thomasville. There he would turn south on 109 and meander deep into the country, with no particular destination

## RETURN TO FAITH

in mind. The further he drove from Archdale, the more it sank in just how easily life would continue in that little town, as if he never lived there, or ever existed on planet Earth.

......

# 5
# When Even Having No Plan Fails

By design there was no plan. Cal would avoid the interstates, stay on rural back roads and see where his curiosity led. His intentions were to follow this method as long as it took to find what he was looking for. The main flaw with that logic, he didn't have a clue what he was looking for, so there was no way to know exactly when he found it.

Cal had several thousand dollars cash strategically hidden throughout the truck. His credit cards were at zero balance. He had remote access to all of his accounts and investment funds. If he spent wisely, it was possible for him to spend the rest of his life seeking answers to who, what, and why he was on this planet.

For as long as Cal could remember his father was a devout Christian who raised him in a structured church environment. His father was never a Bible thumper, but he was a true believer willing to experiment with multiple denominations. During Cal's younger years they spent time in a small Methodist church. Then they moved to a moderately-sized Episcopalian church for two or three years. Lutherans were next on the list, but they spent only two years there.

The next move became their church home, at least for his father, who had heard about a small Baptist church on the outskirts of neighboring Thomasville, NC. The preacher was a solid, Bible-based leader who could keep the congregation's attention on any subject. It was growing rapidly, and the Baxter boys became a vital part of the amazing building program. As a matter of fact, Cal used it as a model to help plan Tabernacle's aggressive building schedule.

The main reason Cal chose Highway 62 out of Archdale was that it would take him by his father's chosen church, which was in Thomasville, on 62, several hundred yards from 109. He pulled into the parking lot and quietly looked at the eight-sided sanctuary that was built when he and his father attended. Those were the good old days when religion and God had a meaningful purpose in his young life.

In those days, God and church were as important to Cal as breathing and eating. They were synonymous. God and church sustained his spirit, while eating and breathing kept his body alive. That simple logic soon became the foundation of Cal's existence and was the main reason he felt led to become a pastor. That was his goal as a pastor, to use that simple logic as the key to surviving in a very unkind world. To keep focused on that simple truth was the solid rock on which Christians must always stand. Just like the refrain in the great hymn, "All other ground is sinking sand."

Then out of the blue, on such a warm and beautiful, sunny spring afternoon, in the middle of nowhere in North Carolina, Cal Baxter asked himself two astonishing questions, out loud: "Did God turn His back and walk away from me, and allow Annie and Taylor to be so cruelly and unjustly taken away? Or, when Annie and Taylor were so cruelly and unjustly taken away from me, did I turn my back and walk away from God?"

On the surface his questions easily sounded like simple semantics. The order in which the incidents occurred, and more importantly, to whom blame was immediately assessed, from Cal's perspective, had always been skewed. He still felt justified in ruthlessly blaming God.

However, for a fleeting second he actually entertained the notion he might have unfairly reacted. Was it possible he allowed his pain and lack of understanding to fester into the cancer that quickly invaded his spirit and so savagely decimated his faith? Quickly that foolish notion faded into the deep blue sky that loomed over the next hill in the distance.

Cal had both windows down. His hair blew in the constant fresh breeze that poured in on both sides. Yet without a hit of conscious suggestion, his sense of smell zeroed in on the aromas that escaped from Gabby's gift box. Then as a bee drawn to a nectar-ladened flower, his hand cut through the air until his fingers could flip the lid open. Without taking his eyes off the road, by sense of touch he located the chocolate covered, cream-filled delicacy he desired.

If he hadn't taken those precious seconds to hold the aromatic treat close to his nose, he would've already taken a sizable bite. Instead, his attention turned to the car on the side of the road with its hood up. He tossed the delectable treat back into the box and closed the lid. It appeared someone needed help, and he would stop to see if they were still there and still in need.

It was convenient that the stranded car broke down on a stretch of rural road with a shoulder wide enough to safely pull over and be completely off the pavement. Gravels crackled as Cal's truck slowly rolled to a stop. There were no signs of anyone in or around the old ratty car. The woods on both sides of the road began a mere few feet from the six-foot shoulder. It was as if the road builders deliberately created a narrow corridor through the forest to preserve as much foliage as possible.

Cal couldn't help but chuckle. He spoke aloud, "This is the time when the audience would say I can't believe he's stopping. There's no way I'd stop there." He chuckled again, "In horror movies, this is the moment the protagonist makes the wrong decision and bad things start happening."

Cal checked the rearview and side mirrors to make sure nothing approached from behind. Since all was clear, he opened the door and stepped out, but looked both ways just to make sure.

He spoke loudly enough to be heard if the driver had stepped up into the thick stand of trees on both sides of the road, "Hello. Do you need help?" He looked around, and at first all he heard were mixed bird songs.

Then a timid female voice sounded from in front of the car. She was either leaning over and looking under the hood, or she wasn't tall enough to be seen over the opened hood.

"Know anything about cars," Megan said as she stepped into view in front of the car. She was in her early 20's, slender, and wore a trashy short black skirt and white halter top. She was very attractive but noticeably distraught.

For all intents and purposes, Cal had denounced God when he left the ministry. His instincts were as if he were still a man of the cloth. Before him was a young woman in distress, not a young woman to take advantage of, or one who had nefarious or lurid intent.

"Are you alone?"

"Yeah," Megan put her hands on her hips and shifted her weight to bring attention to her shapely, tanned legs. "I was out for a nice spring drive. Not really in a hurry...." She kicked at the front of the car to once again draw attention to her legs, "Then this old crappy car decided to die."

"Have you called for help?" Cal realized his eyes focused on the young woman's beautiful legs. He immediately averted his gaze to look her in the eyes. It was obvious she was in no hurry to answer the question. As a man of God, he shouldn't have entertained the thoughts that suddenly flooded his mind. He was no longer a pastor and he hadn't been with a woman in over ten years. He didn't want to be the aggressor, but if she showed interest, this could turn out to be an entirely different movie plot. It could be a sorted tale where the lonely man meets a hot young woman who likes slightly older men.

Megan seemed to sense she had gotten into Cal's mind, perhaps in the way they both wanted. She slightly grinned, "My cell phone died, and I don't have a car charger."

Cal's better judgment kicked into overdrive and he quickly retrieved his cell phone, "Who would you like for me to call?"

"Know much about cars?"

Before Cal realized, he had reached over and gently patted Annie's hood, "Found this old girl rusting away in the woods. We tore her apart and restored her to her original glory."

Megan smiled as she stepped out of view behind the raised hood, "You must be good with your hands. Maybe you can fix it."

Cal was so conflicted, but he stood just far enough in front of the truck to see the custom Annie tag his father had made. That moment of weakness and lurid desire was crushed. No matter how many lonely years had passed, he would always love Annie. At that moment he realized why that old black truck meant so much to him. It had always been a physical reminder, the symbol of the only woman for him.

With renewed conviction he stepped to the front of Megan's car. He would look under the hood to see if there were any obvious causes. Then if the sexy young woman didn't give him a number to call, he'd ask Siri to call the closest towing service.

A quick visual inspection revealed no signs of smoke or steam. "There's no busted hoses, nor any severe fluid leaks." Cal sensed the young woman had eased closer to him, "How about you trying to start it so I can see and hear what happens."

"Ok. But I can assure you it ain't gonna start," Megan promised.

As soon as Megan turned the switch, the engine cranked and sounded normal for such a poorly maintained car.

Cal carefully looked around for any leaks or loose parts as Megan stepped around the front of the car.

"Wow, your hands can work miracles," Megan smiled broadly as she slowly raised a pistol with both hands.

"It might've just overheated," Cal surmised as he straightened up and turned to the unexpected sight. His hands lifted to his chest. "Okay. There's no need for that."

"Oh, I'm afraid there is. Just do what I say and you'll be okay."

Cal had never handled guns but there were two very odd details he noticed immediately. The pistol was a revolver. More importantly, the chambers where the bullets should've been were empty. He could see all the way through them. But was there a bullet in the chamber aligned with the barrel?

"Do you have any bullets in that gun?" Cal asked but wouldn't hear the answer. It happened so quickly he never felt the sharp blow to the back of his head. His body crumpled like limp fabric in front of the car.

Megan shook her head in disgust as she lowered the pistol, "Told you to put the bullets in the gun!" She snapped.

"Would you really have shot him?" Tommy, a scruffy young man with mussed hair asked without looking up. He had already begun to rifle through Cal's pockets.

Megan pondered quizzically, "Not to kill him. But I think.... Yeah, I could'a shot him in the leg."

"That's why there's no bullets in the gun."

"What if he would'a charged at me?" Megan shook the pistol at Tommy. "Was I supposed to say Bang! Bang! And he'd run home to his mommy?"

Tommy stopped searching Cal's body and shook his head

as he finally looked up at Megan in total disbelief, "You're one cold-hearted woman."

"Me!" Megan was offended. "You whacked him pretty hard. Is he dead?"

Tommy put the back of his hand under Cal's nose. After a tense beat he shook his head, "He's still breathing. But we can't leave him here like fresh road-kill."

Megan stuffed the pistol in the waistband of her skirt, lowered to her knees and helped Tommy search through Cal's pockets. "Let's get his stuff and get outta here?"

......

Five minutes later Tommy checked the rearview mirror as he blindly reached for the bag, instead he felt the framed photo of Annie and Taylor. He picked it up, looked at it, then callously tossed it out the window, "Sorry, pretty lady, but there's no room for you and your little girl. Megan will be jealous."

Cal's treasured photograph smashes against a tree. Glass shatters and the photo is torn in half. It was a cruel ending of a memory in which the unthinkable happened. It is something Cal would have never fathomed. Taylor was torn from Annie's loving arms.

Without a second thought, Tommy stuck his hand into the grease-stained white bag on top of the doughnut box. He pulled out the fresh Apple Fritter Gabby snuck into the bag.

Without regard for the mess he was about to make, Tommy glanced down to gauge how wide he needed to open his mouth, then he chomped down and bit off a huge hunk. Golden crumbs coated with a thin sugar glaze rained down on his lap. Some bounced onto the sparkling leather seat, while others littered the immaculately clean floorboard.

With his mouth crammed full he spewed crumbs as he exclaimed, "Man! This is awesome!"

Megan led the way in her cluttered, ratty old car as they sped down the winding country road. She pulled cash, driver's license, and credit cards out of Cal's wallet, then tossed it out the window. It tumbled across the asphalt. Photographs swirled in the turbulence as Cal's truck zipped past. The wallet rolled into a mud puddle. Water seeped in and crinkled the photo of Cal, Annie and Taylor.

## OTIS FARMER

After a quick inspection, Megan tossed Cal's cell phone on the pile of assorted trash in the floorboard of the passenger side. Then she picked up her cell phone.

Seconds later, Tommy tossed the Fritter in the seat, quickly licked his sticky fingers before he snatched his phone from the seat. He nearly lost control of the truck as he attempted to slide his gooey finger across the phone to answer. Moist crumbs spewed from his mouth as he barked, "What?"

Tommy's muffled rebuke concerned Megan, "You okay?"

After a few rapid chews Tommy attempted to respond more clearly, "Eat'n this insane apple thing."

"You hog! Is there another one!"

"Ont'know."

"We may have a problem."

Tommy stopped chewing. His chipmunk cheeks bulged with sweet delight, "What?"

"Bet his cell phone has a tracker."

Tommy's eyebrows rose, and he swallowed hard. His words were still very muffled.

"I didn't understand a word you said. Swallow it, or spit it out." Megan demanded. "We gotta figure something out right now."

Like an obedient puppy, Tommy immediately stuck his head out the window. It took a couple of serious spits to empty his mouth enough to talk. Two blobs of half-chewed fritter went splat on the inside of the tailgate.

"You got his phone with you?" Tommy didn't think before he spoke.

"D'huaa! Doughnut Brain!" Megan shook her head in total frustration, "Why would I bring it up if I didn't?"

"Then chuck it out the window…. Pea Brain!"

"With my fingerprints all over it. We're still too close to where we left him."

Suddenly, the hapless Bonnie & Clyde realized the potential folly of their ill-conceived crime in the modern world, with ultra sophisticated electronic devices.

"What'da you wanna do?"

"Follow me."

It helped that Megan and Tommy were in familiar territory. In the long run, they soon realized they would've been better off to have set the trap a lot farther away from their sleepy little hometown.

Megan slammed her foot on the brake pedal, but Tommy didn't expect such a drastic move. He tossed the phone in the seat and grabbed the steering wheel with both hands. By mere inches the chrome bumper from Cal's truck missed the rusty bumper of Megan's car. With the skill of a seasoned stunt driver, Megan slid the car around to head in the opposite direction. She accelerated while Tommy wrestled to regain control of the heavy, unwieldy old truck that finally slid to a stop a foot from a deep ditch. He snatched up his phone.

"Have you lost your mind!"

Megan's maniacal cackle erupted from the phone's speaker. It unnerved Tommy. He'd never heard that unholy sound from her before.

"You tryin to kill us?"

"Come on, Tommy! Don't be such a little girl."

Moments later, even further off the beaten path, Megan and Tommy knelt on a flat rock by the edge of a small, green slime covered pond. Tommy lifted a grapefruit-sized rock over his head and emitted a guttural "Huuuh!" akin to a martial arts master. Then he slammed the rock down against Cal's cell phone. It took several violent "Huuuh!" charged blows to split the phone into half.

Megan smiled, grabbed Tommy by the cheeks and passionately kissed him on the mouth. She pulled back with a wide grin and bragged, "There you go, Baby! I knew you had it in ya!"

Inspired and encouraged by the misguided praise, Tommy pounded even harder. Small pieces of plastic and glass flew up in the air as Tommy reduced the expensive smartphone into a pile of stupid circuit boards and shards of glass and plastic. Megan had to take hold of Tommy's hand at the apex of his reach.

"That's good." Megan declared with confidence.

Then they giggled like malicious children as they slung a handful of shattered pieces from Cal's smartphone across the contaminated pond. The larger pieces kicked up patches of green gunk as they skipped across the slimy surface, then plopped as they disappeared.

"They'll never find it in there," Megan was confident.

"How much cash was in the wallet?"

Megan was emphatic, "TWELVE HUNDRED DOLLARS!"

"What?"

Megan repeated with glee, "Twelve hundred dollars." She paused. "A man who carries that kind of cash in his pocket probably has a lot more in the bag on the seat."

"He could be a dealer," Tommy became excited.

"Yeah. That means....."

They broke into evil smiles and spoke in unison, "Free drugs too!"

Megan grabbed Tommy by the arm and pulled him toward the black truck, "We might'a just hit the jackpot!"

Megan rifled through the overnight bag and tossed the clothes over her shoulder into the thick bushes. Tommy ruthlessly tore into the glovebox and tossed everything he deemed of no value on the ground. That included the vehicle registration. However, he quickly realized that little piece of paper could be important, so he picked it up and stuck it into his jeans pocket.

Soon Megan let out an excited yelp when she discovered the first of two envelopes tucked away in not so secret pockets on opposite sides of the bag. Each contained two thousand dollars.

Tommy nodded confidently, "He's a dealer. There's probably a lot more."

"Yeah, we just gotta find it."

"Give me your keys," Tommy demanded.

"They're in the ignition," Megan was confused. "Why?"

Tommy bolted to the car, snatched the keys, ran to the trunk, opened it and dug into the jumbled mess. Soon he produced a hunting knife with a long blade. He ran back and showed it to Megan.

"We need the right tool for the job," he declared as he jammed the sharp blade into the soft black leather.

Moments later after a series of barely controlled, violent slashes, the beautifully upholstered bench seat was in shreds. But no hidden treasures were discovered.

Disappointed, yet still wild-eyed and undeterred, Tommy prepared to jab the knife in the black leather door panel until Megan grabbed his hand.

"Wait a minute! I bet this truck's worth a fortune. We can't totally destroy it."

Tommy seemed to come to his senses, "Yeah." He continued sheepishly, "Guess I kinda got carried away."

Megan smiled smugly, "What would you do without me?"

......

# 6
# Forced To Leave The Past Behind

The back of Cal's head hurt. He didn't have a clue why. Nor did it make any sense that he laid on his back in the edge of the woods along a narrow, rural road. The only thing he was sure of, he was annoyed how the late afternoon sun glared in his eyes. Reflexively, he slammed his eyes closed. How long had he been there? More importantly, why was he there?

A sudden series of sniffs and a slight rustle sounded on the right side of his head. It captured his attention. It sounded too small to be a human, but large enough to be a potential threat. He held his breath and made sure to lay perfectly still. Dare he look?

The sniffs and rustle of grass grew louder. Then the rustle silenced and he felt the rapid pulses of air being sucked into tiny nostrils, then the rush of air being blown out of a curious nose.

Curiosity prevailed over the fear and he allowed his right eye to crack open ever so slightly. All was blurry at first, a mass of grayish white with pairs of black dots that shifted as if they had purpose. The curious sniffing continued as his eye opened a bit wider. The black dots were definitely coordinated.

A split second later his vision cleared enough to identify the black dots as eyes. As his vision cleared even more, the eyes belonged to curious baby possums that tightly clung to the back of their equally inquisitive mother.

Had he thought about it a split second longer, he would've stayed silent in hopes the curious little critter would've satisfied her curiosity and moseyed along, with her kids still on her back. Instead, he was ready to negotiate. What a foolish notion that turned out to be.

"Make a deal with you, Ma'am."

At the first hint of his voice, the ugliest creature God

ever placed in the woods bolted away so abruptly two of her kids tumbled off her back and rolled against his tender, slightly sunburned cheek.

Bless the terrified mother's heart, she was ten feet away and ready to race up a small tree when she realized she carried a much lighter load.

By the time the soon-to-be extremely aggressive mother possum spun around, Cal was halfway to his feet, and the terrified babies had scrambled to their paws. The mother and her babies quickly closed the gap while Cal created a safe distance between himself and the happily reunited family unit.

Cal extended his hands as he backed further away while the emboldened, protective mother advanced.

"The deal I was about to offer, I won't bite you, if you don't bite me."

It was an unexpected lesson just how fierce the hiss of a provoked mother possum sounded. She meant business and Cal took her seriously. He quickly turned and swiftly walked away. Seconds later the aggressive momma marsupial realized the tall, lanky creature was equally determined to avoid the physical confrontation she was ready to instigate. As Cal moved farther away, the extremely agitated momma stopped, then turned and victoriously strutted into the undergrowth.

To add insult to his bruised ego, Cal imagined the little brats on their mother's back probably snickered at him. One or two probably boasted, "Way to go, momma! You showed that tall, very ugly, two-legged stinkier whose boss."

Unfortunately, as his blood pressure returned to normal, Cal felt worse by the second. He was very dizzy and realized the back of his head throbbed. A curious reach around and light touch revealed a sticky knot on the back of his head. He was afraid he knew what it was. A quick check of his finger tips confirmed. It was drying blood. He'd obviously sustained some type of blow to the back of his head. But how, and why?

During all the excitement he never realized that woven between the fingers of his other hand was a folded bill, but he wasn't sure of the denomination. He had the presence of mind to pull his trusty handkerchief out of his back pocket and wipe the blood off his fingers. Then he removed the money and unfolded it enough to reveal it was a twenty.

Once again his instincts kicked in and he quickly patted his pockets to see if he had any other assets. There were no keys, no change, no phone, and especially no wallet.

A quick evaluation of his dry clothing led him to surmise he hadn't been out in the weather very long. He gently brushed some dust and blades of grass off the front of his jeans and navy blue polo shirt. There was more on the back, but he couldn't see it so that would stay with him a while longer.

Next on his list, where was he? Equally important, why was he there? For some reason he'd already determined by the angle of the sun there were still a few more hours of daylight.

Unfortunately, as he looked to the right and left, he wasn't sure which direction to walk because he had no clue which direction he was headed when he hurt his head. Cal wasn't sure why, but he made the decision and turned right. Based on his best calculation that would be to the Southwest. He was confident that eventually someone would come along that he could flag down and at least find out where he was. Still the reason he was there was up to him to answer, but at that point he didn't have a clue.

......

More than likely, far less time had actually passed. Cal hadn't seen any sign of human life since he started walking. Based on what he'd seen so far, it was logical to assume he was a long way from any city. Nobody lived on this particular stretch of road in the middle of nowhere. Nor was the road heavily traveled. All things considered, Cal felt justified to be more than a little curious. He hadn't seen or heard any manmade forms of transportation, which included planes or helicopters overhead. He was surrounded with a plethora of Nature's symphonies.

Cal wasn't surprised that the farther he walked the more questions he had. None of this made sense, nor could he answer. Two significant questions dominated his time. Was he dreaming? Or, was he dead? If he were only dreaming, then eventually he would awaken. But, if he were dead, was he doomed to aimlessly wander down an empty road that went on forever? And if he were dead, was he condemned to seek but never find answers to, "Why?"

His mind reverted back to the first thing he could

remember. The glaring sun in his eyes seconds before the encounter with the mother possum and her little ones. That was as far back as he could go. There had to be more.

Then, as if to reinforce he was still alive, he heard a familiar, man-made sound. The distinctive, deep-throated rumble of a large Harley Davidson motorcycle.

Harley riders spanned the entire socioeconomic spectrum. Successful, well-educated professionals to hardcore gang members. The majority of Harley enthusiasts were in-between, average people who just loved the freedom and feel of the wind.

The image that popped over the hill appeared to be the least desirable. The Biker wore all black. Helmet, tee shirt, patch-covered vest, tattered jeans, and shin-high, multi-buckled boots. The muscular, colorfully tattooed arms suggested the Biker was male.

Immediately, the Biker whose helmet was full-faced with a dark shield reduced the throttle. The bike slowed considerably, which made Cal extremely nervous. The Biker's head turned. He apparently studied Cal carefully as he rolled past, but Cal kept his head straight. There was no need to turn because the dark shield hid the Biker's eyes.

Cal refused to look back. He picked up his pace but there was nowhere to run, except into the woods, but he didn't have time to hide. His heart rate increased when he heard the bike's engine reduce to the iconic chopping idle. The tires crunched on loose gravel. The Biker turned the bike around. This could go very wrong really quickly.

Not sure if it were the right thing to do, once again Cal refused to turn and face the Biker as he slowly rolled past. A chilling flash of panic raced from the bottoms of Cal's feet to the top of his head as the Biker eased the bike over on the narrow shoulder. Gravel crackled as it rolled to a stop. The Biker's neat, satin polished boots slipped off the foot pegs and kicked up small clouds of dust as they firmly planted on the ground. The loud thumping lope of the engine silenced, but the Biker just sat there, his head facing forward. Obviously the Biker's intent was for Cal to make the next move.

After a few tense seconds, it was evident Cal would stand his ground. The Biker wore black, fingerless gloves. He lifted his left hand and his index finger wagged the familiar, "Come here" motion.

Right or wrong, Cal quickly assessed that was about as non-threatening as the Biker could've been. The cold hard truth, there still was a 50/50 chance the Biker had ill-intent.

However, on the positive 50 side, at the very least the Biker could give Cal some idea of where he was. Even better, maybe take him into town. At that point any town would be good. The disquieting reality he'd avoided as he walked along suddenly stormed to the front of the line. He didn't have a clue where to ask the Biker to take him. He was in an unenviable quandary; and to make matters worse, he was very hungry.

It was decision time and Cal had only two choices. He could continue by himself on an unfamiliar road that led to a place he'd probably never been. Or, he could take a chance and hope the Biker would give him some badly needed assistance. The Biker appeared to patiently wait.

Cal reached into his pocket and pulled out the neatly folded twenty dollar bill. He walked slightly in front of the Biker and extended the twenty, "This is all I have. Can you please take me to the closest town."

The Biker just sat there, not once did he utter a word or offer to lift the dark face shield.

"I'm sorry. I don't have any more," Cal confessed. By then he feared he just made the worst mistake he'd ever made.

The tense, silent stare-down continued. At least from Cal's perspective it was a stare-down. For all he knew the Biker was a faceless robot that awaited instructions from a remote operator. Or, if he were human, he might be waiting for more of his gang. Perhaps the leader was in the pack that followed.

Then the Biker's black helmeted head barely turned to the right, then back to the center. Did that mean, "No?" He wasn't waiting on more Bikers. Or, "No," I don't want your money. Cal had to consider the Biker might be hearing his thoughts. After all, he still wasn't sure if he was dead or dreaming.

Quite unexpectedly a non-mechanical voice projected from the ominous black helmet, calming Cal so he dared to relax though ever so slightly.

"Keep your money. Hop on."

Cal shook his head. He couldn't believe he was about to do the dumbest thing he'd even done in his life, and he was perfectly comfortable with its absurdity.

Just before Cal swung his leg over the massive machine, he decided this had to be a dream, so he might as well ride it out. Enjoy it to its fullest.

"Ever been on a bike before?" The Biker asked.

"Years ago my wife and I used to ride twelve speed pedal bikes."

"Then you understand the principle of leaning into turns."

"Yes. It might take me a turn or two, but I'll try not to work against you."

The Biker offered a simple suggestion that made perfect sense, "There's a strap on the seat behind me. You'll probably be more comfortable holding on to it, instead of me."

Cal understood because men had issues with touching other men, even for safety purposes.

It was odd that Cal remembered in movies when overstuffed, brawny men mounted their "hogs" then placed their grubby boots on the starter lever and stomped the massive beast's engine into life. He braced himself for the shifting of weight that never happened. This "hog" must've had an electric starter. The engine just thundered into life. It was loud. The thump of the lope and vibration of the engine bolted to the frame provided a brand new sensory experience. It was actually exhilarating and Cal understood how easily people could become addicted.

It was probably a habit all Bikers had to rev the thunderous engine a couple of times before letting out the clutch. The pull away was smooth and Cal barely felt the gear shifts.

Within minutes Cal experienced a profound revelation that defied logic, yet was so liberating. Helmetless, the fresh air that rushed around him and over him seemed to have blown away a heavy burden he'd carried far too long. A burden he couldn't readily identify or even fathom letting go. If this were the reason for the dream, then it had already fulfilled its purpose. Even though he wasn't sure what he just let go, he was so relieved such a heavy load appeared to have vanished into thin air.

By then the sun had fallen behind the rolling hills and Cal realized it must've been later than he thought. Based on his estimate before the Biker appeared, at that moment the sun was much lower in the sky than it should've been. He hadn't been on the bike that long. Or, had he? Obviously he enjoyed himself so much that he lost track of time. He really hadn't paid attention to the number of turns they'd made, or how many different roads they'd been on. As far as he knew, they were still on the same road.

Then the Biker reduced the throttle and down shifted the gears to assist with slowing the bike. Even though they hadn't met or passed another vehicle, the Biker extended his right arm to indicate his intention to make a right turn. Cal coordinated his lean with the Biker for a smooth, comfortable turn on to another country road.

Cal barely noticed the name on the green road sign, Destiny Way. It was an odd name for a road, but he let it go and focused his thoughts on exactly where a "Destiny Way" would lead them. The answer awaited a few hundred yards down the road where streetlights flickered on. At last, Cal was about to return to civilization where hopefully he could start finding answers to his mounting questions. First on the list was this odyssey of a dream about to end?

The Biker brought the bike to a stop about a hundred yards from the first street light. He shut down the engine. The sudden silence was deafening.

"Is this where I get off?" Cal wasn't sure what to do.

"Yes," The Biker replied softly, but with authority. "This is as far as I can take you. The rest is up to you."

"Well, okay then," Cal didn't know what else to say as he dismounted and stepped away.

The black bike thundered back to life and the force of the massive energy vibrated against Cal's chest. It seemed more powerful than before, unnervingly out of this world.

Without so much as a glance to the right, the Biker eased forward, then made a u-turn and slowly thundered away.

Cal lifted his hand and waved, "Thanks. My name is Cal. Nice to meet you."

Eerily, the Biker lifted his arm and waved as if he heard and responded.

## RETURN TO FAITH

As the Biker grew smaller in the dimming light, Cal realized that on the back of his black leather vest was an arched patch, the kind that identified the gang, group, or club the Biker belonged. The entire time Cal was on the bike, not once did he focus on words embroidered in crisp, black letters. He had no clue it read, "Lord of Lords."

Likewise, as Cal turned to face what lay ahead on Destiny's Way, he would never know that the Biker paused at the stop sign and turned back for one last look. The Biker nodded. He had indeed done all he could do for Cal. They had an appointed meeting in the future, and he hoped Cal would be ready. For now, this was the place Cal had chosen to be, so he must face himself and his own demons before he would realize he needed help. The answers he sought were in front of him. It would be up to him to see the way, to accept the truth, and to reconnect with the one thing that could restore him and enable him to fulfill his destiny.

At that point Cal couldn't grasp the impossibility of returning to a place he had never left, nor could he grasp the unfathomable joy of returning to a place he should've never left.

Cal stood alone as the uncertainty of darkness descended. While on the bike with the mysterious Biker, Cal had become so relaxed, secure and actually feeling safe. Now confusion and an unnerving unease settled over him. He was compelled to walk toward the dim light.

Between Cal and the first light pole was an aged wooden sign he assumed was the name of the small community that lay beyond. The faded letters were eye level and at that point only spelled the name of the town. It was very possible he would never grasp the significance of the name. He read the words aloud.

"Welcome To Faith."

......

# 7
# When Past Becomes Both Present And Future

Megan and Tommy found a few more packs of Cal's money hidden in Annie. With eight thousand dollars in hand, they were on top of the world. It was time to live it up. Megan would be the banker and control the cash. They didn't have the guts to actually use the stolen credit cards in public, and they lacked the computer savvy to exploit them online. In what would become their only rational choice that evening, they burned the credit cards, along with Cal's driver's license.

Megan was a speed junkie behind the wheel, and in an often stated rebuke, Tommy drove like a little old lady.

At speeds in excess of 100 mph, Megan led the way on the very familiar back road. Tommy could barely keep Megan's tail lights in sight on the winding strip of asphalt.

While Megan cackled with glee, Tommy cursed and swore under his breath, "She's gonna kill us both, and we'll never get to spend all that money."

They were so wrong for each other. Megan was a free spirit whose mother had abandoned her and her drunken father who became the worst possible role model. Megan loved her father mostly because he allowed her to do what she wanted.

On the other hand, even though Tommy was fatherless, his mother was a devout Christian who struggled to get by. She tried her best to be the mother her son deserved. Much to his mother's dismay, Tommy evolved into a rudderless sailboat with no clear direction in life.

Unfortunately for Tommy, within minutes after they met a few years ago, Megan realized he was easily influenced, and like most men, subject to sexual bribery. She kept Tommy under control with few departures from her game plan. Yet, she was still upset that he refused to put the bullets in the gun. That could've turned out badly had their victim turned hero and charged her. She was sure that she wouldn't have intentionally killed the guy. If he would've forced her to shoot him, it would've been in self-defense.

Megan groaned as she checked the rearview mirror again, "Come on, Granny. Pick up the pace." She knew the old truck wasn't built to lean into the curves and twists in the road, but he could've stayed closer if he really tried. She slowed down. She had a surefire incentive to speed him up.

Tommy was relieved when he realized he was closing the gap, "Okay. Hopefully you've had enough of the Richard Petty game. Now let's take it easy for a while." Tommy's wishful thinking was so misplaced and very unwise. He dared to relax until he rounded the next curve. There sat Megan's car in the oncoming lane, with a long straight stretch ahead. He knew what that meant and he was already shaking his head as he brought the old black truck to a stop beside Megan's hooptie. She revved the engine a few times as she leaned over so she could see Tommy's face.

"Beat me to the end of this stretch, and you can have your way with me," She playfully teased.

"Are you kidding me?" Tommy shook his head, "It would take ten miles to get this thing up to eighty miles an hour."

"Give you a head start," Megan taunted. "You know I'm worth it."

That was all it took. In his eagerness to make the best possible start, Tommy let the clutch out too soon and Annie merely lurched forward before she stalled out. Megan howled with laughter.

"Okay. So I'll give you a do-over," Megan cackled. "Make this one count."

Tommy was embarrassed and frustrated as he turned the key. Annie didn't fail and fired up. This time the foolish young man was less aggressive with the clutch and was actually impressed with how quickly the old truck accelerated. The power had been there all along; he was just afraid to unleash the beast under the hood.

Megan was caught off guard by how quickly the old truck raced away. She stomped on her accelerator and the wild chase was on. Her car had an automatic transmission that changed the gears much faster than Tommy could wind up the old manual gearbox in Annie. The last time she glanced down at her speedometer it had just ticked past 100 mph, but they were nearly at the end of the straight stretch. The next few miles were too curvy to take at that speed.

Confident she had won the drag race and was far enough ahead, she cut too quickly in front of the old black truck.

It was too late. Tommy realized he had neglected to strap the seatbelt across his waist when the back of Megan's car slammed into the front of the truck. He panicked and overcompensated which caused him to lose control. The truck swerved wildly across both lanes. He just about had it corrected when Megan's car on the verge of rolling over slammed back into the truck.

The impact corrected Megan's direction. She had already slowed enough to only lightly skid the tires around the sharp curve. As her car continued to slow, her white-knuckled hands maintained their death-grip on the steering wheel. Her eyes turned to the rearview mirror where she witnessed the carnage unfold.

"No! Tommy! No!" Megan cried out. "What have I done?"

Tommy's luck ran out. The last contact with Megan's car doomed Annie to a straight line through the sharp left turn. Tommy may have had the steering wheel clutched tightly in his hands, but he was a helpless passenger as the truck went airborne off the road, over a shallow ravine. The nose of the truck dipped down as the back of the truck rose. As if in slow-motion, Megan witnessed the headlights and taillights of the truck swap ends twice until it completed a full revolution before slamming back down on all four tires.

From her perspective, Megan had no clue that the violent impact knocked Tommy out, just before the front of the truck crashed into thick undergrowth.

By then the flying truck was completely obscured behind the trees. Megan didn't witness the truck kick up clumps of grass and dirt clouds as it violently flipped end-over-end several times.

Megan screamed as she ran back to where the old black truck flew off the road, "Tommy! Tommy! I'm so sorry!" She was out of breath but ran as fast as she could, "Please be okay!"

Without regard for what she might discover, Megan leapt

into the darkness and thick undergrowth. Her feet became entangled and she fell face first into a fragrant, budding bush. She struggled to her feet and forced her way deeper into the twisted roots and vines until she saw the truck at the bottom of the hill. At least the headlights pointed in the right direction, but was the truck right side up on its wheels, or upside down on its top?

"Tommy! You okay?" Megan was frantic as she stumbled down the hill to level ground. Thankfully, the brush thinned which made it easier to hop over.

So far there was no sign of life around the truck. She assumed Tommy was still inside. As she got close, she heard the ominous hiss of steam. She panicked when she realized the truck was upside down and the top of the cab was crushed down to the dashboard. She thought it odd that the overhead light was still on.

Both doors had been jarred open and crushed as the truck violently tumbled. The engine had stalled but all four wheels still turned. Megan feared the worst. Her voice was meek, heavy with guilt, "Tommy, you still in the truck?" She mumbled as she inched toward the smoking hunk of twisted metal. The hiss of steam grew louder.

As Megan cautiously leaned over, she was terrified that she would probably discover Tommy's broken, mangled, lifeless body. Instead she couldn't help but smile when the cab was completely empty, except for a flashlight that laid on the crumpled roof.

Then another even more horrible thought weakened her knees as she dropped to the forest floor. She gasped. The only way to know for sure was to start looking. She snatched the flashlight and anxiously fiddled with it but couldn't figure out how to turn it on. It was one of those new-fangled, multipurpose light "thingies." Her frustration mounted as she haplessly fumbled.

"Who sits around thinking up these stupid men-toys?" She grumbled until she pushed the right button that ignited the face of the sun. Reflexively she gasped and averted her eyes from the painful light, as she slung the flashlight across the carpet of new Spring growth. She leapt up and quickly retrieved the light. She had to find Tommy.

Megan wildly flashed the bright light around as she

frantically searched for what she feared she would find. The dense, new undergrowth was high enough to cover over Tommy's body, or body parts.

"Tommy! Tommy! Tommy!"

......

As day quietly yielded to night, the streetlights illuminated the quaint little town of Faith, a short walk beyond the faded welcome sign. It appeared to be one of those sleepy little country villages that incorporated into a town. That kind dots rural America.This was a place where out of necessity the generations who built, named and supported Faith had all but died out, and their offspring mostly had abandoned. More than likely, during Faith's pinnacle, in that part of North Carolina the lifeblood of the community was split between large-scale family farming, a cotton mill, a hosiery mill, or small furniture factory. When those industries fled America, and family farming became a losing proposition, many such communities withered and faded into obscurity. A ghost town erupts full of empty, dilapidated buildings filled with many fond memories but no humans left to remember and share. For some reason Faith had been able to hang on.

As fate would have it the very thing Cal was in most need of was the first surviving business he spotted. Red neon letters glowed Faith Family Diner on the sign mounted on a blue pole. Fortunately the lights were on inside the small brick building and a few cars were in the lot.

The rusty spring attached to the wooden framed screen door squeaked as Cal pulled it open. The worn and tarnished brass doorknob was cool to the touch. A little bell attached to the door tinkled as he pushed it open.

The interior walls were akin to a Cracker Barrel, a time capsule filled with objects from the 1940's through the 1970's. It was more of a museum setting, rather than a worn out relic of a bygone era. Cal paused and wondered if it was a functioning diner, or some type of off-the-beaten-path museum? Until the alluring aroma engulfed him answered that question.

A pleasant female voice sounded, "Take a seat anywhere you want. I'll be with you shortly." The voice belonged to Betsy Tate, the head waitress and owner, who refilled the coffee cups of two elderly, blue overalls clad gentlemen, Melvin and Dub, seated at the bar. "Would you like a cup?" Betsy held up the steamy pot. She was in her early forties, slender, and attractive. She reminded Cal of someone but no name came to mind.

Cal pushed the door closed then paused and mumbled to himself, "Do I drink coffee?"

Betsy glanced at her regular customers and scrunched her shoulders while the newcomer considered the offer.

At a table midway along the outer wall sat a husband and wife on one side, with their five-year-old son and seven-year-old daughter opposite. The curious children had turned, climbed up and rested on their knees on the padded bench seat. They were like curious puppies who studied the quiet stranger as the most current oddity.

Questions flooded Cal's mind as he made his way to the wall mounted booth closest to the door. He was unaware he was the center of attention. Seven people watched his every move.

"Turn around," the young mother instructed her reluctant children, but they acted as if they didn't hear.

"Do as your mother asked," The stern voice of their father demanded the children's immediate attention, and they quickly complied.

Cal was confused by the time he slid into the comfortable booth. More questions than he could possibly answer echoed in his mind, like the Niagara River as it poured over the edge.

Betsy figured she'd given her new customer enough time to decide, "You want a cup of freshly brewed coffee?"

Cal stared blankly out the window and didn't realize he whispered his thoughts instead of answering the question he never heard, "Not sure I even like coffee."

"Honey, you okay?" Betsy was concerned.

All eyes turned back to Cal who remained focused on something outside, that neither of them saw.

......

Megan erratically pointed the flashlight as she frantically jumped around in the shin-high undergrowth. She had to find Tommy alive. "Tommy! Tommy!" The longer she searched the more hysterical she became. "Oh, God! What have I done?"

The harsh reality caused her to pause her search. She had been enjoying her usual "it's all about me and what makes me happy," when she made what might have been a fatal mistake. If Tommy were dead, it was her fault. With her record she could face the rest of her life in prison. She really liked Tommy. He was fun as long as he played by her rules, but he wasn't worth her spending the rest of her life behind bars, especially if he were dead.

Of course that mindset was heartless and callus, but it was the best she could do in the heat of the moment. She was who and what she really was, and would always be, so she had to accept the facts and move on.

Megan realized her car sat halfway on the road with the lights on and the driver's door open. "Well, that's not going to be suspicious at all," she rationalized, "If Tommy's dead, there's nothing I can do for him. And if somebody drives by and sees my car like that, they'll call the cops."

It was the moment of truth. She had to make a decision based on what was best for her in the long run. Even the night critters and creatures seemed to have gone silent as if to await her next move. She made one more slow, complete circle as the powerful flashlight beam pierced deeply into the darkness. There was no sign of Tommy. No groans of someone in pain.

"Sorry, babe," Megan slowly shook her head. "I gotta get outta here."

Moments later, without taking time to consider the amount of evidence she would leave behind, Megan laid the flashlight on the side of the road, pointed into the woods. That would identify the spot where the truck went off the road. That was the best she could do. She didn't like it, but she had no choice. She ran to her car and quickly drove away.

As Megan put more distance between herself and the accident site, it dawned on her there was one more thing she could do. In her frazzled mind, she didn't completely think it through. She picked up her cell phone and debated if she should make "the call."

.......

Betsy smiled as she arrived at Cal's booth with the coffee

pot in one hand and a menu in the other. She would try one more time, "Would you like a cup of coffee and a menu?"

Cal still couldn't remember if he liked coffee, but he was nearly ravenous so he shook his head.

"Both?" Betsy didn't want to assume.

Unsure what to say, Cal nodded then muttered, "Yeah. Ahhh, both." He could sample the coffee and then he would know.

Betsy handed the menu to Cal, then turned the coffee cup over and started to pour, "Cream and sugar?"

"Ahh, yeah. Sure."

"We serve breakfast all day, if you're interested."

Again with the options. Cal's frustration mounted. He wasn't sure if he was even fond of breakfast foods.

Betsy had worked with the public since she started as a waitress in the Faith Family Diner as a high school sophomore. Over the years she realized she had an above average ability to judge character when she met new people. She immediately became uneasy because she rarely received the level of mixed signals this new customer emitted.

"We're kinda off the beaten path. Don't get many strangers. You live nearby... have family in town?"

Cal just wanted to get something to eat. He was already consumed with trying to figure out what was going on. If he were alive or dead. He didn't have time, nor was he in the mood to play fifty questions with an attractive, but annoyingly nosy waitress.

Hopefully a quick, ambiguous answer would signal his reluctance to get all "chatty," in an effort to boost her tip, "I'm from up the road a ways."

That didn't work. The waitress persisted, "Didn't notice you drive up. Having car trouble? My brother runs the only garage in town. Always trying to hustle up some business for him."

Cal picked up the menu in an obvious move to avoid answering the current question, or invite the next one, "I'll need a minute, if you don't mind."

Betsy became even more suspicious and took notice of Cal's disheveled appearance, "Sure. Be back in a few."

As Betsy walked away from Cal's booth, she was tempted to call her brother and ask him to come over. This guy may be too embarrassed to admit he didn't have enough money to pay to have his car towed and get it worked on. She doubted he walked from wherever he was from. Hitchhikers were extremely rare around their little town. They were just that far out of the way. Her brother had a big heart and over the years he had helped many strangers who had car trouble on their way to or from anywhere other than Faith.

......

"Nine-one-one, state your emergency?"

Megan panicked. Instead of sounding angry and concerned she went full-blown, over-the-top hysterical, "I'm in labor. Was on the way to the hospital when this maniac in a truck passed me. He lost control, went off the road. I was terrified, afraid to stop, but I did and left my flashlight pointing into the woods where he went off the road."

It was well after dark and the seasoned Dispatcher wondered how the caller knew the driver of the truck was a "he?" But she had to follow a carefully laid out protocol, "Ma'am, I need you to calm down and as detailed as possible help me understand where you are. Miss Allen, are you calling on your cell phone because I'm not seeing an address?"

Megan drew in a long breath. She realized she had to lie. This always came too easily. She calmly responded, "This is not my cell phone. I found it the other day."

"At this point that's irrelevant. Are you still at the scene of the accident?"

"No! I had to leave cause my baby's coming any minute."

"Are you driving?"

"I'm fine. But you need to get an ambulance out to…"

"Ma'am can you give me an address?"

"There ain't no address. It happened on Causey Road, off Highway 64."

"Causey Road is long and winding."

"I done told you…. left his…. I mean my flashlight point'n where he went off the road."

"Ma'am, hold on. Since this happened on a rural county road, let me get an ambulance and the Highway Patrol on the way to the accident scene."

"I gotta go!"

"Wait. I need your name, phone number, the hospital…."

# RETURN TO FAITH

All the Dispatcher heard was. "Click." Something was very wrong with that call. She suspected the caller was involved with the accident and wasn't pregnant. More than likely the caller was also the owner of the phone.

Until recently, cell phone numbers had been harder to verify and confirm their location when used. Now all the Dispatcher had to do was make a couple of calls and she would know the carrier, and the exact tower the phone was closest to when the call was made. The Dispatcher knew the person who actually owned the phone might not be the one who placed the call.

Another thing the Dispatcher didn't know was that Megan was very familiar with the area and had turned up on a narrow dirt road near the accident. She was parked where she had the perfect vantage point of the curve where the truck flew off the road. It was one of hers and Tommy's favorite, secluded, romantic spots.

......

## 8
## The Mystery Deepens

Cal opted for breakfast. Two eggs over-well, smothered with cheddar cheese, two sausage patties not overcooked, hash browns, a bowl of grits, and buttered whole wheat toast. He also tried the coffee which he liked enough to have four cups. Each cup was an experiment. The first was black. The second was with cream only. The third was with honey only. The fourth had both honey and cream. That was his favorite combination. At least the coffee mystery had been solved.

On the other hand, the items of food on the plate just came to him randomly, seemingly out of the blue. The combination Cal wanted wasn't listed on the menu, but the chatty waitress was more than happy to write it up for him.

As a matter of fact, Cal's attitude had softened toward her and they had hit it off. He was actually disappointed when she asked, "Can I get you anything else?"

Cal's stomach was pleasantly stuffed with an amazing meal. He had finally relaxed enough to share his trademark smile before he responded, "No, Ma'am, I'm quite content."

Betsy tried in vain to restrict her smile, but she beamed. She couldn't help it. Her cheeks flushed with embarrassment.

There was an awkward moment where neither knew what to say. The silence was broken by the young father a few booths over. "Betsy, we're ready for our check."

Betsy turned to the young couple whose children had returned to their usual rambunctious selves, "Be right there," she said as she turned back to Cal, "I'll ring up yours too."

Cal nodded as Betsy turned away and walked toward the cash register at the end of the bar, which was next to the door he entered. He thought to himself, "So, her name is, Betsy." That was the moment when an enjoyable evening switched back into the mass confusion that ruled the late afternoon that led him to Faith.

The annoying mystery deepened. He knew the beautiful

waitress' name, but couldn't introduce himself because he didn't have a clue who he was. Equally perplexing, why did he find himself on a road he didn't remember, especially with a knot on the back of his aching head that he didn't have a clue how he acquired.

"Have a good evening," the young father smiled at Betsy as he handed her the signed copy of the bill. Then he and his frustrated wife attempted to herd their tussling children toward the door.

"You too," Betsy replied as she reached for Cal's ticket. She smiled as she rang it up. "Eight, sixty-two."

Cal unfolded and extended the twenty dollar bill. Betsy immediately noticed Cal didn't hold a wallet in his other hand. It wasn't uncommon for customers to hand her cash, then simply place the change, both bills and coins in a pocket. Two customers in particular who handled their money that way were Melvin and Dub. These guys were real-life incarnations of the Walter Matthau and Jack Lemon characters from the hilarious movie, "Grumpy Old Men." Both Melvin and Dub kept their money in their right front overhaul pockets.

Melvin and Dub made no attempt to disguise their interest in Betsy's interaction with the nice looking stranger. They may have been old, but they knew Betsy and still relished fond memories of meeting a special young lady. It was obvious Betsy and the stranger had connected. Melvin turned to Dub and they shared a smile and wink.

Betsy carefully counted the change into Cal's hand, "Here you go, eleven, thirty-eight. Please, do come back if you're gonna be in town a few days."

Not paying attention, Dub reached over to nudge Melvin with an elbow, but instead knocked the coffee cup out of his hand. The "Clank" destroyed the moment. Melvin and Dub awkwardly snatched napkins out of the dispenser in order to stem the flow of the dark liquid on the white countertop. The ruckus demanded Betsy's immediate attention. The long-time friends made sport of each other.

"You should'a wiped the butter off your fingers," Dub accused.

Melvin fired back, "You big Dummy! You need to keep your elbows to yourself."

Melvin's and Dub's clumsy, borderline spastic efforts

failed and coffee splattered on the floor.

"Sorry, I need to take care of this," Betsy apologized to Cal, then wheeled around and headed to the disaster zone. "It's okay, boys. No harm done."

Cal wanted to stay and chat with Betsy for a few minutes, but there were too many things he couldn't explain and far too many questions he simply couldn't answer. He opted for the coward's way out. The spill was the perfect opportunity to escape.

As Cal turned to leave, he revealed the matted, bloody spot on the back of his head. Betsy, Melvin, and Dub were too busy to notice. The bell on the door "tinkled" as he exited.

"Nice go'n Spazo," Dub barked at Melvin.

"He was kinda weird. Probably a serial killer. Betsy'll be better off if he doesn't come back," Melvin surmised.

"Wait a minute, fellas," Betsy paused as she placed the dry mop in the growing pool of coffee on her clean floor. "A stranger comes in for a bite to eat. He'll likely never come back in here again. Cut him some slack."

Melvin nudged Dub and they both grinned as they watched Betsy's eyes cut to and focus on the door.

"I don't know," Melvin grinned mischievously. "He seemed to like your coffee."

"I think he liked his waitress much more," Dub chuckled.

"You guys. Cut me some slack," Betsy set about cleaning up Melvin's and Dub's mess. She couldn't help but look at the door. Two thoughts came to mind. She hoped the stranger would come back. More importantly, she hoped he wasn't a serial killer.

Betsy's thoughtful glance at the door wasn't lost on Melvin and Dub. They were even more hopeful the stranger would come back, and that he wasn't a serial killer. They were too old for Betsy, and she deserved to have a great guy in her life. One who would treat her right.

. . . . . . .

Law Enforcement vehicles and an ambulance were parked near the flashlight that cut a bright path into the stand of trees. Flashing lights clicked on top of the vehicles and sent red and blue streaks across the new leaves. Paramedics carefully loaded Tommy into the back of the ambulance. Two Deputy Sheriffs compared notes with Trooper Daniels. All three were suspicious.

"The Nine-One-One caller's story doesn't add up," Trooper Daniels surmised.

"No sign of a single skid mark," Deputy Karr added.

"We need to track down the caller," Trooper Daniels said. He would get the ball rolling when he got back into his car. "Will one of you stay until the wrecker gets here? I want to follow the ambulance to the hospital."

"The paramedics aren't very optimistic," Deputy Karr felt he should inform the Trooper.

"Yeah. I may not be able to get a statement from him," Trooper Daniels lamented.

From her hidden vantage point on a nearby hill, Megan nervously chewed her fingernails while crouched behind a bush. She drew in a shaky breath as the ambulance pulled away below. The siren blasted into the quiet night.

"Sorry, Tommy. Hope you make it," Megan struggled to keep from howling her frustration at the darkened sky.

......

Cal faded into the dimness beyond the last old-fashioned street light. It was too late to head back out to the road because he didn't have a clue where to go, or why. With a full stomach his body was ready to rest and digest. All he needed at that moment was a dry, sheltered place to lay down and collect his thoughts. If he were to drift off to sleep, that would be okay. Hopefully he would awaken with a clear head.

The low, full moon cast an eerie light and silhouetted a nondescript building one block off Main Street. There were no exterior lights, and no lights on inside the structure. That became his destination. His refuge for the evening.

The undergrowth was unfriendly and painful to navigate the patches of thick briers in the dim light. In the morning he would be able to plot a less brutal course out.

Finally he stepped into a clearing that appeared to surround the building. Now he was able to look up and evaluate the potential shelter. Before him stood a dilapidated wooden church with a tattered roof that appeared to be partially collapsed. A quick scan of the night sky revealed stars as far as he could see, but Spring showers could pop up at any time. He wasn't sure how he knew that, but it was a concern he must address, especially if there were no opened doors or windows.

A passing car on Main Street temporarily distracted Cal before he tentatively placed his right foot on the crumbling brick stairs. He tested the integrity of the bricks on each level of the four steps until he reached the concrete porch slab.

The hall was dim and foreboding. Yet to his right, another doorless entry led to the sanctuary. Moonbeams showed through stained glass windows and created a surreal mosaic of muted colors. One very odd possibility stood out. It appeared not a single panel of colored glass was broken. With the building's current state of disrepair it made no sense that the beautiful windows would still be intact.

The boards squeaked as Cal walked through the doorway, but they felt far more solid and secure than they should've. He was oddly curious. He felt a chilling familiarity to a place he was certain he'd never been before.

Like a moth drawn to a flame, Cal eased into the dim, cobweb draped room. For some reason he was sure he knew exactly how many rows of dusty pews were before him. He was relieved when he glanced up and it appeared the wooden plank ceiling was still intact, even if the roof had partially collapsed.

Cal had relaxed until an unexpected, very ominous growl sounded to his left. It seemed to originate from the pulpit that laid face down on the three-foot, raised platform.

A split second later a second warning sounded and a skinny, female Golden Retriever stepped out of the overturned pulpit. Completely oblivious to the potential danger, six small puppies frolicked and tumbled into their mother who definitely stood guard. The third growl was even more threatening after her babies appeared. The seriousness of the growl ended the play time. One by one the puppies cowered back into the hopeful safety of the dark shadows. However, a few brave pups curiously poked their heads out.

Cal stood his ground and lifted his hands. The words came from somewhere he couldn't consciously relate, "Easy Sheena. Just looking for a place to take a nap." Even more perplexing, he knew exactly why the name came to him.

# RETURN TO FAITH

Sheena Queen of the Jungle, the Fiction House Comic Book character that premiered in 1937, in Britain. Sheena was the first female heroine in her own adventure, but why would this real-life mother dog spark such a reference?

Sheena left no doubt she meant business. She inched closer to the edge of the platform as she intensified her guttural growl. Cal dared to take a few steps backward until he bumped into the end of a pew. Sheena made another threatening step forward until Cal caught his balance and resumed his retreat.

Satisfied she had asserted her position as the Alpha female, Sheena stopped growling and herded her puppies into the shadows of the pulpit.

Totally exhausted and ready to sleep, Cal felt that since the dog had established the boundaries, they could peacefully coexist and sleep for the night, in their own safe spaces. Cal settled down on the front row pew. He knew it was covered with thick dust but at that moment he was too tired to care.

Cal laid down and with a simple fidget and twist, he was stretched out. His exhausted body was comfortable. Mere seconds later confusion and concern for his safety were overpowered by a long overdue sense that everything would be okay.

......

# 9
# No Answers In The Light Of Day

Early morning sunbeams pierced the stained glass windows. The colorful mosaics could never highlight the actual strength of the oak pews that were still securely screwed to the wooden floor. They stood in straight rows like dedicated soldiers ready for active duty.

Unfortunately, the church body had long since died out, and the building was abandoned to a cruel and lonely demise. It was an average morning for the forgotten and neglected old church. Years had marched on and left the interior of the building frozen in time, but the exterior had been ravaged by the merciless elements of wind, snow, rain and intense summer heat.

Cal slept soundly on the front row unaware he had become the subject of intense interest. Six curious puppies followed their keen sense of smell to Cal's makeshift bed. The inquisitive pups had no reason to fear their potential new playmate. They awkwardly lifted their front paws to rest on the edge of the pew. Their tails wagged and their lower bodies squirmed as they lined up and eagerly sniffed. They began to whine. The boldest in the group dared to lick Cal's face.

The flurry of activity around Cal, coupled with the wet tongue that lapped his face, woke him from a deep sleep. He reflexively held his hand as a barrier to eager pup's incessant though well-meant licking. He lifted his head enough to realize he had six new friends.

"Well, good morning, kids. Are you sure your Mom's gonna approve?"

The answer quickly followed. A familiar, ominous growl instantly captured the puppies' attention. In unison they dropped to all fours and spun around. They froze like kids caught with their hands in the cookie jar until Sheena eased out of the shadows and into the doorway with a bulging white, grease-stained bag in her mouth.

# RETURN TO FAITH

The excited puppies' paws slipped on the wooden floor. They ran in place until their claws finally caught traction. Cal was abandoned as the blonde streaks scampered to meet Sheena at the overturned pulpit.

Cal rose, stretched and yawned. He looked around and remembered how tired he'd been the night before and the confrontation with the mother dog. If he were lucky, and the puppies weren't in too much trouble, the protective mother would relax. It was a good sign that she was preoccupied and paid him no attention.

Obviously Sheena no longer considered him a threat to her and her kids, so he swung his legs and lowered his feet to the floor. His attention was drawn to the toppled pulpit. He wasn't sure why he was in the abandoned church, but that could wait a bit longer to figure out. He was hungry.

Cal watched as Sheena carefully tore the bag open and pulled out what appeared to be a wrapped biscuit which she used her front teeth to carefully unwrap and place on the floor. As if it had become routine, three of the six puppies converged and attacked the warm meal.

Sheena reached her snout into the bag, extracted another biscuit and repeated the process. She watched to ensure her hungry brood would mind their manners and share their bounty. Satisfied, she turned her attention to Cal and extracted another biscuit. Without hesitation, as if driven by motherly instinct, she trotted over and hopped down from the platform. She never hesitated as she confidently trotted toward Cal and presented him the wrapped treat. It smelled heavenly, but he was careful not to move too quickly in accepting the gift.

"You're not just another stray. Somebody spent a lot of time with you," Cal surmised as he quickly unwrapped the biscuit, but his attention was drawn to Sheena as she sat down at his feet. She licked her snout as she watched him prepare to chomp down on the thick tenderloin, egg and cheese, stuffed between the fluffy, golden halves of the warm biscuit. "How rude of me. This is the last one... you're sharing."

Sheena whined softly before she licked her snout again. Cal felt guilty that he had been so self-consumed. He tore the biscuit and its savory contents into equal parts. He extended one half to Sheena, who gently took it and returned to her puppies. She tore the half into quarters and her brood immediately devoured the pieces, then licked up every crumb.

Cal decided he really wasn't that hungry after all, "Hey, Momma, come here, girl." He waved the biscuit, then took a few big bites and extended the remaining quarter of the biscuit.

The puppies' ears perked and Cal expected to be mobbed until Sheena growled. The puppies cowered into the shadows of the pulpit as Sheena visited Cal to receive her share of breakfast. This time she took it and stepped only a few feet away before she chewed a few times and swallowed.

It was only after Sheena returned to the platform and laid down that her kids dared to exit the shelter of the pulpit. When they realized their new playmate was still around, they raced over and lavished him with affection.

The Momma appeared relaxed, but she kept a watchful eye on Cal as he sat on the floor and played with her energetic and rambunctious fur balls. They climbed all over him. They licked, chewed and tussled with him relentlessly. It was obvious Momma welcomed the needed break.

......

The paramedics had called the medevac helicopter shortly after they arrived on the scene the night before. They doubted Tommy could survive the ground transportation to the trauma center in Charlotte.

Since there were no safe landing zones close to the accident scene, the paramedics transported Tommy a few miles south, closer to Charlotte, where the chopper could safely land. It was the right decision. Immediately upon Tommy's arrival in the ER, the neurologist determined it best to put him into an induced coma.

It had been touch and go with Tommy throughout the night. The swelling in his brain had been carefully monitored and finally stabilized around 4:00 AM.

Tommy had built a long "wrap-sheet" with the local law enforcement agencies. Due to the numerous run-ins he'd had, combined with no evidence the truck's owner had been ejected from the vehicle in the woods, they determined the truck had been stolen. Odds were the owner wasn't even in the area, let alone in the truck during the accident. The Deputies concluded Tommy had been involved with the theft. Phone records confirmed the 911 call came from Megan's cell phone. The deputies had seen her recently and she was too slender to even be thirty minutes pregnant, let alone in labor.

The truck hadn't been reported as stolen. While at the accident scene, Trooper Daniels sent a text message with a photo of the truck's registration to Trooper Miller, his counterpart in Randolph County. Since they didn't know where the owner of the truck was at the time, the law enforcement officers had to assume the worst, so they had to locate him ASAP. Even though it was the wee hours of the morning, Trooper Miller drove to the address to confirm if the owner was at home. He rang the doorbell. Then after a minute with no activity inside, he turned his flashlight's powerful beam on the realty sign in the front yard. There was no sold sign attached. The smell of freshly cut grass only meant the yard had been mowed recently, but the truck's owner could've moved out long ago.

Trooper Miller called for a Randolph County deputy to meet him at the residence to assist with a welfare check. In extreme cases officers are empowered to burst through doors to make sure the person in question was not incapacitated.

Randolph County Deputy Russell had a battering ram in his trunk and was careful to inflict the least amount of damage when he bashed the door open. Even though it was furnished, it didn't take long for the officers to discover the house was unoccupied.

Trooper Miller and the Deputy Russell consulted with their supervisors who advised them of the steps they were required to take in such a scenario. They had found no sign of Rev. Calvin Baxter by 8:00 AM, the end of their shifts.

The search for Rev. Baxter would be continued by the day shift officers.

......

Megan and Tommy had stopped at the liquor store shortly after they realized how much cash they had to blow. They picked up three half gallon bottles of their favorite Jack Daniels Black Label. The fact that they had consumed a foolish amount of the first half gallon was the cause of their lapse in judgment that led to the accident.

After Megan abandoned Tommy, confusion and fear led her back to her safe space where she hadn't slept under the roof for the last four years. This is where her alcoholic father still lived. Even in the dark and through the bourbon fog she could tell the old two-story farmhouse still needed to have the flaking paint scraped off and fresh paint applied. She doubted her father would ever get around to it.

With what was left of the first half gallon of bourbon in hand, Megan snuck in the unlocked back door. Her father would never change. The TV was on in the cluttered, undusted den where she found her father passed out in his chair as usual.

She was barely able to function by the time she stumbled in the back door. She didn't think to check and see if her father was still breathing before she staggered toward the stairs. She would check to see if he were still alive in the morning. Her last conscious thought was that she would surprise her Daddy, whom she still loved dearly, with his favorite breakfast, once they both sobered up. If they sobered up at all. She wobbled upstairs to her old bedroom where she drank Jack Daniels until she passed out.

Megan's father had been a drunk for as long as she could remember, but he managed to keep his truck, tractor, and farm equipment repair business profitable. At least until he won a couple of million dollars on the lottery. He was smart enough to make some sound long-term investments that if he spent wisely would enable him to never have to work again. Unfortunately, she expected to hear one day that he had finally drunk himself to death. He assured her he had a will drawn up and she was the only person in it, but she didn't expect there to be anything left.

Megan had awakened far too early that morning. Her head pounded. Death would've been a welcomed upgrade to her current condition.

Shortly after her father collected the lottery money, he made a few significant upgrades to the old house, then suddenly stopped. The first remodel was to convert the upstairs bedroom next to Megan's room into a full, modern bathroom and walk-in closet. It was so out of place, like the contractor prefabbed the elegant room, and then stuck it in a cave. The room was perfectly designed; it was just so out of place.

Megan lingered in the warm refreshing stream of the multiple shower heads. The water drops caressed her skin like thousands of rejuvenating fingers on her abused body. She could not even handle the softest massage setting.

It was a relief to find her father still alive, awake and in much better shape than the night before. He was happy to see his daughter, and he always enjoyed when she cooked. They had a special morning, but he could tell something bothered his little girl. He would wait for a while and let her open up, if she felt comfortable.

During his sober moments, when Megan was around, his fatherly instincts kicked in. It didn't take long, the reality of the poor example he'd established sank in. Those were the times he turned up the bottle and drank more, then cursed the shameful person he became.

......

After breakfast Cal's curiosity led him out of the sanctuary, into the dim hall. To his left was the doorway out into the bright morning sun. To his right two doors. Two more mysteries to solve.

The dusty wooden boards squeaked under Cal's weight as he cautiously strode toward door number one. It took several steps before he felt he could trust the integrity of the boards. Soon he heard two adventurous puppies sniff the floor as they closed in on his heels. He turned to the curious puppies, "Okay, Mutt and Jeff, what'da say we check this out?"

The door to the first room took some effort and an assist bump from his shoulder to open. The bottom of the door scraped up a mound of dust before it wedged and wouldn't move any further. It hadn't been opened in years and the room was empty, so it wasn't worth the effort.

Door number two was opened at an odd angle and hung by only one hinge. There were no footprints in the thick dust to indicate anyone had been there in years.

In the center of the dim room a dusty, broken down oak desk captured Cal's attention and sparked his imagination. There was something oddly familiar about the room and desk. Enough to be vaguely annoying, in no way clarifying.

As if on cue and a welcomed distraction, Mutt and Jeff could no longer contain themselves. They leapt into action, a playful, snarling, twisting ball of fur rolled across Cal's feet. He chuckled and side-stepped the fracas to enter the room. Not to be left behind and miss any new adventure, the puppy tussle ended. With noses to the floor they charged past Cal and sniffed around the desk that sat on three legs. It was something new and they sniffed as they circled, while Cal opened and closed what turned out to be empty drawers.

Expecting the same results, Cal pulled on the tarnished brass knob on the lower left drawer. It didn't budge. He tugged a few times but it wouldn't break free. Inset on the center of the drawer front was a corroded, round brass lock.

Mutt and Jeff appeared as interested as Cal, so they rose up on their hind legs and placed their front paws on the draw front. They sniffed, then looked up at Cal as if to ask, "Well, what's the hold up? We wanna see inside too." They followed up with a couple of inquisitive whines.

Then they all heard the unmistakable click of Momma's paws in the hall. Seconds later Sheena's head appeared in the doorway. She "woofed" softly, but unmistakably annoyed the boys had wandered off. Mutt and Jeff immediately dropped back down on all four paws and raced back to Momma and stood behind her. They innocently looked at Cal as if it were his fault they followed him down the hall.

Cal was oblivious the puppies tossed him under the bus. He was totally, but inexplicably fixated on the old desk.

Sheena turned, looked on both sides at her disobedient boys and emitted two ominous "woofs." Message sent and received. The boys scampered back down the hall where they slipped and skidded as they turned back into the sanctuary.

The third "woof" was more guttural as Sheena took a step into the room. Cal looked up. He noticed the dramatic tonal variation but wasn't sure what Sheena meant. He surmised it was either, "Okay, I got the kids out of the way, so continue your mission." Or, "You're wasting your time, so let's go back and play with the kids." However, his last reason would be impossible. Or was Sheena capable of sensing things far beyond his capacity to reason. Was Sheena's last utterance a warning, "You really don't want to find out what's in that drawer."

Sheena stood there as if to allow Cal more time to reason. It was still early and he had more important things to do than fiddle with a broken down desk.

"Guess this can wait for a while," Cal admitted as he straightened back up.

Apparently, Sheena felt as if she had communicated and Cal had received the message she intended, so she backed out of the room and trotted back down the hall.

A few seconds later, Cal stepped in the hall to discover Sheena stood at the entrance to the sanctuary, as if she waited for him. He looked back at the desk, then walked down the hall and followed Sheena into the sanctuary where he was mobbed by elated fur balls.

......

By mid morning Sheena was sound asleep stretched out on the concrete slab of the side porch. Cal led the excited puppies around the corner as they completed their exploratory adventure around the rundown church.

For the most part the puppies stayed under his feet or followed close behind. Frequently two or three would peel off and engage in a little growling rough-and-tumble, but they would quickly catch back up.

Cal unexpectedly paused which caused a puppy pile up behind him. It was an excuse for the six bundles of fur to rough-house again.

From that vantage-point Cal had an unobstructed view back to the edge of Faith. It looked different in the light of day. Last night the dim street lights cast an eerie, otherworldly glow on the quaint little town. By the looks of the more modern structures on the edge of town, it appeared the church had been constructed many years before the town grew so close. As if the church had been purpose-built to be far enough away from the little community to make it a destination. A place one wanted to go. To be further separated from the secular world.

Cal was confused by his curiosity and fascination with the rundown church building and its relationship to Faith. Before his mind could process any rational thought, a knot of growling, writhing, playful fur crashed into the back of his leg. The clump of blonde fur separated into three determined puppies, intent on reengaging in the morning romp. They leapt to their paws and resumed the scrum.

Cal had foolishly hoped the new day would shed some light on the serious issues he faced. He didn't have a clue who he was, where he was from, or where he was going when he found himself on the country road the day before. Did he have a wife and family, or pets who wondered where he was and when he'd be home? He really enjoyed the dogs and they seemed equally enamored with him. The idea there may be living beings that depended on him was a major concern that must be addressed.

As if to drive the point home, in the corner of his view he saw the mother dog's head lift. She started looking around but didn't see what she was looking for. She rose and appeared concerned. Obviously Cal had kept the puppies out of her presence too long.

"We're over here," Cal spoke up.

Sheena turned and immediately scampered down the steps. She emitted an inquisitive woof as she trotted over. The puppy frolic ended. The kids were excited to see their mother. They ran to her and lavished her with licks and attention. She sniffed each puppy from head to tail to ensure they were her babies and were in good shape. Satisfied, she eased over, sniffed, and then licked Cal's hand reassuringly.

So many thoughts raced through Cal's mind. In less than twenty-four hours this suspicious, protective canine mother had accepted him, a stranger who invaded their sanctuary. More importantly, he sensed she just reassured him that she could trust him with her babies. That was significant, but he wasn't quite sure how he'd earned that right. Obviously her mothering instincts were heightened, thus explaining why she would so willingly take in a stray, needy being.

Sheena sat down beside Cal on the porch while the puppies rolled and tumbled nearby. Cal looked down as the revelation clarified in his mind. "You just adopted me. Didn't you?" That had to be the answer.

It was as if Sheena understood. Her expressive eyes spoke volumes when she looked up reassuringly.

"What do you know about me that I need to know?"

......

## 10
## Is Truth Absolute?

At the shift change that morning Deputy Russell handed off the search for Reverend Cal Baxter to Deputy Tucker, the new kid on the block. Randolph County regulations required Deputy Tucker be considered a rookie, even though he'd excelled in the Army for six years as a Military Police Officer. His instincts were keen and he was eager to make a difference. Law Enforcement was his desired career path. It was his calling.

Shortly after lunch Deputy Tucker arrived at the home of Sadie and Ralph Jenkins. It was obvious the elderly couple was very fond of Rev. Baxter, so they were concerned. Sadie tried Cal's cell number but it went to voicemail.

Sadie was as fanatical about keeping a neat and clean house as she was in her devotion to her church and her God. Every visitor who graced the doors of their home was as welcome as any visitor to their church. Something to drink and snack on was never really an offer, it was more of an insistence the visitor couldn't refuse.

Sadie was contemplative as she served Deputy Tucker a saucer with a steamy cup of hot green tea and four double-stuffed Oreos. "Sunday was his last sermon, which will be the last sermon at Tabernacle," she explained as she glanced down at the saucer. She'd served a wide array of snacks and treats to visitors over the years. This odd combination selected by the baby-faced deputy was a first. When the young fellow accepted her offer for a snack, then made the unappetizing request, she assumed he really didn't want anything. This off-the-wall combo had to be his way to politely decline without saying, "No. Thank you." At least that's what she thought until the young lawman wasted no time in devouring the first fat cookie and then washing it down with a few sips of steamy tea. This day and age, kids must eat anything.

"Wish we could help you, but he didn't tell us where he

was going," Ralph volunteered as Sadie sat attentively on the edge of her chair beside Ralph's identical chair.

Deputy Tucker was amused and amazed by the not so subtle symbology of the matching chairs placed side by side in the room they apparently spent the most time while at home. The widescreen TV was left on, but the sound had been turned down.

"I haven't been able to find any family members in the area," Deputy Tucker lamented.

"He didn't have any living family members around here," Sadie informed. "His wife and infant daughter were killed in a tragic accident," she turned to Ralph for conformation, "bout ten years ago."

Ralph obviously didn't hear well, "Bought what ten years ago?" he responded to the question he thought he was asked.

Sadie raised her voice considerably, "Annie and Taylor died in the accident ten years ago, right?"

Ralph shook his head and turned to Deputy Tucker, "Yeah, it was about that long."

"But Annie's Momma and Aunt run a doughnut shop in town," Sadie added, then provided the name and location.

Granny's Doughnuts would be Deputy Tucker's next stop. On the drive over the young deputy followed his intuition and contacted Lieutenant Decker and asked him to run a "ping report" on Rev. Baxter's cell phone number. Verizon would be able to provide them with the day, time, and location of the last tower his phone pinged.

.......

In the ICU of the Charlotte Trauma Center, Tommy looked like he could've fallen victim to an evil plumber's experiment. Plastic tubes and hoses connected him to electronic boxes that beeped, hissed and clicked. Each one an engineering marvel of modern life-support equipment. Two nurses stepped in for the third time in fifteen minutes to monitor the electronic readouts. Concern was etched in their youthful faces, and rightfully so. Tommy's vital signs had been alarmingly erratic the last hour.

"Dr. Peterson wants an update on his brainwave activity every fifteen minutes," Shift Supervisor Donna Engle instructed.

"The dramatic fluctuation is probably causing his irregular heartbeat," Tina Barton, a first year RN surmised.

"Is his mother still here?"

"She's down the hall in the waiting room," Tina paused. "Seems he's in some serious trouble."

The senior nurse shook her head, "At this point, issues with the law are the least of our boy's problems."

Down the hall, Deputy Karr and Tommy's mother, Samantha, were the only people in the Critical Care Waiting Room.

Samantha was an average middle-aged mother of a troubled son who would rather be in the ICU room because he could pass away at any moment. She had tremendous respect for the law, but unfortunately, over the last six years she had gotten to know Deputy Karr far too well. Tommy's bad decisions generated far too many negative encounters with local law enforcement agencies.

Eventually Samantha requested that Deputy Karr refer to her as Sam, instead of Ms. Forrester. The heartbroken mother knew Deputy Karr really cared about her son and had tried many times to encourage Tommy to turn his life around. Just like he had dramatically changed the direction of his life when he was Tommy's age.

"Sam, I realize it's not a good time for this. But, the truck we suspect Tommy was driving is registered to Reverend Calvin Arthur Baxter from Archdale, North Carolina. Is he a relative, or family friend?"

Sam fidgeted and tried to focus on the question at hand. She wasn't intentionally short, just eager to get back down the hall to be at Tommy's bedside, "I've never heard that name before. Did you say Reverend?"

"Yes. Reverend Baxter from Archdale."

"I doubt very seriously Megan's allowing him to hang out with a preacher."

"Sam, this is serious. Seems Reverend Baxter is missing."

Sam gasped, and cupped her hand over her mouth.

"We've recovered portions of Reverend Baxter's cell phone and some of what we believe are part of his clothes, and an overnight bag."

"Where?" Samatha shook her head, "Was Tommy's finger prints on it?"

"I'm not at liberty to share much at this point."

Lieutenant Decker called Deputy Karr while he was on his way to the hospital to remind him not to relate key details. Because Reverend Baxter's life was in danger, Verizon expedited the Randolph County Sheriff Department's request. They provided enough information that led Decker to the exact location where they found the clothes and few pieces of Cal's phone beside the little pond.

"This much I can tell you. Divers recovered most of a destroyed iPhone. Our detectives confirmed it matched the one owned by Reverend Baxter. This proved our suspicions that foul play was involved in his disappearance," Deputy Karr needed to stress the seriousness of the situation.

"You accusing Tommy?"

"There's no trace of Rev. Baxter around the accident site. Divers are searching the pond for his body now," Deputy Karr had to be blunt. "If Tommy knows anything and tells us the truth, it will help him in the long run."

Sam gasped, "No! No! My Tommy's made some very bad decisions, but he's not capable of murder."

"I'm not saying they intended to kill Reverend Baxter, but sometimes things go horribly wrong. That's why we need to find out where he is and if he's still alive."

Sam was stunned, then indignant, "I've told Tommy a million times that girl is trouble. She's gonna ruin his life, but he just won't listen."

"So you think Megan's involved?"

"She controls him. She's destroying my boy."

......

Shadows lengthened as the late afternoon sun dipped lower in the western sky. Cal sat on the side porch beside Sheena. The puppies slept in various positions at the foot of the steps. Cal turned to Sheena and she appeared to stare blankly into the distance. Her offspring had completely worn themselves out. The silence was golden, and the rare inactivity was precious. Clouds blocked the sunset so there was no spectacular ending to the day.

"If you don't mind, I'm gonna hang out with you and the kids for a couple of days. See if I can figure things out." Cal ran his fingers through the fur around Sheena's neck. There was no collar. "Looks like we've both lost our way and our identities."

It was the witching hour when the sky grew dim. Not knowing why, Cal decided to explore the charming, small southern town. Even though he didn't have the slightest nefarious intent, he felt like a burglar prepared to case his next series of targets.

"I'll be back in a little while," Cal promised as he rubbed Sheena on the head. She never moved and he was careful not to wake the youngsters. Equally important, there was still enough light to safely navigate the thorn infested brush.

In Cal's favor, small towns usually had light traffic and fewer people walked the streets after dark, only making strangers stand out much faster. He decided to stay a block off Main Street where there were fewer overhead lights and only walk up to every other corner of Main Street. He did his best to remain in the shadows.

It didn't take long to discover the town was much smaller than Cal anticipated. Only five blocks long, with three quarters of the buildings empty. He wondered how many years before Faith would finally die out and become a ghost town.

Cal was on the way back to the rundown church and his new four-legged friends much sooner than anticipated. He discreetly leaned against a wall in the shadows across the street from the Faith Family Diner. It was then he realized the only thing he'd eaten all day was the quarter of the tenderloin biscuit Sheena provided.

Oddly, he wasn't hungry and that was okay. Yet he reached in his pocket and pulled out the small clump of money. That was all he had to his name, so it had to last at least a couple of days. At that point, if he still couldn't remember anything about his past, he'd have to make some serious decisions. He would have no choice but to ask for help.

Cal placed the money back in his pocket. He would take the chance that Sheena's breakfast run was a daily occurrence.

That encouraged Cal because it would make it easier to extend his stay at the church a few more days. Then if as on cue, Sheena strolled up and sat down at the door to the Faith Diner. Moments later, as if on schedule, Betsy opened the door and presented Sheena a bag that appeared to contain a styrofoam carry-out box. Sheena allowed Betsy to pet her on the head before she stood up and turned to head back toward her refuge.

There were several cars in the parking lot and Cal suspected Betsy ran a one-woman operation, plus a cook in the kitchen. He waited a few seconds to give her enough time to be far enough away from the door, and more than likely taking care of one of her regulars. Then he followed Sheen but didn't call out to alert her he was close behind. She was mission-focused and appeared unaware of his presence. Still he was close enough to catch a scent that something tasty was in the bag.

Cal was more confused than ever when he arrived back at the abandoned church. In the darkness he dreaded the painful trip back through the brier patch.

Clouds had covered the full moon. Yet he was surprised when he stepped back into the very dim sanctuary. Sheena sat on her hind quarters on the platform with the bag still in her mouth. The ravenous puppies harassed their mother to share the bounty. Instead, Sheena rose, stepped off the platform, then growled at the kids as they started to follow. They stopped and watched longingly as their mother led Cal to his pew.

Cal accepted the evening meal box from Sheena. He opened it and in the dim light held it close to his face. Upon close inspection he determined there were multiple pork chops and several pieces of cornbread. He took one of each and placed the box on the floor. A simple "woof" from their mother and the hungry brood leapt down from the platform and raced toward the evening meal.

Cal expected carnage akin to a school of ravenous piranhas attacking a hapless victim that stepped in the wrong part of the river. Quite unexpectedly, the puppies skidded to a stop and lined up to await their mother divvy up the grub.

"Oh, you're good. Really good," Cal reached down and rubbed the top of Sheena's head.

Dinner was orderly and delicious. As an added bonus, Cal allowed the puppies to lick his fingers. Then he added his bone to the pile for the puppies to gnaw on.

Cal wasn't sure how much food he was accustomed to

consuming on an average day; but the tender, thick pork chop was delicious, and combined with the crispy-crusted, country cornbread was most satisfying and filling.

Much to Cal's surprise, Sheena and her adorable offspring curled up in a knot beside his pew. They were asleep within a few minutes.

So many things should've demanded Cal's attention, most importantly, how to unlock his memory. Everything would have to wait until morning. He was exhausted and followed his canine friends example. The moment he stretched out and got comfortable his eyes closed. He fell into a deep sleep.

......

Sid Williams was one of Betsy's favorite customers. He was in his late sixties. Ellen, his seemingly healthy wife of forty years, had suffered a debilitating stroke that forced him to place her in an assisted living facility, thirty miles away. Even though Ellen was an excellent cook, they ate breakfast in the diner at least four times a week.

Unfortunately, Ellen unexpectedly died a month ago, thus devastating Sid. He was actually a good cook, but he had grown dependent on Betsy for more than physical sustenance. Betsy had long since reduced Sid's meal cost to half which he appreciated.

The day Sid had to admit Ellen into the facility, he opted to sit at the bar, and from that point on, he couldn't bear the thought of sitting at a table without his beloved Ellen to smile across from the other side. On that night, Sid was missing Ellen more than ever. He faked reading the newspaper as long as he could.

Betsy was busy with one of the tasks considered "side work" in the restaurant biz. She refilled salt and pepper shakers in the booths along the glass front wall. A female figure walked by the window and captured her attention. She shook her head, "This can't be good news."

The bell on the door tinkled as Megan slowly pushed it open. She was reluctant to enter. Her eyes fixed on Betsy, "Hi, Aunt Bet. Can I come in?"

Betsy placed the container of pepper and the pepper shaker on the table, "Haven't seen you in a while."

"Gotta head out of town. Not sure when I'll be back."

Sid turned innocently enough to look at Megan, but she didn't appreciate his intrusion into her conversation, "Mind your own business, Old Man!"

Betsy pointed at the door,"Young Lady, you can just turn yourself around and march right back out that door. You don't talk to my customers like that."

Sid was more stunned than offended. He turned as Betsy arrived behind him and placed a hand on his shoulder.

Megan lowered her head in mock contrition. Her tone was less than convincing, "Sorry, Aunt Bet."

Betsy gently patted Sid on the shoulder, "Mr. Williams is the one you owe the first apology."

Megan barely looked up. At least she made an effort to sound meek, weak as it was, "Sorry, Mr. Williams."

Mr. Williams nodded then turned back to the paper.

Betsy and Megan sat across from each in a window booth. Megan was nervous and faced the door. She shifted her eyes from the door to out the window to identify and track the few cars as they passed.

"I need to get out'a town for a while," Megan confessed.

"Your mother said the same thing - last time I saw her - in this very booth - twelve years ago. She had to get out of town for a while. Haven't heard from her since."

"She's never attempted to get in touch with me either."

"Your mother was my best friend since kindergarten. But she changed when she met you dad," Betsy felt the need to remind. "He was the absolute worst thing that ever happened to her."

"But he gave her - me - the best thing she claimed ever happened to her," Megan held out both hands palms up. "But where did that get me? She ran off and left the best thing that ever happened to her with the worst thing that ever happened to her. Makes sense, right?"

"Meg, let's not go there again. We've had this same conversation a thousand times, and we always wind up back at the same place."

"I know. I know. It's my own fault I turned into such a royal screw up. Yeah. Yeah. And so on. And so on. I can't blame my parents for my bad decisions."

"Sounds like great advice a loving god-mother would give to a little girl she prayed would grow up better than her roots."

"There you go with the God thing again."

"Hey. I didn't invite you here. Remember, you play by my rules when you step on my property, both at home and here."

"I didn't come here to argue with you, Aunt Bet."

"Then exactly why did you show up, out of the blue. Unexpected, and unannounced?"

Megan's face flushed with an equal surge of embarrassment and resentment. She abruptly started to rise until Betsy reached over and took hold of her hand.

"Sit back down." Slight pressure from Betsy's hand gently prompted Megan to ease back on the soft booth seat. "Okay, let's make nice."

"You're not even blood kin, but you've been more of a mother than she ever was." Long since buried pain resurfaced in Megan's voice and dredged up years of psychological sewage that had pooled and rotted out her heart.

Betsy reached over and took both of Megan's hands. She was genuinely compassionate but ironically unapologetically direct, "Charlie and I've done all we can to help. But you have a nasty habit of rejecting sound advice."

Megan's eyes narrowed. Her jaw tightened. She hoped she would remain civil. The last thing she could afford to do was inflict more damage on an already strained relationship. "I'm sorry. I probably should've just slipped out of town, then called you in a week or so."

Betsy sensed she might've been a little hard on the troubled young woman, "How bad is it? The reason you're in such a hurry to bug out?"

"Bad," Megan was hesitant. Her eyes wandered, "Real bad."

"Too bad to even tell your Auntie Bet?"

Megan drew in a long, pensive breath, "Tommy and I...." Without warning, her attention shifted out the window. She panicked and bolted from the booth, "Gotta go."

Betsy looked out the window and spotted what must've terrified Megan. A Sheriff's patrol car passed by at normal speed. It didn't appear the deputy behind the wheel had any intentions of entering the parking lot. Yet Megan sprinted toward the back door like a rabbit from a fox .

......

## 11
## By Accident, Or Divine Intervention?

Next morning, Cal awoke to a symphony of sniffing noses and scratching paws on the edge of the pew. His eager new furry friends were ready to play. Meanwhile, Sheena was headed toward the door when Cal called out, "Hey girl, come here."

Sheena stopped, turned around but stood her ground.

"Come here, girl. I want to talk to you for a minute."

As soon as Cal swung his legs over and his feet hit the floor, six sets of eager front paws impacted his jeans.

A "woof" from Sheena ended her offspring's incessant pleas for attention. The writhing blonde fur around Cal's legs parted like the Red Sea.

Sheena trotted over and sat down on her hind quarters like an obedient service dog.

"Somebody has indeed spent a lot of time working with you," Cal smiled as Sheena leaned her head toward him to meet his hand halfway. "Okay, so you're fond of having your head scratched. Why don't you stay here and watch the kids this morning? Let me take care of breakfast."

......

Fifteen minutes later, the bell on the front door tinkled when Cal entered the Faith Family Diner. He was more disheveled than the night he wandered in off the street for the first time, and he still wore the same shirt and jeans. His hair was greasy and mussed. His unshaven face was shadowed with a couple days' growth. He had no reason to be embarrassed by his appearance because he didn't have a clue what he looked like in the past. As much as pastors might've tried to be regular people, as the leader of a church, it came with the territory to always be presentable in public. On that day Reverend Calvin Baxter was well below his meticulous standards.

The breakfast crowd had cleared out and only six people

were scattered about the room. Since Betsy was caught up on her beverage refills and Sid just exited the door on the other side, Betsy focused her full attention on Cal. Her eyes narrowed as she studied the scruffy man who was still a handsome hunk.

"Welcome back," Betsy smiled. "Didn't see you yesterday. Wasn't sure you were still in town." She pointed, "Your usual table?"

Cal nodded and sat in the same booth. He waved off the offer of a menu, "How much are your steak biscuits?"

"Plain steak?"

Cal pondered for a second, "With egg and cheese."

"For a promising new customer - two dollars each."

Cal glanced down at his opened hand conveniently hidden below the table. In his palm were the crumpled ten and one dollar bills, and some loose change. He wouldn't try to count the change. Also he wouldn't give any thought to how he could secure more money once he spent what was in his hand. His eyes turned back to Betsy, "What's the total on four steak, egg, and cheese biscuits to go, and a cup of coffee while I wait?"

Betsy replied without the slightest hesitation, "Eight dollars, and as part of my special offer, coffee's on me. I'll even pay the tax."

Cal placed the ten dollar bill on the table, "Not to take advantage, but at those prices, what would ten bucks buy me?"

"I can deal with that. Ten bucks'll get you five premium steak, egg, and cheese biscuits, and one cup of freshly brewed coffee while you wait."

Cal placed the one dollar bill and change on the table, "And here's your tip."

Betsy leaned toward the long, narrow opening in the wall behind her, where the Hispanic cook awaited, "Five of our best steak, egg, and cheese biscuits, to go."

Betsy approached Cal's booth with the pot of coffee. She wasn't sure if she should be impressed or concerned that this handsome man didn't appear bothered by his unkempt appearance. What she chose to focus on was that for some reason, against her better judgment, she was attracted to this good looking stranger. It made no sense. She had worked so hard to build an impenetrable wall around her. One that no man would ever be able to breach, or blast a hole through. She was extra careful not to spill a single drop as she filled the cup she sat before Cal. There was no way she would allow herself to appear flustered, or nervous, even though she was a whole lot of both.

Unfortunately, she suspected but couldn't confirm that the handsome stranger was equally inhibited by the same human insecurities. Betsy was first to stumble through her reluctance to make small talk, while Cal sipped coffee to avoid being the ice breaker.

Betsy still wondered how Cal got around. She was busy telling Sid bye and could've easily missed Cal as he drove into the lot in his car, or truck. She didn't want to appear suspicious, but her curiosity was about to get the best of her. She would pivot and go another direction to see if she could find common ground. A good start would be the name of the person or persons he visited.

"You stay'n close by?" She justified what she considered innocent chitchat.

Cal nodded but was evasive, "Yeah, with some new friends, not too far from here." He told the truth, just not enough to identify Sheena and her pups who lived at the abandoned church, a short walk from there. He smiled as his brain churned to produce anything to talk about that didn't involve him, but would enable him to learn more about her. Unfortunately, he was incapable of a quid pro quo, where he would divulge equally informative tidbits about himself.

"Betsy, can I get a to-go order?" A male voice sounded from the farthest stool at the bar.

Betsy turned toward the request, "Sure. Be right there." She faced Cal, "We'll have your biscuits ready shortly."

Cal was relieved yet even more frustrated. The main reason he wanted to pick up breakfast was to see Betsy again. He knew it was a fool's errand before he stepped out of the sanctuary, but it was too late. There he was, the "silly rube" who just set himself up to go down in flames.

Cal didn't leer, but he was compelled to watch Betsy walk away. There was an eerie familiarity with her graceful stride and body movements. Not overtly seductive, just pleasing. All of the parts were perfectly proportioned, at least compared to his concept of the ideal female frame. There was no doubt all the parts fit well and functioned properly as a working unit. Then it dawned on him how oddly sterile he just evaluated a living human being, to himself, in terms akin to how an engineer would've a robot's initial test walk. Why, in the privacy of his own mind had he been so careful not to sexualize her natural beauty?

So there he sat, in a small diner, in a tiny town in the middle of nowhere. He just questioned his motive and method for admiring a woman he barely knew, just after he committed to spend the last money in his pocket. On what, and why? Did it make sense it was for a single meal he'd share with a mother dog and her six ravenous pups? The answer was a resounding "no." That much he was certain of, even though he didn't have a clue who he had been a couple of days ago before a mysterious Biker dumped him at the edge of Faith.

That was all he knew about himself, not a single important fact in regard to his identity, or where he came from.

Everything around him felt, smelled, sounded and tasted real. His connection to reality was clouded by a shroud of secrecy, not by his choice. It was as if his past had suddenly become irrelevant. The who, what, and why of who he used to be, suddenly ceased to be cause and effect for who he had become. Urgent questions emerged, "Why had he become who he was at that moment?" More importantly, "How long would who he is even be relevant?"

Fortunately, before his dizzying dilemma spiraled out of control, he was distracted when the Cook slipped a bulging, white bag through the slot in the wall. He tapped the button on a silver bell. DING.

Betsy scooped up the bag and happily headed toward Cal's booth. As she approached, Cal had to avert his eyes so he wouldn't question his own motives for being there. The awkward move sent the wrong signal to Betsy, who battled her own mixed signals and emotions.

What had begun for Cal and Betsy as an innocent, hopefully productive exploratory visit had gone completely off the rails. It was the look on Cal's face when he turned away. Was it her looks? Had she done or said something out of the way? Or was it simply that he liked her looks, but couldn't allow himself to be interested in a "waitress?"

Within a split second, Betsy was offended. How dare this scruffy, though still handsome man look down his nose at her. She'd worked hard and bought the diner and land it sat on several years ago. With cash money, Buster. That's right! This little country girl didn't need a loan. As a matter of fact, she had a couple more productive revenue streams. She didn't need the approval of any man. Thank you very much!!!

Needless to say, Betsy had worked herself into quite a snit by the time she reached Cal's booth. Unfortunately, the head of emotional steam she'd built up on the way over melted her pleasant smile. By the time Cal had guts enough to face her, he was greeted by the stern glare of a woman who would rather he take his bag and vanish off the face of the earth.

Cal was confused. He couldn't think of a thing he'd said or done that could've been construed as offensive. Then he did the absolute worst thing. Without a word, he extended the ten dollar bill. That only seemed to make matters worse. Betsy's once pleasant, almost enchanting eyes narrowed, and without a word, she accepted the money. Cal hesitated when he reached to retrieve the dollar bill and change from the table.

"That's okay. I'll get it when I wipe off the table."

It was time to leave. The damage, whatever caused it, had been done.

"Thanks for the deal on the biscuits," Cal rose from the booth and dared a glance at Betsy as he headed toward the door.

Betsy did nod but there wasn't even a hint of a smile.

A serious question arose as Cal neared the door. During his little "walkabout" Faith the other night, he didn't notice another eating establishment. That little necessary piece of information foreshadowed the need for a few more uncomfortable visits back to the diner. This situation could shorten his stay in Faith. Where would he go? And why would he go anywhere else?

The overwhelming conundrum was as if he never existed, anywhere, until he opened his eyes in the edge of the woods on the side of that country road. He was still mystified how he knew so many things, but absolutely nothing about himself. He didn't even know why he paused before his hand reached for the door knob.

It was during that split second Betsy was compelled to cut her eyes for one last look at the man she prayed would come back, until he did. At that moment she hoped he would never return. She stopped short of asking God to keep him away because she noticed something odd about the back of his head. Her mouth slipped open when her eyes zeroed in on the silver dollar-sized dried blood spot centered on the back of his head.

In an instant she plummeted from the lofty perch of a justifiably insulted woman to the depths of a scum-of-the-Earth, unjustifiably, unfairly judgmental female. It was a swift, horrific descent to a humbling impact that generated a seismic event. It rocked her to her core. Overwhelmed with guilt she opened her mouth to speak, but the right words wouldn't form in her mind. "Hey, I'm sorry for being such a jerk. What happened to your head?" Would've been an excellent conversation re-starter.

The bell tingled as the door opened, and from Betsy's location she noticed a blonde bundle of fur that rose from a seated position on the concrete walk.

Cal immediately leaned forward and extended his empty hand, sending the puppy's hind quarters into a twisting gyration.

Betsy was captivated by the display of affection exhibited between the man she feared she had misjudged and the innocent puppy that obviously adored him. At that point Betsy was miffed at herself for having allowed her cynical, toxic attitude toward men to crush her better nature.

Cal stepped outside and allowed the spring on the door to pull it closed. He welcomed Mutt's unconditional love that he was unable to contain. Until Cal spoke the truth as he scratched the little fellow's back, "You're gonna get us in a heap'a trouble."

Mutt's ears perked. He looked up as if he understood Cal's ominous prediction. He cowered but his hind quarters refused to be still, and his little tail swung wildly. Then his ultra sensitive nose picked up the heavenly aroma that wafted from the bag in Cal's other hand. Mutt sprang into action. He spun and jumped, no longer worried about how mad Momma would be.

Betsy stepped to the doorway and watched Cal and Mutt walk toward the edge of town. "So that's who he's staying with." She wasn't sure where the Momma dog kept her brood, but it appeared she had taken in a stray human as well. She reached for the knob to open the door and offer to give them a ride.

Ding.

"To go order up," the Cook called out.

Betsy turned to take care of her customer who was in a big hurry so she missed Cal and Mutt make the left turn on First Street, aptly renamed in 1965 when it became the first paved street in Faith. When the little community started naming roads in the early 1900's, it was called Muddy Road, due to an overactive spring. The spring was the main reason Faith Covenant Church was built on that location.

Shortly after they turned on First Street, Mutt sniffed out what Cal first thought was a piece of trash, until the little fellow brought it to him. He bounced and pranced around Cal in an attempt to taunt him into a little game of "you want what I got, come get it."

When Mutt stood still long enough for Cal to focus on the little fellow's mouth, the suspected piece of green trash was a worn and soiled twenty dollar bill.

"Well, looks like the universe just smiled down on us," Cal suggested. Then he wondered why he made such a statement.

It took a small corner chunk of a biscuit to lure Mutt close enough and willing enough to drop the money.

Cal stepped into the dim sanctuary with Mutt on his heels. Sheena had huddled the remaining puppies inside the toppled pulpit and guarded the way out. She wasn't about to allow another pup to wander off.

Sheena frantically bolted out of the safety of the shelter and rushed to sniff Mutt to ensure he's okay. She emitted a guttural, chastising growl that cowered the guilty pup, and sent him in a humbled scurry to the pulpit. He was greeted by his relieved and happy siblings who mobbed and licked him.

The look of utter disappointment and betrayal in Sheena's eyes stunned Cal, "Hey, I didn't invite him to go with me." He felt silly that he expected the relieved mother dog to actually understand what wasn't an apology, just an explanation.

As if to move on and get to the important business at hand, Sheena gently took hold of the aromatic biscuit bag with her front teeth. She led Cal to the edge of the pulpit platform.

All was quickly forgiven as Sheena and Cal tore the biscuits into scrumptious morsels they evenly dispersed to the piranha-like feeding frenzy. Then Cal pulled the last biscuit into equal halves. He consumed one and Sheena the other.

Cal decided to hang around the church that morning to relax and play with the pups. By early afternoon he felt like a good nap would help clear his head, but he had no intentions to sleep long.

......

## 12
## When The Time Is Right

Just after the dinner crowd thinned out, a well-maintained, 1989 Chevy wreck truck pulled into a parking space in the middle of the nearly empty lot. The vintage wrecker was so at home in the sleepy little town of Faith. Itself a place either lost, or at least frozen in time.

The driver's door swung open and out slid Charlie, an average man in his 40's. He wore a clean, modern gray uniform with bright yellow reflecting stripes on the shirt and trousers.

The bell sounded when Charlie swung the door open and entered the diner. His routine was a quick scan of the room to see if there were one or more people he should speak to or go shake their hand.

Betsy stepped from behind the counter and eagerly accepted Charlie's bearhug. As usual, he lifted her and spun her around.

"How's my little brother?" Betsy smiled down.

"Desperately need'n some fresh brewed coffee and a wide slice of his sister's famous pecan pie," Charlie boldly proclaimed as if it were a canon law straight from Vatican City, declared by the Pope himself.

Betsy giggled while hoisted in the air, "But that'll spoil your dinner."

Charlie grinned, "I'm such a rebel."

"You're a heathen child, and I should'a raised you better."

"Yeah, it's your fault."

Betsy's face beamed. She loved her little brother so much, "Well, unless you put me down, it's gonna be your fault you don't get your pie before dinner."

Charlie lowered Betsy and gave her a playful kiss on the cheek, "I'm star'vin."

Bobby Albertson a tall, lanky, youngish seventy-two year old entered from the other side. His long strides made it appear he loped to the middle of the bar, where he landed on his usual stool. He'd recently joined the ranks of the unemployed, via retirement from the United States Postal Service. During his forty plus year career, Bobby was Faith's and the surrounding community's mail carrier. He knew things. He heard things. And while on his daily routes he saw things. At times there were things he knew best to forget, or at least, never share with anyone. He was a great conversationalist with broad interests. As a well-read man Bobby could hold his own with anyone.

Charlie patted Bobby on the shoulder before he plopped down on the stool beside him, "Morn'n Bob'a'lew."

"Want your usual, with a cup of decaf," Betsy smiled.

"What if I said, no?" Bobby appeared serious, catching Betsy and Charlie completely off guard. He gave them a moment to ponder, then answer. Since neither Betsy nor Charlie appeared to have an answer, he decided to end the suspense. "Just wondering what you'd say if I did," he grinned. "Yes, Ma'am, the usual. Thank you!"

"Anything going on around town we need to know about?" Charlie inquired.

Since he retired, Bobby had more time to listen to his police scanner throughout the day, "Any news about the guy that owns the old truck you hauled to the county impound?"

"It was totaled. I just found out more details a while ago. They think Tommy Forrester was driving it when it wrecked. They don't understand how he survived."

"Who owned the truck?" Bobby asked.

"A Baptist preacher from Archdale and the Cops aren't sure where he is. But they're pretty sure Tommy was involved with stealing the truck."

Betsy stepped up on the other side of the bar with Charlie's wide piece of pie, "You keep saying Tommy. Megan's, Tommy?"

Charlie nodded, "Yeah."

"When did this happen?"

"Night before last."

"Why didn't you tell me yesterday?" Betsy really wasn't upset, she just wanted to know.

"Like I said, I just found out a while ago."

"That explains why Megan came in here last night. Hadn't seen her in months. Something was really bothering her, but she got spooked and bugged out before she explained. She did say she was going out of town for a while."

"Tommy's in ICU. May not make it," Charlie explained just before his cell phone rang. He retrieved it from a pocket on his trousers and looked at the screen, "Well, well. Wonder what she wants?" He slid his finger across the screen and held it to his ear, "Megan. Long time."

Megan dusted off her sweet, innocent voice, "Hi Charlie. Been meaning to drop by and see you."

"I'm at the diner, going to eat some of Betsy's pecan pie."

"It's the best, ever."

"Sure is," Charlie turned to Betsy, "How's your Dad?"

"Same as usual," Megan paused. "Did Aunt Bet tell you I came to see her last night?"

"Yeah. Everything okay?"

Betsy shook her head in disagreement as Charlie played along to see what Megan would say.

"Well, not really. My car's acting up and I need to go out of town for a few days."

"What's wrong with your car?" Charlie pressed. "Want me to look at it?"

"Well...." Megan took a deep breath, "I'm a little short of cash right now. Can't afford to get it fixed." There was another pause, but Charlie decided to wait it out. Megan had to make her move, "Was hoping I could borrow a car for a couple of days. You keep several around."

"Where do you need to go?" Charlie wasn't comfortable with the request.

"Ahh, well, on the other side of Raleigh. There's a job I might can get. Pays pretty good too," Megan lied.

"Why don't you bring your car over? Let me take a look at it. I might can fix it, then you can go on over to Raleigh. We can talk about any charges later."

"I'm already at your garage. Daddy dropped me off before he started drink'n. I've been stay'n with him for a few days, and when I'm there, he tends to wait until the even'n's to start drink'n"

Charlie shook his head. It was time to end the farce, "Megan, Tommy's in the ICU. You know that, right?"

Megan wasn't prepared, nor did she want to hear any more; but she had to play along to hopefully get a car, "No. I didn't know. What happened? We had a fight a few days ago. Haven't seen or spoken to him since." At least she told a half-truth.

"He was in a wreck. Totaled a truck the police suspect he stole. You don't know anything about that?"

The long, silent pause clenched Megan's guilt for Charlie and Betsy, who had her ear close to his phone. Charlie allowed Betsy to take the phone.

"Megan," Betsy was genuinely concerned, more importantly, nonjudgmental, "Megan, you were with him, weren't you? That's what you were ready to tell me until you bolted like a scared rabbit. Honey, Tommy might not make it. Can you live with yourself if you don't go see him?"

"What did Tommy say?" Megan's tone was unnervingly calm, detached from consequence.

"What would he say?" Betsy didn't want to make it too easy on Megan.

"Is the police there?"

"Why would that matter if you weren't with him?" Betsy held firm.

Megan was torn. It was her idea to ambush a driver and steal their vehicle, and it was her stupidity that caused the accident that could take Tommy's life. She didn't have the courage or integrity to stand up and face the consequences of her actions, "I gotta go."

"But what about your car," Betsy asked before she handed Charlie his phone.

"I'll get one."

"From where?" Charlie asked as he bolted from his stool.

"Thank's Charlie. I'll take good care of it," Megan said as she ended the call.

"Megan, stay there until I get there," Charlie ran toward the door. "You don't have permission to take either one of my cars."

"Charlie," Betsy trotted after her brother, "Wait. I think the guy that owns the truck was in here earlier today."

"Where'd he go?" Charlie paused with his hand on the door knob.

"Not exactly sure," Betsy was hesitant, "There's a good chance he won't be back."

"Why?"

## OTIS FARMER

"It's a long story. I'll tell you when you get back," Betsy motioned Charlie out the door. "Don't let her take one of your cars."

"Have no intentions of letting that happen," Cal promised on the way out. "Call Deputy Karr. Have him meet me at the garage."

"You gonna have her arrested?" Betsy asked.

"I've had enough."

......

Sam listened intently to the monotone voice of Dr. Ben Roberts, a studious neurologist who during fifteen years of practice had yet to develop a warm bed-side manner. Odds were that would never happen, but he had the most successful case record with severe head and brain trauma patients.

"Even though the concussion was pretty serious, the MRI doesn't show signs of permanent brain damage," Dr. Roberts' chocolate brown eyes glanced up from the clipboard in his hand, "But there's several more tests we need to perform. More importantly, we simply have to wait and see how things develop."

Sam hadn't left Tommy's side except to talk with Deputy Karr in the waiting room. She was desperate for any nugget of hope to latch on and hold tight. The nurses had warned her that Dr. Roberts was often short and direct, but her son was in the best hands on the East Coast. In Sam's struggle to rationalize, that assurance excused his seemingly detached demeanor.

Sam was exhausted and hadn't slept since she arrived the night of the accident, "It's a miracle. From what the paramedics told me, he should be in the morgue. The police want a statement from him if they can get one."

Dr. Roberts was unmoved, "I've already handled the law enforcement. I understand the life of another human being may be in danger if they can't find him; but your son is my patient, and I have to first ensure his survival, then oversee what will more than likely be a long and difficult recovery."

"Do you think...?" Sam wanted so much to at least hear a hint of hope in Dr. Robert's voice, but he cut her off in his usual droll tone.

## RETURN TO FAITH

"Ma'am, most often what I think is exactly not what patients or family members want to hear. In the early stages, I advise patients and family members to allow me to study test results and present them the facts. Inadvertently giving false hope can set vulnerable people up to be devastated when reality rears its ugly head."

Sam drew in a deep, unsure breath, "I want the facts."

"The facts: your son's badly bruised from head to toe, and we're keeping him heavily sedated, in an induced coma until we see if his brain is going to continue swelling. You can talk to him. He may even be able to hear and understand some of what you say; but he is definitely not going to be able to communicate with you, or the police, especially for the next couple of days. If you're religious, I encourage you to pray."

"I'm a Christian."

Dr. Roberts nodded, "They tend to speak the most effective prayers." He paused then added, "They're going to post a guard outside the entrance to ICU. That's as close as I'm going to allow them. Told them it's a waste of time because he's not going anywhere anytime soon."

Sam thanked Dr. Roberts for his update. He was right. He hadn't said anything positive that she could cling to. All she had was her faith in her God, and the mercy and grace she'd been praying for since she received the call that changed her life forever.

The broken-hearted mother would spend the next several hours in a very uncomfortable chair, holding the hand of her only child. She would repeat one repentant prayer several times, "Lord, I've failed You and the child I begged you to bless me with. I'm so sorry. Please forgive me, and allow me another chance to help lead him to the right path in life."

......

By the time Charlie arrived at his shop, he wasn't sure if a crime had already been committed and the criminal was miles away, in any possible direction. At first glance he couldn't determine which, if either of his eclectic collection of vehicles were missing. The five out front were still there. The more rare and valuable were inside, and the bulk were around back.

Megan never revealed who taught her how to pick locks,

or outsmart basic alarm systems. In the past she mentioned those unladylike skills, but Charlie never took her seriously. Regardless of what he was about to discover, he had decided to call and have a more sophisticated alarm system quoted.

The second positive sign, Megan was courteous enough to have closed the office door. A simple turn of the knob revealed that in her obvious haste she wasn't concerned enough to turn lock when she left. Charlie cautiously opened the door to the dim room. He paused in the doorway. "Megan?" He would rather be safe than sorry. She was probably desperate and like a wounded animal, she could be dangerous. Especially if she were as cash strapped as she claimed.

Charlie flipped on a row of overhead lights. The small office was in order. Megan had left no visible clues she had disturbed anything in the office. She knew where he kept the large key rack.

Charlie stepped through the office door into the moderate sized shop that was clean and orderly. He flipped on more lights to reveal several vehicles in various stages of repair. Through an opening that led to another room sat two older race cars in dim shadows.

The moment of truth would come soon enough as he rounded the corner to the room that was the most recent addition to his shop where he installed new machinery. Hidden behind a sixteen-by-twenty inch photo of him in a race suit beside his first race car was a custom built key rack. He moved the photo and spotted an open hook. He knew exactly which car key was missing. He called Betsy.

Betsy snatched her phone from under the counter. It was a call she expected, "Surprise. Surprise. She's not there."

"Neither is my sixty-five, convertible Mustang."

Betsy reluctantly shook her head, "We can't help her, if she don't want help."

Charlie was livid, "When Andy gets here, I'm filing a stolen car report. We'll be over there as soon as we finish."

Thirty minutes later Deputy Karr's patrol car led Charlie's classic black '72 Corvette into the diner parking lot. Deputy Karr carried a tan folder into the diner where he and Charlie sat beside each other at the bar. Betsy poured them a cup of steamy hot coffee, then took the plastic wrap off Charlie's pie and sat it in front of him.

Charlie smiled and excitedly rubbed his hands together, "Oh yes, I need this."

"So you think the man who owns the truck has been in here the last couple of days?" Deputy Karr inquired.

Betsy nodded while Deputy Karr opened and slid the folder to her. She picked up the enlarged copy of Cal's North Carolina Driver's License.

"Is that the guy?"

"Yeah."

"Name's Calvin Baxter. Rev. Baxter from Archdale."

Betsy nodded as she lowered the piece of paper. She was concerned, "So he's a preacher?"

"Appears to be," Deputy Karr said before he took a sip of coffee.

Charlie had another fork full of the sticky pie ready to shove into his mouth, "Let me see," Charlie reached for the photo.

Betsy handed the photo to Charlie, who responded almost immediately, "Never seen the man." He said as he handed the photo back and stuffed the pie in his eager mouth.

Betsy turned her attention back to Deputy Karr, "He had blood on the back of his head."

"Fresh?"

Betsy shook her head, "Looked like it was a couple of days old."

"Has he been in today?"

Betsy nodded and glanced toward the door, "This morning around breakfast."

"Do you know where he is?"

The Cook tapped the bell. Ding, "Order up." He announced.

Betsy turned, accepted the white bag from the Cook who had stuffed two styrofoam to-go boxes, then motioned for Charlie and Deputy Karr to follow her. She glanced out the door and nodded as she exited. Charlie and Deputy Karr followed.

Sheena sat patiently. Her tail wagged as Betsy stepped toward her with the white bag in hand. Without looking she raised her empty hand to Charlie and Deputy Karr, "Stay back. I'm always alone when she's here."

Charlie and Deputy Karr turned to each other. Both were confused.

Sheena sniffed and cautiously eased toward Betsy. The new humans behind Betsy made the mother dog suspicious.

"Come get it, girl," Betsy extended the aromatic bag.

Sheena gently took the bag in her mouth.

Betsy turned to Deputy Karr, "Over the years I've worked with service dogs, and I'm sure she's one... or she used to be one." Sheena allowed Betsy to pat her on the head. "She wandered up a month ago, ready to explode with puppies. Took a while to trust me... to get close enough to take food from my hands."

Deputy Karr appeared ready to wait for further explanation.

Charlie was impatient, "What's this got to do with Rev. Baxter?"

Betsy pointed as Sheena turned and trotted away, "Follow that dog."

Deputy Karr instructed Charlie to stay at the diner, then he followed Sheena in his Sheriff's car. The mother dog meandered along and turned her head several times as if to ensure the car was still behind her. Deputy Karr was skeptical as Sheena led him to the abandoned church, where she climbed the steps and waited for him to park and exit the vehicle.

Deputy Karr shined his flashlight into the dim hall before he dared to enter. He pointed the beam at Sheena, in the doorway to the sanctuary, as she seemed to wait for him with the bag of food in her mouth.

"Are you inviting me to have a candle-light dinner with you?" Deputy Karr asked.

Sheena turned and trotted into the dim sanctuary. The stained glass windows were muted in eerie shadows.

The flashlight beam preceded Deputy Karr and illuminated the anxious puppies as they hopped around their Mother who brought dinner.

Deputy Karr decided to scan the room for any signs of a human body. He started in the far corner, on the other side of the fallen pulpit. "Okay, girl, what next?"

Sheena opened one of the styrofoam boxes and allowed

her little grub grabbers to dive in while she trotted to the edge of the platform and hopped down.

Deputy Karr followed Sheena with his powerful flashlight until she sat beside a dusty pew where Cal lay with his face to the back. He focused the flashlight on Cal and discovered Mutt curled up asleep at his head. At some point Cal lifted the little fellow up because he refused to leave him alone. Mutt's little fury head popped up and his sleepy eyes opened. He yawned.

Deputy Karr shifted into investigative mode. He stood his ground in case the dog led to a crime scene, "Rev. Baxter?" There was no response, "Rev. Baxter?" The lawman asked as he surveyed the area with the flashlight while Sheena sat her ground.

Mutt rose and sniffed Cal's motionless head, as Deputy Karr focused the flashlight beam on the back of Cal's head where he saw the dried blood Betsy described. He activated the chest mounted radio mic, "This is thirty-two. I may have located the owner of the truck."

A Female Sheriff Dispatcher's voice crackled through the radio mounted to his belt, "What is the situation?"

"Standby one," Deputy Karr cautiously stepped toward the pew, careful not to disturb the scene. Mutt jumped into action as if to alert Cal. The little pup frantically licked Cal's face, while Deputy Karr checked Cal's neck for a pulse. He talked into the mic.

"Dispatch twenty-eight to my location. Code four. Condition unknown."

Cal stirred and reflexively reached up to take hold of the source of the frantic, moist attention. With the wiggling ball of fur securely in hand, Cal slowly rose and looked around as he swung his legs and placed his feet on the floor. The flashlight beam was too intense and forced him to shield his eyes. Deputy Karr lowered the flashlight, then activated the mic, "Dispatch, this is thirty-two. Subject is responding now."

Cal was confused while Mutt wiggled around in his arms. All the while, Sheena sat patiently as if she wasn't concerned.

Deputy Karr leaned over and took a closer look into Cal's eyes, then scanned his body for additional injuries, "Are you okay, sir?"

Cal's mind was lost in the lingering fog of a deep sleep.

He nodded, but didn't convince Deputy Karr.

"Can you give me your name?"

Cal's silence and confused gaze concerned Deputy Karr, "Are you Rev. Baxter?"

Mutt crawled up and put a paw on both sides of Cal's neck and eagerly licked his face. Cal pulled Mutt back down to his lap as he leaned back against the pew. He stared into the distance, "I'm not sure who I am."

"That's okay. I have medical personnel on the way. Can you remember how you got here?"

"I remember riding a motorcycle."

......

## 13
## One Step Closer To Nowhere

In the ER hall, outside Room #35, at Charlotte Trauma Center, Deputy Karr listened intently to Dr. Roberts.

"Temporary amnesia is more common than you'd think, even with mild head or brain injuries."

"I'd like to ask him a couple of questions," Deputy Karr requested.

Dr. Roberts opened the door and peeked in, "As soon as they finish suturing and bandaging the wound. Other than slight dehydration, he seems to be in good shape. In my medical opinion, he wasn't in his truck when it wrecked. He would've been pretty banged up."

"Then Tommy was at the wheel."

"I can't determine that, medically."

"How soon before we can talk with Tommy?"

Dr. Roberts slowly shook his head. It was bad news, "The next twenty-four to forty-eight hours will determine if he's going to live."

......

At that very moment, Megan sped south on Interstate 85. She was so consumed with guilt that she never noticed the "Welcome To Georgia" sign she zipped past. Traffic was moderate and she managed to keep enough attention focused on driving to not be a danger to herself and others.

The windows and convertible top were down. The wind tossed her hair. Her left arm rested on the door, with her forehead cupped in her left hand. The music blasted, but she couldn't outrun the truth and consequences of her actions. The horrible reality stayed with her, no matter how fast she drove.

Even though she knew it was a last-ditch effort to drown out her beleaguered conscience, Megan turned the music wide open. Instead of the badly needed relief she desperately sought, the loud music combined with the wind was a sensory overload that became unbearable. She abruptly swerved to the right and accelerated up the exit ramp. Gripping the steering wheel with both hands, she wasn't sure she would take her foot off the gas pedal. She stomped the pedal to the floor board. This could be a way to make it end.

As the speedometer raced over 100 mph, Megan realized she had a few seconds to make up her mind. Was she going to live or die? She had refused to put on her seatbelt so any head-on collision was guaranteed to be fatal.

Without any conscious effort on her part, her right foot leapt from the accelerator then jammed the brake pedal to the floor. The sensation was instantaneous. As smoke billowed from the rear tires, Megan's forehead slammed into the steering wheel with enough force to stun her.

The new tires screeched as Charlie's prized Mustang slid sideways to a stop, in the middle of the road at the top of the off-ramp. The music blared. Megan stared straight ahead. Fortunately, no traffic was headed toward her as the classic car came to rest, pointed in the opposite direction of the lane.

The emotional dam burst. Like an unstable volcano, Megan erupted in a guttural scream that burst from the depths of her ruptured soul. She pounded the steering wheel in unbridled anguish and utter frustration.

"NO! NO! NO! What have I done?"

......

Cal was stretched out on the bed and wore a hospital gown. His head was bandaged.

Deputy Karr made notes as he questioned Cal, "You have no memories prior to being picked up by that strange guy on a motorcycle?"

Cal shook his head, "I don't remember much before seeing the motorcycle come over the hill."

A male voice crackled through Deputy Karr's radio, "Thirty-two, this is Twenty-six. Can you step outside?"

Deputy Karr responded in his mic, "Be right there."

Fifteen minutes later Cal was asleep and awakened by a gentle knock on the door. He was slightly startled, "Come in."

Deputy Karr grinned while he eased in the room, "They found something at the accident site. Might help." He said as he entered with Cal's scuffed black Bible in hand. "It has your name on it."

Cal was unaffected, yet reached for the Bible, and carefully examined it. Deputy Karr looked on expectantly, until Cal frowned and shook his head, then laid the Bible on the bed.

"If, as you say, my name is Cal Baxter, it does have my name on it; but it doesn't mean anything to me."

Deputy Karr was openly disappointed, "Doesn't mean anything to you?"

"I'm sorry. But I don't remember owning this book, or fathom why I would've ever owned it."

Deputy Karr's head tilted with curiosity, "Do you know what the book is? What it's about?"

Cal nodded, "It's the Bible. People who believe in God claim it's His divinely inspired word."

"But you don't believe?"

Without hesitation, Cal shook his head, "Have no reason to believe in fairytales. Do you?"

"At this point my beliefs aren't important," Deputy Karr had many more questions but sensed they would be fruitless to ask.

A knock on the door provided a welcomed distraction.

Cal was equally relieved, but wasn't sure why, "Come in."

Dr. Roberts stepped in with a chart, "Mr. Baxter... is it okay to call you Mr. Baxter?"

"That's what it says on the driver's license with my picture on it, so I guess so."

"We're going to admit you for a couple of days, just to keep an eye on you," Dr. Roberts informed, then turned to Deputy Karr, "Can I see you in the hall?"

Out in the hall, the door to Room #35 was closed. Dr. Roberts led Deputy Karr over to another Doctor who wore a white lab coat. "This is Dr. Simmons."

Dr. Simmons was in his late 50's, graying, ruddy complexion, average height and build shook hands with Deputy Karr. "I'm the resident neurologist, and I've evaluated Rev. Baxter's X-rays, EEG, and MRI. The good news, other than some slight bruising, his brain appears to be functioning normally."

"But he has amnesia," Deputy Karr was confused. "And

at this point, I don't think he'd appreciate being called Reverend."

Dr. Simmons nodded respectfully, "I'll keep that in mind. As to his condition, there's no medical reason he suffers severe amnesia. I've asked a psychologist friend to come by. Severe emotional trauma can trigger amnesia."

"I've reached out to some of the senior members of the church where he used to preach. He resigned recently. Appears to have given up the ministry. He was pastor there for a number of years."

"Where's the church?" Dr. Simmons inquired.

"Here in North Carolina. About an hour north."

"Have you contacted his family?"

Deputy Karr shook his head, "Local officers spoke with his mother-in-law in Archdale." He paused, "Guess she'd be his ex-mother-in-law. His wife and baby daughter died in a car accident ten years ago. He was driving."

"Any other family?"

"Not to my knowledge, they're still looking."

Dr. Simmons turned to Dr. Roberts, "You're going to keep him a few days, right?"

"At least two, maybe three days."

"I'll try to get the psychologist to visit him this afternoon, or by tomorrow. Have a feeling he's going to recommend we have someone take him to his old church, then have him visit some people who knew him best. The familiar faces, voices and landmarks could go a long way to sparking a memory that could open the floodgate."

Deputy Karr was pensive, "Let me check with my Sergeant. I'll be glad to handle that."

Deputy Karr was more than an investigating officer in a crime. Now he had a vested interest in Tommy's future. The troubled lad had become a mission for the lawman with a troubled past. He was determined to help turn Tommy's life around.

Over the next couple of days, zero progress was achieved on the investigation into how Rev. Baxter was separated from his truck. Most important to Deputy Karr was if Megan and Tommy were actually involved in the theft, or if they came into possession of the truck after the fact. All three of the people authorities agreed should know what happened were unable to answer questions. One had simply vanished and was being sought for car theft, one was in Intensive Care and could die at any minute, and the victim claimed amnesia.

Needless to say, Deputy Karr had never been involved with a case he was so personally involved. Talk about conflicts of interest. It would be best not to let his superiors know the extent of his intentions for Tommy. In the eyes of the law it would be best if he recused himself from the case. Most judges and prosecutors, due to personal involvement would question his ability to remain an impartial law enforcement officer.

However, with his department's current short-staffed status and his superiors support of his genuine humanitarian effort, they were willing to allow him to walk a very thin line within reason.

The entire Sheriff's Department was aware that Deputy Karr had taken such a personal interest in Tommy. He wasn't the only lawman in the world, or in his country, who had a heart and really wanted to make a difference. More importantly, he was certain that his reputation proceeded him so his integrity wasn't the issue. It was imperative he did no harm to his position in the department, to his fellow sheriff's deputies, and the responsibility of his superiors, especially Sheriff Coffee, who was in the middle of an election year.

......

A couple of days later, Deputy Karr picked up Cal at the Charlotte Trauma Center for a day trip to Archdale. Cal still had the bandage wrapped around his head.

Betsy purchased Cal some new clothes to wear, which were bolder colors and more stylish than what he had on when he arrived in Faith. These were especially more updated than the clothes they found in his overnight bag. Cal was willing to give them a try. Deputy Karr could add clothing delivery man to his job description. Cal was very complimentary, "Obviously, this is not what I would've chosen, but I like what she picked out. She has good taste."

As Deputy Karr prepared to pull out of the parking lot, Cal spoke up, "I honestly don't have the slightest hint of a single memory from living in Archdale. And at this point, I don't really see the importance, or even the need for me to remember anything," he confessed.

"First, and foremost, let's enjoy the drive. It's a lovely Spring day, and we're getting you out of that sterile environment for some fresh air, and a couple of good meals. Courtesy of the sheriff's department."

"Since I doubt I've ever lived in your county, it's not my tax dollars at work. You sure your boss is okay with this?" Cal quipped light heartedly.

Deputy Karr chuckled. He took it as a very positive sign that even though Cal claimed he couldn't remember key facts about his life, his sense of humor functioned and carried over. Although, Deputy Karr had no clue if Cal even had a sense of humor prior to the event that stole his memory.

"I have the good fortune to work for a Sheriff who has a heart, and even though we're short of help, he's very supportive. The only thing I had to do was find an off-duty deputy to cover my shift today. And that was easy."

It was a thirty mile jaunt up Interstate 85 to the exit that led them to their first stop, the accident site, where Cal's classic truck was destroyed. It took Cal only one minute.

"I don't remember anything about this place. Don't believe I've ever been here."

"None of the road looks familiar?"

Cal studied the road and shook his head.

"I'm going to drive you to the intersection in this direction, then we're going to turn around and drive back to let you see it from the other direction."

Cal shook his head, "Don't think that's going to help. I'd say let's go to the next location."

Cal intently searched for any familiar landmarks; an unusual building, or geographically significant setting. Unfortunately, everything he saw was for the first time.

Then Deputy Karr pulled his patrol car off the paved road. Gravel crackled as they drove the short distance on the narrow dirt road, to the small, green pond.

Cal followed Deputy Karr as they strolled around the slightly overgrown bank.

"So, this is where they found my phone, and other items?" Cal looked around.

"Yes, your phone was in several pieces. It was no accident. Someone intended to destroy it," Deputy Karr explained.

Cal shook his head, "I'm pretty sure I've never been here either. Nor do I have a clue why anyone would bring my phone here and pound it to pieces."

Cal squinted his eyes in the bright morning sun.

Deputy Karr was about to turn toward his car when Cal nonchalantly picked up a rock and skimmed it across the green water. For some reason that seemed odd to the curious lawman. Especially when Cal turned to him and causally shrugged his shoulders. It seemed to be a random impulse to which he yielded.

From that point on, Deputy Karr watched Cal carefully for any sign he wasn't telling the truth. Even the most practiced liar could slip up when placed in unexpected locations and situations. Pathological liars were often arrogant control freaks who methodically mapped out every tiny detail of the truth they wanted all to believe.

At that point, as far as law enforcement was concerned, Rev. Cal Baxter could have any number of reasons to pull such a stunt. To have his truck destroyed for insurance purposes. Perhaps he wanted to disappear in plain sight. To escape from a crime he'd committed, or was about to commit. If he convinced the right people he was incapable of comprehending the deed, or deeds, then he couldn't be held responsible. He had dealt with some very smart crooks who tried to pull off dumber stunts.

Rev. Baxter could've easily driven his truck to an out-of-the-way location, abandoned it, hit himself on the back of the head, then melted into a small town like Faith. Then he was an instant victim of a crime who couldn't remember a single thing about his past, prior to being hit in the head, and his prized truck stolen.

In such a scenario, Tommy's propensity for making bad decisions, would've made it too tempting to pass up. Even a "no questions" asked "black market" sale could fetch a hefty price. Since Megan was suspected of being involved, her wild, push-the-limits personality could explain a reckless joyride.

Deputy Karr was uncomfortable with both scenarios, but to do his job effectively, he had to consider all possibilities. More importantly, he had to make sure he wouldn't be tempted to skew his investigation in a well-meaning attempt to minimize Tommy's culpability. It was imperative as a lawman he remain objective and impartial throughout the investigation. He must carefully observe and evaluate, not observe and judge, either Tommy or Rev. Baxter, especially since he was predisposed to come down on Tommy's side.

As soon as Cal got back into the patrol car, he expressed his discomfort with the idea of going back to the place he'd come from. The remainder of the drive up Interstate 85 was relatively quiet.

······

## 14
## When Reality Collides With Duality

The small community of Archdale, North Carolina, chose to incorporate into a city in order to avoid being annexed into High Point, its aggressively expanding neighbor. The move wasn't petulant or vindictive; it was a genuine effort to preserve the close-knit community's sense of identity and individuality enjoyed in a small town atmosphere.

High Point was considered the Furniture Capital of the World, where twice a year the Spring and Fall Furniture Markets hosted the world's furniture dealers. Sixty to eighty-thousand dealers flocked to High Point from around the world to view and buy the next season's hottest introductions. For five days in April and October, High Point's streets and sidewalks were converted from sparse small southern town foot traffic to the hustle and bustle of crowded sidewalks and streets akin to New York on an average day.

Even though several new, modern hotels sprang up on both sides of Interstate 85, the heart of downtown Archdale's Main Street was occupied by locally owned small businesses and restaurants. Several of the most notable businesses had been handed down to the second generation. A few were recently taken over by the third generation.

Deputy Russell, the case officer from the Randolph County Sheriff's Department, wanted to meet and begin Cal's visit at the parsonage. He had already made arrangements for some of the Tabernacle Baptist Church members to meet at certain times and locations.

Several miles south of High Point, Deputy Karr turned the volume down on the navigation app in his phone and followed the visual cues to turn up the exit ramp. He kept a watchful eye on Cal to see if he would give any indication he recognized what should be familiar surroundings. Near the top of the ramp Deputy Karr pulled on the right side of the white line and parked on the wide shoulder.

Deputy Karr carefully evaluated every facial expression and every eye movement as he asked, "Can you tell me which way to turn to go to the parsonage?"

Cal sat silent for several seconds. His eyes slowly scanned, then his head turned for a broader look in both directions. Eventually he shook his head, "Sorry, Deputy Karr, but this is all new to me."

"How about taking a guess."

Cal looked in both directions and diligently searched his mind, then turned defeated eyes to Deputy Karr. He reluctantly shook his head, "If I had to guess, I'm not certain we're even at the right exit."

"So this is not the exit you would've taken?" Deputy Karr thought for a fleeting second they might be on the brink of a meaningful breakthrough.

Cal's head slowly shook, "No, Sir. I honestly don't know. None of this looks familiar."

Deputy Karr called Deputy Russell and informed him they had just pulled off the highway and were about to turn onto South 311. They would arrive at the location in less than ten minutes. Deputy Russell was already on scene.

From the moment they exited the highway, it was all new to Cal. He didn't recognize the parsonage from the outside. He was impressed with the Avalon, but didn't remember driving it. Nor did the interior of the parsonage spark the slightest hint of a memory. Not even the master bedroom where Cal and Annie loved to cuddle and talk until the wee hours.

Then Deputy Russell opened the manila folder and pulled out the "big gun," a photo of Annie holding Taylor, that Gabby had given him to show Cal inside the parsonage. Gabby was sure that would crack the wall.

Cal studied the photo intently for several long seconds before he turned to Deputy Karr, "This was my wife and daughter?"

Deputy Karr nodded.

"Wow. She's gorgeous. Wish I remembered her. And my daughter's a little angel," Cal shook his head. "And they died in an accident?"

Deputy Russell nodded.

"What happened?" Cal asked.

## RETURN TO FAITH

The psychologist in Charlotte who recommended the visit also warned the authorities not to share too much information with Cal during the initial visit, "The sensory overload could exacerbate his condition."

Deputy Russell spoke up, "At this point, I don't have all of the information."

Then Deputy Karr took charge, "Let's move on to the church. As I understand, there's some people who want to talk with you."

Deputy Russell suggested they drive all the way through Archdale, then turn around at the edge of High Point, and drive back to the road that took them to the church. They slowly drove by and pulled into a few parking lots, but none of the businesses or landmarks were familiar to Cal.

Cal spoke up as Deputy Karr followed Deputy Russell's car and made a left turn onto Madison Street, which would take them to Tabernacle Baptist Church.

"I'm sorry, Deputy Karr. I really appreciate all the trouble you guys are going to, but I honestly can't remember anything you've shown me so far." He held up the photo, "Especially these two gorgeous girls." He turned his head sideways, "But Annie." He turned to Deputy Karr who was very hopeful, "She reminds me of a younger Betsy." He held up the photo for Deputy Karr to see.

At first glance, with his attention focused on the road ahead, Deputy Karr couldn't formulate a fair comparison. Mostly because Deputy Russell just flipped on his right turn signal and pulled into the cracked parking lot at Tabernacle Baptist Church.

As they pulled into the parking lot Cal noticed the "For Sale" sign in front of the glass faced, brick structure that held the church sign.

"They're selling the church?" Cal asked as his head and shoulders turned while he focused on the odd sight. A "For Sale" sign beside a church sign that still had the date and information about the last service to be held, which was less than a week ago.

Safely in the parking lot, Deputy Karr stopped the car and accepted the photo from Cal. He had known Betsy and Charlie his entire life, and a chill raced up his spine. Cal was spot on. Betsy could've easily been Annie's older twin-sister.

He turned to Cal and shook his head as he handed the photo back, "That's spooky."

"Did he give me this to keep?"

"He didn't say her mother wanted it back."

By then, Deputy Russell had parked and exited his car beside the Jenkins' car, and they were slowly climbing out. Deputy Karr parked on the far side of Russell's car and turned to Cal, "Well, let's see if there are any surprises awaiting inside the church."

Cal half shrugged his shoulders, "Got nothing to lose." He started to open the door, then turned back to Karr, "Who are we meeting?"

"Don't know. Let's get out and see."

As usual, Sadie took charge and closed the distance to Cal at her granny pace, with extended arms, which caused Cal to become uncomfortable and take a half step back.

Sadie was stunned, borderline hurt by Cal's reluctance to accept one of her famous hugs. She cut her eyes to Deputy Russell, who held up his hand and shook his head. She wasn't sure if that meant to stop her advance, or not to take his reaction to heart.

Ralph was stunned as well and was reluctant to extend his hand to Cal.

"Oh, my dear boy," was all Sadie could mumble.

"Mother, don't crowd him," Ralph suggested.

Sadie lowered her arms and flashed a stern glare at her well-intended husband.

Ralph realized he was in trouble as he looked back to Deputy Karr and released his hand.

Deputy Karr was compelled to step forward and defuse the unexpected tense and very awkward moment. He extended his hand and Ralph immediately shook it, "I'm Deputy Karr, from the Rowan County Sheriff's Department."

Ralph turned and watched Sadie awkwardly step back from Cal. He motioned to Deputy Karr, "Mother, this is Deputy Karr, from Rowan County."

Sadie couldn't help herself, "I heard him, Ralph. Remember, I hear much better than you." She shook Deputy Karr's hand, "Nice to mean you, young man."

"This is my wife, Sadie," Ralph just made another

mistake.

"Ralph, why don't you just stand there and look like the fool you are."

Deputy Russell spoke up, "Ms. Jenkins, as I explained to you and Mr. Jenkins, Reverend Baxter is suffering from amnesia."

Needless to say, Sadie did not receive Deputy Russell's kind reminder in the spirit in which it was intended.

Sadie's voice was more of a growl with a serious bite, "Young man, I may be in my eighties, but my mind is still sharp as a new razor blade."

"And your tongue is even sharper, more dangerous," Ralph dared to suggest.

Deputy Russell wasn't about to allow the situation to devolve into the same kind of verbal joust he endured on his visit to the Jenkins' home, "Yes, Ma'am," he struggled to recover, "Please forgive me. I didn't mean to insinuate you didn't."

Cal felt bad for the ruckus he'd caused and immediately extended his hand, "Ms. Jenkins. I'm sorry I didn't remember you. I didn't mean to offend you."

As usual, Sadie took hold of Cal's hand with both hands, "It's Sadie, dear boy. Obviously you don't remember I taught you it was okay to call me, Sadie. Not Ms. Jenkins."

Cal was emphatic, "Then Sadie it is."

Deputy Karr looked at his watch. They had a tight schedule to keep, "Well Sadie and Ralph, we certainly do appreciate you taking your valuable time to meet with us here today."

Sadie was taken aback by Deputy Karr's misappropriated familiarity and tipped her head back, "Young man, you don't know us that well."

Sadie turned her attention to Cal and stepped toward him with a cautiously extended hand. He allowed her to gently place her fingers on the bandage around his head. "My dear boy, does your head hurt?"

"No, Ma'am."

"Thank the Lord, you're okay, Rev. Baxter. So you don't recognize me, honey?"

Cal was silent. His expression was blank, "I'm having a bit of a problem grasping I was a preacher. And no, I'm sorry, I don't remember either one of you."

Sadie nodded compassionately but felt she needed to point out, "Well, I'm Sadie Jenkins and," She pointed to Ralph, "This annoying old man is my husband, Ralph."

Cal's expression remained blank.

Ralph spoke up, "Careful, Sadie, you don't want these nice young deputies to arrest you for spousal abuse."

Sadie reached over and patted Cal on the arm, "You know I'm telling the truth. That man I married is the Devil incarnate. You and I have prayed for his soul a million times." She winked and grinned.

After a second Cal grinned, "I honestly don't remember, but somehow I suspect this has become a fun game between you."

Sadie giggled mischievously, "It's been years since our frisky life ended. This is the only way we can raise each other's blood pressure, at our tender ages."

"She's still a spunky little gal," Ralph confessed.

Sadie and Ralph shared a genuine look that revealed the truth, a deep love and respect for the other.

"Reverend Baxter, does this church look familiar?" Deputy Karr asked.

Cal was noticeably uncomfortable as he turned to Deputy Karr, "With all due respect, Sir, at this point I'm really not comfortable with being called Reverend."

"I'm sorry, Mr. Baxter."

"Your friends called you, Cal," Ralph spoke up.

Cal nodded and contemplated as he lightly chewed on his lower lip before he responded, "Cal." He nodded again, "I can live with that. I can be a Cal," he confessed as he surveyed the scene, which to him was for the first time. He slowly shook his head and spoke absentmindedly, "Sorry. I don't remember ever being here."

Sadie gently took Cal by the arm, "Come on, Dear Boy, let's take a look inside."

Ralph had called the realtor and she met them there earlier to open the building and turn on the lights. She was excited to share that she had just gotten off the phone with an investor who was very interested. Ralph and Sadie were stunned, outright offended by the plans the wealthy man had in store for the property. They would recommend the impressive offer be rejected. Sadie and Ralph just couldn't fathom their church turned into a family style restaurant named, "The Bread Basket."

Sadie responded in kind when Cal slowed the pace as they neared the side door, the entrance he would normally use. They stopped twenty feet from the first step. Sadie released Cal's arm and took a few steps back. She sensed he didn't want to be pressured to go up the steps and enter the church.

"The door is unlocked, and the lights are on," Ralph informed.

"We'll follow you, when you're ready," Sadie assured.

Deputy Karr, Sadie, Ralph, and Deputy Russell stood in silent support behind Cal. They couldn't see his face while his head eased to the left, then back to the right, so he could take in the length and height of the church with its tall, white steeple.

Cal struggled to find at least one tiny thread of a memory he could latch on and pull it into focus. But there wasn't so much as a trace of recognition or associated thought. More importantly, he had no desire to enter.

Oddly enough, the fact that he didn't want to step into the church was the very reason he must overcome his reluctance. There had to be something inside those four walls that would prompt a memory. If he were indeed a preacher, the interior of any church should be a refuge. A place to seek answers.

After a few tense seconds Cal took a deep breath, and without looking back, he mustered the courage to take the first step. Once he reached the top platform it was imperative he continue. If he stopped, that would be it. He would never step foot back inside a church again.

Cal thought it odd that the door knob didn't feel familiar to his hand, which it should have. And after years of taking hold of the knob, then physically stepping through the door, his feet should've felt comfortable, at home. But they didn't. He was a disassociated stranger in a world he didn't belong.

Several long, tense seconds passed. It was the moment of truth. How badly did he want to remember? And what logical reasons did he have to remember?

Sadie nudged Ralph and they eased forward to flank Cal in the hallway. It was their way to assure Cal they were with him. They supported him and desperately wanted him to return to the place he should've never left. Not necessarily to that structure, but to the solid foundation of the strong faith he had when he first entered that very door as their new pastor.

In a matter of seconds the first memory unexpectedly connected with the present. It was a recent memory. Too recent to be the first step backward to the past he'd lost touch with. If he were to spray a thick coat of dust on the ceiling, walls and floor, then rip a few doors mostly off their hinges, he would have been in the hall of the dilapidated church he'd spent his first few nights, in Faith.

Somehow it made sense. The fact that it was so very wrong made it right. There he stood an unwitting, unwilling participant in a twisted duality. No matter how many years of Sundays he had spent in that building, they no longer mattered because he no longer belonged there. Nor did he feel connected to the purpose he must've fulfilled while under that roof.

There was one more thing he needed to see, so he pushed the door open to the sanctuary. As expected it was eerily similar to the one in the rundown church in Faith. He turned to Sadie, "I've seen enough. I'm ready to go."

Ralph shook his head and pointed down the hall, "There's your old office, where we had many'a powerful prayer session. Let's step in there for a second before we leave."

"We're here. What's it gonna hurt?" Sadie smiled. "Give us five more minutes. That's all we ask." Sadie's face morphed into the innocence of a child who couldn't possibly be told, "No."

As badly as he wanted to get out of that place, Cal couldn't be so cold, "Even though it goes against my better judgment, and I doubt this is the first time, I'm going to let you have your way."

Sadie cut a sly grin at Ralph, who shook his head. "You don't have a clue what you're getting yourself into," he warned.

The room was equal in size to the empty office in the abandoned church. However, it looked smaller due to the amount of furniture and bookshelves that covered two walls. But what caused the muscles in the back of his neck to tighten, the placement of the disturbingly similar desk in that office. If the room were to be stripped of everything else, that desk appeared to sit in the exact location on the floor, at the same odd angle to the right. He was the only one who knew, and there was no need to share the eerie similarities, especially with Sadie. No doubt, she would conjure up all sorts of obscure meaning.

Much to Cal's chagrin, moments later he was compelled to turn and enter the sanctuary, instead of exit the side door. He was drawn to stand behind the pulpit, where his hands firmly gripped the sculpted sides of the Bible stand on top of the pulpit. Exactly like he did when he began his last sermon.

Seated on the front row were the smiling faces of Sadie, Ralph, Deputies Karr and Russell.

"Now that's the Reverend Baxter we know and love," Sadie clutched her hands to her chest.

There was no way Cal would share what he actually felt, or what was really on his mind. There was absolutely no connection to that pulpit, the white book on it, nor to the purpose of that book's meaningless significance to his life. Those wonderful, sincere people didn't deserve the stench of his disassociation to what they so ardently believed and accepted as real and meaningful in their lives.

"Rev. Baxter, our members voted to allow you to move back into the parsonage, at least until it sales," Ralph was pleased to offer.

"That will allow you some stability until we can get you back on track," Sadie added hopefully.

Cal was respectful enough to take a few moments to appear genuinely considering the offer. He discretely stepped away from the pulpit, "Thank you so much. I really appreciate the kind offer. But at this point, I don't believe it's the best thing for me." He continued as he descended the three steps from the platform, "If all I've learned in the last few days is true, obviously the reason or reasons I left Archdale are the very same reasons I shouldn't come back."

Moments later, the lights in the church were off and the doors locked. Cal and Deputy Karr stood beside the passenger door of the Jenkins' car.

Sadie reached out and took Deputy Karr's hand, "Don't hesitate to call us, if there's anything we can do." Then she reached and Cal took her hand, "My dear, we will always be here for you. If and when you need us."

Cal nodded, "Thank you so much. I really appreciate it. And please, don't take any offense. I know you and every one of the members are sincere. I just need some time to sort things out."

Ralph leaned over from the driver's side, "Be sure to stop by Granny's Doughnuts, on Main Street. Gabby wants to see him."

"That's our next stop," Deputy Karr promised.

......

## 15
## The Best First Step Back Might Be To Walk Farther Away

In an attempt to spark a memory, Deputy Russell stopped in specific parking lots on their first drive through Archdale. Granny's Doughnuts was the first location, but Cal showed no sign of familiarity.

Cal was quiet on the short drive from the church to the doughnut shop, "I'm really not comfortable with stopping by this place," he finally spoke up as they pulled in the lot.

Deputy Karr stopped the car and turned to Cal, "It's entirely up to you. We can head back now."

Cal inhaled deeply and exhaled slowly as he stared straight ahead, "I'm kinda tired. I've really racked my brain, trying to find the slightest detail of something I remember." He turned to Deputy Karr, "Have you ever been mentally exhausted? Not sure this is a good analogy, but imagine taking your brain out and holding it in your hands. Then in total frustration whacking it on the edge of a counter like a stopped up salt shaker. But it slips out of your hand and bounces into the cat's freshly used litter box."

Deputy Karr chuckled, then quickly gathered his composure, "Sorry. My wife has three cats."

"You and your wife separated?"

"No. We live together, and we love each other more than the day we were married. But those evil little furry creatures are hers. They hate me, and I hate them. We maintain an uneasy truce. So I understand perfectly, you're in a real crappy situation."

"Yeah, I really want my brain back, without all the crap around it."

The visceral visual imagery was actually hilarious and the comic relief was welcomed. The good laugh they shared was the best thing that had happened to Cal all day.

"Deputy Russell told me they make the best coffee and

Apple Fritters in the state," Deputy Karr was less than subtle.

"Out of respect for you, my good man, I'll skip the obligatory 'doughnut shop' joke."

"Well, Mr. Baxter, in light of your situation, I'll give you a 'get out of jail free' card on that one."

"Cal," was all the former pastor said.

Deputy Karr waited for more, then asked, "Excuse me?"

"Please, feel free to call me, Cal."

"Okay, Cal. Please allow me to buy us a cup of coffee and a couple of those Apple Fritters, if the shop's not overrun by law enforcement."

They chuckled again.

"When we pulled in this lot earlier, none of the signs or shops even piqued my interest."

"I'm game. It's up to you."

"Apple Fritters? Hummm, do you hunt'm, and shoot'm, before you cook'm and eat'm?"

"Let's find out."

Cal noticed the sign on a pole twenty feet in the air and he reads it aloud, "Granny's Doughnuts, Voted Best, Fresh Apple Fritters in North Carolina."

"That's a sign from above," Deputy Karr said then immediately shook his head, "Sorry."

"We might as well poke fun at preachers too," Cal grinned.

Deputy Karr opened the door for Cal, who didn't know what to expect after the bell over the door announced their entry. His eyes were immediately drawn to Jenny behind the counter as she rang up a customer. The customer was a tall black male in his forties in a black suit, white shirt and red tie. He looked at Cal and Deputy Karr and nodded. Cal wasn't sure if the customer acknowledged someone he knew, or exhibited genuine Southern Hospitality. Either way, Cal respectfully nodded back. If the stranger were someone who knew him well enough in his past life he would've spoken, or headed toward them to shake Cal's hand and speak. Instead, he turned and walked in the opposite direction.

Little did Cal realize the customer was the new Branch Manager of his bank, who started last week and was in a meeting when Cal stopped by on his way out of town. They never met, but the manager did see him briefly through the glass wall in his office. The problem for the new manager was he'd been bombarded with hundreds of new faces and Cal did seem familiar; but at that point he chose not to speak, or introduce himself. Right or wrong he opted to remain silent, pick up his box, then exit the other side door.

As the door closed, Jenny was surprised and visibly unhappy to see Cal headed toward the counter. As much as she loathed Cal, she loved her sister more, so she made a silent vow to be civil. That decision had nothing to do with the Deputy Sheriff to Cal's left.

Gabby had informed Jenny earlier that Cal was going to be in town and she requested the Deputy bring him by before they left.

Jenny turned her head toward the swinging kitchen doors, "Gabby, you might wanna come out here." She cut a harsh stare at Cal, "She'll be out in a second," Jenny barked before she forcefully pushed through the doors, and they swung dramatically. Click-Click! Click-Click!

Jenny's apparent hostile reception caused Cal and Deputy Karr to stop and stand their ground. They looked at each other, both were surprised and caught completely off guard.

"And we came here for...?" Cal wondered aloud.

"Your mother-in-law and her sister run this place," Deputy Karr reminded. "Was that your....?" Deputy Karr started then realized it was probably a waste of time to even ask.

"My mother-in-law? I hope not."

Deputy Karr made no attempt to lower his voice, or disguise his disgust for the way they were greeted, "If you would rather leave, I understand."

Gabby heard Deputy Karr as she extended both hands to stop one of the swinging doors. "Hold on. Please stay," She was humble and sincere. "Forgive my sister," She paused at the edge of the bar, totally unprepared to see Cal with a bandage wrapped around his head. "Oh Cal, my dear boy." She addressed Deputy Karr, "Please forgive my sister, but I'm afraid she has issues."

Cal turned to Deputy Karr, "What haven't you told me yet?"

Deputy Karr held up his hand. This wasn't part of the plan. Deputy Russell didn't tell him there was friction between Cal and his wife's family. Russell got a call and couldn't join them for that visit. Karr was concerned if Cal was about to learn something he shouldn't know yet.

Gabby was embarrassed by how rudely Jenny greeted them, with the misguided intent to make them feel unwelcome. She was unsure what to do or say next, until she was overwhelmed with the desire, the need to hug Cal. She slowly crossed the room toward him unable to gauge if her advance would be welcomed or rebuffed. Her arms naturally assumed a loving, hopeful cradle for the man she would never blame for the death of her daughter. She would always love and cherish him and remained hopeful that one day he would at least be able to like himself again. Jenny was a lost cause, but she refused to give up hope for Cal. She prayed for him every day.

At first Cal was a bit reluctant to receive the hug, that was as much for Gabby, as for him. Gabby refused to be deterred, or denied, "We're gonna get you through this, my Dear." She whispered as she felt her grip tighten around Cal. It took a couple of seconds until she smiled when she felt more pressure from Cal's arms. It was only a hint of the bear hug he always gave her before Annie's death. But it was a good start. More importantly, it was stronger than the last, reluctant hug he gave her on the way out of town the other day. She was prepared to stay in his arms as long as he hugged back. It ended much too soon. She stepped away and extended her hand to Deputy Karr.

"I'm Annie's mother. They call me Gabby."

Deputy Karr was relieved when he felt the deceptively firm grip from such a petite woman. And how the little sprite gently she cupped her left hand around his right hand. He'd learned over the years that was a natural gesture attributed to those with genuine, tender hearts. The unexpected visit began on a sour note, but it was about to end on a double sweet note. His mind switched back to looking forward to the famous sugary fritter.

"We're also searching for his closest kin, so we can get him on the path to remembering who he is," Deputy Karr revealed.

Cal felt like a stranger in someone else's life, only to realize he was the very stranger in his own life.

## RETURN TO FAITH

Gabby slowly, disappointedly shook her head, "He was an only child, and his mother left when he was young. His father did a few years after he and Annie were married. As far as I know, both his parents were only children too. So he had no aunts and uncles. To my knowledge, we were his only close family."

"Mr. and Mrs. Jenkins told us Cal was welcome to stay in the parsonage for a while," Deputy Karr stated.

"They said all my personal belongings were in a storage unit, but they didn't know where," Cal injected.

"We're gonna visit all the local units we can on our way out of town today."

Gabby smiled hopefully as she reached over and took hold of Cal's right hand, "Honey, you can stay with me for a while." She became excited and the words danced out of her mouth, "And you can help us around the shop too."

Jenny had eased back into the room and held one swinging door opened as she eavesdropped. She didn't trust her sister's judgment and was prepared to stand up for her. She was unable to hold back her harsh objection, "Oh no, you don't…" She slammed her right hand over her mouth as she wheeled around and disappeared back into the kitchen. The doors Clicked, but didn't drown out what she muttered and sputtered in disgust.

Gabby took hold of Cal's other hand, "Don't you worry, Sweetheart. I own fifty-two percent of the shop. You can work on my side, if Miss Grumpy Apron wants to show her sourdough."

Cal and Deputy Karr chuckled, "Thank you… Miss… Miss."

"I'll always be Gabby."

"Thank you, Gabby. But I don't think that'll create the proper atmosphere for this type of establishment."

"Oh, I can handle her. Don't you worry bout that." Gabby's shoulders lifted and her eyes narrowed with bullheaded determination.

"There's no doubt in my mind," Deputy Karr chimed in. "Absolutely no doubt."

Deputy Karr politely declined to sit with Cal and Gabby. He settled in the small, identical booth on the opposite side of the room to savor his mouth-watering pastry and hot coffee. The sign definitely wasn't false advertising. After he licked his fingers and used the wet-nap, he dried them with a regular napkin before he stepped outside and called his boss. "Yes, Sir, Captain, we're going to make a few more stops on the way in. Should be back by six."

Gabby was appreciative of Deputy Karr's kind gesture to allow her some private time with Cal, even though Cal would've preferred a little back up. Not that he was intimated by the spunky little woman. Cal felt like a punch-drunk fighter still wobbling and weak-kneed after a vicious headshot.

Once again, Gabby reached across the table and took hold of both of Cal's soft hands. Her eyes were hopeful, "Maybe a fresh start is just what you need."

Cal couldn't disagree, and they left with two dozen of Granny's Doughnuts best pastries. A few would be eaten on the drive back to Charlotte. Cal insisted Deputy Karr take the rest to share with his family.

When all was said and done, it was a good idea for Cal to visit Archdale. Even though no memories were jogged. More importantly, as far as Deputy Karr could tell, no real damage had been done. Neither mentioned the need for another visit in the near future.

Stops at the three of the largest storage facilities around Archdale proved futile. Nobody named Calvin Baxter had rented any space recently. Neither of the clerks recognized Cal and he didn't recognize them either.

......

Megan had landed in a less than desirable fleabag motel in a small community well off Interstate 85, about thirty miles north of Atlanta. She picked up a large pepperoni pizza, a two-liter Coke, and dared to risk a bucket of ice from the grungy dispenser in the sheltered snack machine area.

She had four new half gallon bottles of Jack Daniels and just scarfed down the second large slice of pizza. She was actually impressed by the taste and quality from the little dingy pizzeria named, Fred's Pizza & Spaghetti, a short walk from the motel. Not bad for a "biker bar" with a menu. Fred's close proximity was convenient since Megan had been drinking heavily all day. Had she been sober, she would've never dared walk there and back, especially alone.

Lack of money wouldn't be an issue for a while. She still had thousands in cold hard cash. And thanks to the steady stream of rowdy, oversexed bikers she could keep her monthly motel bill paid with seven tricks a week. The "pimping" bartender at Fred's already added her to his little stable. With Megan's looks and fine body, she would rocket to the top. He had already added a fifteen dollar surcharge for an hour with Megan.

A steady flood of bourbon washed away the guilt and disgust for the potential death spiral she'd entered. She would be terrified if she allowed herself to sober up for two minutes. Then she would realize how quickly she accelerated to terminal velocity in a few short days.

Megan was so mixed up and in over her head. She was like an inexperienced student pilot who arrogantly jumped into the cockpit of a modern, high performance jet fighter. She was determined to take on the entire enemy air force, without a clue how to harness and control the awesome machine she strapped into.

The sad reality, Megan had no vision or understanding of who or what she was, or why she existed on this planet. The next drink was half bourbon and half Coke, with very little ice. Megan polished that drink off in short order. Mercifully it became the magic bullet that would put her out for the rest of the evening.

......

Meanwhile, Deputy Karr returned Cal to the Charlotte Trauma Center, where he quickly showered and went to bed without ordering dinner. He was exhausted. All day long, instead of his brain humming along on all twelve cylinders like a finely tuned Ferrari engine, his brain sputtered, misfired, smoked, and rattled like a rusted and abandoned Studebaker.

Neither food, nor a satisfactory resolution to the mystery of who this Cal Baxter guy really was didn't matter at the end of such a frustrating day. Every fiber of his being craved sweet, uninterrupted sleep.

......

Deputy Karr opted to stop by and have a cup of coffee

with Betsy, instead of going straight home after he deposited Cal at the hospital in Charlotte. He loved and absolutely adored Deb, his very average wife of fifteen years. He also loved the best son and daughter any woman would have borne. At the moment he met Betsy, a switch flipped and lit up a part of his soul Deb would never reach.

It wasn't sexual. Not once had he lusted after her flesh, even though she was much prettier and better built that Deb. There was an instant connection. A spark of life that was missing between him and Deb. It was the same every time he was around Betsy. Circuits deep inside him were energized and made each day he interacted with her much better.

Divorce wasn't even an option, and Betsy was too fine of a woman to consider a physical affair. In reality, he was having an affair with Betsy. More than likely Betsy never knew as it was probably one-sided.

Nonetheless, if Deb were to ever realize how he felt, she would be devastated, beyond betrayed. And jealous, oh dear Heavens! The worn-out saying "Hell hath no fury as a woman scorned," would describe the unholy storm that would ruin his marriage and life.

"Hey, Sweetie, want me to freshen up that cup?" Betsy asked as she swept by on her way to deliver a steamy plate to the gentleman at the end of the bar.

Deputy Karr knew he wasn't special. Betsy called everyone "sweetie." She would've called Cal sweetie had he joined him at dinner. The conflicted lawman always chose to believe it carried more meaning when she called him, "Sweetie." He knew it was wrong and foolish, but it was his little fantasy and he was good with it.

"Yeah, thanks. Appreciate it," Deputy Karr smiled, even though he knew Betsy was too busy to even look back and enjoy his broad, genuine effort.

"When I get a break, I want you to tell me how your day went with Reverend Baxter," Betsy couldn't help but smile.

At that moment, Deputy Karr felt something he never considered a possibility. He just experienced more than a twinge of jealousy. The fact that this troubled stranger had stirred something in Betsy didn't set well with him. He should've been happy for Betsy, instead of being childishly annoyed by the potential rival for the attention Cal didn't deserve.

To make matters worse, Deputy Karr considered it might be in his best interest to back off trying to help Cal. The time he took with Cal that day was his choice. The real quandary was evident. The pledge he'd made to Tommy's mother could wind up causing him to have to spend more time with Cal than he would prefer. The only possible out would be if Tommy were to die. That could happen at any second. Deputy Karr prayed that the Lord would spare the young man's life.

The tinkle of the bell on the door disrupted Deputy Karr's inappropriate conundrum. Charlie entered and by the look of his uniform shirt, he spent a long, hard day under the hood of a car with a serious oil leak. His hands and arms remained clean.

In typical Charlie fashion, he playfully brushed a clean arm against Deputy Karr's back as he passed behind to settle on the empty stool to his left, "You ain't gonna find my Mustang hanging around here chat'n up my sister."

Without looking, Betsy quickly responded, "Be nice. He's here on official business."

Deputy Karr fought to control his expression and to conceal how Betsy's defense of him destroyed the myth he secretly fostered, "Yeah. Try'n to get an update on that hoodlum niece of yours."

Charlie shook his head in total dismay, "She's no blood kin to me. Her and Betsy adopted each other. I just got roped in. Have been kicking and screaming from day one."

Betsy paused as she wiped the bar and turned her head sideways. Her eyes narrowed and her lips pursed, "Don't you dare go there. You really care about that troubled soul."

Charlie shook his head and his eyes told the truth, "Her troubled soul, yes. But, the crazy, mixed up body and mind that carries it around drives me crazy." Charlie glanced around, then turned to Deputy Karr, "Speaking of mixed up, where's your new friend?"

Reverend Cal Baxter was the last thing the conflicted lawman wanted to think about or discuss. It would take an Academy Award winning performance to muster a convincing, non-bias answer. The spotlight was on him and four very involved ears awaited what they expected would be a concerned lawman's response. He opened his mouth and hoped for the best, "The trip to Archdale wore him out, and he wanted to go back to the hospital. Said he was going straight to bed."

"I hauled what was left of his truck to the impound lot. Did he do the restoration?"

"According to what we learned today, he did most of the work himself. A friend of his let him use some garage space, and he methodically worked through it," Deputy Karr explained.

"Looks like he completely stripped it down to the frame and reworked everything."

Deputy Karr nodded, "But he don't remember a single screwdriver turn."

Charlie and Betsy exchanged a glance and wisp of a smile. Deputy Karr knew it meant something, but decided it wasn't anything he wanted to know, so he remained silent.

"Can you bring him to my shop in the morning?" Charlie asked.

Deputy Karr was caught off guard, "I don't know. I'd have to check with my lieutenant and captain."

Betsy smiled, "Would you mind? It could be a good thing for him." She knew exactly what was on Charlie's mind.

It would have been easy to let it slide if Betsy hadn't jumped in and made the request with such an eager smile. He wasn't sure if the favor would be a good thing for Cal, or for her. Either way, he dare not say, "No." So he responded, "Of course I'll see what I can do. But I just spent most of today with him, and we're already short-handed."

Deputy Karr told the truth. He just didn't tell the whole truth. He deliberately omitted that this patrol area was actually boring, due to a consistently low incident rate. His superiors would be more than willing to allow him to possibly help restore Cal's memory. However, to make himself the hero, he would have to convince Charlie and Betsy, especially Betsy. He needed to make it sound like it took some serious effort on his part to convince his supervisors he wanted to perform an important community service.

"Can you go ahead and call'm now?" Betsy inadvertently sounded off, which even surprised Charlie, who turned to Deputy Karr.

"Yeah, go ahead and call. That way I'll know now how to plan my day for tomorrow," Charle turned up the pressure.

Much to his dismay, Deputy Karr was off the phone in less than a minute. All he had to do was ask, and both of his superiors wholeheartedly encouraged him to honor the request. The only requirement was that he be back on duty by 2:00 PM.

Deputy Karr's simple call made him a hero to Betsy, but it wasn't nearly the magnitude of the accomplishment he would've preferred.

......

## 16
## The First Steps Back Can Be The Worst Steps Forward

After a few days of binge drinking and constant snacking, the small, grungy motel room was transformed into a starter kit for a garbage dump. Empty soda cans, candy bar wrappers, wadded chip bags, and several pizza boxes with varying numbers of uneaten slices were scattered about on the double bed, floor and heavily worn furniture.

Over the last few days Megan quickly learned that it was wise to remain drunk, rather than sober up and pay the price of a cruel, head pounding hangover. She had only one task to accomplish. She was already extremely drunk.

It was 8:30 AM and the best she could do was aim her body at the wall on the other side of the room. If she made it, she would turn around and try it again, with her cellphone to her ear. It wasn't really a walk, it was an unstable weave.

With a slurred voice she argued with an operator at the Charlotte Trauma Center.

"I'm sorry, Ma'am, HIPPA laws forbid me giving out information on patients, unless they're on an approved list of family members," the volunteer operator had about reached the end of her patience with the rude, and obviously intoxicated caller.

"You can't even tell-l-l me if Tommy'zzzz in your stink'nnn hoz-pital?"

"Ma'am, I've already told you he's in the Intensive Care Unit. That's all I'm permitted to share with non-family members. Ma'am, you've refused to give me your name, or the password, so I don't know if you're even on the list to receive information."

"Hizz wicked mother wooo-uld never let me be on no stink'nnn list." Megan complained.

"Ma'am, I'm going to hang up on you now," The

# RETURN TO FAITH

Operator said before she pushed the button to end the call.

Megan heard the click and became indignant, "Oh no! You didn't!" She barked as she crashed into the door and stumbled back a few steps. It took three violent yanks on the door before she realized she hadn't slipped the chain lock out of the slot.

Once the door was open, Megan staggered out on the sidewalk and slung her phone across the parking lot, "That'll teach'cha to mess with me."

The unprotected phone slid under the tire of an eighteen-wheeler truck's front tire as it rolled past. By the time the last tire on that side of the truck rolled over the thin phone, it was crushed and useless.

After a few seconds to think, Megan turned, staggered back into the room and slammed the door, "That might not've been smart."

As she kicked the wall it dawned on her that she would have to sober up long enough to drive to the closest Walmart and buy one of those cheap pay-as-you-go phones. The upside was the Walmart phone would be much harder to track.

......

"There's no way I can tell you how much I appreciate all you're doing to help me," Cal shared with Deputy Karr as they drove up I-85 toward Faith.

When Deputy Karr got home the night before his loving wife greeted him at the door for her customary hug and kiss. Then she turned and announced, "Daddy's home!" She intentionally didn't mention he had two large doughnut boxes.

Seconds later they heard the thump of little socked feet as they pounded down the hall. It was the evening routine in the Karr house as he was attacked by his loving kids.

On that evening the doughnut boxes were noticed but would be celebrated after the loving kids showered the father with affection. The kids had one doughnut each after dinner.

Every night when Deputy Karr walked through that door, within thirty-seconds he was reminded how lucky he was to have a wife and family who adored him, and cherished every minute they spent together. They made his life worthwhile, and they deserved no less from him.

It wasn't that his wife and kids made him forget how special Betsy was, they diverted his attention to the important things in his life. They reminded him about his responsibilities as a loving husband, and father.

On that morning, for the next few hours Deputy Karr's responsibility as a lawman and decent human being was to lend all the assistance he could to a man in dire need of help. Cal's genuine show of appreciation drove home the realization.

"No problem," Deputy Karr turned and smiled. "Glad to help," he said, and was very pleased that he was sincere.

"I'd like to buy you breakfast, but I don't have enough money," Cal admitted.

"Don't worry about it. Today's on me."

Cal was suddenly distant, in deep thought.

Deputy Karr became concerned, "You okay?"

After a few tense moments Cal shook his head, "I don't know. The only two things I have to prove who I used to be are a beaten up Bible and the picture of my driver's license you gave me."

"Yesterday your mother-in-law gave you that photo of your wife and baby girl."

"But I wasn't in that photo, so it doesn't really connect me with them."

Cal's heartbreaking reality heaped additional hot coals of guilt on Deputy Karr, but it made him more determined to control his unhealthy fascination with Betsy.

"How about we stop at the diner? We'll call Charlie to join us if he can. Then we'll run over to his shop."

"What does he want to show me?"

"Don't know. They wouldn't tell me."

"They?"

"Betsy and Charlie."

Cal smiled, but it quickly faded, "They're going to release me in the morning, so I've got to decide what I'm going to do."

"From what you said yesterday, going back to Archdale's not an option. Or, have you reconsidered. You have the option of two places to stay up there." Deep down Deputy Karr wanted Cal out of the way, but he dared not show his hand.

# RETURN TO FAITH

Cal shook his head, "At this point I don't know. But one of the first things I've got to do is get my driver's license replaced, then check on my insurance coverage. I'm not sure the truck was covered enough to replace it. And this few days in that high tech hospital is going to cost a fortune."

"At this point, since we can't connect you to the accident that destroyed your truck, your regular health insurance may have to take over."

"I don't even know if I have any of that either." Cal turned to the lawman, "And if I do, I don't even know who I have coverage with."

"The Highway Patrol's got your vehicle registration. I'll call them and see how soon we can get it back to you. It'll have your vehicle insurance company's name and policy number. We can start there."

A few minutes later they were seated in a corner booth at the Faith Family Diner and sipped coffee from a fresh pot Betsy brewed just for them.

Cal had to get something off his mind, but he seriously doubted it would help. Unfortunately for Deputy Karr, he was the closest, most convenient target, "I feel like a newborn baby who was born into a grown man's body. It's so frustrating because I know everything a grown man should know, except who and what I am."

Deputy Karr sat in silence for an awkward moment, "They didn't cover that one in B.L.E.T."

"B.L.E.T?"

"Basic Law Enforcement Training. It's taught in just about all of the Community Colleges in North Carolina. It's a crash course in how to deal with real people in the real world when it involves local, state, and federal law."

"I don't understand why my situation's not covered in that curriculum," the first hint of the old Cal's sense of humor slipped out.

The odd, off-the-wall-response caught the serious lawman off guard. The unexpected laughter went a long way to continue dismantling the wall Deputy Karr had unintentionally erected between them.

On that morning, several very complicated and deep-seated interpersonal dynamics were in motion in that small town diner. The three people involved were aware to varying degrees.

Betsy was extremely happy Deputy Karr honored her request and brought Cal in for breakfast. But, overnight she became very uncomfortable with a significant complicating factor. Deputy Karr let something significant slip during his coffee visit the afternoon before. It had to do with the photo shown to him by Cal's ex-mother-in-law. It was unnervingly creepy that Cal so quickly realized how much Betsy looked like his dead wife. That was a ghost story she had no desire to become part of, so she remained noticeably standoffish. Still she was very glad to see Cal.

At the same time, Deputy Karr recognized how uncomfortable Betsy was with him and Cal at the same table. Deep in his mind, the conflicted lawman couldn't help but hope Betsy was uncomfortable because she had some deep-seated feelings about him. As much as he attempted to quash that pipe dream, it just wouldn't go away.

On the other side of the table Cal was even more confused and conflicted. As far as he knew when he first saw Betsy, he had an instant, unexplained attraction to her. The evening they met he was unaware he'd lost all memories from his past. As far as he knew, his innocent attraction was pure, and he was content not to have a clue why. Until he did, which suddenly "weirded" him out and complicated matters. He felt guilty about an attraction to a woman he'd never met, only to discover a few days later she could've easily passed for his dead wife's older twin. It was an unholy twist to the plot that had become the beginning of the rest of his life.

Charlie couldn't break away from the shop so Cal and Deputy Karr went ahead and ordered breakfast. As they finished, Betsy came over to refill their coffee cups and clear the table.

There was an awkward exchange of uncomfortable looks between three individuals now entangled in an odd triangular relationship, that neither one was aware of at the moment. The tension wasn't perceived as adversarial, but the look in each other's eyes and the energy each emitted was undeniable and restrictive.

To make matters worse, Cal and Deputy Karr wanted Betsy to sit with them for a while, and she really wanted to. She dare not choose which one to sit with and leave the other alone on the other side.

Her dilemma, if she sat beside Cal, he might think she was interested in him, which she was, but dare not let him know. If she sat beside Deputy Karr, then Cal would probably take that as a sign she wasn't really interested in him. To make matters worse, if she chose the King Solomon approach and dragged a chair over to sit at the end of the table, both could easily misconstrue her intent.

At that moment, the best thing would be for them to pay the check and get the heck out of there. For a long time Charlie had given Betsy a hard time and was serious that Deputy Karr had a "Thing" for her. It was only once or twice a month when the two of them were alone. Yesterday was the first time, as far as she knew, that he said anything to Deputy Karr, at least in front of her. Fortunately Deputy Karr played it off like it didn't sink in, so it didn't seem to matter. It was just a part of the constant fun banter between long-time friends.

"Thanks guys," Betsy's smile was more relaxed, and she was relieved they were ready to head out the door. She hoped she wasn't too obvious.

"Great food, as usual," Deputy Karr nodded and turned toward the door, but out of the corner of his eye he noticed Cal lingered. It was tough but he continued toward the door without looking back.

Cal and Betsy focused on each other's eyes for a couple of long seconds. Neither wanted to be the first to speak and possibly tip their hand.

Finally Cal nodded and couldn't help when the corner of his mouth turned up in a sincere grin.

Betsy was relieved. Cal gave her the opening she hoped for. She felt her face relax which allowed both sides of her mouth to draw a welcomed grin across her tensely pursed lips.

.......

Cal and Deputy Karr followed Charlie out of the office, into the first of three interconnected work rooms. Last month he switched out the old-fashioned fluorescent tube lights with highly efficient LED tube lights. He was amazed by how the change of bulbs in one room had significantly reduced his power bill. That morning he ordered enough fixtures to convert the rest of the shop.

"Wow," Deputy Karr looked around, then up, "It's so much brighter in here."

Charlie held up the index finger on his right hand, "Used the same number of fixtures. Hang tight, until I get the lights on in there." He pointed straight ahead, then stepped over and flipped several breakers.

There was a dramatic contrast between the new, brilliant white lights in the room where they stood, which made the old lights in the next room appear to be dull, yellowish antiques.

"There's an amazing difference," Cal admitted, then turned to Deputy Karr and spoked barely above a whisper, "Reckon that's what he wanted to show us?"

Charlie heard Cal but never let on as he motioned, "Follow me." He instructed then paused beside a dusty, canvas covered object. He pointed, "Grab that end."

Deputy Karr stepped over and bent down to take hold of the canvas' lower corner. Whatever was underneath would be as new to him as it would be to Cal.

Dust clouded away from the canvas as Charlie and Deputy Karr pulled it off and exposed the rusted cab and bed of a 1957 Chevy pickup truck. The body sections weren't connected, but were slid against each other on a makeshift wooden rack. It looked like the wheels had been removed from the hopeless mess too far beyond salvageable.

Cal nodded, "I'd probably keep that covered up, too."

Charlie shared a sly grin with Deputy Karr as he led them over to the rusty, greasy chassis, "It'll take about a year to restore... by myself. But with some good assistance, maybe seven or eight months." He said with a smile.

Cal was caught off guard, "You want me to help you try to put that rusty Humpty Dumpty back together again?"

Charlie nodded, "It's the same year, make, and model you restored and drove."

Cal took a step back and lifted his hands, "You do know that I don't remember that guy, right? And I may never have his desires or skills." He warned. "So I wouldn't count on my help. At this point, I'm more concerned about where I'm going to sleep tomorrow night."

Deputy Karr turned to Charlie to see how he would respond.

"I have a furnished apartment over my garage at home. Rent free, if you wanna stay and help me out for a while."

"If Archdale is out of the question, then at least Charlie's offering you a viable, if nothing else a temporary solution." Deputy Karr couldn't believe how quickly and easily that thought came to his mind and raced out of his mouth.

"We're only an hour from Archdale. We can get you up there anytime you need to go," Charlie assured.

Cal was pensive, "What about that kid?"

Deputy Karr took charge, "Tommy?"

"Is he the one who stole my truck?"

"From a legal perspective," Deputy Karr felt the need to explain a few parameters, "Allegedly stole your truck. And by law, he's innocent until proven guilty. The law requires us to give him the benefit of the doubt. We're pretty sure he was driving the truck, or at least was in the truck when it was wrecked. We have no proof he stole it. But from what we've been able to deduce so far, he's the prime suspect."

Cal nodded, "I'm not sure why, but I want to meet him."

Charlie and Deputy Karr exchange ominous looks and Charlie deferred to Deputy Karr.

"He's in the ICU, at the same hospital you're in. It doesn't look good. I don't think he's going to make it."

Cal stood silent, in deep thought for a few tense seconds, then nodded his head, "Okay, so my first priority is to secure a place to stay for a while. And at this point a homeless shelter is not an appealing option. So, thank you very much. I'll take you up on the offer to bunk in your garage for a couple of weeks."

Charlie smiled and cut his eyes toward the old rusty Humpty Dumpty, then back to Cal whose head slowly shook.

"If you'll be so kind, I'll have to get back to you on that impossible project. Although, since I'm out of the preaching business, I need to find a job of some sort."

Charlie grinned and nodded, "I'm good with that." However, he would never tell Cal, and especially Deputy Karr what just crossed his mind. Charlie knew his sister better than anyone else. She desperately needed a worthwhile project, and for some unknown reason he determined Cal might be the perfect project for her to take on.

......

On the drive back to Charlotte, Cal insisted he wanted to see Tommy. Deputy Karr didn't think it was wise. Cal really couldn't explain the gnawing desire, but he refused to seriously consider Deputy Karr's professional opinion. Against his better judgment, the reluctant lawman agreed to take Cal to the ICU for a few minutes. They stepped into the waiting room.

"You need to meet his mother first. We can't just pop into ICU unannounced," Deputy Karr insisted.

"I'm good with that."

"You're not going to do anything stupid, are you?"

"You say I used to be a preacher. What do you think?"

"As you're so keen to remind us, you can't remember being a preacher. So what does that mean?" Deputy Karr paused, then said, "I'll go get her."

Cal stood silent as he waited. He had gotten his way but wondered if the battle of wills had been worth the victory. He didn't expect Deputy Karr to insist he meet the boy's mother first. What could he possibly say to the mother of the boy who at the very least probably stole his truck and may die as a result of a reckless joyride? Problem was that he'd made such a big deal about seeing Tommy, he wasn't about to back out. Regardless of how uncomfortable he was about the encounter about to happen, he was committed.

Moments later, Deputy Karr opened the door for Sam. She was exhausted and too concerned for her son. She didn't care that she was sans makeup, or that her eyes were puffy and bloodshot from frequent tearful pleas to God. Nor that her hair wasn't in perfect order, or that she had caught only a few moments of fitful sleep since she arrived at the hospital.

Deputy Karr was very compassionate and concerned about Sam's well being, "This is Samantha Forrester, Tommy's mother. And Sam, this is Cal Baxter, a former pastor."

Sam misinterpreted the purpose for the visit and reached out for Cal's hands. Cal didn't appreciate Deputy Karr's approach and was angry that he set him up, but he did accept Sam's shaky hands.

Sam was seconds from tears, "Will you ask God to show mercy to my son? He really is a good boy."

Cal was in no mood to carry on a farce so as sincerely and understandingly he replied, "I'm sorry Ma'am. I'm no longer a pastor."

Sam was confused as she turned to Deputy Karr, "He's the one who owns the truck."

Sam became indignant and yanked her hands from Cal's light grasp, "What's he doing here? You going to arrest Tommy now?" Sam burst into tears as she leaned against Deputy Karr who so casually and naturally embraced the heartbroken mother.

"No, Sam, Mr. Baxter just wanted to see Tommy," Deputy Karr kept his arms around Sam as he turned to Cal, "Sam and I have a mutual project."

Cal nodded. He understood. Now Deputy Karr's intentions became suspect.

Sam sniffed as she pulled away from Deputy Karr and turned to Cal. She nodded and was barely able to speak, "My boy can turn his life around, if we can get him away from that wicked girl. You were a preacher. You understand."

Cal remained silent and exchanged a quick glance with Deputy Karr. They were definitely going to talk about this.

Sam perked up. She sniffed again as she wiped her eyes with her left hand and extended her right hand to Cal, "You're alive." Cal was a bit confused but felt it best to shake Sam's hand. She gripped it tightly then cupped her left around it and held on. "They didn't know where you were. Said you might be dead." She shook his hand vigorously, "So glad to meet you."

Cal didn't know what to say and looked to Deputy Karr for clarification.

"When you turned up, the list of potential charges Tommy faces reduced considerably," Deputy Karr clarified.

Sam's energy level ramped up, "Tell me you sold Tommy your truck, or at least you let him drive it before you were going to sell it to him." Her desperation was predictable, but sadly her futile grasp for a nonexistent truth was wasted.

Cal searched for the right words to answer the wrong question until Deputy Karr came to his rescue.

"He has amnesia," Deputy Karr began. "He sustained

some type of head injury."

Sam pointed, "Then he could've been driving the truck." Sam became excited, "Maybe my boy was a passenger, and the truck wasn't stolen."

Deputy Karr's head slowly shook, "We've already concluded Mr. Baxter wasn't at the accident scene."

Sam stepped back and became defensive, actually insulted, "How'd you come to that conclusion? If he can't remember, then he could've been driving. He could've been dazed and just walked away after the accident."

It was too late for Cal to admit he should've listened to Deputy Karr. Regardless of the stunt Deputy Karr pulled, a visit to the ICU was the absolute worst thing they could've done.

"Sam, the facts just don't add up to that conclusion," Deputy Karr attempted to explain, but Sam held up her hand and cut him off.

"Now, hold on!" Sam pointed toward the ICU doors, "My son's in there fighting for his life, and this man claims he can't remember. And just because my boy had problems with the law, and at this moment can't defend himself, suddenly he's guilty." The pitch of Sam's voice rose a few octaves and cracked with raw emotion. "Is that what you're say'n?"

Deputy Karr remained calm, "No, Sam. That's not what I'm saying."

"Sure sounds like it to me."

"Sam, you're upset and...."

"Upset! You think I'm upset! Don't you think I have a good reason to be upset? My son might be taking his last breath while I'm in here wasting my time defending him, while you're defending the man who could be responsible for the accident that might take my son's life. Just because this guy claims he can't remember, you expect me to say it's okay, when you believe a total stranger. I'm not going to accept Tommy did it, just because this guy claims he can't remember if he didn't." Sam was livid, but deep down she knew she had unfairly overreacted, and said several things she already regretted.

Cal was now more upset with himself than with Deputy Karr. There wasn't a thing he could say that would defuse the tense situation. He wisely opted to remain silent in the hot glare of an emotionally charged mother, determined to defend her critically injured son.

"We need to let you get back in there with Tommy," Deputy Karr suggested. There was nothing left for him to say in his or Cal's defense. In fact, there was no reason to mount a defense at all. Sam needed a lot of space and some quiet time alone to calm down and think more clearly. Less emotionally, and far more rationally would help.

Sam nodded, "Yeah. Probably would've been better if you didn't bring him here."

Deputy Karr nodded toward the door and without a word Cal led the way. He knew it best to keep his mouth shut and not even extend his hand.

Sam tightly crossed her arms against her chest and focused her eyes on the floor as she took another step back from Deputy Karr.

"We'll stay in touch," Deputy Karr promised.

Sam looked up and flashed a stern look of utter contempt. It spoke cavernous volumes. The jest of which was an insult easily translatable to, "Don't waste my time. You have no right to stand in judgment of my son, and dare to convict him when you refuse to even consider viable evidence he might not have done anything wrong. I thought you really cared about Tommy and wanted to help him."

At that point, no matter what Deputy Karr said, it would be wrong, and yet he must respond. To have remained silent would've been an even more destructive insult, "Sam, I really do care, but I'm a law enforcement officer, and I have to follow the letter of the law."

Sam held up her hand again, "Save it. I'm in no mood to be lectured about the law." And with that said, she spun around and hustled out of the waiting room.

Cal and Deputy Karr briefly glanced at each other while on the elevator ride upstairs. Cal was very disappointed with himself. This whole debacle wouldn't have happened if he hadn't insisted on seeing Tommy. They didn't speak again until they were back in Cal's room.

"Wish I could remember, and it be the exact opposite of what you believe happened that night," Cal lamented.

"I've been trying to help Tommy for a while, so believe me, I wish more than you that we were wrong. Unfortunately, reality doesn't care what we think, or how we feel. Real will always be real and will cut no slack for those who deny it, then lie to themselves."

"Hey, I'm so sorry I didn't listen to you on the drive back," Cal humbly admitted.

Deputy Karr waxed philosophically, "In the long, we might've done Sam a huge favor."

Cal didn't expect that logic, "Was that something you learned in that B.L.E.T. course? How to push a distraught mother over the edge?"

Deputy Karr shook his head, "For a few tense moments, we presented a good mother with two ready-made targets she could use to unload her anger and frustration."

"Not exactly an item that was on my bucket list for today."

......

## 17
## When The Tide Rolls In Be Ready To Put To Sea

Sam's emotions were still at a fever pitch when she stepped back in the room with Tommy. Her eyes were focused on the white tiled floor as she mumbled under her breath all the way over to the bed. To the average person her rant would've sounded illogical. A plea to a nonexistent entity, rather than to her loving God. She still believed He was very real, even though He remained hurtfully distant and silent.

It wasn't until she nearly bumped into Dr. Roberts who reviewed a chart as he stood beside Tommy's bed. Only then she realized someone other than her comatose son was also in the room.

The look on the poised medical professional's face revealed a truth Sam would've rather not learned. As a reluctant observer, he witnessed and heard every hateful word she sputtered during her nearly incoherent rant as she stomped across the room. It wasn't the worst he'd ever heard, but it ran a close second.

All in one abrupt motion she stopped and stumbled back at the same time. She gasped and shivered as she blurted, "Oh, my goodness! You scared me half to death!"

"Sorry to startle you."

"No. No." Sam stammered, "I'm… I'm sorry. Just had a bad meeting with the law."

"Well, you arrived at the right time to hear some encouraging news," Dr. Roberts glanced back down at the chart. "The last EEG readings were very encouraging."

"Really," Sam was confused. "I was here when the nurse came in and I asked her how he was doing. She said he was holding his own. No emotion. No sign anything had changed."

Dr. Roberts nodded, "I've given strict instructions not to

react or share hopeful, or especially negative results. In his extremely delicate condition, it's best not to raise any false hopes, or cause any undue worries."

"What's going on? Can you tell me now?"

"It's hard to say. I just got here moments before you arrived," Dr. Roberts admitted. "I wanted to come in and check him out for myself."

Sam didn't expect Dr. Roberts to lay the chart on the side of the bed. She had been constantly talking to Tommy and playing him soothing nature sounds, as if she hoped he would hear. The nurses had suggested the more she talked to Tommy and encouraged him not to give up, to keep fighting, the greater the odds he would hear her and respond positively.

Sam stepped up to the bed and reached over to gently stroke her son's bruised cheek, "Honey. Did you hear that? Your EEG is showing some improvement." She turned to Dr. Roberts, "He probably doesn't have a clue what an EEG is."

The simple, unfiltered honesty in the distraught mother's eyes and tone deeply impacted the nearly robotically inclined doctor. His stayed, "business only" expression dared to crack with a slight grin, "It's not important that he knows what it is. Just that it's a good thing. Now I want to check his pupils."

Sam leaned to step out of the way until Dr. Roberts' soft voice sounded, "You stay right there where you can keep touching him, and he can hear you." He said, then he reached behind her and pulled out two light blue latex gloves from the medium box. He methodically put the gloves on as he respectfully walked around to the other side of the bed.

Sam likened Dr. Roberts' bedside manner to that of a car mechanic who casually walked around to the other side of the broken down vehicle to check for it out from that perspective. To the worried mother, on that bed lay the battered, wired, hosed and monitored body of her only child.

Dr. Roberts stood beside the respirator that hissed and clicked as it gently pushed pure oxygen into Tommy's badly bruised lungs. After a few seconds to allow maximum absorption, the machine precisely sucked the residual carbon dioxide back out. That intrusive, noisy machine unnerved Sam, but Dr. Roberts acted as if he didn't hear the incessant, mechanical hiss, pop, click, pause, hiss, pop, click, over and over.

Dr. Roberts pulled the penlight from his white lab coat, and with his other gloved hand he gently lifted Tommy's right eyelid. He briefly shined the bright light into the wide open pupil. Sam didn't know what to look for or to expect. From her perspective on the other side of the bed, she didn't see how quickly and dramatically the pupil shrank in diameter. The methodical doctor performed the procedure a few more times without reacting or even uttering a sound.

Then he clicked off the light and gently lowered the eyelid back in place, "Tommy, can you hear me?"

Immediately Sam noticed movement under Tommy's eyelids, as if he were looking to his right and left. She got so excited she nearly burst into tears, "Tommy. Honey. It's Momma. Can you hear me?"

"He won't be able to talk with the tube down his throat, so he'll probably panic. Ask him to squeeze your hand if he can hear you," Dr. Roberts calmly instructed.

Sam was careful not to grasp Tommy's hand too firmly, but she couldn't contain her joy when he immediately managed to put some pressure on her hand, "He heard you and understood you." She said before erupting into an emotional burst of uncontrollable crying. "Thank You! Thank You! Thank You, Lord," was all she could say, again, and again.

Dr. Roberts quickly cautioned Sam not to get too excited, or hopeful, "We've only begun the early stages of Step One."

Sam wiped her eyes and sniffed, "What do you mean?"

"We're going to start cutting back on the medication and see if we can slowly wean him from the respirator."

"How long will that take?"

"At least several hours. But be prepared for a couple of days or more if necessary. We may even have to put him back under several times before we're able to drastically reduce both the medication and mechanical life-support."

That very real diagnosis blasted the sheer joy from Sam's battered heart, but she had to remain optimistic and be careful to sound extremely positive while in the room.

"Honey. Did you hear what the doctor said?" Sam's teary eyes immediately shifted to hers and Tommy's tenderly entwined hands. She felt the slight pressure.

Sam wouldn't dare leave Tommy's side over the next several, exhausting hours. She was encouraged and exuberantly thanked God every time the nurses were able to successfully maintain three step-downs with the meds and life-support machines.

By midnight, Sam was sound asleep, the best and deepest she'd been able to manage since the accident. Her head rested on the side of the bed, gently against Tommy's shoulder.

Earlier, when she rested her head on the bed she was well aware that if she went to sleep, her neck would be extremely sore in the morning; but she didn't care.

To keep the pressure off Tommy's right hand, she slid her right hand between his hand and the bed. That way he could also move his hand or fingers without restriction.

At fifteen minutes after midnight, the nurse came in to monitor Tommy's vitals. She was very pleased and leaned over to whisper in his ear, "Good job, Tommy. Good job. Keep it up, buddy. Let's make your Momma's day when she wakes up."

The battle-hardened nurse had worked in ICU for fifteen years and eventually built up a high tolerance to extreme shifts in patients' conditions. She was capable of emotionally controlled delivery of the worst and best news to her patients' concerned family and friends. But on rare occasions the simplest of positive signs would overwhelm her. Like at the very moment she whispered in Tommy's ear, "Your Momma loves you very much. She hasn't left your side."

Ever so slightly, but the most movement yet, Tommy's index finger gently stroked the top of his sleeping, unyieldingly loving Mother's hand. If only she knew how much he loved her too.

When the nurse walked out of the room, both cheeks glistened with crocodile sized tears and tracks. It had been years since she was so deeply and profoundly moved. It was time for her fifteen minute break which she spent in the bathroom crying her eyes out. She had allowed this patient and his mother to enter her danger zone. She had heard enough about their situation; and even though it flew in the face of proper protocol, she couldn't help but allow the troubled patient and his deserving mother to slip into her heart. She cared. The situation with this young man and his sweet mother just became very personal.

......

Dirt and gravel crunched under the Mustang's tires on the narrow dirt road near the motel. Megan had sobered up enough for a very early morning drive. She was distraught and exhausted from the lack of proper sleep. A few hours of fitful sleep here and there, along with the tremendous stress of knowing she was responsible if Tommy died had overwhelmed her. Along with excessive alcohol consumption, she had devastated her young nervous system. She knew that if she continued her current pace, she raced headlong toward an epic meltdown. If she could get only a few hours of uninterrupted, sound sleep. That could be the first step back to where she was a few days ago, before Tommy's accident.

Megan was smart enough to make one sound decision that morning. She left the liquor bottles in the room. It was a noble intent to sober up for at least a few hours. Even in her self-induced debilitated state, she knew it was time for a serious assessment of her future. There was no way she wanted to be trapped in a destructive lifestyle and demean herself to the wasted existence of a low-rent, alcoholic prostitute.

The classic Mustang came to a stop well off the paved road where Megan hoped she would have complete privacy. She switched off the lights and made sure the doors were locked, then she curled up in the back seat. Instead of thinking things through, mercifully she fell asleep.

Several hours later a light breeze carried occasional bird chirps through the treetops. Safely cocooned in the Mustang, Megan's eyes slowly opened. It took a few seconds to realize where she was, but her head immediately throbbed as the hangover ravaged her body and made it difficult for her to rise. Her hair was a mess. She was stiff and very grumpy.

The Mustang was out of its element and had invaded the territory of a large, aggressive male deer with a sizable rack. It was rutting season and the odd blue creature demanded the alpha male's immediate attention. He lowered his head and sniffed the ground as he cautiously approached. The majestic creature's nostrils flared as they sniffed and inhaled an unfamiliar scent. That massive blue creature was much larger than a husky buck. It was unlike any rival he'd ever encountered and he dare not underestimate it, or take it for granted. It could be an unwelcome rival for the females in his small herd.

The wily alpha male closed the distance and then pawed the leaf-covered ground as it snorted. There was no reaction from the unwelcome intruder. It stood silent, motionless. To further assert its authority, the resident alpha presented its antlers and tapped them against the side of the Mustang. If the rival intended to challenge, it would respond with a few probative taps of its antlers against the alpha's. But the intruder remained motionless and silent. So, the alpha snorted loudly. It was the master of that territory's final warning.

Megan froze in fear when she heard something bump against the side of the car. She didn't know if it were made by man or beast, until she heard the ominous snort. She looked at her watch, "Oh my!" She never intended to spend that many hours in the woods. She cautiously rose and came face to face with the curious deer as its moist nose smudged the driver's door window. She let out a long sigh of relief, it was an agitated deer, not a stalking serial killer.

The stag boldly, more confidently sniffed the car. Fortunately a thick canopy of green leaves blocked direct sunlight and only a hint of the deer's head and rack reflected on the outside of the driver's window. Megan hoped the aggressive animal wouldn't charge the window and shatter the glass with its broad spanned, sharp-pointed antlers, especially when it appeared to notice her climb from the cramped back seat into the driver's side bucket seat.

Megan was so stunned that she spoke aloud in a normal tone, "What are you looking at?" She immediately cupped her hand over her mouth. Little did she realize the buck's seasonal heightened senses immediately identified the source of the voice was female. Though definitely not a deer, or potential mate. The source of the voice wasn't a rival, or adversary.

The magnificent buck snorted then casually resumed its search for its next potential mate.

．．．．．．

Later that morning, Charlie locked his shop. He had strict

orders to stop by for a cup of coffee and a piece of pecan pie with Betsy, who had something important to say.

"It really creeps me out that I look so much like his dead wife," Betsy confessed when she followed her brother outside. She leaned against the driver's door of his classic Chevy. "I really want to help him, but I have to keep telling myself that he's probably seeing his ex-wife, instead of me. And that makes me really uncomfortable."

"Would you rather we back out of the deal? If you're gonna have the 'heebeegeebees' when he's around, then that's not fair to you."

Betsy shook her head, "No, it's not that. I think I can handle being around him, well, until he looks at me a certain way."

"Do what?"

"It's the way he looks at me. From the first time he laid eyes on me when he walked in. Like he knows more about me than I want to be known. Especially by a man I never met."

At first, Charlie didn't know how to respond, "Say what? I'm not sure we're in the same boat. Or even on the same lake, using the same bait. Or that we're even angling for the same fish."

Betsy exhaled in frustration. Her lips pursed as she turned her head to the side and narrowed her eyes, "Hello. He caught me off guard. He really got my attention."

Charlie nodded, but appeared even more confused, "And that's a bad thing? Sounds like you got his attention too."

Betsy shook her head, "No. I didn't get his attention. She did."

"Sis, I'm afraid we're still on different lakes, on opposite sides of the world."

"His ex-wife. She's the one that got his attention. Not me."

"You think he's seeing ghosts?" Charlie failed to prevent a twitch in the corner of his mouth. It was the beginning of a grin and he knew that she knew.

"You making fun of me?"

"No. I suspect you're overthinking, which is causing you to overreact."

"Over the last few years I've managed to wrap myself in

this comfortable, very safe cocoon."

"And he made you peek out."

Betsy shook her head, "He reached in and yanked me out."

Charlie smiled, "Good for him."

"Whose side are you on?"

"Both. What's it gonna hurt to be nice to the man? He's got some serious issues to deal with. And he has amnesia. Probably don't even remember a thing about his wife." Betsy opened her mouth to speak, but he cut her off. "Don't go full-blown psycho-logical on me and try to analyze everything he does and says. Especially the way he looks at you."

The side door to the diner opened and a male customer stuck his head out the door, "Hi Charlie. Can I borrow your sister? I need to pay my check and get to work."

Betsy leaned in and kissed Charlie on the forehead, "Can't make any promises. But thanks for hearing me out." She said before she turned and headed back toward the diner.

"Hey, you."

Betsy paused and turned around and pretended to be miffed, "What?"

"Still want me to bring him by for lunch?"

"No. But bring him anyway."

"Sure you don't mind me letting him stay above the garage?"

"That's between you and him."

"You gonna make nice when we get here?"

"Guess you'll have to take your chances."

Charlie chuckled. But deep down he knew too well the heartaches his sister had endured over the last ten years. There were some real jerks in this world. Unfortunately, his kind-hearted, and loving sister had run afoul of more than her share. In the short-term, the least he would be was extremely overprotective of his sister's heart. He wouldn't hesitate to step in and set Cal straight if he had any issues with how he treated his sister, who just happened to double as his best friend.

As long as he could keep Betsy focused on the main goal they'd established to step in to help Cal. It was important for Cal to reconnect with life, and hopefully his memories, then move on to whatever was next in his life.

## RETURN TO FAITH

Charlie was blindsided by Betsy's heartfelt confession and was so preoccupied he nearly drove past the onramp to south bound I-85. His immaculately restored 1958, black and white Chevy Bel Air had ample power and quickly accelerated to 75 mph and merged into the traffic flow. His next stop, the Charlotte Trauma Center.

......

Just as Charlie got up to speed on the highway, Cal was still asleep on the bed in his room. He had no reason to expect Candy Troxller, an administrator over the billing department, would visit him. She was a pleasant, no-nonsense woman in her mid-forties who often dealt with confused and exasperated patients. She hated to wake Cal, but insurance companies were notorious for instant claim denials. Worst of all, often the claims department would quickly follow up a denial with a series of complicated processes designed to delay and deter all claim payments as long as legally possible. Even with undeniably legitimate claims. Candy had been forced to expect the majority of those patient conferences to end with more questions asked than answered.

Candy gently awakened Cal and gave him a couple of moments to gather his wits. Then she introduced herself.

"Mr. Baxter, until provided proof you were in the truck at the time of the accident, your automobile insurance company has denied responsibility for your treatment. In addition, since Mr. Forrester is suspected of having stolen your truck, the company has also rejected the claim for his treatment." Candy paused to allow what she hoped was fairly straightforward information to sink in, but she was disheartened by the glassy stare in Cal's eyes. She had no choice but to continue, "We understand and have compassion for your current condition and that you are still in the process of attempting to locate your personal insurance information. But before we release you from the hospital, we are required to have you sign this acceptance of financial responsibility for your charges."

To say the least, Cal was confused and more than a bit miffed. He sat up and swung his sock-covered feet over the edge of the bed. He rested some of his weight on his hands as he slightly leaned toward Candy, "You mean I'm going to have to accept responsibility to pay for my treatment, and the boy who stole my truck, before you let me out?" He shook his head, "I realize I've lost my memory, but I seem to have retained my common sense. I don't see how that's fair, or even legal."

"Mr. Baxter, I'm afraid that fair and legal are mutually exclusive when it comes to most insurance companies' business models."

Cal understood completely and shook his head, held up his hand and refused to accept the form to sign, "With all due respect, Ma'am, I'm not going to be foolish enough to sign such a document."

"No, no. You didn't allow me to finish."

Cal was extremely skeptical and unapologetic, "I'm not accepting responsibility. I don't even know what happened; and the only person who can shed any light on it is barely clinging to life in your ICU."

Candy leaned closer and turned the multi-paged document to Cal, "We have a program that covers these types of situations, provided the patient qualifies."

"Go on."

"From all I've seen and heard, you definitely qualify. The fact that Mr. Forrester appears to have committed a serious crime and has a long rap sheet, I doubt he'll be accepted."

"It'll pay all my medical bills?"

"No, but it will cover all of your hospital bills," She turned her head to the side and appeared hopeful. "At this point, there's no way to predict how long it will take to recover your memory. And there's the real possibility you never will."

"Whose actually paying the bills?"

"A private foundation established to prevent well-deserving patients from being financially ruined by catastrophic hospital and medical bills. All you have to do is sign this acceptance form, then take the application home, fill it out and send it to the address required."

"How long does it take?"

"Up to a month. They'll notify us, and we will contact you."

"But what if they turn me down? Then I've signed a paper that I'll be responsible for mine and that young man's

# RETURN TO FAITH

hospital bills."

"They seriously consider our recommendations." Candy smiled, "We're over ninety-nine percent sure you'll be accepted immediately."

"What about the young man in ICU?"

"His mother will be required to sign an identical form."

"What are her options?"

"As a rule, I'm not supposed to tell you; but in your case, I'll give you an overview. Since she's Mr. Forrester's mother, and as I understand has power-of-attorney, she can file on her behalf, as the one our lawyers would take to court if she refuses to pay. But don't you worry about them," she said as she reached over and touched Cal's right hand. "We want you to ride out of the hospital free of worry and concern about your medical bills. You already have enough to overcome."

Candy was spot on. Cal was amazed how relaxed he was when the orderly arrived with the wheelchair to roll him to the elevator to take down to the lobby, where Charlie awaited.

As Cal was rolled out to Charlie's classic car, all Cal needed to think about was what he needed to move into the apartment above the garage at Charlie's house. Before they pulled away, Charlie handed him the keys. Now he had to pick up a few bags of groceries and some simple household necessities.

"Do you own a car that's less than thirty years old?" Cal chuckled as he admired the beautifully restored car.

"Yeah, but they're no fun to drive."

Charlie stopped at the last Walmart on the way out of Charlotte. As he pulled into a parking space, he turned to Cal, "This isn't the best place to buy serious work shoes, or boots, but at least we can get you a pair to get you started with the truck restoration. If you stay with it and want a better pair, I'll take you to the place I buy mine. I think you can wear some of my work uniforms, so we don't have to worry about that now."

Cal grinned, "And your sister seems to have zeroed in on the new style of clothes I should adopt."

Charlie nodded and was thoughtful as he smiled, a bit on the cautious side.

Cal noticed and let it pass. He still hadn't fully committed to stay in Faith, and especially to jump into a long term, very greasy restoration project he might hate. Or to show any interest in or pursue a relationship with Charlie's sister. Instead, he addressed the obvious, "You're spending money I don't have."

Charlie grinned and pointed, "Open the glovebox. There's a little package."

Cal was more than a little curious as he pressed the button and lowered the door.

"It's in that clear plastic wrap."

Cal removed the package, "In here?" He asked as he turned it over to examine. On the other side was a rip that revealed the package contained cash, "Whose is this?"

"It was dark when we pulled your truck out of the woods. Once we had it beside the road, we turned it back over on its wheels and the package fell out. I was lucky to be standing where I could see it. We already had quite a tussle pulling that thing out, and we still had to get it up on the flatbed. I picked the package up and tossed it into the flatbed's cab. Didn't know it bounced off the door on the other side, and slid under the seat. It was two in the morning and I was exhausted and simply forgot about it by the time I delivered the truck to the impound lot. Found it early this morning when I was looking for something under the seat."

Cal turned concerned eyes to Charlie. He was dead serious, "Hope I'm not a drug dealer who masqueraded as a preacher."

Charlie smiled comfortingly, "Doubt it. You're not the type."

"How can you be sure?"

"My sister's been blessed with a scary ability to sense people's true character."

"Is she ever wrong?"

"Rarely."

"Let's hope I'm not one of her rare mistakes."

There was eight thousand dollars in the package. Cal spent very judiciously, actually only $253.62 dollars.

......

## 18
## Life Is Precious But Oh So Fragile

By late afternoon Tommy's medication had been reduced to the point his eyes slowly opened for the first time. Sam was seated beside his bed and held his hand. She fought back tears as she quickly rose and leaned closer. She had to be strong for her son, "Hey, Honey. Welcome back."

The nurse who whispered encouragement to Tommy after midnight had just stepped in to begin her next twelve-hour shift. She turned away from checking one of the life-support machines. There was no need to let them know that she had spoken to Tommy while his mother slept beside him. Her reasons and her passion were her own. She smiled as she stepped beside the bed.

"Well, hello there, Tommy. I'm Rachael, your nurse. You're coming along very well. We're going to keep waking you up."

Tommy's hand slowly reached up and touched the apparatus that was taped to his mouth and to which the respirator hose was attached.

Rachael took hold of Tommy's hand and gently pulled it away, "Yes, sweetheart, I know it's very uncomfortable. But you keep improving and we'll be able to get that nasty tasting plastic thing out of there real soon."

Sam's voice quivered with raw emotion, "Thank you so much for all you've done. And especially for what you said this morning."

"I thought you were asleep," Rachael was a little embarrassed.

"I was praying for the Lord to spare my son and to guide his doctors and nurses to do the right things to save his life." Sam sniffed and struggled not to cry, "Your voice was like an angel in the night. A comforter that God sent to reassure me He was in control, and everything was going to be alright."

Tommy drifted back to sleep as the two women clenched

hands and shared a very special moment. Sam would never know that five years ago, Rachael was on the other side of a hospital bed, and held the hand of her precious nine-year-old daughter when she slipped into eternity. Rachael knew too well the dark shadows of the never-ending pain she'd asked God to spare Sam from living through. It took a loving mother to know the heart of another loving mother.

......

Charlie also had strict orders to stop back by for Betsy to serve Cal lunch, on the house. They didn't stay long because Charlie had a full afternoon planned for Cal. It worked out well because Betsy was slammed and really didn't have time to spend with them.

It took Charlie only five minutes to show Cal the layout of the apartment and give him a rundown on where the switches were and how to set the thermostat.

Charlie went downstairs and over to his house while Cal changed, then hung up the few shirts and pairs of jeans he bought. He couldn't remember if it were important to him in his past life, but he was compelled to neatly fold his new underwear and socks and carefully arrange them in a certain order. Charlie assured Cal the new steel toed work boots would soften as they broke in. Charlie kept calling them work boots, but they looked more like high-top hiking boots. He'd insisted on the steel toes because he wasn't sure if Cal were a klutz who would constantly drop tools.

Within twenty minutes Cal stood in front of the floor length mirror, dressed in one of Charlie's two-tone gray work uniforms, and it was nearly a perfect fit. He was ready to go to work. What an odd comparison came to mind. From preacher man to antique automobile restorer. At least a temporary restorer. Who knew where he'd be in the next few days, weeks, or months?

One thing was certain, Cal already had a sense that he would find many odd comparisons between preaching and turning wrenches to convert a rusted, worn-out heap of metal into a work of drivable art.

Then a few profoundly important thoughts surfaced. Would he ever remember who he had been? More importantly, even if he did, would he want to resume where he'd left off?

The door downstairs opened, "You ready? We're burn'n daylight," Charlie called up.

All mechanics had their own methods and reasons for this to be here, and that to be over there. Charlie gave Cal a brief rundown of the shop, but didn't expect him to retain a great deal from his first day. He showed him where and how all of the truck parts were stored, in a logical order.

"You're serious. You've completely taken this thing apart," Cal mused.

"Yep. And I don't intend to have any left over parts. We're going to have to replace a few, and might even add some pieces the original never had. But it's going to have the same number of original parts."

Cal shook his head, "How in the world do you remember where all these pieces go, and how they fit together?"

"They'll fit together better and function more efficiently once we get'm cleaned up." Charlie explained as he wiped his greasy index finger on the sleeve of Cal's uniform. "Welcome to the club," Charlie grinned as they stood beside the grease and grim covered engine block that was still mounted on the equally grungy chassis.

Charlie rolled a red engine hoist in front of the chassis, then pushed an empty engine caddy beside the chassis, "Our first task is to remove the block and mount it on this caddy so we can finish tearing it down."

That was the instant Cal realized he'd made a terrible mistake. More than likely, this would be a quick, hard-learned lesson that would provide crystal clear insight into what he didn't want to do with the rest of his life.

Cal looked at the fresh grease smudge on the shirt, "I don't think I bought enough soap."

"You'll be surprised how quickly you'll get used to it," Charlie grinned slyly.

After they pulled the engine out and mounted it on the caddie, they rolled it out of the way. Charlie and Cal used putty knives to scrape grease and grime from the engine compartment. The longer they work the dirtier and grungier Cal became. But much to Cal's surprise, he felt oddly satisfied. "Wow. I feel like we really accomplished something," Cal admitted.

"Then you're gonna come back for a full day tomorrow?"

Cal grinned and reluctantly nodded, "Can't believe I'm actually going to come here and do this again, on purpose."

Charlie chuckled, "You probably really enjoyed converting that old truck in your former life."

"Might just learn to enjoy it in this one too."

Before they left the shop Charlie introduced Cal to the special gritty soap mechanics used to wash off the grease. It did a great job, except for around and under his fingernails.

"From tomorrow on, you'll have the option to wear mechanic's rubber gloves," Charlie informed.

"Why not today?" Cal paused washing off the stubborn grease and grime from his elbow.

Charlie grinned, "You're not a real mechanic until you get your hands dirty."

"But I got into it way over my elbows and we didn't fix anything."

Charlie chuckled, "Yeah, but you sure got your hands dirty."

Cal looked at his hands, "Yep. Sure did."

"When student pilots take their first solo flight, their instructor cuts off part of their shirt, and that shirt signifies a right of passage. Most pilots keep that shirt in a very special place. It's a prized sacrifice. I've heard some student pilots even have the piece of shirt framed and hung with their student pilot certificate."

"It's your shirt. Are you going to cut part of it off and give me a certificate?"

"Want one?"

Cal chuckled, "Not really."

……

Later that evening in his new apartment, Cal exited the small, steamy bathroom, and entered the open living room and kitchen area. He toweled his hair. It felt so good to be clean, except for the black outline of grease around his fingernails. Charlie promised that eventually it would wear off. That was if he decided not to work on old cars and trucks the rest of his life.

Cal paused for a moment and looked around. His mouth formed a satisfied grin as he surveyed the nicely furnished apartment. This would be a very cozy place to stay for a while. He sat down on the comfortable tan leather sofa and quietly pondered his options, which were many and widely varied.

He had to consider what led him into the ministry in the first place, especially since he detected during the visit with Mr. and Mrs. Jenkins at the church, that something very bad changed his attitude about his life's calling. He supposed that every day good people had justifiable reasons to step away from the pulpit. Before he twisted his brain into a headache with a million possible scenarios, one thing Charlie said stood out.

"You probably really enjoyed converting that old truck in your former life."

At that point, it didn't matter if Charlie intended to draw a meaningful comparison to preachers using the Bible to convert lost human souls into Christians, to a man who saw the value of salvaging, and converting lost, broken and abandoned vehicles into beautiful new creations.

On the surface, the conversion scenario Charlie chose was a powerful metaphor. If Cal decided to stick with the dirty project, he and Charlie would completely rebuild the truck from the inside out. More importantly, it would actually be better than the original. But it wasn't going to happen overnight. It would become a long, very patient, and extremely detailed endeavor. It would be a messy job to scrape away all the dirt and grime to overcome the misguided neglect. Had the truck been left alone, it would've rusted away and been lost forever.

There was a gentle knock on the door downstairs. Cal descended the stairs, turned on the porch light, and opened the inner door to a pleasant surprise. Under the aluminum cover stood Betsy, Charlie, Sheena and six wiggling puppies.

"Can we come in?" Betsy asked with a hopeful grin.

Cal opened the storm door to a flood of blonde fur. Mutt led the charge that swarmed around his feet and jumped up to put their front paws on his legs to beg for attention. It got really crowded in the small entryway at the base of the steps.

"Can they go upstairs?" Cal asked.

"That's why we brought them over," Charlie admitted.

"You moving them in too," Cal was caught off guard.

"No," Betsy clarified. "We thought you might like to have a roommate."

Cal was silent for a moment.

"Don't feel like you have to," Charlie chimed in.

Mutt sniffed the first step behind Cal, then eagerly, though awkwardly struggled to climb the stairs.

"Guess you have a volunteer," Betsy chuckled.

Cal turned, "Mutt, what are you doing?"

The exuberant little critter briefly paused. He turned, looked down at Cal, then became even more excited as he struggled even harder to climb the stairs faster. It was as if he wanted Cal to chase him.

"Do you have anything of value laying out that he can get a hold of?" Betsy was mildly concerned.

"Don't think so," Cal turned and hustled up the fifteen stairs. "But it's best not to take any chances."

Cal easily caught up with and passed the determined pup. Behind them, on various steps, a mass assault of blonde fur was underway. Betsy and Charlie followed, and Sheena stayed in the rear to redirect any wayward pup.

By the time Mutt reached the top of the stairs his little tail was in high speed wiggle gear. The boundless bundle of energy raced toward Cal. It appeared all was clear so Cal turned to the onrushing blonde bullet of joy. "So, what do you think?" Cal lowered to his knees and opened his arms. Mutt didn't even attempt to hit the brakes. At full speed the little fellow leapt into Cal's opened arms.

However, a blonde stampede raced toward Cal.

Betsy reached the top of the stairs in time to witness the adorable collision of love, "Looks like we have a winner."

Cal was surrounded by jealous, hopping and barking puppies demanding their share of attention. Cal was unable to show Mutt's siblings any attention because he could barely keep a grip on the bundle of excitement that gyrated in his arms. It quickly became an exercise in futility to keep his face away from Mutt's anxious, rapid fire tongue, "Mutt, have you already made my decision?"

With short attention spans, the jilted puppies soon fanned out to explore the new environment.

Seemingly secure and with his rivals dispersed around the room, Mutt calmed and surveyed his new domain. He was content he had exerted his dominance.

Cal chuckled as he watched the puppies sniff and rush back and forth across the room like blonde balls that bounced off the walls of a pinball machine, "Thanks for bringing your sisters and brothers over."

All the while Sheena patiently sat guard by the top of the stairs. She wasn't about to let one of the kids sneak downstairs alone.

Betsy dodged the blonde projectiles as they bounced back and forth. She leaned over to pet Mutt, "It's time to find the puppies a home. We wanted to give you first choice... if you want one."

Immediately, as if the little fellow understood Betsy's words,
Mutt excitedly wiggled around in Cal's arms and lovingly licked his face again.

"You can bring him to the shop every day," Charlie assured.

"Then I guess that seals the deal. Right Mutt?" Cal asked.

As if on cue, Mutt yipped his approval.

Betsy and Charlie hadn't planned to stay long. During the short visit, Mutt would not budge from Cal's arms as he sat on the sofa. The little fellow soon dozed off.

The rest of the excited puppies cuddled up in a knot of heads and tails beside Sheena as she slept beside the sofa.

"Sheena, you ready to go?" Betsy turned to the sleeping mother.

Sheena rose and took a quick inventory of her sleeping babies and once satisfied they were all there and safe, she stepped over and placed her head on Cal's knee. She stared at Mutt. She knew she was saying goodbye.

Cal, Betsy, and Charlie sat in stunned silence as they witnessed such an amazing display of love. Sheena let out a gentle "oooff" which awakened Mutt. Mother and son looked into each other's eyes. The humans could only wonder the level of communication exchanged between two animals. After a few precious moments, Sheena leaned toward Mutt, and he responded in turn to allow his mother to lick him one more time.

Not long after their company left, Cal and Mutt returned to the sofa and were soon fast asleep. They quietly napped into the end of a long day. Their first night together was only the beginning of many good days, weeks, months and years to come.

......

The doctors were amazed by how rapidly Tommy improved throughout the day. They instructed the nurses to continue reduction of the meds. The respirator was removed just after midnight. They wanted to see if Tommy could breathe on his own. More importantly that his lungs would function properly and absorb a sufficient amount of oxygen.

Rachael gently knocked on the door before she entered to record the first blood SpO2 level.

"What is it?" Sam asked.

Rachael smiled, "Ninety-four. He's holding in the normal range. Now we monitor his respiration to see if we can leave him off the machine."

"How long before you know?"

There was a light knock and Dr. Roberts entered, "How's our boy?"

"His SpO2 is 94," Rachael answered.

"Excellent. The rest of his vitals?"

"All good."

"Has he been awake yet?" Dr. Roberts directed the question to Sam.

Sam shook her head, "Not while I've been awake."

Dr. Roberts put on a pair of rubber gloves and pulled out his trusty penlight and leaned over to pull one of Tommy's eyes open. He paused when both eyes slowly blinked.

Tommy was groggy, and confused, "Who are you?"

"I'm Dr. Roberts. You were in a bad accident."

"How's Megan?"

"As far as I know, they brought you in," Dr. Roberts looked over at Sam.

Tommy slowly turned his eyes to Sam, "Mom?"

"Honey, we don't know where Megan is. Nobody's heard from her. Was she in the truck with you?"

Tommy had to think for a second. Then his head slowly moved from right to left, his voice was low and weak, "No. She was driving her car."

Sam had to know, "Were you driving the truck?"

# RETURN TO FAITH

Tommy reluctantly nodded.

"How did you get the truck?" Sam couldn't help herself, she had to know.

Dr. Roberts put his fingers around Tommy's wrist to check his pulse, "Ma'am. If you don't mind… can that wait until I'm finished?"

Rachael stood beside Dr. Roberts and remained professional as Dr. Roberts placed Tommy's arm back on the bed, "Can you make a fist?"

Tommy looked at his hand and his fingers slowly curled into a loose fist.

"Can you make a fist with your other hand?"

Tommy slowly turned his head and focused on his left hand, which curled into a loose fist. Then he turned to Sam, "Where's Megan? Is she Okay?"

Sam glanced at Dr. Roberts who reluctantly nodded, so she focused narrow eyes down at her critically injured child, "Son, she left you… She left you to die in the woods." Sam reached to touch Tommy's cheek, but looked to Dr. Roberts for permission.

Dr. Roberts nodded and knew it would be best to let his patient get those questions answered and off his mind, so he could continue with the exam.

After Sam lovingly stroked Tommy's cheek, she gently took his hand. Even though she whispered, her voice couldn't mask her concern, "The police wanna to talk to you. Did you hurt that man? Steal his truck?"

Tommy's eyes turned toward Dr. Roberts, then back to his distraught mother.

"I don't care what he hears. I didn't raise you to do such things."

Dr. Roberts felt the need to speak up, "Ma'am, I'm going to have to inform the police he's conscious, and that we're probably going to be moving him to a step-down room in a few hours. And based on how quickly he's progressing, into a regular room in the next day or so."

Sam's eyes swiftly shifted back to Tommy, "I don't have the money to get a lawyer."

The tense looks between Tommy and Sam revealed their very rocky relationship.

"Is Megan here?" Tommy was fixated.

Sam tossed her hands up in utter frustration, then reflexively turned and muttered as she stormed across the room, swung the door open and stepped into the hall. Her emotions were so churned up she had to get out of the room and try to calm down. She was a millisecond from an epic explosion.

Without missing a beat, Dr. Roberts remained calm, totally unaffected by the drama as he stepped back up to the bed, "Can you lift your right leg?"

Tommy's right leg lifted under the sheet.

"Now your left?"

Tommy's left leg lifted under the sheet.

"You're a very lucky young man."

Tommy immediately averted his eyes. He was embarrassed and dared to ponder what would happen to him over the next couple of days. No matter what, he couldn't get his mind off Megan. From what he could gather from his Mom, the law didn't know where Megan was; so if she spent wisely, she could still be a free girl when he got out of the hospital. Then they could run away and have some fun. At least until the money ran out.

......

## 19
## When God Moves It's Not Fate, It's His Will

The room was dim. Keys jingled and a lock clicked. The door slowly swung open and flooded the concrete floor with bright sunlight. Two sets of human feet entered. Both were male, one wore scuffed, black ankle work boots. The other wore brand new hiking boot style work shoes. Four furry blonde puppy paws trotted closely behind into Sunshine Racing & Auto Repair.

Charlie paused and turned on the lights in the office, then he led Cal and Mutt into the shop area. He turned to Cal, "I'll be right back," He said before he disappeared around the corner. Seconds later, light switches were flipped on and the left side of the shop lit up.

Cal looked down at Mutt seated beside his feet, "He's up to something."

Before Cal got the last word out of his mouth, Charlie turned the corner with a satisfied grin as he tossed a set of keys to Cal.

"You need something to drive for a while."

Moments later, in the side lot outside Charlie's shop, Cal sat behind the steering wheel of a very special orange car.

"What is this thing, and how old is it?" Cal asked

"It's a 1968 GTO Judge, one of the iconic GM muscle cars of that era."

"And you want me to drive it? You sure about this?" Cal asked.

"Your truck had an aftermarket floor mounted shifter. Did you convert it from the steering column?"

"I honestly don't know. Can't remember driving that truck."

"No worries. It's like riding a bike," Charlie encouraged.

"When I was seven, I tried it once. Fell off. Broke my arm. Haven't been on another bike since."

"How do you remember that but can't remember driving your old straight-drive truck?"

"I honestly don't know. It just came to me. And to be perfectly honest, I'm not sure if it's true, or it just seemed like it was."

Charlie waved his hand, "Don't worry, you can't fall off this; it has four wheels. So, start'er up and let's give it a go."

Cal reluctantly turned the key in the ignition switch. As soon as the starter engaged, the powerful muscle car lurched forward, like an eager thoroughbred would leap out of the starting gate. Cal's and Charlie's heads snapped back which caused Cal to panic; but it was too late when he switched off the ignition. Their weight was slung forward; and they heard a thump in the back floorboard, followed by a yelp from Mutt. It was a good thing Charlie had insisted they go ahead and put on their seatbelts and shoulder harnesses.

Charlie glanced in the back floorboard where Mutt cowered in confusion as he looked up as if to ask, "What was that all about?"

"Relax. It's okay, Little Buddy," Charlie chuckled. "He'll get better."

"Yeah. Sorry Muttly Doright, I'll do better," Cal shook his head. "I hope."

"You gotta push the clutch in," Charlie reminded.

"I did."

"But you have to hold it in while the car is stopped. Then you let it out slowly as you press the gas pedal to make it go."

"Oh, I'm supposed to hold it in to start."

"Tends to work better that way."

"Okay," Cal turned to Charlie as Mutt placed his front paws on the console and looked up at Cal. "Sure you want me to do this?" Cal asked.

"Of course, he does," Charlie chuckled.

"I was asking you," Cal clarified.

"Of course, I do."

Cal placed his left foot on the clutch and pressed it as far as it would go, then turned the key in the ignition switch. The engine turned over several times, before it fired up with the distinct deep rumble of a high performance engine.

Charlie nodded with satisfaction, "It has an awesome cold start. And I love the exhaust note. Nothing sounds better than an idling classic GM muscle car."

"It's kinda loud," Cal offered.

"The exhaust's not stock," Charlie explained as he pointed toward the exit, "Once around the block, my good man."

Cal shook his head, "You asked for it." He warned as he attempted what he hoped was the right combination to slowly release the clutch as he applied pressure to the gas pedal.

By then Mutt's head popped up in the opened back window behind Cal. His little nose eagerly sniffed. He was ready for the new adventure.

Once again Cal's and Charlie's heads were forced back as the car lurched forward. Mutt's head disappeared as the engine stalled. There was another thump in the back floorboard.

"Breakfast's on me, if you can get us there," Charlie offered.

Cal fired up the engine and the tires screeched as the car lunged forward, but this time Cal was able to keep the engine running and the car continued forward. The ride was a bit jerky until Cal got the hang of it.

Within a few minutes Cal was able to stop the car then take off again and change gears as smoothly as a pro. From first to fourth gear as if it were an automatic transmission.

"Told you it was just like riding a bike. Your brain might not remember, but your muscles didn't forget."

Something unexpected happened when Cal turned the bright orange car on Destiny Way where the mysterious biker dropped him at the Welcome to Faith sign. There was no reason Cal would've known the old abandoned church existed. Or, that the dilapidated building might become significant in his life.

All that mattered on that morning, at that moment, Cal was overwhelmed by an inexplicable urge, "Mind if we make a slight detour?"

Moments later the Judge's tires crackled on the gravel on the road's shoulder beside the abandoned church.

"So this is where you spent your first few days in Faith?"

Cal was silent for a few seconds, "It doesn't make sense that I chose this place."

"When alone and in trouble, where else would a preacher go other than a church?"

"That's where I'm having trouble making sense of it." Cal

turned to Charlie. "According to what I found out in Archdale, the reason I left the ministry would've made a church the last place on Earth that I would've sought shelter. Although, with the steeple gone, I didn't know it was a church until I got inside."

"This old building should've been torn down years ago, but Betsy and I never could bring ourselves to pull the trigger," Charlie admitted as he opened the door and stepped out. "Our Great Granddad built this church back in nineteen-hundred."

"Your family built this?" Cal checked for traffic before he opened the door, pulled his seat forward, and retrieved the excited pup from the back seat.

Charlie leaned against the side of the Judge, "Our Great Granddad was the preacher, and he also drew up the plans. His little congregation saved up their money to buy the land and get started. Then they paid for the construction as they went along. Betsy has the original, handwritten ledger. Land included, it cost nine thousand dollars."

Cal carried Mutt around the front of the car and leaned against it beside Charlie.

They looked at the rundown structure until Charlie realized something was on Cal's mind. So he decided to remain silent, allow Cal to think.

"When did they shut it down?" For some reason Cal was more than a little curious, but couldn't explain the need to know.

"After years of neglect the building was looking rough as the members continued dying out. It was in sad shape when Grandad passed in nineteen-eighty. Dad took over then, and Granny died in eighty-one. Then Mom left Dad in eighty-two. She'd had enough of being the wife of a struggling preacher who was doing a lousy job of supporting her and their two kids. She wrote him a scathing letter we never knew about, until we went through his things after he passed. Dad finally shut the doors on the church in eighty-three. The last time I was in that building was for his funeral, in eighty-five. That was the last service to be held in the sanctuary."

"Did he quit preaching?"

"It wasn't that he just quit. He totally abandoned his faith and took a job at a hosiery mill in Salisbury. He was never the same. He grew distant, pitifully hollow, and bitter. He died a miserable man in eighty-five. Betsy was nine, and I was seven. We didn't find out until years later that he committed suicide."

Cal nodded, "I'm still not sure why I had to stop by here this morning."

Charlie nodded, "Betsy and I regret that we've allowed what could've been such a beautiful building to become such an embarrassing eye-sore."

Cal shook his head, "I feel like I have a lot to think about, but I don't have a clue what it is, or why I do."

Charlie pointed to the classic orange car, "Then while you think about it, if you can use this to get us from here," he pointed in the direction of the diner, "to there, I owe you breakfast." Cal appeared conflicted, but Charlie chose to play a different card, "Aren't you hungry?"

Cal bent over and let Mutt loose to sniff the ground around their feet and car tires, "Now you stay right here with us." He wondered if it would be best to stare into space rather than look Charlie in the eyes and try to gauge how he received what Cal was about to say, "Please bear with me for a few minutes." He opted to direct his eyes just over the top of the abandoned church, "I still can't figure out who that biker was, or why he was on that road that day. He seemed to know where to take me, and exactly where to stop and let me off. Just close enough to the Welcome sign to clearly see it, but far enough away where I'd walk by this road on my way to the diner. It wasn't until this morning when we approached the welcome sign, that something became so clear. I didn't realize it until then. I remembered that for some reason as I walked past this road that evening, the silhouette of this church was in my peripheral vision, but didn't register until after I had eaten and walked out of the diner. That's when it really hit me. I needed to find a place to sleep for a while, but I knew I didn't have enough money to get a hotel room. Now here's the kicker, instead of walking toward the safety of the lights downtown, I was led into the darkness on the outskirts. Not exactly what a preacher would do."

Charlie had two serious concerns. Where was Cal headed with this increasingly weird revelation, and had he made a serious mistake to invite this man to stay on his property? To be fair, Cal had sustained a head injury that at least temporarily deprived him of significant memories. It would be the Christian thing to at least hear him out a bit longer, before he determined if it might be best to take him back to the hospital. So, he remained quiet and a great deal more attentive. Not only to what Cal said, but how he said the words.

To complicate Charlie's predicament, Cal suddenly changed gears, "But as far as all that goes, there's plenty of time to figure it out. The issue I must address today and moving forward, what am I going to do with your sister?"

To say the least, Cal had Charlie's undivided attention, and had definitely piqued his curiosity, "With my sister? It would help if you'd be a little more specific."

Cal turned to face Charlie. It was time for direct eye contact, "I know you and Betsy are good friends with Deputy Karr, and I'm not accusing him of breaking the law, or violating any trust; but I'd say it's a safe bet he told you, and probably Betsy, that my mother-in-law gave me a picture of my deceased wife and daughter."

Charlie nodded, "And I'll go ahead and save you some time, it really weirded her out."

That response didn't catch Cal off guard. In fact, he would've been surprised had Charlie not responded accordingly, and bluntly. "When I walked in the diner my first night in town, I was instantly attracted to her."

"To Betsy. You're referring to my sister, not your wife, right?"

Cal didn't miss a beat, but he would be careful to clearly distinguish between the two women from that point on. "Yes. Your sister. At the time, it seemed organic. An unexpected meeting that more than likely would result in only a memory I couldn't understand, or explain. One of those rare chance encounters where you're so intrigued by someone who entered and exited your life in a flash, but touched you so deeply, even though you never spoke. Someone who instantly affected you so deeply at a glance. Someone you may never know their name, but you'd remember the rest of your life."

Oddly enough, that made perfect sense, "I can admit to you, but not my macho male friends, I know exactly what you're talking about. I've had a couple of those moments in my life," Charlie was comfortable to confess.

"At first I thought I'd see Betsy only a few times then be gone. But it hasn't worked out that way. I'm not sure how long I'm going to stay, but you could play a major role in my future," Cal was headed in the right direction. He just hadn't got there yet. But Charlie was about to close the distance in short order.

"Somehow, I think my sister is going to play a much larger role in this developing drama."

Cal reflexively chuckled, "Let's hope the drama is minimal."

"Well, we're two grown men. As long as you treat my sister with the respect she deserves, we won't have any problems. But, as far as Betsy, she's been through the wringer several times in the last few years. On the surface she comes off tough as nails, but she's very vulnerable and fragile. So tread softly."

"Trust me, I'm not exactly a tower of strength that's constructed on a solid foundation."

Charlie grinned slyly. It was time to lighten the mood, "And that's supposed to instill confidence in you?"

Cal grinned. They had made their points and both understood the significance of the situation. There was no need to extend that conversation, but they knew either one was free to reopen it at any time.

At least the air had been cleared between Cal and Charlie, or at least they had reached an initial understanding. On the other hand, there was Betsy, who was more pressing. Before the day was over Cal was confident that Betsy would know that he knew the issues they must work through. More importantly, Charlie would be sure to inform his sister that Cal knew Betsy would know he knew that she knew he knew she knew. And that was the most important accomplishment of that little talk.

For the most part lunch was uneventful. Since most of the lunch crowd was gone, Betsy insisted they bring Mutt in and the little fellow soon fell asleep at Cal's feet after he scarfed down the lunch Betsy slid under the table.

Once all of the remaining customers had full glasses and cups, Betsy felt comfortable and slipped in the booth beside Charlie, "So, what'da think about the apartment?"

Cal nodded and was able to flash a genuine smile, "It's great. All a man really needs. I think my new roommate and I are going to be very comfortable." He hoped he just said the right thing all three of them needed to know.

"Yeah, it was all I needed while I was going through a very nasty divorce a few years ago," Betsy hoped she just said all that Cal needed to know.

By then, Charlie had become an innocent, but very involved bystander. He was glad the three people at that table had kind of cleared the air, and set a few parameters as they embarked on a very interesting human experiment. One in which could take many directions and involve untold depths of human emotions. He hoped that both Betsy and Cal were up to the challenges they faced.

One way or the other, Charlie was prepared and committed to be there for both of them. As if on cue, the fourth entity reminded them he would be an important member of that select club. Mutt had awakened and was ready to play.

......

After a successful day in the shop the 1957 Chevy pickup's chassis was the cleanest it had been since new. At least the grease and grime had been scraped away. It still needed to be sandblasted, primed and then painted. Those steps would come later.

Mutt slept most of the day and was fully charged when it was time to leave. He wagged and gyrated as he followed Cal across the pavement to the Judge.

"Want'a meet me at the diner and grab a bite before you head to the apartment?" Charlie suggested as he grasped the cord to pull the garage door down.

Cal stopped, but Mutt was unable to stand still, so he circled him like a curious fly as he spoke, "Actually, I want to take Mutt on a little ride, see if I can get us lost before we go home."

Without any thought, Cal referred to the garage apartment as, "Home." Charlie smiled. The more time he spent with Cal, he realized that his new shop volunteer was really a good guy. At that point it was less important Cal couldn't remember who he used to be. Who he was at the core of his being would more than likely surface eventually. It was a good thing that so far he appeared to be a good man.

The jury was still out on how Cal and Betsy would get along. At least, Charlie felt more confident Betsy would soon realize that like him, she had made a good friend. Of course, that would be determined by how Betsy and Cal managed their feelings and emotions.

Cal stopped beside the passenger door as Charlie stepped out of the shop, pulled the office door closed and checked to make sure it was locked.

"All afternoon, I've had this odd desire to cook dinner tonight." Cal confessed as he held up his hands and tilted his head. "Not sure where that came from, but I want to give it a go."

"Good thing I keep the insurance up on that building," Charlie jabbed. "Enjoy. See you in the morning."

......

As the Earth continued to tilt toward its Summer Solstice, the sun stayed up one minute longer each day. It had been an awesome day so far.

"Where you want to go, Little Buddy," Cal asked as he lifted Mutt and placed him on the passenger bucket seat.

Mutt extended his snout toward Cal's face and licked the air. It was obvious the excited pup didn't care, as long as they were together.

To be over fifty years old, the Judge surely drove and rode well. The steering was tight and responsive, the brakes didn't squeak, and there were no annoying rattles. Based on Charlie's attention to detail, Cal was sure every component of the classic muscle car's suspension, engine, and body had been thoroughly prepped and refurbished before he reassembled the car.

Mutt spent most of the time with his front paws on the armrest, and his super active nose thrust as high as possible. He was too short to stick his head out the window, but he inhaled every scent possible that poured through the opened window.

There was a good thirty minutes of daylight left as Cal turned on Destiny Way that first led him to Faith. The shortest distance to his new home was to turn just before the

Welcome sign and pass by the old church. That would become the longest way home as he stopped beside the church.

Mutt sensed they were about to exit and dropped his front paws back down on the seat and excitedly turned to Cal.

"Yes, we've got a little mission to accomplish before we get home," Cal announced.

Even though Charlie never was a Boy Scout, his motto had always been, "Be prepared." Before he turned the Judge over to Cal, he put a few essential items in the glovebox and trunk. In the glovebox was a multi-function Prepper's Peak flashlight. The Swiss Army knife of flashlights.

Mutt wagged his tail as Cal exited and closed the driver's door. The little fellow couldn't contain his joy and resumed his stance against the door. Had the little fellow's tail been a rotor, he would've hovered above the seat. He would have to wait a bit longer as Cal opened the trunk and the toolbox inside to pull out a few tools.

Then Cal led the eager Mutt on the freshly worn path through the thick undergrowth. After a few steps on the path Mutt's keen sense of smell detected the familiar trail and he bolted past Cal, a blonde blur of fur.

Cal assumed his little buddy believed his Momma and siblings awaited inside the abandoned church. Sure enough Mutt scampered up the steps and charged into the shadows. Seconds later he slowly emerged back onto the concrete platform. He was confused.

The hallway was already dim so Cal switched on the bright flashlight. Several of the old boards squeaked and Mutt's paws clicked as they entered the second office. Cal was purpose driven and hadn't given much thought to how similar the interior of Faith Covenant Church was to Tabernacle Baptist.

The bright flashlight became a spotlight on the dusty old desk. Cal crossed and placed some tools on the desk, and kept a screwdriver in hand. He turned to his curious companion, "Never really considered a career in larceny."

Confident Cal could handle whatever it was he intended to do, Mutt switched into Sherlock Holmes mode, and placed his nose to the floor and began a thorough inspection of the room. Side to side. Corner to corner.

# RETURN TO FAITH

When Cal and Charlie leaned against the Judge, Charlie divulged what was more than likely not an often shared part of his family's history. The suicide of his father. The last pastor of this church. For some reason, Cal thought about the locked drawer in the office. Why was it locked? More importantly, why was the desk the only piece of furniture left in the entire building, other than the oak pews in the sanctuary?

Cal's first thought was to attempt to use the tip of the flathead screwdriver to pry the locking bar down so he could open the drawer. But he needed to wiggle the drawer and see how much of a gap he had to work with.

He pushed the drawer to the left which revealed the drawer was much less restricted than when he tried to open it before. "Interesting," He muttered as he decided to pull the knob. "Well," he said as the drawer pulled open with no resistance.

Immediately, Cal spotted a dusty, yellowed envelope. He removed it and blew off the loose dust. The writing was either printed or written by a very steady hand. He read it aloud, "This Letter Is Intended For You."

Cal turned the envelope over to discover the flap was loose and appeared to have never been moistened and sealed. With great care he extracted the letter, unfolded it, and pointed the flashlight on it.

As if he had no choice, Cal read the letter aloud, "September 27th, 1985. To the one who opens this letter, God has a special purpose. He selected you to restore this, His house, to its fullest glory. Rest assured, regardless of your past, your future is cradled in God's loving hands. Your path will lead you back to your faith, in which you will discover a renewed courage, strength and determination.

As you may have already discovered, I chose to end my journey on Earth. It wasn't a decision I made lightly, but it was the right thing for me to do.

You see, my wife lost all faith and hope in me, not just as a preacher, but as a man. Our church had been failing and dying out, long before my father passed, and I inherited the pulpit.

It was bad enough that my wife abandoned me, and the church. What ripped through my soul, she also left our children for me to raise alone. You see, my wife was the love of my life; and when she left, she took my will to live. How cruel of her to not only abandon me, but to saddle me with the burden and responsibility for our children's future.

I was humiliated. Our family's legacy was this church, and I had allowed it to be destroyed, along with what would more than likely be the future of my children.

Closing the doors of Faith Covenant Church for the last time as its pastor, destroyed my will to live. I don't expect you, or anyone else to understand, or condone my actions. I have made peace with my God. I'm ready to meet Him face to face. You see, I've been diagnosed with terminal cancer, and the pain has become unbearable. I have a friend who has supplied me with some medication that will allow me to leave this world in peace.

Most importantly, I've arranged for a fine man and his wife to adopt my children. They have no children of their own, and they are well established in this community. My children will grow up with far more opportunities than I could've ever provided them with the meager living I was making working in the hosiery mill."

Cal had to lower the letter. The content boggled his mind. He had to lay it down. A chill raced up his spine. It felt as if he held the broken heart of the letter's author in his bare hands.

Thankfully, Mutt had sufficiently investigated the room and grown bored. He hopped up and put his front paws on Cal's legs. The distraction was welcomed. He tussled with his little buddy for a couple of minutes, until the letter slipped off the slanted desk top.

Mutt leapt on top of the paper as if it were a new toy tossed into the fray. Cal quickly rescued the paper before the sharp teeth of his companion snatched it up and started to chew. At that point the need to know overpowered the reluctance to learn, so Cal resumed reading, "Today, I preached my last sermon, at what I fear is the last service at Faith Covenant Church. I held on as long as I could, until life crushed the last grain of my hope in Faith. It's time for me to step away. And when you read this, it will be time for you to step in and make right my wrong. To pick up the cross I had to lay down, and carry it to victory. May God lead you with

# RETURN TO FAITH

His grace and hope that I was forced to abandon in this place. God Bless You! Pastor Allen Tillman."

Cal sat in silence. At his feet, Mutt seemed to sense play time was over, and his human friend was troubled. The young canine didn't understand the human words, but he understood the tumult in his human's tear filled eyes. He rose, lifted his front paws and gently placed them on Cal's legs. His whine was low, heartfelt, and compassionate.

On the drive to the apartment, Mutt refused to stay in the passenger seat. He curled up and snoozed in Cal's lap. Once they got upstairs, Cal decided to delay cooking dinner. Mutt had stayed at his heels and wanted in his lap when he sat down on the sofa. Fortunately, Cal managed to keep his uniform grease free that day. He would take a hot, refreshing shower in a few minutes. At that moment, he just needed to sit quietly for a while and try to absorb the letter he held in his hand.

Rejuvenated after the hot shower, Cal had to contend with a compulsion that made no sense. He retrieved the scuffed Bible that Deputy Karr returned to him in the hospital. Mutt wouldn't leave Cal alone, so he picked up the pup and allowed him to curl up and sleep with his head in his lap. Mutt had to be in contact with his human to comfort him.

Cal decided not to chop fresh vegetables and start dinner. He invested the next two hours on an adventure he found so foreign yet eerily familiar. He opened the King James version and turned to Genesis. Where better to start than with Chapter One, Verse One? He read aloud, "In the beginning God created the heavens and the earth. Verse two: And the earth was without form, and void, and darkness was upon the face of the deep. And the Spirit of God moved upon the face of the waters. Verse Three: And God said, Let there be light, and there was light. Verse Four: And God saw the light and it was good. And God divided the light from the darkness. Verse Five: And God called the light Day, and the darkness he called Night. And the evening and the morning were the first day."

Okay. That made sense. For the sake of argument, he admitted there would be justification for those who chose to believe in a higher power to accept those verses.

He decided to randomly flip through the book he couldn't remember if he'd read. Yet, as a preacher more than likely he would have memorized numerous scriptures.

Cal didn't have a clue what to look for, so there was no logical search criteria. He got lost on an adventure into an ancient world where incredible events happened to people with names most Americans couldn't pronounce, in oddly named places on the other side of the world. None of which had any relevance to his modern world, nor his current situation.

He picked up Pastor Tillman's letter and read it again and again. Okay, so until shortly before he lost his memory, then was unwittingly dumped on the outskirts of Faith, he had been a preacher, or pastor, or minister. The operative theme was "had been." Whatever the reason he opted out, he was ready to accept as justifiable to step away from the pulpit. Most important, at that moment, in his current life he had no desire to return to any pulpit. Especially one in a rundown church, in a sleepy little southern community known as, Faith. How corny and insane was that unlikely scenario?

Then the distraction began as an irreverent comic relief. It was subtle at first, then gradually intensified as if Mutt suddenly discovered the art of a humorous snore. As the seconds ticked off, the little canine became more proficient and intense.

Eventually, Cal succumbed to a snicker that morphed into a chuckle that quickly intensified into a hearty, stress relief laughter. Mutt was startled awake. The innocent little buzz saw silenced. His head sprang up as his eyes popped opened to search for the source of the rude intrusion into his precious nap time.

"Sorry, Little Buddy, couldn't help it. You've become a pro snoring machine right in front of my eyes and aching ears," Cal explained.

After his late dinner that turned out pretty darn well, Cal decided to call it an early night. He knew he'd made a serious mistake when he hoisted Mutt up on the bed. The moment his little paws touched down on the clean sheet, it was on, freestyle twirl and spin with a corner of the top sheet locked between his teeth.

The sudden explosion of energy, combined with the

events of the long day soon put Mutt into a deep sleep coma. Finally the little critter was too tired to even whimper a snore.

At one point during the night, Cal awakened and abruptly sat up, which startled and awakened Mutt. Cal turned frustrated, disgusted eyes Heavenward, "Obviously I'd had enough of you. Why can't you accept that and leave me alone?"

No thunderous answer boomed or roared down from on high by an angered God. Nor did Cal hear the slightest whisper of understanding from a kind, loving, compassionate entity. By the time Cal laid back down he was frustrated enough to doubt he would ever receive a logical, acceptable response.

By then Cal was totally exhausted and easily drifted off, but never slipped into deep, restive, restorative sleep. He suffered through a fitful night where he tossed and turned. The next morning he was even more tired and out of sorts.

......

## 20
## The Time Was Right To Learn The Whole Truth

Charlie could tell Cal wasn't on top of his game as soon as he walked in the shop. Mutt wasn't his usual frisky self and refused to leave Cal's side. Charlie dared not assume he had the right or justifiable need to meddle.

The morning's task was to complete the tear-down of Charlie's '57 Chevy Truck engine. This truck was also a 3100, like the one Cal had restored in his previous life. Instead of a six cylinder engine, Charlie's had the more powerful 283 cubic inch V8, with a "Turbo-Fire" twin-barrel carburetor. Brand new, Charlie's truck rolled out of the factory with 185 horsepower. It was considered powerful in those days, but was far under modern standards. The popularity of the 3100 model, and 8 cylinder engines meant there were plenty of used parts still available. Charlie's source had some lightly used pistons, rods and lifters he'd already ordered and expected to be delivered any day.

Cal had been unusually quiet so when he finally spoke up, Charlie took note, "Mind if we take a break for a while? Head over to the diner and have a cup of coffee with Betsy?"

Charlie glanced at the antique Ford clock on the back wall that still kept perfect time. It was 10:00 AM. "Now would be perfect. This is when she usually sits down, has a cup of coffee, and catches her breath before getting ready for the lunch crunch," Charlie immediately took off his black rubber gloves.

After they washed up, Cal offered to drive them over in the Judge.

"You're driving this thing like you've owned since it was new," Charlie was sincere.

Cal nodded, "It's odd how comfortable I feel behind the wheel. Somehow I just don't see myself having ever wanted to own a car like this. They showed me the Toyota Avalon that the church supplied me to drive. It was quite a different animal."

"I'd say." Charlie chuckled. "Seeing you behind the wheel of this beast, I can't imagine you driving a preacher mobile."

"At this point, neither can I."

Charlie called Betsy while Cal washed up and used the restroom. Betsy agreed it was best that Cal not know she'd been given a heads-up.

Betsy played her role perfectly and convinced Cal she was pleasantly surprised and glad to have the company while she took it easy for a bit.

Of course Mutt was welcome. However, both Betsy and Charlie noticed how subdued the usually rambunctious critter as he stayed cozied up to Cal in the booth.

Charlie saw Cal pull a yellowed envelope from above the sun visor before they exited the Judge. He wondered how much the contents consumed both Cal and Mutt. Since this was Cal's show, Betsy and Charlie opted to remain quiet and leave the direction up to him.

Betsy brewed a fresh pot and served up three steamy cups at what had become Cal's favorite booth. She and Charlie patiently sat opposite and watched Cal take a pensive sip.

Cal nodded, "Good stuff."

"Thank you," Betsy was eager to respond, mostly because she wanted Cal to know she genuinely appreciated his compliment. Also, it was their side's first effort to break the ice.

Cal set the coffee cup down and glanced at the envelope that was turned face down to hide the writing. Betsy's and Charlie's eyes followed Cal's gaze.

"Did you know there's an old oak desk in the second office of the church?"

Betsy and Charlie both shook their heads.

"It's been so long since I've been in there, I couldn't tell you much," Charlie confessed.

Betsy waxed nostalgic and dared to allow herself to grin, "I remember one time Daddy told me how proud he was of the old desk in his office. That it was a gift from a friend, who'd bought it at the factory in High Point, and donated it to the church." She shook her head, somewhat stunned she remembered so quickly. "Wow. That one came from deep in the shadows of a cobwebbed corner of my memory."

Cal turned his eyes to Charlie's, "The other day you told me some of the history of the church, and how involved your family had been since before it was even built."

Charlie nodded, then shared a "what's this all about" look with Betsy.

"Please bear with me," Cal immediately wished he would've chosen a better lead in; but it was too late and it would serve no purpose to stumble and stammer to find a better way. He continued, "There's so much I don't understand and have no hope of grasping at this point in my life. It's like my life began when I found myself on the side of that road not far from here. What makes no sense is the life I'm living now began in the middle of another man's life. What's hard for me to grasp is that the other man's life appears to have ended when I realized I was there.... alone on the side of that road." He shook his head as he pondered, "I feel like two completely different men who share the same body and identical past, but I'm the only one who will continue after the new beginning." He shook his head, "I know it sounds nuts, but...."

Betsy's hand eased across the table before she could even think to stop it, then it gently floated down to rest on Cal's hand. Foremost in her mind echoed a stern warning, 'whatever you do, don't call him honey, or sweetie.'

Charlie raced to his sister's rescue, "Hey, you're among friends. We may be new friends, but we're here for you."

Betsy nodded and gently patted Cal's hand, which was all the physical contact she dared make, so she awkwardly pulled her hand back. In fact it was too much contact and it happened too easily and too quickly. She would have to be careful not to accidentally send any wrong or mixed signals, "Yeah, you're among friends." That was absolutely the wrong thing to say. It could've easily been construed as condescending, more like an adult's attempt to console an overly sensitive child.

Cal didn't appear affected. Betsy was relieved when Cal smiled and turned his attention to the envelope that he picked up and kept face down.

"This is where it really goes off the reservation. Yesterday, while on the way back in from trying to get Mutt and me lost, I had no choice. I had to stop at the church where I went straight to the office, to the desk with tools in my hand. The reason I had tools was because on the first or second day I spent in the church, I discovered the desk and looked in all but one drawer, which was locked. What makes no sense was yesterday, the drawer was unlocked." He held up the envelope, "And this is what I found inside." He turned the envelope to reveal the fancy writing to Betsy and Charlie.

Immediately, like a lightning bolt, Betsy's right hand flew to cover her mouth as she gasped. Charlie became concerned and reached for his sister, who quickly waved him off with her other hand.

"What is it?" Charlie all but demanded.

Betsy was unable to tear her hand away from her mouth as she shook her head to indicate she was also unable to speak. Charlie turned desperate eyes toward Cal for some kind of explanation.

"I have good reason to believe the letter in this envelope was written by your father," Cal explained.

Betsy's eyes flooded with huge tears that tumbled down her cheeks and pooled around her fingers and hand. She slowly nodded affirmation.

Charlie looked at Betsy who continued to nod, so he reached over and took the letter from Cal.

"So you've read it?" Charlie asked as he turned the envelope and to examine it carefully .

"Yes. And it appears there's a very specific message and direction for me that looks like it could link us together in a common cause. As well as contain a long overdue explanation for both of you," Cal focused on Betsy's eyes, "You okay?"

Betsy nodded and was finally able to lower her hand, "He had the prettiest handwriting. He didn't write, he drew."

The same quandary encompassed both sides of the table. Cal wanted so much to reach over and comfort Betsy as much as she wanted to do the same for him. Instead, they just sat there and kept their hands to themselves. They looked like two socially challenged children who could only awkwardly stare at the other, while Charlie slid out the letter and read.

Charlie remained stone-faced as he read. When he finished he dared not even peek at his curious and anxious sister. He casually folded the letter and laid it on top of the envelope. He pondered, then sighed, "I'm not so sure you need to read this yet."

"What do you mean?"

Charlie turned to Betsy, "It seems our loving, adoptive parents meant well, but may have done our father a significant injustice."

"They've been dead for ten years. Don't see how getting mad at them now would serve any purpose," Betsy offered.

"According to this letter, in our father's own words, they neglected to tell us a few vital facts, and they mischaracterized others," Charlie held up the letter. "If we would've known all the facts contained in this letter, we would've grown up with a different, more positive perception of our father."

Betsy was pensive, "I always thought they went out of their way to treat us like we were their natural born kids."

"They did leave us a substantial inheritance," Charlie turned to Cal, "Part of which is the church and land it's on."

Betsy nodded and pondered, "They did make a point of telling us they'd bought the property and would leave it to us in their will." Betsy said as she extended her right hand palm up, as she arched her eyebrows.

Charlie reluctantly handed over the letter. He was impressed with how well Betsy took the new information as she read, even though her eyes filled with tears as she gently replaced the letter in the envelope. Then she glanced at her watch before turning to Charlie.

"We've got time to visit Dad's grave before the lunch bunch rolls in," Betsy suggested.

Charlie handed Cal his key to the shop, "We need to get you one made. Go on back to the shop and start scraping the engine block. I'll be there in a bit."

......

Betsy and Charlie didn't spend much time at their father's grave, but they finally made peace with his decision to take his own life. More importantly, they forgave him for abandoning them. It would've been better had their father felt comfortable telling them the truth, but given his circumstances they weren't sure what they would've done if they were in his shoes.

"Daddy, we never stopped loving you," Betsy said as

Charlie put his arm around her.

"And we promise to visit more often," Charlie added.

It wasn't important for anyone else to know what they really thought about their father. But it mattered to them. Children who grew up with healthy relationships to their parents tended to mature into more confident, self-assured adults.

For as long as she could remember, Betsy had battled self-esteem issues and feelings of inadequacy. Several years before she had sought professional help, and after several sessions the psychologist told her, "There's a good chance you don't think you're worth being loved by any man because your father chose to die instead of staying to love and raise you."

For whatever reason, Betsy's and Charlie's adoptive parents opted not to tell them their father had terminal cancer. Or, their father never told them why he was going away, or how he intended to go away, when he asked them to raise his children.

Betsy made a very wise suggestion as they drove away from the cemetery, "We owe it to our father and our adoptive parents to give them both the benefit of the doubt."

"But on the other hand, I'll always have an issue with our mother," Charlie confessed. He could never bring himself to call her, "Mom."

Betsy sat in silence a few seconds then spoke up, "There's so many things I could say about her, but they're best left unsaid."

They agreed they owed their father an apology, even though it was posthumously. But they had no respect for their absentee mother.

Betsy suddenly turned to Charlie, "It just dawned on me. Have you told Cal about what's supposed to happen next week?"

Charlie was focused on the road, "Next week. What'da ya mean?"

"With the church?"

Charlie's eyes widened, "Dad's letter kinda changes things. Don't it?"

"Think we should at least talk with Cal about it?"

"Let's run by the shop."

Betsy looked at her watch, "I really need to get back to the diner. Why don't you drop me off, then go get him."

Charlie nodded, "We do need to discuss this with him."

......

"I'm sorry. Didn't mean to ruin our whole day," Cal felt the need to apologize as he slid into his booth.

Betsy and Charlie sat opposite Cal, and Betsy turned to Charlie for him to take over, "Technically, it is your fault, but not your doing."

Cal shifted his eyes back and forth between Betsy and Charlie in hopes one or the other would explain.

Charlie nodded slowly, "That letter was most unexpected, and has the potential to cause some dramatic changes in," he gestured, "all of our lives."

"You see," Betsy was compelled to join in, "A while back we were approached by three local volunteer fire departments to do a controlled burn over the course of four days." Betsy handed off to Charlie.

"They explained how important it is to do regular live-fire drills to keep their guys proficient in actual safety procedures," Charlie continued. "We committed, and set the dates; then we had a few dry weeks; and on the day of the first scheduled fire, the winds were too high. The forecast for the next few days was gusty, so they cancelled,"

"All three fire departments were there and geared up, ready to set the first fire which would've been in Dad's office. They were going to start the fire under the desk." Betsy added one important detail. "Would you like to take a guess when that first burn was supposed to happen?"

Cal was a bit reluctant before he responded, "Since you're asking me, I'd say the day I arrived."

Betsy and Charlie nodded. "And the day after tomorrow is the rescheduled date," Charlie informed.

Neither Betsy, Charlie, or Cal wanted to speak because all three had been significantly affected by the letter that, by the grace of God, would've more than likely gone up in smoke.

"Our adoptive parents were very good people but not too keen on going to church. And after Daddy took his life, we kinda lost our hope in a faith that couldn't save our Daddy," Betsy revealed.

"I wouldn't say that we stopped believing in God," Charlie tried to explain, but hit a roadblock and turned to Betsy.

"I'd say we turned our backs on God, just like we believed He'd done on us," Betsy turned back to Charlie who nodded in agreement. "At this point, we're very confused," She confessed. It was evident they'd spoken their piece and were ready to hear Cal's thoughts.

"I didn't sleep very well last night; and sometime up in the morning I remember telling God that I'd obviously had enough of Him and to leave me alone," Cal confessed. "And guess what?"

"He hasn't," Betsy surmised.

"Not in the least. I'm having a real problem with this whole, 'God thing.' Can't settle in my mind if He's real or not. I can't remember a single thing that would give me a reason to believe in Him." Cal was noticeably conflicted, "But at the same time, I can't really justify a single reason I shouldn't."

After a few tense, quiet moments Betsy spoke up, "Seems we have a serious decision to make."

Cal shook his head, "No, not we. You and Charlie. Don't bring me in on this. I don't belong here."

Betsy shook her head, "I'm sorry, you might not have belonged here before, but you're right in the middle of it now."

Charlie nodded, "It appears that God, regardless if we believe in Him or not at this moment, has sent all three of us a very clear message."

Cal obviously disagreed and opened his mouth to speak until Betsy lifted her hand, "Let's do ourselves and God a favor, and at least think about it the rest of the day, and not discuss it among ourselves. Then let's talk about it over breakfast in the morning."

As far as Cal was concerned, that was the least acceptable option. What he would rather do would be to rise from the table, thank Betsy and Charlie for their understanding, their generous hospitality, and for offering him a place to stay. He was also appreciative of the car to drive while he tried to get a handle on what he should do with the rest of his life. But that was the problem, he didn't have anywhere else to go, or any way to get there; so at least in the short term, he was an unwilling participant in a drama that should've remained solely in their family.

By then the regular early lunch crowd started to trickle in and greet Betsy. The newly minted trio had run out of time. Out of respect, Cal gave in and accepted Betsy's suggestion.

······

## 21
## When The Path Ahead Is Divine, Not Random

Charlie was charged up early the next morning and called Cal just before his alarm went off, "If we're going to meet our deadline on the truck project, we're going to have to maintain a tight schedule. I'm not even going to ask if you've ever sandblasted, and go ahead and inform you that this morning you're going to learn. At the bottom of the stairs, open the door to your right and hanging on the wall to your left is a clear plastic face shield. Bring it with you." Charlie paused and was ready to hear Cal's response. Instead, he remembered one more thing, "Oh, and thank you."

There was one very necessary item Charlie didn't mention on the phone, but handed to Cal before he fired up the enclosed sandblaster. A pair of ear plugs, and boy were they welcomed as the tiny glass beads forced at high-speed through the nozzle sounded like a jet engine that randomly flew around the room.

On a positive note, though slightly off key that morning, Cal had to admit over the last few days he'd come to realize busy hands at work was very therapeutic. The task he performed that morning required a level of concentration that wouldn't allow his mind to wander.

The highly specialized machine Cal had his hands and arms buried in up to his elbows in thick rubber gloves was capable of two stages to sandblast smaller pieces. The first step was to use actual grains of sand that were abrasive and came in different sizes, depending upon the need. The second step was to follow up with tiny glass beads to smooth the surface after the sand applications. Cal had switched over to the glass beads to smooth up the metal engine mount brackets.

Even though the enclosed machine provided a thick

safety glass through which to view the process, Charlie insisted on using a high grade plastic face shield as well. Cal was engrossed, actually amazed at the transformation he'd achieved in such a short time. The grimy, grease and gunk encrusted bracket now looked like a freshly cast piece of steel that was ready to be sprayed with gray primer and painted black.

Cal watched through the glass shield while he guided the nozzle that spewed a narrow stream of fine glass pellets into a corner of the bracket. He'd forgotten Deputy Karr's call on the drive to the shop. He had dreamed up this harebrained scheme he wanted to explain further, in person, with both Cal and Charlie.

Mutt was still in protective and comfort mode for Cal and refused to venture away from his human companion. The little canine would have to be convinced his human was no longer in crisis. That didn't mean his juvenile canine behavior would be totally ignored and stored for later release.

On the contrary, Mutt had been very active around the sandblasting machine and was smeared with grease streaks from head to tail. He growled and playfully slung a greasy rag around that he clenched tightly between his teeth.

Deputy Karr walked into the room unnoticed due to the loud hiss of the sandblasting machine. He located Cal and cautiously stepped around so Cal could see him approach, rather than come from behind unseen and unexpectedly. Mutt was too involved on the other side of the noisy machine to see Deputy Karr.

When he noticed Deputy Karr, Cal immediately lifted his right foot off the pedal that allowed the air to force the glass beads through the nozzle. The jet-like hiss silenced, which startled Mutt, who dropped the rag and turned to the sound of the footsteps. The pup's natural instincts kicked in and he assumed a defensive posture between Cal and Deputy Karr. The junior guard dog emitted his most convincing "Yip," followed by an ominous puppy growl, that was more cute than protective. The undersized protector would have to grow into a deeper, more aggressive bark and throaty growl.

Cal withdrew his arms from the sleeved gloves, stepped back, pulled up the visor, and chuckled as he shifted his eyes down to his eager watch-pup in training, "It's okay, Muttly

Doright, he's a lawman. He's a good guy. At least I thought he was. We'll have to hear him out."

As a dog owner, Deputy Karr was very comfortable around puppies and dogs, so he leaned over and offered his hand for Mutt to sniff. He spoke as if to a young child, "Oh my goodness, you're a ferocious little critter."

Mutt growled and backed closer to Cal who chuckled, "Careful, you might lose an arm." He looked down at Mutt, "He's okay, go get'm," he added with a sweeping motion of his hand.

The positive tone and physical invitation was all Mutt needed to launch into a wiggle-waggle toward Deputy Karr.

"He's a bit greasy," Cal warned.

"That's okay, I know where the Gojo is," Deputy Karr said as he squatted to tussle with the willing ball of fury energy. Then he stood up. "Just got off the phone with Charlie. He's on his way back here."

Cal nodded, "Did you share your nutball idea with him?"

Deputy Karr grinned, "He wasn't too sure about it at first, but he soon came around. We agreed Tommy's biggest problem is Megan. And I think both he and Betsy wished they could've been a better influence on her."

"If he agrees, then I really don't have a choice," Cal wasn't ready to tip his hand that he was 50/50 if he would stay in Faith much longer.

"Oh, but you do. He said it was contingent on your being willing to take on the challenge with him."

"Great, put the pressure on me. Let me ask my assistant," Cal turned his eyes down to Mutt who sat at his feet and looked up expectantly. "What do you think?"

Mutt's tail wagged because Cal paid him attention, not that he grasped Cal's question, so he only mustered a half-hearted, unenthusiastic "woof."

"I don't know. He doesn't sound too convinced," Cal said, then turned serious. "Please don't misinterpret my ill-timed attempt at humor. I really applaud both of you wanting to help this troubled young man, but I don't know him, and I'm not comfortable taking on the challenge, or responsibility right now."

Deputy Karr nodded, "Fair enough. But we don't even know if Tommy would be interested. Let's at least give him the opportunity to say "no," before you do. Then the pressure's off you."

Cal pointed at Deputy Karr, "Pretty slick. It's almost criminal how quickly you twisted my concern into guilt." Cal accused as he wiped the grease off his hands and looked down at his greasy uniform. "Probably need to take a shower and put on clean clothes first?"

Charlie pulled the car into the garage and exited, "What's the verdict?"

Deputy Karr turned to Cal, "I'll swing by the apartment in thirty minutes and pick you up."

"Better give me forty-five," Cal suggested.

"I'll take care of the Mutt'ster," Charlie promised.

Cal shook his head then looked down at Mutt, "You coulda got us out'a this."

Mutt was suddenly energized by the prospect of three playmates to frolic with, so he leapt into a wag fest and barked excitedly.

......

During the last twenty-four hours Tommy progressed so well Dr. Roberts gladly signed off on his transfer from ICU Step-down to a regular room. Tommy was aware he had company on the way, but was less than thrilled.

Deputy Karr and Cal paused out in the hall.

"It's not too late to change your mind."

Cal didn't waste any time and shook his head, "But I may come to regret this."

Deputy Karr slowly opened the door and led Cal into the room. Sam was very uncomfortable and still embarrassed by the way she treated Deputy Karr and Cal in the ICU Waiting Room. That was before Tommy came around, and she learned the truth from her unrepentant son.

To Sam's right stood Benny Timmons, the court appointed public defender, who looked every bit the timid bookworm his name implied. Behind his deceptively boyish face was a shrewd, very aggressive, razor sharp legal mind. He graduated with honors from a well respected law school in the Northeast. A future in politics was his ultimate goal, his dream career. He wanted to travel through a Public Defender's office on his way to Washington, DC. He was determined to establish an impressive record and build a reputation as a champion for social justice. A noble cause had it been birthed and nurtured in a humble, ethical legal mind.

Shortly after he walked into his office that morning, Benny was informed of the meeting he was required to attend with his client. It was unexpected and suspicious. He was girded and ready for battle by the time he arrived at the hospital. He would watch every move and pick apart every sentence the lawman uttered. He was a young, ravenous lion ready to pounce for his cause, more so than for his troubled, misguided client's best interest.

Tommy's head was still bandaged. There was no way for the socially inept lad to conceal his reluctance to the court ordered meeting. Nor how nervous and uncomfortable he became when Deputy Karr and Cal entered. He refused to make eye contact with the two men who were about to make him an offer he would be a fool to reject.

On the other hand, Benny was eagle-eyed and laser-focused, determined to assume control of the meeting from the outset. He asserted himself in the role of aggressor and stepped around the bed. He confidently approached Deputy Karr and Cal and was first to extend his hand, but to Cal, not Deputy Karr. That was carefully planned.

"I was informed this morning that Judge McEntire and the prosecutor are willing to accept Deputy Karr's recommendation, but I haven't had a chance to review it, so we're not prepared to agree to, or sign anything."

Sam was caught completely off guard, "But I...." She paused when Benny lifted his hand. "We request a couple of days to review the language in the plea deal."

Deputy Karr was a no-nonsense kind of guy and wasn't the least bit impressed with, nor intimidated, by the reputation the young lion had already garnered during his short tenure in the Rowan PD office. "Excuse me?"

Benny never suffered from a lack of confidence and was rather proud of his outsized ego, "I would like to review the language in the document to ensure there are no...."

Deputy Karr nodded as he interrupted, "Umm Hummm. I see. Well, first of all, it's written in plain English, so even the simplest minded attorney can read it and understand. And as a matter of discovery, I've known Sam and Tommy since he was six years old. So for a number of years, I've been trying to help him find and establish a solid foothold on a positive path. My advice to you, young man, is to step down off your high horse and let's get down to a serious discussion, right now."

"Deputy Karr, for your information, I have the right to review every comma and period. Every "if," "and," or "but." So I'd advise you to mind your manners, or I will file a complaint with your superiors," Benny bristled with confidence.

Deputy Karr countered as he retrieved his cell phone and tapped the screen several times, then held the phone to his ear. After a beat he spoke, "Yes, Captain Thomas, are you available to meet with Cal and me, with Tommy Forrester and his attorney at the hospital?" He listened, "No, Sir. It's not signed. He wants to review it a couple of days," He explained, then listened again before he answered, "Yes, Sir. He's right here," Deputy Karr said as he extended the phone to Benny, who was ready to battle Karr's superior.

"Yes, Sir. Captain Thomas, is it?" Benny tapped the speaker icon to show off for his client and his mother, as he put the lawmen in their place.

"Yes, this is Captain Thomas. What's the problem?"

"Captain Thomas, this is Benny Timmons, I'm Tommy's P.D. And there's no real problem, Sir. It seems Deputy Karr is taking issue with me reviewing the plea deal."

"Do you have me on speakerphone?"

"Yes, Sir. We have nothing to hide. Do you?" Benny smirked at Deputy Karr.

"Okay. I see how it is. I'm getting ready to step into court and testify in a murder trial, so I'll be brief. The problem isn't having the plea deal reviewed, it's that you're doing the review. Your reputation precedes you. Now listen very carefully, I was invited to join Deputy Karr when he made the recommendation to the judge and prosecutor. And for your edification, they were against this from the start, and it was Deputy Karr who stood up for Tommy until he wore the judge and prosecutor down and won them over. You can do what you want, but I would advise you to think long and hard about nitpicking this deal to death. You'll probably discover how quickly the judge and prosecutor are ready to set a court date."

Benny maintained his stern glare and defiant tight jaw as he pondered.

"Hello. Hello. Mr. Timmons, Deputy Karr, you still there," Captain Thomas' voice sounded through Deputy Karr's phone speaker.

"Yes, Sir, Captain Thomas, we're still here, and I'm sure we'll be able to reach a common ground," Benny responded, then handed the phone back to Deputy Karr.

"Deputy Karr, I'll call you when I get out of court," Captain Thomas' confident voice reassured.

"Yes, Sir," Deputy Karr responded then ended the call. He replaced the phone in its clip on his belt, then turned his attention to Sam and Tommy, "I'm going to be straight with you, Tommy. You're pretty much out of options. You blow this deal, and you're probably going to face some serious time. I'm not going to bat for you anymore."

Sam turned to Tommy in desperation, "Son, the judge called the prosecutor and me into his chamber yesterday afternoon. We had a very short, but serious conversation. This is your last chance." She turned to Benny, "I'm sorry, but I'm going to ask the judge to replace you."

A number of brilliant insults raced to the tip of Benny's tongue, but he was smart enough and wise enough to swallow them, along with his battered pride. Without a word, the overly inflated ego nodded and departed the room without a word.

Deputy Karr and Cal stepped closer to the bed as Sam sat on the edge on the other side. She shook her head, "Deputy Karr, I'm really sorry about that, and for the other day. I'm just...."

"You don't owe me any apologies," Deputy Karr said, but deep down he really appreciated her strength and character to do so in front of her son and Cal.

Sam shifted her attention to Cal, "And I'm really sorry for the way I treated you that day too. How's your head?"

Cal smiled, "Thanks. I understood you were under a lot of pressure at the time." He touched the back of his head, "No pain the last few days. But no memories either. Doctor told me there's a fifty-fifty chance I'll never regain a single memory."

"Look at him, son," Sam pointed.

Tommy reluctantly turned his head toward Cal, but it was impossible for him to look into Cal's eyes.

"Deputy Karr told me on the drive to the hospital that you face your own fifty-fifty possibility," Cal relayed.

Tommy turned to his mother, "Momma this meeting was supposed to be between you, me, and my attorney."

"Honey," Sam pointed to Cal, "Mr. Baxter's agreed to not press charges."

Cal spoke up, "Tommy, your mother's right about the charges, but I was referring to you may never be able to walk without a cane or walker."

Tommy became angry and found the nerve to face Cal, "Guess that makes you happy. Serves me right for whacking you in the back of the head."

"If your attorney would've stayed here, and on the case until he was replaced, he would've probably advised you to not make such incriminating statements," Deputy Karr warned.

"Mom just said he's not going to press charges, and he's even asked the judge to drop all state charges. Heck, he can't even remember. Bet you've already told him what you think I did."

Cal made quick eye contact with Sam and Deputy Karr, who nodded for him to speak. Cal had made up his mind what he should say, "Son, I...."

Tommy angrily pointed his index finger at Cal, "You ain't my father," he barked.

Sam launched from the bed and lifted her hands in disgust, "Tommy, for your own good, will you please shut your mouth and open your ears! You need to listen and comprehend, instead of hear and immediately react."

Tommy drew a deep breath and forcefully exhaled in total frustration. But he did keep his mouth shut.

"Okay, I'm not your father," Cal admitted. "Wasn't trying to be. But let me get said what I wanted to say. Yeah, they told something along the line of what you just confessed to, but I don't have any memories of you. So as far as I'm concerned, what happened was between you and another man, who may no longer exist."

Tommy turned to Sam with an arrogant smirk, "I think I

hit him a little too hard."

"That's it," Sam stormed toward the door. "I gotta get out'a here for a while."

Deputy Karr held up his hand, "Sam, hold on a sec." He turned a stern glare at Tommy, "If your mother walks out on you now, we're gonna follow her." He paused to allow Tommy to grasp the seriousness of the moment. "We'll be out the door behind her, and you'll end up in jail."

A gentle knock on the door broke the tense silence. The door slowly opened and a young Male Orderly pulled a wheelchair as he backed into the room, "Mr. Forrester, it's time for your physical assessment."

Tommy turned concerned eyes to Sam and she clarified, "Dr. Roberts wants to run a series of dexterity tests."

Tommy forcefully pushed the sheet down and quickly sat up. He forgot he only wore the tie-in-the-back hospital gown, "Let's do it. I'm ready to get out'a here." Tommy said as he spun and slung his legs over the edge of the bed as the Male Orderly rolled the chair into position.

"Woooh! Slow down there, chief," the Male Orderly became alarmed and reached for Tommy.

It was too late. As soon as Tommy's feet hit the floor and his weight transferred, he wobbled and crashed back on the bed.

"Oh, my gosh. I think I'm gonna get sick. My head is spinning," Tommy moaned.

Sam shook her head and was totally unsympathetic as she strode to the cabinet, opened the narrow door and removed a pair of light blue pajamas. She walked over to the bed and laid them across Tommy's stomach, "While you're down there."

"Mom, will you give me a hand with these?" Tommy finally made an attempt to sound the slightest bit contrite.

Sam motioned to Cal and Deputy Karr to follow her into the hall, "Ask the Orderly to help you. You don't seem to really want or need our help for anything that really matters."

Out in the hall Sam looked Heavenward, "Lord, give me strength."

"What do you want us to do, Sam?" Deputy Karr asked.

Sam turned her eyes back to Cal. Her tone and intent was informative, "He didn't know how bad he's hurt."

"I'm really sorry, Sam. This whole stupid idea was mine, and I'm afraid all I've managed to do is waste everybody's time," Deputy Karr confessed.

"Well, you convinced me, and I was willing to give it a try," Cal admitted.

Sam was sincere, "I really appreciate both of you wanting to help Tommy. But I think it's about time I accept the truth. He's never gonna change. I'm afraid it's better for him to know what he's actually facing. And the sooner the better. My heart, and my nerves can't take it any longer. I am not going to protect him any longer."

Deputy Karr looked at his watch, "I gotta get back on duty."

"I'd like to stay a while longer," Cal unexpectedly requested.

Deputy Karr turned to Sam who was caught off guard but quickly recovered. She answered but wasn't sure she meant what she said, "I can take you back. I need to leave in a couple of hours."

Deputy Karr smiled. Sam was single. Cal was single, and they had a mutual interest in her son, as problematic as that would probably be. They just might slip into a relationship that could lessen his interest in Betsy. It was silly, down right foolish to entertain such a thought, but desperate times require desperate measures. The lawman wasn't sure how much his jealousy of Cal's appeal to Betsy played in the development of his harebrained scheme. He felt guilty he even entertained such a thought, because he really wanted to help Tommy and was sure Cal did as well.

A half hour later, Sam and Cal were concerned as they sat in chairs along the back wall in the therapy room. They watched as the beautiful Asian female therapist put Tommy through a series of dexterity and balance evaluation tests, none of which went well. Tommy's frustration intensified. In large part because his mother dared to sit with the enemy. The man Tommy could've accidentally killed when he and Megan stole his truck. The preacher claimed he wanted to help him, but Tommy was suspicious. Megan was the only person, other than his Mom who ever really cared about him.

The Asian therapist's name was Adia. She was young and her dark tan highlighted her flawless skin against the light blue scrubs. To say the least, Adia had definitely captured Tommy's attention. He soon became more intent on impressing her than being angry at his mother and the unwanted, intrusive preacher.

They had just wrapped up the least stressful challenge in Tommy's overall evaluation, especially since he was able to remain seated in the wheelchair.

Tommy was already grumpy because his vision was a bit fuzzy and his depth perception was lousy. Simple hand-eye coordination and basic dexterity tests with both the left and right hands hadn't gone well. The next series of tests would physically challenge Tommy.

Tommy's poor performance in the preliminary test didn't bode well. Adia and her male associate, Miguel, who was in his second day on the job, didn't look forward to what lay ahead. However, Miguel had been successful with his overt flirtatious behavior directed at Adia. She was definitely interested and did her part to encourage more, which annoyed Tommy to no end.

Sam and Cal were close enough to be privy to the little drama as it played out before them.

Sam chuckled, "At least I know his mind can be taken off that evil Megan, at least for a little while." Sam was hopeful.

"So, she's bad news," Cal was more than casually interested.

"Only on an epic scale."

"Is she coming to see Tommy?"

"I've been here most of every day since the accident and I haven't seen her yet. Hope she's fled the state and never comes back."

Even though Adia was receptive to every one of Miguel's overt cues, they remained extremely professional and didn't miss a beat during their evaluation.

"Okay, Tommy," Adia was required to explain every move before her patient was to attempt to execute. "I'm going to be right beside you, and Miguel will keep the chair behind you, so we gotcha covered. Okay?"

Tommy nodded.

"I understand you're having trouble standing. Keeping your balance?"

"Yes, Ma'am," Tommy dreaded the thought he was about

to embarrass himself in front of such a pretty girl.

"Well, let's give it a go. I'm going to put my arm under your right armpit, and Miguel will help on the left. We'll assist you to stand up. Then, let's see how that goes."

Tommy could feel Adia and Miguel assist him up, but he panicked when Adia said, "Okay, we're going to ease off on the pressure and let's see what happens," Adia warned. "But don't worry, we're each holding on to the wheelchair."

"And we have the brakes locked," Miguel promised.

Everything was fine until Tommy was forced to shift his weight from left foot, to right foot, to maintain his balance. He panicked because he couldn't find the balance point. His body had always functioned on autopilot, but suddenly the autopilot was switched off. As soon as he was forced to maintain his balance on his own, he became dizzy and almost sick to his stomach. His knees collapsed before he could warn the therapists. Fortunately, they were pros and even though Miguel had to make some quick adjustments, Tommy safely landed in the right spot on the seat of the wheelchair.

"Not exactly what we were hoping for," Adia lamented.

Sam turned to Cal, "Sure you wanna get caught up in this mess?"

Cal was already caught up in "this mess" but his face and eyes revealed his heartfelt concern, and unexpected compassion. He witnessed a tragic, real-life drama unfold. Such a vital young man with so much of his life yet to live, may be forced to experience it from the restrictive perspective of a wheelchair. The Universal Law of Cause and Effect, or as some referred to it as the "iron law of the universe," had mercilessly injected its premise in two once unrelated lives. There was no doubt Tommy's decisions were the direct cause of the negative effects to his and Cal's existence. Tommy's bad decisions inflicted limitations they could be forced to deal with, but never fully overcome. One thing was certain, Cal felt zero satisfaction. The young man struggled in vain to even stand on his own.

"Not exactly sure what I want to be sure of," Cal admitted. "But I've got some serious thinking to do, and some serious decisions to make."

......

## 22
## When God Communicates, It's Often Without Words

The narrow space was dark and dank. It wreaked of stale, trapped air. A bright flashlight beam illuminated the bottom side of the wooden floor. Insulation wasn't widely used in rural 1900 era construction. A hammer and some purposeful taps confirmed the hearty "thunk" of solid oak beams. More than likely the subfloor would remain reliable for another hundred years, or more.

Amazingly, the mix of brick and stone pillars on which the subfloor rested were intact and remained sound. Whoever had laid out and dug the foundation knew what they were doing. There were no cracks or signs of sinkage. The substructure was out of place under a building that from the outside appeared unworthy of renovation. Based on the exterior, this foundation should've been riddled with rot and decay.

There was a lot to be said and considered in regard to the strength and integrity of a solid, well anchored foundation. That was what drove Cal under the abandoned church. He had to see for himself.

At some point in his previous life, as a pastor, a supposed man of God, he must've stood confidently on a solid foundation. There had to have been a driving force that motivated him to take on the awesome challenge to lead a body of believers.

As Cal crawled on his belly in the putrid air, he experienced a sobering revelation. He inched his way toward the brilliant light that poured in from the exit. The light ahead was a promise of hope. Once he emerged from this dark and dreary place, he would once again be in the beautiful world God had created for mankind. It was outside of his current self-induced journey into a place unfit for human existence.

Cal paused halfway to freedom. He was overwhelmed. A

power beyond his grasp permeated the interior of this long since abandoned church. A power that could only emanate from a superior being, but more importantly, could only be understood and accessed by a willing and humble human soul.

Cal's amnesia had been forced on him, and justifiably or not, his apparent strife and war with God was his to continue, or seek peace. At that point Cal was far from tossing his hands in the air and shouting, "Hallelujah, amen, let the healing begin," but at least he accepted that option might be viable.

As Cal resumed his crawl out of the darkness, he realized the moment the epiphany occurred, a couple of hours earlier when his heart broke as he witnessed Tommy struggle to stand on his own. It was impossible, but sadly, the young man, due to his own folly, caused an accident from which he may never fully recover.

On the other hand, Cal had to consider if he ever wanted to fully recover his memory. Or, if it would be best for him to start all over?

Mutt sat patiently outside the crawl-space door, seemingly befuddled by the noises Cal made as he dragged his body toward the exit. Mutt had eagerly followed Cal under the church, but after a few sniffs of the foul air, he backtracked and opted to wait outside, where the scents were more to his liking.

After what seemed forever, the shifting bright beam from the flashlight blended into the light of day. Shortly thereafter Cal's dusty head and shoulders emerged through the opening. Mutt's little tail switched to wag mode. The excited pup demanded attention before Cal could fully extract himself from under the old church.

Mutt followed Cal as he walked around the exterior of the rundown structure to make one more visual inspection. The paint was cracked and much of it had fallen off, and the exposed planks had weathered gray; but they hadn't cracked and split.

Inside, Cal studied the ceiling. For the steeple to have been ripped off by a tornado a few years ago, there appeared to be no water leaks in the ceiling. The most logical assumption was the original roof was constructed without a steeple, and when one was added later, it was attached over the shingles. The jagged edges of the remaining steeple base were easily misleading. It would've been logical that rain water poured into the church.

Cal walked the length of each row and checked the integrity of each pew. He sat on and leaned back against each pew at multiple locations. It appeared that all they really needed was a thorough cleaning and healthy coating of polish.

......

Megan got up that morning and decided as guilty as she felt about Tommy's accident, the best she could determine, even though she couldn't get any details, Tommy was still alive. Her decision, she would keep drinking and stay as numb as she could, and still manage to function.

One of two things would eventually happen, and at that point either would be okay. She would either drink herself to death, or she would finally forgive herself and seek help. That conclusion led to another long gulp of bourbon.

......

The bell on the door rang as Cal entered. He managed to pat most of the dust and grime off the uniform he had quickly become accustomed to wear, but he still looked rough.

Betsy paused when she first saw Cal. What a dramatic transformation in such a short time. He'd gone from a dashing man who could've been a movie star, a doctor, or bank president in casual clothing, to an average man who worked with his hands for a living. But to her, he was still as handsome. She was amazed at how easily people judged at first glance. Herself included. She wondered if she would've seen the same handsome man had Cal first walked into the diner dressed like that, and as grungy as he was at that moment?

Instead of heading to his booth, Cal walked over and plopped down on a stool at the bar. He'd learned the best times to visit Betsy when she would have a few minutes. As she approached it was obvious by her smirk she had something to say, "What can I get for you, a cup of coffee, or a towel and bar of soap?"

Cal nodded and grinned. He got it, and he took it in the way she hoped he would, "Both."

"Are you hungry?"

"I should be, but I'm not. I've spent the last hour under and all the way through the church," Cal explained.

"And?"

"My vote, we refurbish the building and see if we can find a picture we can use to build a replacement steeple."

"Then what?"

"I'm not sure. Sell it, or rent it to a group that wants to start a church. Turn it into a museum. I don't know. But one thing I'm sure of, it would've been a travesty if it had been burned down."

"Where's your little side-kick?"

"In the car, sound asleep. I'm going to run by the shop and tell Charlie I'm heading up to Archdale, to do some banking stuff."

Betsy's head dipped, "Like that?"

Cal looked at his dirty arms and dusty uniform, "What's wrong with the way I look? I earned it honestly."

Betsy reached under the bar and pulled out a fresh towel she used to wipe down the tables, "Here. There's soap in the bathroom. At least wash up your face, arms and hands. Other than that, as far as I'm concerned, you're ready to go to the bank."

"Okay, Momma."

Betsy tossed the towel on Cal's head. "Go wash up, or I'll put you in time out."

After Cal removed the towel from his head, he and Betsy looked into each other's eyes. They seemed to reach a mutual agreement; they should relax around each other. They could be friends. Whatever might develop later would happen on its own. In the short term, they and Charlie had a mission to accomplish. There was a building to give new life, and with the interruption of a puppy bark, a rambunctious canine to keep out of trouble.

"Seems somebody's hungry," Betsy said with a chuckle.

"He even dreams about eating."

"You, go clean up and I'll put a snack together for you boys to eat on the drive up."

# RETURN TO FAITH

Twenty minutes later the orange Judge cruised up I-85 with a man and his dog who enjoyed their scrumptious snacks. Once Mutt had devoured his, he assumed his favored position of paws on the armrest and nose toward the opened window. His little sniffer worked overtime.

"Hey you," Cal spoke sternly, which garnered Mutt's attention, so he dropped down and stepped to the side of the seat. Cal pointed his finger, "No more jumping out the windows, not even with the car is sitting still."

Cal figured Mutt didn't understand the words, or know what he meant; but the way his little head lowered, he knew he'd done something wrong. He sat in silence and wouldn't look up until Cal spoke again. This time with his normal tone that Mutt was accustomed, "Okay, put your sniffer back to work."

For the rest of the drive Mutt would sniff for a while, drop back down and rest in the seat, or want Cal to pet him, then repeat. As soon as they stopped at the top of the off ramp, Mutt leapt up and resumed the sniffer position. The air was thick with brand new scents.

Mutt's nose was in high gear when the orange Judge pulled into the bank parking lot. Cal leaned over the passenger seat, which Mutt reasoned was to be licked, but it was to hand crank the wind up enough that the curious pup couldn't escape.

"You stay here. I'll be back shortly."

Like all dogs who realized they were about to be left alone, Mutt turned his best "poor pitiful me" face to Cal.

Cal shook it off, "Not gonna work, Bud."

Cal had to glance back as he walked toward the door of the bank. Sure enough he saw the tip of Mutt's nose appear then vanish as he hopped up and down in the seat.

One of the things Cal had yet to grasp was that he had gone without a cell phone since Megan and Tommy stole his truck. Then once inside the bank, he realized that he didn't recognize a single face. He knew that was his bank because it was the only branch in Archdale.

He was certain that was the bank because Sadie Jenkins told him that he'd long since switched his personal banking to the same bank that had Tabernacle Baptist Church's accounts. He should've dropped by the day Deputy Karr brought him to town. At least he would know who to talk with. He stood just inside the door and was ready to step over and introduce himself and ask who he would need to speak with to start a new account. Then he heard his name and the question from across the room, in a strong Southern Accent.

"Good afternoon, Reverend Baxter, how can we help you today?" Ms. Randell, the Branch Manager waved from the door of her office. She had no idea that Cal had been in an accident. He'd stopped wearing the bandage on the back of his head the day before.

Cal made his way over and shook the awaiting hand from the cute, full-figured woman in her forties.

"How are you doing on this awesome Spring day?" Ms. Randell inquired.

Cal nodded, "Doing well. Hope you are as well?"

"Lovely, and tonight my wonderful husband is taking me to dinner to celebrate our twenty-fifth wedding anniversary."

"Congratulations," Cal smiled, but realized immediately he didn't respond in the manner she anticipated. An uneasy moment of silence followed, until Cal realized he probably needed to inform her, "I'm really sorry. But, I don't remember you. I've had an accident and lost a great deal of my memory. And I would prefer if you'd be so kind and call me Cal, instead of Reverend Baxter."

Ms. Randell was stunned but very understanding as she motioned for Cal to enter the office and take a seat at her desk, "Oh my, what happened?" She asked as she closed the door.

It took several minutes to explain enough for Ms. Randell to understand what happened and why he dropped in unannounced. Within fifteen minutes from the time he'd entered the bank, Ms. Randell had used the driver's license number off the photocopy Deputy Karr provided him to produce pages of statements for his multiple accounts. Then she went through the stack and explained each account and summary balance at the bottom.

"You've done very well for yourself. You've made some very sound investments. You really don't have to worry about your retirement. You'll be able to enjoy it quite well," the happy Branch Manager was also very proud. "And I'm so happy I was able to help guide you on a couple of your better yielding accounts." She really didn't have to brag, but she wanted Cal to know that if he wanted future advice, she was available. Especially since she received commissions as the branch's certified financial advisor.

Cal grinned sheepishly, "I'm impressed. We did good."

Ms. Randell chuckled, "I'd say we did awesome. You were brave enough to make some very aggressive investments that would've frightened away the average investor. But they've paid off handsomely."

Cal nodded as he quickly reviewed the summary page she handed him. It was an impressive number, "Some of that's going to come in handy. I have another bold investment I'd like to make."

"Cha Ching!" The cash register echoed in the Financial Advisor's vault of a brain. She snatched up her pen, "Are we talking stocks, bonds, mutual funds, or real estate?"

Cal nodded, "Real estate."

"Commercial property or private residential?"

"Private, non-residential."

Oooops! Obviously that was not a category rich in commissions. The consummate professional Ms. Randell had been was knocked down a significant notch, but she was still curious, "Okay. Give me some details so I can help you with the first steps."

"We're going to remodel a small church in Faith," Cal explained. "I think I want to set up an account just to handle the expenses."

"We? Are you starting a ministry?"

Cal shook his head, "I'll be working with the people who own the property. And as far as I can see, a ministry's not even a remote possibility."

"Are you going to form a 501c with these people?"

"Why?"

"For tax purposes," Ms. Randell was surprised, but more concerned Cal appeared to have made a very rash, uninformed, under-researched decision. She feared what she was about to learn would evolve into a bottomless money-pit. She assumed the decision was probably based on emotion, rather than sound logic. Worst yet, the people he worked with may have ensnared him in some kind of scam. This was so irrational, so unlike the Reverend Baxter she developed such a strong, successful, and trusted relationship with over the ten years he came to her for advice.

Cal was blunt, but very respectful, "Right now, I just want to do it. I can't explain it, and to be perfectly honest, shouldn't have to. It's my money, and no more than I plan to spend, won't even scratch the outer shell of my nest egg."

Ms. Randell wasn't comfortable with the new account, but she set it up and explained that he would receive the checks and debit card within five to seven business days.

Once the bank closed at 5:00 PM, Ms. Randell invited Cal to bring Mutt into the office, so he wouldn't have to keep going outside to check on the little fellow. Cal and Mutt eventually left the bank at 5:45 PM.

The very involved process took much longer than anticipated to complete all the required paperwork. They switched the information on all of his accounts and restarted the mailing of paper statements that would be delivered to the garage apartment.

Out in the parking lot, Cal walked Ms. Randell to her car and extended his hand, which she readily accepted, "I'm so sorry to have been so difficult today," Cal was sincere.

"We've known each other too long for that kind of apology. I'm here to help you in any way I can."

"Even though you disagree?"

"Even though I may strongly, and urgently disagree, as long as everything you want to do is legal, and ethical," Ms. Randell assured.

"Even if you deem it foolish?"

That question was harder for her to answer. She slowly, reluctantly shook her head, "Even if I have to hold my nose."

......

During the return to Faith that evening Cal wanted to call Charlie and invite him to the diner, so he could treat him and Betsy to dinner. They had a great deal to talk about. There was one minor issue. He should've gone to the Verizon store before he left the High Point area. That wasn't amnesia's fault, that one was on him.

Cal went straight to the diner and Betsy called Charlie to come over for dinner. Charlie and Cal could talk for a while, then they could go into more detail after she closed for the evening.

First thing Charlie wanted to do was talk about the truck restoration. He'd come across another parts supplier they might need to call on.

"Yeah, I'm glad you brought that up," Cal smiled, "I can pay for the parts, and I'll be glad to pay you what you paid for the truck."

Charlie was caught off guard, "Who asked you to pay anything?"

"Nobody. I just discovered I'm in pretty good financial shape, and if I'm gonna own the truck after it's finished, I want to pay for the parts and outside sourcing we need."

"I'm not even going to whisper any disagreement, except for paying me for the pile of junk I brought to the table. We're gonna turn it into a work of art, but I'm going to donate the unassembled parts," Charlie extended his hand, "Deal?"

Cal smiled and shook Charlie's hand, "Fair enough."

After Betsy locked the doors, the boys pitched in and helped her with enough of the side work so she could spend some time with them to discuss the old church. Cal had never heard the term "side work," things like roll the spoons, knives and forks in napkins, refill salt and pepper shakers, and wipe down certain items that must be cleaned every day. Betsy was very appreciative and brought her helpers a cup of coffee, and a fat slice of her famous pecan pie.

"Ooohh, now that's what I'm talk'n bout," Charlie rubbed his squeaky clean hands together, "Let me at that beautiful thing." He used his fork to sever an oversized hunk, "Come to papa," he added as he opened his mouth wide and stuffed the sweet treat in.

Betsy shook her head, "You're an animal." Then she pointed to Cal, "And you're insane." She sat in silence for a few seconds, "You actually transferred money into a special account."

Charlie lifted his fork and used it as a pointer. His mouth was still full of delectable goodness, "You should've waited and let us talk about it."

Betsy playfully swatted her little brother on the shoulder, "Don't talk with your mouth full. I taught you better than that." Then she turned her attention back to Cal, "You're probably not going to start on the church until you finish your new truck. Right?"

Charlie nodded as he chewed, then swallowed, "Yeah, and there's only two of us, which equals four hands."

"What if I could get each one of us another hand?"

Charlie looked over at Betsy with a mischievous grin.

"Don't you dare," Betsy warned, then she quickly faced Cal. "Don't encourage this juvenile delinquent."

"On the drive back from Archdale, I was thinking, if we can get one more full-time helper on the truck, I can break away and start some of the preliminary steps at the church," Cal shared.

Betsy and Charlie sat in silence. They really tried but couldn't think of a single fault in Cal's logic until Betsy asked, "Who you got in mind to be your helper?"

Cal was confused, "Tommy. We already agreed with the judge and prosecutor."

Betsy and Charlie exchanged uncomfortable glances, "We've been talking about that ever since Charlie agreed," Betsy began.

"Yeah, Bet and I think it's a great idea; but we doubt even if he agrees, more than likely he won't show up," Charlie shook his head.

"And even if he does show up, he won't last long," Betsy tried to grin. "I'm sorry we're such Debbie Downers."

Cal sat back and remained silent but deep in thought. Betsy and Charlie glanced at each other and opted to remain silent. After a few seconds, Cal nodded, leaned forward, rested his elbows on the table and rested his chin in his palms. "Please hear me out," he requested before he drew in a slow, deep breath, "Today didn't go well."

Betsy nodded, "We know. Andy, that's Deputy Karr, stopped by and visited both of us."

"I don't think you'll mind he did that." Charlie implied.

Cal had to regroup, "That'll save me some time."

"That's what we want you to consider...." Betsy started until Cal lifted his hand.

"I wasn't finished. On the surface, this sounds as foolish to me as I'm sure it will to you." Cal could tell both Betsy and Charlie were about to burst to tell him to not waste his and

# RETURN TO FAITH

their time, but like the true friends they had become, they remained respectfully quiet, and genuinely attentive. So he continued, "Deputy Karr left before Tommy went into therapy. And I believe that for the first time in his life, Tommy was forced to come face to face with the ugly reality of who and what he has become, and where he's headed at the speed of light."

At that moment, Cal's sincerity touched Betsy much deeper than she'd ever been reached. There was so much more to Cal than she allowed herself to imagine.

"Perhaps the former preacher I'm still fighting so hard to keep repressed is fighting back, determined to reemerge. Because I saw in Tommy a young man who wants so badly to get back to normal, but he's terrified he will go back to the same guy that whacked me on the head and stole my truck."

Charlie and Betsy were glad they decided to hear Cal out, and not try to talk him out of something that would be worthwhile, if they could pull it off.

"I'm not going to paint a beautiful sunset, I know at best we have a fifty-fifty chance this'll blow up in our faces. But I'll never forgive myself if I don't at least try." He added, then leaned back.

Charlie spoke up, "You finished now?"

Cal nodded. There was so much more he could say, but he'd probably already said way too much.

"Okay," Charlie glanced at Betsy then turned back to Cal, "Since we're being honest, I believe this will become a colossal waste of time. I'm convinced Tommy won't last a week. But out of respect for you, and the long-term friendship we're building, I'll support you. And I promise to do my best not to say, 'I told you so,' even after I'm justified to take that strut."

Cal smiled victoriously as he leaned forward, "Now, here's the kicker. The moment I realized Tommy, even as the damaged, and severely flawed human he's become, he's worth the effort. To his credit, he helped me see that old, worthless church is worth restoring to its original glory." Cal said as he smiled with great satisfaction, "And when we accomplish both, I'll do my best not to gloat and strut when I say, 'I told you so.'"

......

## OTIS FARMER

Early the next morning, the room was dim. Tommy's eyes were closed. He appeared to be in fitful sleep. His head was still bandaged. There was a significant sign trouble brewed; his mother was not in the room. In fact, the night before, she left before 9:00 PM.

There was a light knock on the door, but Tommy didn't respond, or even react. A few seconds later the door slowly opened. Cal cautiously entered, quietly crossed the room, then sat in the chair beside Tommy's bed. He studied the troubled lad as he slept.

A few moments later, Tommy awakened and looked around as if to confirm he was still in the hospital. When he realized he had an uninvited visitor, he sat up, and became noticeably hostile, "What do you want?"

Cal remained silent as if Tommy hadn't said the right thing or asked the right question.

"You come here for an apology? Want me to say I'm sorry for whacking you on the head - stealing your old truck?"

Cal remained stoic and studied Tommy's body language.

Tommy turned away in an overt show of contempt for his unwanted guest, "Don't hold your breath, preacher man. I'll do the time."

Cal remained silent.

"You preachers, Sunday School teachers are all the same. Try'n to shame folks, make us feel stupid, and you play on our guilt, so we'll keep giving you money."

Cal was very calculated. It was time to test the waters and speak, "I'm not the same man you 'whacked' on the head. In fact, I wasn't even a preacher when you tried to kill me."

Tommy refused to look at Cal, "I didn't try to kill you. If I did, you'd be dead."

"You may actually have done me a huge favor."

"So, I knocked some sense into your thick skull?" Tommy was confused, but very reluctant to turn and face Cal, "We've already had this conversation, and I'm not in the mood for riddles and mind games, preacher man."

"You need to keep up, young man," Cal had to show strength and stand strong against his adversary. Push his buttons. "You seem to think it's an insult to call me, preacher man."

# RETURN TO FAITH

Tommy turned to face Cal, "Then you're not try'n to save my miserable soul from Hell's Fire?"

Cal was careful, but honest, "Not sure what I believe. I'm still sorting out the whole God thing."

Tommy chuckled, "Ain't this rich? I knock a preacher man on the head, steal his truck, now he's thanking me for helping him see the light. But that light ain't com'n from his god."

"Let me be perfectly clear, I'm not thanking you for anything. You committed a few serious crimes. I could've died, and you could've been charged with First Degree Murder. The prosecutor might've even gone after the death penalty. Right now, you're just facing Attempted Murder and vehicular theft, along with assorted lesser charges."

Tommy abruptly turned away, "You've cheered me up enough for one day. You can go now."

Cal remained defiant, seated and silent.

The longer Cal sat there the more it agitated Tommy, "I'm gonna call the nurse and have her kick you out."

Cal didn't flinch.

"What do you want from me?"

Cal dared to crack a grin, "Maybe it's time for both of us to make a fresh start."

"Even if I wanted to start over, you wouldn't be involved."

Cal was satisfied. That was a good start. Tommy definitely had given serious thought to a change of lifestyle. "Fair enough. It's your choice. I can and will respect that," Cal rose and walked toward the door, which revealed the bald spot that was shaved around his injury.

Most unexpectedly, and unable to hold it in, Tommy revealed a crack in his "Bad Boy" facade, "How's your head?"

Cal paused and to conceal his satisfied grin, he continued to face the door, "As you can see, it's healing very nicely."

Tommy scrambled to reassert his perceived control of the situation, "Good. You can go now."

......

## 23
## Do The Right Thing, Even If It Feels Wrong

Cal and Betsy sat in his booth along the outer wall. It was the first time Betsy sat beside Cal. They sipped cups of coffee while Betsy instructed him on how to navigate her iPad.

"Bout time you joined the Twenty-First Century. Now, what do you want to search?"

"Service dog best suited for someone with a balance issue."

Betsy couldn't believe her ears, "You're kidding me, right?"

Cal sipped coffee and refused to offer a feeble attempt to answer.

"Thought you told Tommy you respected his desire that you leave him alone?"

A slight nod was all Cal offered.

"Well, then what's this all about?"

"I did promise to respect it, not to honor it," Cal flashed a sly smile.

Betsy grinned and shook her head, "I'm going to have to watch what I say around you." She quipped as she typed. A few seconds later several links appeared on the screen and she selected the one at the top, "Well, well, well. Golden Retriever's at the top."

Cal and Betsy looked at each other, "You said…." Cal began.

"Yeah, I said Sheena had to have been some kind of a service dog," Betsy assured.

"How many puppies you have left?"

Betsy smiled, "Gave the last one away yesterday. And bless her heart, this morning she got up and roamed through the house, like she was looking for at least one of her babies. When I left, she was laying on my back porch, just gazing into the distance. I think her heart is broken."

# RETURN TO FAITH

"She still wants to be a mother," Cal assumed.

After Betsy closed for the evening, she and Sheena paid a visit to Cal's apartment. They were on a mission.

It was impossible to tell which one was happier to see the other. Mother, or one of her rambunctious baby boys. From the moment they saw the other the wrestling commenced and was still in action as Betsy and Cal attempted to talk over the WWE World Championship Dog title match that took place between them.

Finally Cal raised his voice and asked, "Did you get it?"

Betsy cupped her hands around her mouth, "Yeah. It's in the trunk."

"Has she seen it yet?"

Betsy rose, "She's about to."

While Betsy was downstairs, Cal was entertained by the adorable tussle until Betsy appeared at the top of the steps carrying a walk-assist harness.

"Sheena," Betsy calmly said as she held the harness where Sheena could see it. Play time ceased and confused Mutt, who turned to the rude human who dared to interrupt. Immediately, Sheena's demeanor changed. There was no doubt she recognized what Betsy held. Cal was curious and slid forward to the edge of his chair.

Betsy was calm and deliberate, very business like, "Come here, girl."

Sheena looked down at Mutt, who took the cue and dropped down. He excitedly wiggled, ready to pounce, but Momma had transformed before his eyes. He was confused as his Momma walked away and toward a human with an odd contraption in her hand. Mutt sprang up and followed. He jumped up and nipped at his mother's fur in an effort to provoke another round of raucous play. She ignored him.

"She knows exactly what that is," Cal smiled as he mused.

"She sure does," Betsy lowered the harness for Sheena to sniff and inspect, before she looked up as if to ask, "Am I going to work?"

"Yes, Sheena. You're going to work," Betsy confirmed as she patted her right thigh. Sheena dutifully walked around and assumed the ready position on Betsy's right side.

Mutt was persistent but unsuccessful in his attempts to draw his Momma back into play mode. She simply ignored him as Betsy placed the harness on Sheena's back.

"You seem to know what you're doing," Cal was impressed.

"I've got skills beyond the kitchen," Betsy suggested.

"Have you worked with service dogs?"

Betsy paused and appeared reluctant to answer.

"That's alright. It's not important."

Betsy straightened up and looked at Cal, "Yes, it is. Actually, it's very important. My ex-husband used to train people to work with service dogs. And let's just say he checked his compassion for people at the door when he got home every evening." She explained, then quickly added as if she were embarrassed, "Maybe I should'a kept that to myself."

That came so far out of left field Cal didn't know what to say, or even how to react. His pastoral instincts had abandoned him years before the whack on his head stole his memories.

"I'm so sorry." Betsy felt really foolish, and worried if in defense of future standoffish behavior, she just fired a warning shot across Cal's bow. Did she just declare, stay back Buddy, this target is out of range? The lighthearted and expectant atmosphere instantly morphed into an uneasy silence, where two adults, with major issues, suddenly let those issues seize control.

As if by Divine intervention, Mutt leapt to the rescue when Betsy paused. He was ready to play again when Betsy no longer focused on the gadget she'd put on his Momma's back. How was he to know it wasn't play time again? He excitedly barked and resumed the nip and tug on his Momma's fur, but to no avail.

"Mutt, come here, boy," Cal attempted to distract the insistent puppy, but it took a couple of tries before the furry ball of energy abandoned his disinterested Momma. He charged to what he was sure would be a fierce tussle with Cal.

Betsy straightened up after she was satisfied the harness was snug but not too tight around Sheena, "Let's see how she reacts," Betsy suggested as she pointed to Cal in the recliner. "Go help him up, Girl." Sheena looked up at Betsy to confirm the command. "Go on, Girl. Help him up."

Sheena walked over and positioned herself beside the

recliner. Bless his little heart, Mutt thought Momma was ready to play again, but she ignored his pleas for attention.

Betsy lowered to her knees, "Come here, Little Buddy."

Mutt was overwhelmed with potential playmates, but was so confused as to which one was serious and was ready to satisfy his desire to "go at it with purpose." He just stood there, not sure what to do.

Betsy spoke as if to a child, "Come here, Little Buddy."

Too charged up to stand still for long, and too easily bored by inactivity, Mutt charged and leapt into Betsy's arms.

The experiment with Sheena was a success. They hooked Mutt up to a spring-loaded leash and took the dogs for a long walk. It was impossible to know how long it had been since Sheena was in harness and at work. She had no problem making the adjustment.

On the walk away from the apartment Betsy suggested Cal keep Sheena through the weekend and work with her in harness. That would include taking her to the shop on Thursday and Friday. Cal agreed.

On the walk back, Mutt was enthralled with the new sights, sounds, and the endless scents to sniff. Sheena was in full "on-duty mode." Since it was dark, she was even more aware of her surroundings and made sure the lay of the land was suitable for her partner.

Betsy and Cal relaxed and let their guards down a bit. Regardless of how hard they fought and resisted the truth, they really did like each other's company. There was so much yet to learn about the other, and after this evening together they both hoped it would be easier to allow the other to feel free enough to open up and share.

However, there was one very important question Betsy had to ask. It was imperative to know where she stood, at the outset of this new journey, "Your second wife or girlfriend gonna have a problem with you hanging out with two single women?"

Cal chuckled because that was the last question he expected to hear that evening. He didn't remember that before he lost his memory, he rarely discussed his past with many people. He didn't have any "go to" answers. One thing he was sure of, "I'm certain Sadie Jenkins would've known if I got remarried, or had a girlfriend."

That didn't really answer Betsy's question, "And?"

Cal chuckled, "And she didn't mention either when I was in Archdale."

The reason Sadie came so quickly to mind, after Cal left the bank in Archdale, he paid a brief, surprise visit to Sadie and Ralph Jenkins. He needed to ask a few very personal questions about Annie and Taylor. In retrospect, he wished he would've waited to ask, or better yet never have asked. He drove away with a greater understanding of why after he lost so much of his memory. It was still difficult to reconnect with how and why he ever had faith in a God, who would allow such an awful thing to happen.

Fortunately, on the drive back to Faith for the highly anticipated meeting with Betsy and Charlie, Cal managed to bury the painful truth in the deep shadows of his mind. Until Betsy's seemingly innocent question flipped on a powerful spotlight. He spoke before he fully framed his thoughts, "From what Sadie told me, I haven't dated since I killed my wife and daughter." He immediately realized that was the absolute worst way to state the facts. He just exposed the unvarnished truth. Betsy was sharp and she would not miss the blatant reality - Cal loathed himself for the deed he would never forgive himself. He just revealed he was a man with an extremely fragile psyche. How would Betsy handle that golden nugget?

Once again, Mutt to the rescue. The easily bored puppy had stood still long enough. He hopped up to put his front paws on Betsy's leg.

"Looks like someone is ready to get back upstairs," Betsy suggested.

"I'm sure he's ready to eat again."

Betsy's cell phone rang and nearly scared the life out of her, and startled Cal. It was Charlie.

"Where are you guys?" Charlie sounded reluctant to ask.

"We took the dogs for a walk."

"I came over to see how things are going, and couldn't get anyone to the door. You know me, I didn't, well, didn't know…"

"Put a dirty sock in your dirty mouth to match your dirty mind," Betsy quipped.

"Well, a, well I didn't want to…"

"We're just down the road and almost back."

"He has a key. Tell him to let himself in and go on up," Cal suggested.

"Just got out of the shower, so I'm squeaky clean. So I can sit on the furniture," Charlie was his usual self.

Once upstairs, Sheena was happy to be out of the harness, but Mutt was confused that suddenly his Momma paid attention to him again.

Betsy, Charlie, and Cal had a great conversation about the first steps in the church renovation project. Cal would write up a rough punch-list for the first couple of weeks. Then they would sit down and establish a long-range plan.

"Now, let's talk about Monday," Betsy took charge. "Since I'm closed all day, I'm available early."

Charlie shook his head, "I'm sorry to be 'Negative Ned,' again, but I don't see Tommy following through on this one. Even if he agrees with the judge's deal. Just to keep out of jail for a while. I just don't see this new plot happening."

Betsy and Charlie turned their attention to Cal and waited for his thoughts. He knew both of them were very skeptical and held out little to no hope for a positive, long-term outcome with Tommy.

"I have to believe something good will come from our efforts," Cal encouraged.

"Spoken like a true preacher man," Charlie jabbed.

Cal was polite, but direct, "I don't think I'll ever be comfortable being called that again."

Message sent. Message received.

.......

Early the next morning, long before his alarm was set to go off, Cal was awakened by the playful growl and tumble fest at the foot of his bed.

"Oh, great. The kids are up," Cal mumbled.

It was the same on Friday, Saturday, Sunday, and Monday mornings. Thank goodness. If things went well, Sheena would have a new home before the day was out. It would take Mutt a few days to once again learn how to exist without his Momma around.

Betsy was right on time and in the kitchen where she whipped up an amazing batch of her famous scrambled eggs, along with freshly cut bacon, and equally fresh ground sausage, straight from Carson's Farm. Country liv'n sure did have some awesome advantages.

An unexpected delay in Tommy's Monday therapy session forced Cal and Betsy to shift their surprise visit to the hospital until late afternoon. Betsy took the dogs to walk the lightly traveled sidewalks of Faith. It would be a good thing to familiarize Sheena to the city where she would probably spend most of her time assisting Tommy. Provided things went well at the hospital in Charlotte.

Cal opted to take Mutt to the shop and work on the truck. Charlie had his hands full with customer cars and trucks that needed immediate attention. For the next couple of weeks, Cal would mostly be solo on the project truck; that was, if things didn't go well at the hospital with Tommy.

Cal rinsed off the last remnants of grease from a few brackets that had been loosened and partially dissolved by the powerful degreaser. He placed the parts on some rags to dry. He was quite proud of his efforts. The parts looked brand new, as if fresh out of the casting sand mold. The first thing he did that morning was spray the frame with the same solution. He had to spray it twice and wait for it to dry before he repeated.

Charlie stepped up and nodded his satisfaction.

"What next?" Cal was eager.

"You're really getting into this," Charlie was impressed. "We send them to Allen's shop to be sandblasted. Then they'll go to the paint shop for a couple coats of primer, then get painted."

"You know, the more I think about it, the more I like the idea of painting the engine block matte red, instead of a gloss," Cal mused.

"Yeah, and I like your idea to paint the engine compartment flat black, instead of gloss, like we're going to paint the rest of the frame," Charlie admitted. "It'll help contrast the gloss black body paint."

Cal extended his hand to shake Charlie's, but Charlie opted to offer his fist to bump. They laughed.

"We make a great team," Charlie suggested.

Cal rolled his fingers into a fist and lightly bumped Charlie's fist, "Yep."

## RETURN TO FAITH

Charlie led Cal over and pulled the dusty tarps off the rust truck cab and bed, "Now's when our patience is about to be tested."

"So, they're gonna be real beasts?" Cal lowered his head to get a different perspective on the sad-looking body parts. There were several dents and some waves in the thickly rusted sheet metal.

Charlie chuckled as he rubbed his hand on the rough surface of the hood and created an audible scratch across the rust, "Yes, they'll be hard to tame. Gotta make'm smooth as glass since we're paint'n'm gloss black." He confirmed as he lowered his head, and looked across the hood toward the grimy windshield. "Black'll show every dip and tiny imperfection. But, then you already know that."

Cal grinned and revealed his appreciation of Charlie's attempt to jog his memory, "Wonder how long it took me to prep the first one?"

"If it was in the same shape as this one, a very long time."

......

## 24
## It's Hard To Do The Right Thing, When It Feels So Wrong

Cal called down as he stepped out of the bathroom, shaved, showered and dressed, ready for their uncertain journey. "Come on up, the door's unlocked,"

Needless to say, Cal was stunned when Betsy and Sheena reached the top step. Betsy's hair was down and styled; she was absolutely gorgeous, a freshly opened rosebud. She wore a little makeup and a light shade of lipstick. She made an amazing transformation from her usual hair up when she came over for breakfast, until it was time to head down to the hospital in Charlotte. Cal had never seen her hair down nor the light application of makeup. He just officially met the "off duty" Betsy, with the "on duty" Sheena.

Betsy struggled to hold back a satisfied grin. It was obvious her sneak attack caught Cal completely off guard. More importantly, she knew she'd blown him away. Mission accomplished.

On the drive down from Faith, Cal couldn't help himself, every few seconds he looked over to admire the results of the minimal effort Betsy invested. He was amazed how she had so easily elevated herself from beautiful to gorgeous. Cal dared to say only one thing, "I really like your hair down."

That was enough. Message sent. Message received. Betsy would wear her hair down more often. She was a little iffy about the makeup.

The door opened inside the large therapy room. The Male Orderly pushed Tommy's wheelchair inside.

Tommy immediately held up his hand and the Male Orderly stopped. Sam anticipated Tommy's reaction and opted to wait just inside the room. Tommy shook his head in disgust.

"Was this your idea?" Tommy barked at his frustrated mother.

"I just found out a few minutes ago," Sam told the truth.

"Is this why my therapy got switched?"

"Honey, I have no idea. I had to go to work this morning. I can't afford to lose my job. My Boss has already been extremely understanding," Sam was in no mood to battle her disrespectful son. "Listen," Sam paused, but Tommy was focused straight ahead, "Look at me, Tommy Forrester." Tommy finally though reluctantly rolled his eyes up. There was no doubt she was at her wits end. "Don't you embarrass me. Better yet, don't embarrass yourself. You're going to let this nice young man roll you over there. You're going to listen to what these kind people are going to offer. Then you're gonna say 'thank you,' and you're going to do your best. Got that, young man?" Sam's eyes narrowed. She meant business and expected her son to do as told. The look of contempt in Tommy's eyes warranted a stern rebuke, "Yes, you're an adult, and old enough to make your own decisions, but you've been making a lot of very bad decisions that's about to ruin my life. As long as you live under my roof, you will start doing better, or else." She paused to ensure he understood the gravity of the situation. "We'll discuss that after we get you out of the hospital."

With a nod from Sam, the Male Orderly understood who was in charge, so he didn't bother to confirm with Tommy. His embarrassed patient would just have to deal with it.

Tommy's therapists, Adia and Miguel, apologized for the unexpected schedule change and were eager to get started. They stepped back to allow Cal and Betsy to make their offer. Adia and Miguel were 100% in favor and ready to assist.

Sam followed closely behind the wheelchair. She would stay back and let Tommy stand, or rather sit on his own. He refused to acknowledge Cal and Betsy. Cal held Mutt in his lap, and Betsy was seated to his left with Sheena seated on the floor beside her, in harness, in work mode.

Sam refused to allow Tommy to be disrespectful very long, "Son, you have visitors."

It was difficult for Tommy to face Cal, and he was less than respectful, "What's this all about?"

Sam didn't have time to allow Tommy to play "Mr. Tough Guy," she stepped in front of Tommy so she could make eye contact. "We've discussed this with your doctors and they want you to try this therapy. And you will at least give it a try."

The Mother and Son stare-down didn't last long.

"Alright, but does the preacher have to be involved?"

Sam drew in a deep, frustrated breath and leaned over. She would've much rather taken Tommy aside for this conversation, but she was fed up, and had to be back at work in an hour. "Son, I'm gonna make it short and not so sweet. The other day your doctors told me odds are you would need some kind of assistance with your balance the rest of your life. One option is a service dog, but I checked and my insurance won't cover it, and I can't afford to pay it out of my pocket." She pointed to Cal, "Reverend Baxter," She caught her mistake, "I mean, Mr. Baxter and his friend, Betsy, had access to this dog. If you and the dog can work together, they're willing to give her to us."

Cal remained stoic and refused to avert his determined stare away from Tommy's increasingly rage filled eyes.

"Can't they just give us the dog, then leave us alone. I really don't want to work with him."

Sam's face flushed with a crimson mix of anger and total embarrassment. Cal had seen and heard enough. He spoke up before the humiliated mother could form some sort of apology.

"Young man, there's one thing you need to understand and get your hardhead wrapped around. The Judge and prosecutor don't care what you want." Everyone in the room was stunned by Cal's stern tone. "It's their way, or the highway straight to prison. The choice is yours to make."

Sam couldn't take it any longer. She straightened up and looked at Cal, "I'm so sorry both of you wasted your valuable time. Thank you," She stepped over and shook Cal's and Betsy's hands. "I might as well go on back to work." She turned to Tommy and it broke her heart to inform her son, "I'm gonna have to call the prosecutor's office on the drive back. Instead of being able to take you home when you're ready to be released, Deputy Karr will officially arrest you and take you to jail to await trial." She leaned over and gently took hold of Tommy's cheeks. Her hands trembled, "Son, I love you very much, but I'm sorry, you'll have to stay in jail, because I'm not going to bail you out."

"Or," Cal quickly countered, "I've already been given the

court's and your doctor's permission, to help supervise a portion of your rehabilitation."

"What'da you know about rehabilitation?"

"Tommy," Sam was ready to explode by then.

Cal spoke up, "That's a valid question." Then he grinned slyly, "We'll learn together." He suggested as he pointed to Betsy and Sheena.

Betsy was caught off guard, but couldn't help but grin like a nervous schoolgirl, who just realized a boy she really liked was actually interested in her.

"Well?" The frustrated Mother asked.

For the first time in his troubled life, Tommy realized he was in serious trouble that could lead to a very long prison sentence. But the tough guy in him was prepared to hold out a bit longer to prove how "bad" he really was, until his mother spoke up, then turned to walk out of the room.

"Who are you trying to impress, Megan?" Sam held out her arms in frustration. "Where is she, son? If they don't catch her, she'll be running around free, while you're locked up behind bars. Do you honestly think she'll wait for you?"

The look of contempt on Tommy's face suggested his mother may have gone too far, "Leave Megan out of this." His tone was borderline threatening. Fortunately, the angry son appeared to have immediate second thoughts. His tone softened, "Sorry. Mom."

That was a promising start. Her son was so rarely sorry about anything.

"Bye, Tommy," Sam walked toward the door.

It took a few tense seconds before the tough guy released Tommy's tongue, "Wait, Momma. Please stay."

A few minutes later, Sam was seated beside Cal, and Mutt sat in the chair Betsy had occupied. Sam was very emotional. She reached over and firmly grasped Cal's hand. He gently squeezed to affirm his support as the moment of truth had arrived.

Adia stood in front of Tommy while Miguel held the wheelchair in place from behind.

"Would you stand for me, please?" Adia asked as she held out her hands.

"You know I'll lose my balance."

"I'm right here," Adia assured. "We've been doing this the

last couple of days."

"And I keep losing my balance."

Miguel spoke up, "But you're able to stand longer each day."

"And you're getting a few more steps in each day."

To delay a bit longer, Tommy looked to his left where Betsy stood and smiled as she held Sheena's harness.

"I don't see how that dog's going to help me walk," Tommy said and turned to Sam. "Mom, do I really have to do this? People will make fun of me if I have to use a dog to get around."

Sam exhaled in frustration and lowered her face into cupped hands, then a couple of seconds she raised her head, "Tommy. It's this, or jail."

"Can the judge really make me do this?"

"He's not going to make you do anything. He's giving you a choice," Sam explained.

"Some choice," Tommy grumbled.

Cal decided it was time to lay it out one last time. If Tommy refused to get it, and at least be willing to try, he was done. He rose and spoke as he walked over and stood beside Sheena. His voice was incredibly calm and nonjudgmental. It was the voice and tone of a truly compassionate man who had every right, under the law, to show no compassion or forgiveness. He genuinely, from his heart, wanted to help Tommy. "You made the choice to hit me over the head. Steal my truck, with a lot of money in it. We've already talked about this - but that blow to my head erased a lot of my memory. Memories of my life I may never recover. Then you wrecked and total-lost my truck. I'll never drive it again. I'll never see that money again. And I could've died. Tell me how many of those were good choices?"

Betsy was nearly moved to tears. She doubted she could've found it in her heart to be so willing to take such a chance to help someone who had done all of that to her. She could've forgiven him, but go to the lengths Cal appeared to be committed. No way.

Cal had one more thing to say, and it may be the only concept the mixed-up young man could grasp. It was risky, and could make matters worse, but he went there, "Tommy, look at me." It took a few seconds before Tommy dared to face him. "You owe it to me to at least try. And I mean really try. Because if you turn this down, as much as I hate to, I'll turn it over to the court, and walk away from you." He paused. "Today."

Sam had walked over and stood beside Cal. She was shaky yet defiant, and meant every word, "Me too, son. I won't abandon you. I will come visit you in prison. But you will serve your time."

Adia and Miguel were noticeably uncomfortable and deep down they really hoped Tommy would turn his life around.

Tommy realized as soon as Sam's last word sounded, all eyes in the room focused on him. He was the one who was mad and lashed out. Everyone else appeared sympathetic to his distraught mother. Especially Adia, and her opinion mattered most. Even on his best days, a girl like Adia was way out of his league. Tommy had become a man he was ashamed to be, which was lightyears away from the fine young man his mother always encouraged him to become. That young man would at least stand a chance with a girl like Adia.

For the first time in his life, Tommy was embarrassed and humiliated. No matter how harshly he lashed out at his loving mother, and the old preacher, he had nobody to blame but himself.

Over the last few days, while flat on his back, unable to get out of bed and walk, Tommy had spent many hours in deep thought. Every time he arrived at the same conclusion. As a result of his stupidity, more than likely, he would live the rest of his life as a handicapped man.

Tommy couldn't fathom the compassion in Adia's eyes. Especially for him, such a worthless loser. Could it be possible his anger was very misguided? Adia was always happy, a joy to be around. She was a beautiful young woman with purpose, and he had been treated to her genuine, selfless love for people. How did she manage that? Megan was the exact opposite. It was all about Megan, and would always be about Megan.

Even though Tommy really didn't like the old preacher, and more than likely never would - the preacher man was right. Tommy did owe it to him to at least try, to really put his heart into it. Even though his motivation was to impress

Adia, in a feeble attempt to prove he was worth her time, he would repay part of the debt he owed to the preacher.

So, Tommy drew in a deep breath and reluctantly placed his hands on the arms of the wheelchair. He looked around at the people who were committed to help him, "Some of you might want to step back. This could get a little messy," he playfully warned.

Sam cupped her hand over her mouth and couldn't hold back bittersweet tears. Those were the kind of things that used to come from the mouth of the son who made his Momma laugh all the time. When he was younger and "PM", "Pre Megan."

Cal put his arm around Sam and walked her out of the way.

The fact that his Momma stepped away from him and out of his view was unacceptable. He spoke up with the most heartfelt, sincere confession of his life, "No, Momma. Go in front so I can see you. I owe it to you most of all."

At that moment a "Momma's Pride and Unyielding Love," motivated Sam to once again set herself as an example to follow. She paused ten feet in front, "Is this far enough."

"Perfect," Tommy actually smiled, and it was real.

Sam was ready to spend the rest of the day and through the night, as long as her son needed her and was genuinely ready to accept her help.

Tommy slowly rose. His legs trembled, but he kept his eyes focused on his Momma as she clenched her hands into tight fists and whispered encouragement. It was as if heavy scales had fallen from Tommy's eyes. He was no longer blinded to anything, other than what Megan wanted. The troubled young man struggled to maintain his balance. He bravely waved Adia off as she reached to assist.

Sheena was incredibly intuitive and looked up at Betsy, who nodded, "Go help him, girl."

Sheena very calmly, reassuringly stepped beside Tommy as he began to sway, seconds from falling back in the chair.

"Take hold of the harness," Betsy encouraged.

Tommy's voice quivered as he weakened, "Adia, you sure about this?"

Adia nodded and smiled, so Tommy clenched the harness. His first step was wobbly and unstable. Miguel made sure he kept the wheelchair right behind Tommy, ready if he fell backward.

"You're doing great, but if you feel weak or dizzy, just drop back. I gotcha."

Adia was ready to spring into action, either left, right, or forward to steady Tommy if he tipped too far in those directions.

After a couple of uneasy strides, Tommy collapsed back into the wheelchair. He was embarrassed. He shoved the harness and Sheena away. He was frustrated and angry, "I can't do this!"

Sam took a step toward Tommy. Cal abruptly held up his hand and shook his head. She stood her ground.

Sheena remained calm and repositioned herself beside the wheelchair, where she patiently waited. Everybody anxiously watched to see what would happen between Sheena and Tommy. Sheena turned to look at Tommy who was staring at the floor. The Momma dog who was also a therapy dog leaned over and gently licked Tommy's hand. Then she nudged his arm a couple of times. Everyone was amazed and encouraged.

Cal sensed something was out of place. Mutt should've been in a wiggle around his feet, but to his surprise his Little Buddy sat perfectly still in the chair. The normally active clump of fur was most attentive, as if fully aware of what transpired between his Momma, and the new human, who desperately needed his Momma's help.

Cal decided. Sheena didn't just wander up and drop her puppies in that abandoned church. She was a very special creature. It was at that moment Sheena, the service dog, might have just encouraged Cal to take his first serious step back toward God. Even though it was a short, uncertain stride.

Over the four days Sheena spent with Mutt and Cal, the puppy learned that when Momma wore the harness, playtime was over. In the hospital his Little Buddy automatically knew it was a no-play zone. Cal was certain, but still reluctant to admit, something far beyond human comprehension was at work. That particular little pup wasn't average. He knew more than any human, or normal pup could imagine. But God, in his infinite wisdom, would keep the little creature an innocent mystery to Mankind. There was no way Man, with all of his flaws, would ever earn, or appreciate the right to grasp the depth of knowledge, love, and compassion He endowed in that little innocent pup.

Cal stepped over to Tommy, "You did good. You got a few steps in. Rest for a bit and then see if you can make a few more."

Tommy looked at Sheena, then turned defeated eyes up to Cal's understanding smile, "The muscles in my legs are quivering, and I'm pretty dizzy. Probably need to go back to my room and lay down for a while. Need to be there if Megan comes looking for me."

Sam shook her head, "Tommy, I know you don't want to hear this, but I hope she never comes back. You took some steps with the dog. Let's give you a few minutes to rest, then try again."

Cal leaned over, "I tell you what. We're going out for a while and leave you alone with Sheena and your therapists. You don't have to perform for us."

Tommy looked up and the corner of his mouth twitched a hint of an appreciative grin. Why did this man care so much? It didn't make sense. More importantly, how did this man know Tommy felt the immense pressure to please everyone. He was about to buckle under the unbearable weight of performance anxiety. He was a proud young man who should be able to walk with no assistance. It was humiliation, not lack of desire, that was about to chase him back to his room with his tail between his legs.

Megan was the flimsy, ill-chosen excuse to abandon the therapy session. Little did Tommy realize at that moment, Megan was a grimy mess, who drank heavily in a filthy, rundown room in a small town north of Atlanta. She had depleted only a small amount of the cash scattered on the table by the window. She could stay underground for a long time.

Adia was the perfect person to reinforce Tommy with an encouraging smile, "You're doing great. I'm proud of you. Let's see how many more steps we can get in before our session's up today."

Pumped up by the beautiful young woman who bragged on him, and a few minutes to allow the muscles in his legs to

# RETURN TO FAITH

calm down, Tommy was ready to try again. After the next two steps, and another rest, he was ready for the next two steps.

Adia was a professional, but she was also a woman who knew the right amount of attention and praise from her would produce better results with men than women. It wasn't sexist, and it wasn't an ego thing, it had become a valuable tool in her line of work. What really mattered, Tommy responded, real progress would be made, and that was rewarding.

......

## 25
## The First Step Of True Faith Must Be Taken Blindly

Outside in the hall important decisions were discussed and made.

"I'd say let's give it a week and see what happens," Cal suggested.

"But they won't let the dog stay in the hospital, and I can't keep her, then get off work to bring her down here every day."

"I'll keep Sheena with me, and bring her to the hospital until they release him," Cal promised.

Sam still couldn't believe how genuinely committed Cal appeared to be, "But I can't afford to pay you for your time."

Cal smiled, "I don't recall asking."

"Wish I could take the time to be here," Betsy was sincere.

"You can do Mondays," Cal smiled.

Cal and Betsy walked across the parking lot closer together than they walked in. Sheena and Mutt flanked on the outside.

As they reached the car, Cal pulled the keys out of his pocket and moved with flair to unlock the passenger door. He leaned the bucket seat forward as Betsy unstrapped the walk assist from Sheena, before she hopped in the back seat. Mutt decided it was playtime.

Cal mimicked the boisterous voice of a Worldwide Wrestling Announcer, "Now, let's get ready to rumble," as he was forced to pour the wiggle machine into the back seat. The growl and tumble began.

Then after he pushed the setback into position, Cal motioned for Betsy to enter, "My Lady."

Spoken with an exaggerated, 'true Southern Belle' accent, "Why, thank you, Kind Sir," Betsy curtsied and eased into the seat.

Cal poured on his Southern Charm, "You're quite welcome, Ma'am."

Once inside, Betsy rolled her window down, then smiled at Cal as he happily settled into the driver's seat, "You're very pleased with yourself."

Cal smiled, "Yes, Ma'am. I sure am, but I'm not exactly sure why."

"You're doing a good thing, and for all the right reasons. I'm very proud of you."

"It's nice to do the right thing, and to have the right reasons; but it becomes wasted time and energy if you invest them into the wrong person."

The words just came to Cal and he spoke them without thought. But once they hit the fresh air, they could've easily turned sour. He hoped Betsy heard what he meant, not what any of his insecurities could've twisted them into. The worst thing at that point would be to expose his insecurity and try to explain why he said what he said.

There was one thing he needed to do and it would help both of them if he took Betsy to get it done.

"I've been thinking," Cal opened up.

"Is this a new trick you've learned?"

That was an excellent come-back. Apparently, Betsy didn't misinterpret his last statement. He needed to play it off and get to the point, rather than engage in a fun little banter.

"Since we're teaming up to help Tommy, it would be a good thing to be able to reach each other."

Betsy smiled and looked up the closest Verizon store, where they hooked Cal up with the latest iPhone, and an iPad Pro of his own. Along with help from the salesperson, Betsy persuaded Cal to purchase two iPad essentials, the Apple Pencil, and a Logitech back-lit keyboard/cover.

Cal held the door to the store open for Betsy, who tapped on the screen of Cal's new smartphone, then handed it to him with a big smile, "Okay, now you have my digits."

As they walked toward the orange Judge, Cal quipped, "So, I'm no longer a Neanderthal?"

Betsy smiled, "That remains to be seen."

......

Over the next few days, Tommy had his moments where

he was able to take more steps with Sheena. Then he was very frustrated when his legs and balance just wouldn't cooperate. Progress was slow at first and eventually Tommy's outbursts when things went wrong became less intense and profane.

Yesterday afternoon Cal was pleasantly surprised when Tommy actually smiled and genuinely seemed glad to see him and Sheena. Well, definitely Sheena. As reluctant and headstrong as Tommy had been against the therapy in the beginning, Sheena had worked her magic and made a new friend on day one.

......

By the following Monday, which was Betsy's second visit, Tommy's confidence had grown tremendously. He motioned for Miguel to stay back and not move the chair with each step.

"I want to know I can do this," Tommy requested. "If the chair is right behind me, it'll be too easy to give up and sit back down."

Adia and Miguel weren't thrilled by the request, but sometimes that one little thing was all it took to spark the effort and belief to propel a patient's rehab to the next level. They agreed, but it wasn't swift. They had to do more than sound positive when they responded.

Adia took five long strides, then turned and smiled, "And your new goal is." She pointed to the floor, "Here."

Miguel's voice reassured from behind, as if he believed it were possible, "You got this, man." Tommy would never know that Miguel had positioned his body and feet to be able to bolt and race to Tommy's aid if necessary. He knew Tommy could see his reflection in the mirrored wall to his right, but he hoped his patient was too preoccupied with the tasks at hand to notice. He wondered if Tommy's top priority was to successfully accomplish the goal, or to impress Adia. At that point it really didn't matter as long as the goal was achieved.

Tommy looked down at Sheena, "Okay, girl. It's you and me against the world."

The atmosphere in the therapy room was tense. Betsy reached over and took hold of Cal's hand, as much to support him, as to seek comfort for her own concerns. After the first few steps the tension eased. Tommy wobbled and paused.

"I'm okay. I'm okay. Nobody panic," Tommy assured as he resumed his quest.

Adia had allowed Tommy to slip underneath her professional barrier and she was nearly in tears by the time he reached the goal she set for him. It wasn't strictly forbidden, but it was highly frowned upon for therapists to engage in physical contact beyond that which was required in the performance of their services. Adia tossed all professionalism aside and hugged Tommy, who to say the least was very surprised. In her heart she knew Tommy would continue to work to earn her praise and another hug.

"I'm so proud of you," Adia gushed. "You're doing great!"

After that extended walk, everyone agreed that Tommy should sit in the chair and rest for a few minutes. He rubbed Sheena on the head, "Good girl. Couldn't have done it without you."

Miguel rolled Tommy over to the row of chairs along the back wall so Betsy and Cal could flank Tommy.

"Cal and I've been talking. Sheena was named after a comic book character that was created long before either of us were born; but if she's going to be your dog, we think you should name her."

"She's mine?" Tommy was stunned, "You're really giving her to me?"

"Do you want her?" Betsy asked.

Tommy turned to Sam who smiled and nodded her Momma's approval.

Sheena placed a paw on Tommy's knee which made him smile and rub her head.

"Of course, I want her."

"Looks like she wants you too," Cal was pleased. "But there's a few things that need to happen first."

"We've got to get her checked out by a vet, then get her certified as a service dog," Betsy turned to Cal. "We believe she was a service dog, or at least had been trained, so that shouldn't take long."

Tommy's smile faded, "How much is that gonna cost?"

"Will she have to be spayed?" Sam was concerned about

additional costs.

Betsy shook her head, "The ADA, the Americans With Disabilities Act, doesn't require service dogs be spayed or neutered."

"She will be delivered to you ready to go to work, at no cost," Cal promised. He sounded so much like a used car salesman, but he was referring to an amazing living creature.

"Sheena," Tommy nodded. "My dog's name is, Sheena."

"Then, Sheena it is," Cal concurred.

......

One week later, Tommy was still a little unstable, but he had improved dramatically and was released from the hospital. Betsy and Cal were pleased to officially hand over ownership of Sheena to Tommy. She was a week away from being officially certified as a service dog.

Outside the hospital, Betsy reviewed with Tommy the bags of goodies and treats she and Cal pitched it to provide the first-time dog owner. Tommy was like a child on Christmas morning.

While Tommy was distracted, Sam pulled Cal aside, "You have no idea what you've done for my son. There's no way I can ever thank you enough. Or, ever repay you." She was in tears.

"You don't owe me a thing," Cal assured.

"Tommy's never taken responsibility for anything, so I'm cautiously optimistic by how engaged he is with Sheena now."

"On the other hand, Tommy does owe me big time. Not a single penny, but he does owe me."

"I hope he never loses sight of the tremendous responsibility you and Betsy have given him."

"We'll know soon enough," Cal responded.

"We'll see you around nine in the morning," Sam promised.

Cal remained quiet, but turned up a sly smirk.

"I don't think Tommy fully grasps what this rehab is all about,"

Sam's head slowly shook, "I'm very concerned about what he's gonna learn once he walks in the shop."

"It gets real in the morning," Cal promised.

......

## 26
## Let The Payback Begin

Every morning over the last two weeks, Cal had developed a routine. He got up and took care of Sheena's and Mutt's needs. Then he fixed breakfast for three. With breakfast dishes cleaned, he took both dogs to the shop so he could work on the old truck parts until 12:30 PM. Then he loaded up the dogs and went back to his apartment where he cleaned them up, took a shower, dried his hair, then headed to the Faith Family Diner. During the mornings, Betsy would send Cal a text with the day's special. If he wanted it, she would have it ready when he arrived. If he wanted something different, that would be hot and ready when he walked in the door, which was always just after the lunch crowd thinned out. Sheena and Mutt seemed to be happy with their usual lunch, but Betsy would give them a surprise or two. Then Cal packed up the dogs and headed south to the Charlotte Trauma Center for the afternoon therapy sessions with Tommy.

......

Yesterday Cal and Betsy handed Sheena over to Tommy and Sam. That morning, Cal only had to take care of and feed Mutt and himself.

At nine sharp on that Tuesday morning a loud, high pitch whirr filled the garage. Cal wore a respirator mask and goggles. He was covered in a brownish tan dust, spewed in the air by an abrasive rotary sander. He kept an even pressure as he rotated the device in overlapping circles on the rusty hood. Sparks flew once the sandpaper cut through the thick rust and chewed on the raw steel surface.

Mutt hid under a car nearby. The high pitched whirr was very unpleasant to his sensitive ears.

On time, as promised, Sam, Tommy, and Sheena entered the opened garage door. Tommy was still unsure on his feet and made deliberate, measured strides. It was obvious how dependent he was on Sheena. Once Tommy realized what caused the offensive whirr, and how dirty Cal was, his enthusiasm vanished. He became apprehensive as he focused on Cal, who was engrossed with his project and had lost track of the time.

Mutt scrambled out from under the car and ran to greet Momma, in hopes she could make the bad noise go away.

Charlie had to walk over and tap Cal on the shoulder to break his concentration. Cal looked up and took his finger off the trigger of the grinder. The sparks and high pitch whirr ceased. He lifted the goggles, pulled the respirator mask down, then checked the Ford clock on the wall.

"We're off to a good start," Cal was pleased.

This was the moment of truth. Over the course of the therapy sessions Cal and Tommy had formed an outwardly respectful relationship. At least from Tommy's perspective. The threat of prison wasn't an issue during the therapy sessions. It lurked in what seemed like a distant future. The decision time had roared back to the front of the line. Today was the start of the trial period that would determine Tommy's fate. All the previous evening, into the morning, Tommy worked himself into an unhealthy state of mind. He was terrified about how the first day would go. Too much rode on the outcome. Adia wouldn't be there to encourage Tommy, or for him to impress. He was on his own. Well, he and Sheena were on their own.

Charlie invited Sam and Tommy to join them.

When Tommy realized what Cal was up too, he was even more uneasy about what he had actually gotten himself into. Defensively, he attempted to take control, "I can't stand up very long."

Cal rolled a shop stool around the truck cab, "Gotcha covered."

Tommy turned a last-ditch "pitiful faced plea" to Sam, "Sorry, if you want to change the deal, you'll have to take it up with the judge."

Suddenly it just got very real. Tommy felt betrayed by Cal, and worst of all, his own Mother. This whole thing about giving him the dog was to butter him up before they subjected him to forced labor. More insulting, it would be dirty, grimy, forced labor.

Cal sensed his budding positive relationship with Tommy had just flown off the rails at twice the speed of light. There wasn't going to be a comfortable direction forward. He would at least test the shark-infested waters with a dip of his little toe. "Don't think of this as punishment. Think of it as a chance to head in a new, positive direction. Possibly a new career."

By the look on Tommy's face and the hatred that bolted from his eyes, if true, the old worn-out "if looks could kill" was just transmitted to a dead man. Either way, the game was on. All that remained, who would win? And, who would lose?

Sam hoped to defuse the situation, "Honey, all your doctors agree exercise will help you regain your balance sooner."

Tommy was driven by an impulse that leapt from a very dark corner of his wounded pride. It was sharp and pierced like the cold steel of an ice pick, straight into a warm heart. It pierced his Mother's heart, not Cal's. His glare was fixed on Sam, "They also said I could be this way the rest of my life."

Tommy immediately regretted the hurt he just inflicted on his Mother, especially in front of other people. It was too late, and in the long run, the fact that she willingly took part in the great deception made her a justifiable target.

Like too many times before, Sam refused to openly react and would absorb the pain quietly, internally. Unfortunately that very reaction had allowed her son to victimize her again, again, and again.

There was so much Cal could've said, and should've said, but realized it was best to keep them to himself. He refused to enter into a verbal joust with the troubled young man. Instead, he picked up two sanding blocks and slid his hands under the straps. He motioned clockwise with his left hand, "Smooth up." He motioned counter-clockwise with his right hand, "Then more smooth up. Have you seen 'Karate Kid,' Daniel-son?" Cal asked then demonstrated the opposite circular motions on the hood. "We need to use some good old-fashioned elbow-grease to remove the course grit scratches," He explained then slipped the pads off his hands and laid them on the hood. He smiled and picked up two more sanding pads and slipped his hands under the straps. He pushed on the truck cab and it didn't move, "Got it securely locked down, so you can lean on it to keep your balance."

Charlie wasn't about to stand by and allow the understandably upset young man disrespect Cal and his own Mother with the silent treatment. Tommy was going to have to speak and actually say, "No!" He placed a new, white particle mask over Tommy's head and covered his nose and mouth. Then he gently adjusted the elastic straps around the back of his head. He slipped a pair of new safety goggles over Tommy's eyes.

Sam took hold of Sheena's harness, but Tommy was reluctant to let go. Intense anger was displayed as panic filled Tommy's eyes.

Charlie picked up Mutt, and slowly backed away when Tommy cautiously released his grip on Sheena's harness and slammed his hands on the hood with loud pops.

"Use the sanding pads for support," Cal suggested.

"Jail's starting to look more appealing right now," Tommy snapped before he turned a betrayed look at Sam. "At least I'll get to sit around."

Sam was visibly disappointed, but she had been relentlessly pushed to that point she never dreamed she would arrive. She was ready to step back and let Tommy destroy his life if he was so determined, "That's your decision."

Cal laid his sanding pads on the hood, "Okay. He doesn't wanna be here. I respect that." He said as he motioned to someone hidden in the shadows of the next room. "Go ahead, he's all yours."

"I can handle that," Deputy Karr stepped out of the shadows. He was resolute, very professional in his tone and demeanor, "Judge asked me to make sure Tommy intended to honor his end of the deal."

"I never agreed to do forced slave labor," Tommy argued.

Deputy Karr reached around and lifted his stainless steel handcuffs from his belt and addressed Tommy as an arresting officer, "Mr. Forrester, you agreed to actively participate in a rehabilitation program approved and sanctioned by the judge and prosecutor, supervised by Mr. Baxter, and Mr. Webster. You were advised that your refusal to participate would result in you spending your time in jail, awaiting your trial."

## RETURN TO FAITH

Tommy was stunned, "What's with the Mr. Forrester stuff? You've never called me that before."

"Mr. Forrester, in the eyes of the law, you're an adult male, and therefore, out of respect for your person, Sir, I'm required to communicate with you in such a manner." Deputy Karr spoke with tremendous regret, but he was resolute. It was time he and everyone refused to handle Tommy with kid gloves.

"Obviously, he's having second thoughts," Cal surmised as he pulled the respirator up over his mouth and nose, then slid the safety goggles down over his eyes. He lifted the grinder and switched it on.

Cal turned away from Tommy and stepped on the other side of the truck cab. Sparks flew as Cal buzzed across the remaining rusty section of the hood.

Tommy couldn't believe Cal walked away from him. He glanced at Deputy Karr who prepared the cuffs, and spoke loud enough to be heard over the grinder. "If you put those things on me, I won't be able to hold the harness." Tommy complained as he faced the truck body with his hands on the hood to maintain his balance.

"Spread your legs," Deputy Karr instructed and placed the cuffs on the hood with a clank, just to further intimidate. "I'm gonna have to pat you down."

Tommy turned his head and located Sam as her eyes filled with tears. He looked at Cal, who ignored him and continued to grind, which created more sparks than before.

Deputy Karr explained Tommy's rights as he began to pat him down, "You have the right to remain silent. Anything you say can and will be used against you in court." He completed the Miranda rights, then stepped over and took Sheena's harness from Sam. "You're right, Tommy," he explained as he walked Sheena over and nodded for Tommy to take hold. "It would be unsafe to cuff you, but you're officially under arrest. Now I have to transport you and your dog to the jail for processing."

Charlie gently hugged Sam as she placed her hand over her mouth. The tears of a broken-hearted mother flowed.

Tommy and Deputy Karr stood their ground, engaged in a brief, tense stare-off. Abruptly Tommy turned, slid his hands under the sanding pads' straps, and spastically thrust the pads across the hood.

Deputy Karr grinned and winked as he handed Sheena's harness handle back to Sam.

Sam offered a brief grin and nodded her head. It was all she could do without a flood of uncontrolled tears.

Cal appeared uninterested as he continued to grind away, but out of the corner of his eye he paid close attention to what transpired. He grinned with tremendous satisfaction under the cover of the mask. After a beat, he lifted the grinder and watched Tommy for a couple of seconds. Then he turned the grinder off.

All that was heard in the shop was the scratch of the sandpaper on the pads Tommy awkwardly rotated on the bare metal hood. He dare not look up and give Cal the moral victory. Nor would the young man witness the satisfied smiles from his mother, Charlie, and Deputy Karr behind him.

Without another word, Deputy Karr stepped over and retrieved his handcuffs from the hood. There was one thing the lawman had to do. He reached over and gently patted Tommy on the back. Then without waiting to see how Tommy would react, he returned to his patrol.

Tommy did pause for a brief moment of reflection, evaluation, and justification. He didn't "chicken out." He was still a tough guy, but a tough guy who wasn't on his way to jail. It wasn't a moral victory, but it was still a win/win situation.

After that quick assessment, Tommy was confident enough to pause his reluctant task. He could look Cal in the eye at that point, and it was imperative that the ex-preacher not perceive him as weak, a pushover for his inevitable Bible mumbo-jumbo.

Tommy and Cal stared at each other through safety goggles, their eyes agreed on a temporary truce. After a beat, Cal slipped his hands under the straps of his sanding pads. He and Tommy soon achieve a matching rhythm.

......

By design, Charlie opted to be busy at lunch. He took Mutt with him, which afforded Tommy and Cal some time to talk. Tommy was a little sloppy as he ate, and occasionally reached food under the table to feed Sheena. He paused when he realized Cal casually observed. "What?" Tommy asked as if he thought Cal disagreed with Sheena being fed at the table.

"How old are you?" Cal caught Tommy off guard.

"Do What?"

Cal maintained eye contact but instead of a response, he took a slow, deliberate drink of water.

Tommy took the hint, "Twenty-four. Why does it matter?"

Cal swallowed and set the sweaty glass back down in its pool. "Can't remember what my goals were when I was twenty-four. Was probably already preaching."

Tommy's eyes narrowed as he rested his hands on the table. The fork was full. "Sometimes I think I hit you too hard."

"Just hard enough."

Tommy was a cross between confused and annoyed, "You seeing a shrink, right?"

"I'm not ready to jump back into this God thing headfirst into the deep end, but I can't help but wonder if a higher power, of some sort, brought us together on that country road."

Tommy looked around to see who might be close enough to hear, "I'll believe Sheena's a moose, before accepting your god is real."

Cal nodded slowly, "Can't argue your logic."

"Then where you head'n."

Cal was calm, deliberate, "Seems I've found myself on a new journey of discovery. What remains to be seen, for whatever reason, you've become my reluctant companion on this mysterious new quest."

Tommy stared blankly at Cal as he struggled for an adequate response. "It's none of my business where you're head'n on this new quest you're on. But I can assure you, I ain't interested in no new discoveries. I just want to do my time with you and stay out of jail."

Cal was unfazed, which made Tommy even more suspicious, "I don't wanna come back tomorrow, if you're gonna go all religious on me."

"I'm not sure exactly where I'm going, but you need to keep one very important thing in mind, Deputy Karr loves his job." Cal not so subtlety stated.

"Is that a threat?"

Cal was stoned-faced and took another sip of water.

Tommy felt his blood pressure rise, but he managed to keep his tone a few notches above an insult, "So, you own me?"

Cal remained silent for a tense beat, "Let's make a deal. Work on the truck, until the last detail is finished, then you're free'n clear."

"No more prosecutor, no more judge? And no more threats to have me arrested?"

Cal didn't hesitate to extend his hand across the table, "As long as you keep me convinced you're giving me and the project your absolute best effort."

Tommy eagerly reached across, then yanked his hand back, "Can I trust you?"

Cal pulled his hand back, "The real question is, can I trust you?" He paused for a second then added, "You're welcomed to take all the time you need to make that important decision. And if you'd prefer, we can arrange it so you can ponder your options from the comforts of your well appointed accommodations in the county lock up." Cal grinned.

Tommy was stunned and silent for a tense beat, "To be a former preacher, you have a cruel, evil streak."

Cal's grin broadened into a wide, satisfied smile.

. . . . . . .

At 8:45 AM the next morning, Tommy entered the opened garage door with the handle to Sheena's harness firmly in hand. His deliberate strides were a bit more confident as Sheena led him into the quiet shop.

Charlie stepped out of the office and looked at his wrist watch, "You're either fifteen minutes early, or my watch and wall clocks are fifteen minutes slow."

"It's too quiet in here. Where's the noisy preacher?"

"Take'n care of some business. Said you know what to do."

Charlie smiled as Tommy put on the white mask and safety goggles, then slipped his hands into the straps of the sanding blocks. The life-long mechanic and race car builder smiled as Tommy methodically rubbed the hood on the old truck.

Charlie was compelled to stand back and observe what appeared to be an amazing transformation in process. Charlie was a man who was passionate about attention to details, even when he mowed the yard. It was more than a chore, it was an opportunity to showcase his property's natural beauty.

Therefore, Charlie could spot that same passion in how a person approached any task. Tommy had the passion. He may have just discovered his calling in life. It was imperative to reinforce and build his confidence, then guide him to refine the techniques. Tommy had the raw ability.

Charlie stepped over and leaned down to look across the area Tommy focused on. He slid his hand across the raw metal surface and shared a genuine smile with Tommy, "It's get'n there. Keep it up."

.......

Meanwhile, Cal talked with Terry Stafford, who owned a very successful construction company located north of Charlotte. His office was exactly halfway between The Queen City and what used to be the sleepy little town of Mooresville, that had rapidly grown into the home base for most NASCAR race teams. Related businesses flocked to create the Mecca of the sport. Fortunately, Terry's company had become the first choice for many teams, team owners, and drivers.

Terry was a ruggedly handsome man in his forties who dressed like a heavy machine operator, which allowed him to appeal to the down-to-earth, real men in the tight-knit racing community. His "good ol boy" persona stripped away any preconceived notion of the owner of a multi-million dollar construction company. He was a man who loved to get his hands dirty.

Cal and Terry stood beside the large bulldozer he had delivered to the abandoned church the afternoon before.

Cal nodded and motioned with his right hand, "Yeah, everything goes, except those two trees."

"You got it, Boss," Terry said, then shook his hand and climbed up on the giant yellow machine.

"Take this nasty patch of briers out first," Cal requested.

Cal stayed and watched for a while. The property would

look very different the next time he saw it. Stripped bare and ready to start all over.

......

Cal was on a tight schedule. Terry gave him a "thumb's up" as he pulled the orange Judge away from the church. "That's one clean, mean machine," Terry complimented.

It was the perfect time of morning for Betsy to step away from the diner, and leave her cook to work alone on the lunch prep. The attorney had the 501c papers drawn up and wanted to meet briefly with Cal and Betsy before they signed and filed the documents.

The attorney's questions were answered in short order, and Cal invited Betsy to sign the application first. Then he followed. They were all smiles.

"I'll take the papers by for Charlie to sign, and have them back before the end of the day," Cal promised.

"That way you can mail them today," Betsy was excited.

The wise old lawyer leaned back in his squeaky office chair, "You do remember this is going to the IRS to be reviewed before it can be accepted, or rejected?"

Betsy and Cal nodded, determined to remain positive.

"It can take several months, up to a year, or longer."

Cal smiled, "As of twenty-five minutes ago, I had a bulldozer start clearing the property. We're moving forward, and will continue, regardless if the 501 is approved."

The realist attorney picked up the application and read the organization's proposed title out loud, "Return To Faith," he chuckled. "On the surface, it doesn't sound overly political. So, I don't foresee any hold ups on that front."

"We're gonna do what we're gonna do, and spend what we're gonna spend, either way."

Betsy reviewed the multiple page application as they walked across the parking lot. She made no effort to reach for the door handle because she'd learned Cal was a true Southern Gentleman. It was his job to open all doors and pull out all chairs for a Lady.

However, before she climbed in the Judge, she extended her hand to Cal, "Nice do'n business with you, Preacher man."

Cal pondered for a moment, then nodded, "Okay, I'll let

you have that one. Even though, that's not who I am today, and may never be again."

Betsy smiled, "Good enough."

On the drive from the attorney's office, Betsy called Charlie and asked him to meet them at the diner to sign the papers to save Cal some time.

"How's our little project coming along?" Cal asked.

"I'm assuming you're referring to our two-legged project, not the four wheeled one?"

"You are wise beyond your tender years," Cal joked.

"Have to admit, I'm pleasantly surprised."

"And hopeful?"

"Very hopeful. Very hopeful indeed," Charlie said as he watched Tommy lower his head and do a sight-line to the windshield. Then he ran his hand across the surface to feel just how smooth it really was. Charlie could tell that was the determined Tommy who really wanted to do a great job. It wasn't a troubled boy who wanted to impress somebody.

......

After Charlie left, Betsy handed the 501c application back to Cal and followed him out the door of the diner. She walked him to the Judge, "I didn't want to say something inside where anyone else might hear. When Sam comes to pick Tommy up this evening, how about bringing them over for dinner. She missed a lot of work while Tommy was in the hospital. I'm sure it's going to be tough on her for a while."

Cal nodded, "She's a proud and stubborn woman."

Betsy smiled, "Me too."

"I'm learning that," Cal quipped. "Okay. But only if you let me pay."

"We'll go Dutch," Betsy winked and turned before Cal could respond.

"As a mule," Cal intentionally mumbled loudly enough for Betsy to hear.

Betsy heard but refused to turn around. Instead, she smiled as she approached the door, "Do what?"

"You heard me. You're stubborn as a mule."

"Yep. My hearing's pretty good too."

......

## 27
## That Feeling When A Plan Starts Coming Together

A week later, a routine had jelled in Sunshine Racing & Auto Repair, in the lives of the individuals involved with the restoration of the old Chevy truck.

Mercifully, Sheena and Mutt would be put in the office when the grinder was in use. No matter how hard Tommy tried to conceal his true feelings, when his mask was down, or off, he couldn't hide his smile when he saw how much progress they made each day.

Tommy still missed Megan, and thought about her every day, but he soon realized that she came to mind less and less throughout the day. He was also surprised how quickly he found himself eager to harness Sheena, and get out of bed as soon as he woke up each morning.

Sam made a deal with her boss to make up the time for her to take Tommy to the shop in the morning. She realized she could learn to swallow her pride for a while and accept Betsy's and Cal's standing invitation to provide them dinner on weekdays for the next couple of months.

Charlie had worked alone in the large shop for so long that the sudden addition of two humans, and two dogs, was an uncomfortable invasion of his privacy. However, as the new arrangement continued, he found himself with a sense of dread at the thought of when the last screw would be turned on the old truck. Was he going to be able to adapt after Cal drove his freshly rebuilt truck out into the real world?

Every other day, Cal would leave the diner after lunch and work on little projects in and around the abandoned church. The first was to have the building inspected and the power turned back on, so he could work until well after dark. The wiring and lighting fixtures were sound enough to carry a full load. Eventually, as the building was brought up to Twenty-

First Century standards, the entire wiring system would be updated in stages.

The night before, Cal asked Betsy to come over after she closed the diner. They used his new iPad to pick out modern commodes and fixtures for the Women's and Men's restrooms. She allowed Cal to pick out the styles of the items for the Men's room. She immediately played the veto card when Cal suggested they put a light blue commode in the Men's Room.

"Why is it women feel entitled to make most of the design decisions when they're involved in a building, or remodeling project?" Cal asked.

"Because men make decisions like putting a blue commode in the Men's Room of a public building."

"Duhh!" Cal wagged his head, "If only men go in there, why should women care?"

"Because we do, and you don't."

Suddenly, something about what Betsy just said, and more importantly, how she said it, was eerily familiar. A chill raced up his spine, and exploded in his mind. He wondered if it were a ghost memory of how Annie would've reacted, and would've said the exact same thing the exact way as Betsy.

Betsy totally misconstrued the slack-jawed expression that consumed Cal's face. "Oops. Don't take it personally. I was just kid'n around."

Cal closed his eyes, lifted his right hand, and slowly shook his head.

Once again, Betsy scrambled to understand, "Did you just have a flashback?"

Cal shook his head, "Not a flashback." He opened his eyes and was obviously confused, "A question." Was all he said.

After a few moments of confusion and silence, Betsy had to know, "About what?"

"I don't know if I should tell you."

"Well, if you don't, I'm gonna worry about everything I say to you."

"I'm sorry. I'm not sure I can explain," Cal confessed.

"At least try, for both of our sakes."

"Promise you won't think I'm nuts?"

Betsy giggled, "Too late."

"Okay. But let me begin with, I really like you," Cal started, until Betsy lifted her hand.

"And I like Butter Pecan ice cream, but I'm not interested in having a personal relationship with it, not beyond the temporary satisfaction I feel after I eat my fill."

Cal was sufficiently confused and his eyes narrowed as he nodded, "Umm, Humm. I understand what you mean, but I'm having trouble connecting Butter Pecan ice cream to our situation."

Betsy smiled with tremendous satisfaction, "No, you just nailed it."

Cal shook his head, "Then the hammer bounced off the nail and whacked me right between the eyes, knocked it right out of my brain."

Betsy formed her most sincere expression, "I really enjoy our little word games, but this one's not helping either one of us," Betsy was serious, but not upset.

Cal nodded, "Then here goes. I'm not sure if it's what you said, or how you said it. Or, was it both. Either way, it wasn't that I had a flashback and saw Annie's face, or remembered a specific day, time, or incident. It was the dumbest question I'd ever asked myself, 'Would Annie have said what you said at that moment?' Until then, I don't remember the last time I even thought about Annie, or Taylor. It's like they never existed. But yesterday I got a package from Gabby. She sent me a photo of Annie, Taylor and me together."

Betsy took hold of both of Cal's hands, and she spoke the most sincere words she'd ever uttered, "I can't imagine what you're going through, how confusing and frustrating things are, or will become. Regardless of who she was to you, as long as I'm convinced you don't want me to be her, I can understand and deal with your confusion."

"That's all I can ask. And I promise…."

Betsy held up her hand and Cal stopped, "Don't make promises you might not be able to keep," Betsy requested.

Cal nodded and opened his mouth to speak, until Betsy held up her hand again, "I'm going to hug you right now, because I really want to. But don't make too much of it. Okay?" Betsy felt foolish about the silly request.

Cal wanted that hug really bad, "Deal."

# RETURN TO FAITH

The hug was amazing for the hugger and huggie. To have unexpectedly slammed into a potentially damaging wall, Betsy and Cal escaped with only minor bruises. They would realize later that incredibly awkward moment was the last barrier between them to be demolished.

......

Over the next couple of weeks, Cal continued to keep Tommy out of the loop in regard to the church renovation. He didn't want to risk tossing a grenade into the middle of what he considered an important and consequential friendship, on many levels. It was imperative Tommy wouldn't feel pressure. Tommy had to know where he stood, and in no way fear his freedom was contingent upon participation in the church renovation. The church project would never be mandatory, or in any way attached to the deal they reached with the Judge and prosecutor.

On that morning, Cal wore his goggles and a white particle mask. He and Tommy had spent weeks grinding, sanding, and using minimal body filler on two minor dents, and three small places they sanded holes in the metal to remove all traces of rust. Rust was to metal like cancer was to the human body. Unless it is removed or destroyed, it would continue eating away until it had eaten away its host.

The steel body panels on the cab and bed of the old Chevy truck were smooth as glass. They still had to sand down the dashboard and some additional interior parts before they could send the entire body assembly to the paint shop. Charlie had already told Cal and Tommy that on the day they rolled the cab and bed up on Charlie's rollback, and after they delivered them to the paint shop, on the way back, they would celebrate. Milestones were important to mark with special occasions.

However, for the rest of that day, Tommy's task was to finish sanding the front and back bumpers. Then as a team, they would make the final decision to send the bumpers to the paint shop, or to be chromed. It was a major decision. Originally, the bumpers on that truck had been factory painted white. Would they remain original, or be stepped up to chrome?

"What about the bumpers?" Charlie took charge.

Cal spoke up, "I say we stay original and paint'm."

Tommy shook his head, "I say we chrome'm."

Cal and Tommy turned to Charlie who just became the tie-breaker. He shook his head, "Sorry, Preacher. I have to go with the Kid on this one."

Tommy pumped his fist, "Yeah! And it only makes sense to chrome the wheels to match."

"Oh really?" Cal snapped his head back. "But it takes dollars to make that kind of sense."

Tommy didn't get it at first, "Oh, I see." He turned to Charlie, "The Preacher's going tight-wad on us now."

The good natured banter was followed by a healthy laugh.

"Seriously, guys," Cal nodded. "I was kinda leaning toward chrome, but was thinking about if we ever wanted to enter the old girl into the 'original restoration' category of a car show."

Charlie shook his head, "We're not creating a 'garage queen' are we? A truck that will rarely see the light of day, unless it's at a car show, or on a sunny day? Are we?"

"Say it ain't so," Tommy chimed in.

There was no need for Cal to hesitate, "Not in the least. As I understand, I drove the other one about every day. My mother-in-law told me my wife loved it. And she used it as her primary vehicle."

"Then chrome it is, bumpers and wheels," Tommy pumped both fists in the air.

"Then someone has a lot of work to do to smooth up the wheels," Cal turned to Tommy.

"I'll be on'em like green or grass in the morning," Tommy promised.

"That means all five. Spare too," Cal clarified.

"Now he's Mr. Big Bucks," Tommy quipped.

......

Early that afternoon Cal returned to the shop after another one of his mysterious disappearances.

Since lunch, Tommy had settled down on the rolling shop stool, clad in his goggles and a white particle mask, even though they weren't required. He wet-sanded an area on the front right fender because it just didn't feel smooth enough. Sheena and Mutt slept on a blanket nearby.

Cal was impressed with how engrossed Tommy appeared to be with ensuring the body and cab were perfect. He didn't want to startle the young man so he walked around to compliment him after he'd gotten his attention.

However, when Tommy looked up, his curiosity finally overpowered his intent to remain uninterested, "Where do you go when you disappear like that?"

Rather than waste valuable time to explain, Cal suggested, "Let's knock off a little early today."

"Why?"

"I'll show you where I go, and explain why I go there."

Tommy stopped sanding, "Why can't you just tell me?"

"This you need to see."

So around 4:30 PM, Charlie gave his blessing for the boys to take Sheena and Mutt on a little field trip. Even though Mutt was usually Cal's shadow, when it came time to leave, the little guy paused and sat beside Charlie's feet as he leaned under the hood of a car.

"You staying with Charlie?" Cal asked as he, Tommy, and Sheena paused in the opened garage door.

Charlie raised up and looked over the covered fender, "You stay'n with your Uncle Charlie?"

Mutt's tail wagged.

Charlie turned to Cal, "That's interesting."

Cal nodded but was focused on how to explain, and to what degree was necessary to introduce Tommy to the church project, "Okay, Little Buddy. See you when we get back."

On the short drive, Cal's attention remained on several oddities he continued to notice about Sheena and Mutt. For the most part, they were just dogs, and all dog owners were convinced their dog was the smartest and most intuitive animal alive. Sheena and Mutt had something special, and he hesitated to even silently admit it to himself. Yet, the more time he spent with those two animals, he was about to accept they at least had psychic powers. He was convinced they could read human minds, especially his and Tommy's.

Cal still wasn't convinced God had placed Sheena and Mutt in his and Tommy's lives. In order to grasp who he had become, Cal had to be fair about who he had been. The only way to begin was to invest some quality time to read and sincerely attempt to understand the Bible. Recently, he read

Numbers, Chapter 22, verses 21-39, where God gave Balaam's donkey the ability to speak. Cal didn't expect Sheena or Mutt to suddenly strike up a conversation; but after he read that scripture, he was inclined to seriously consider Divine involvement.

Gravels crunched as Cal pulled the orange Judge off the road, onto the gravel patch he had poured and packed down, so vehicles could safely park off the road. In the background, a few scattered piles of brush remained from the twisted vines, weeds, and small trees that years of neglect allowed to consume the land around the abandoned church.

"Wow! That looks different," Tommy opened up and was way too comfortable. He would realize immediately that he probably said too much, "Me and my buddies used to get high in that old church all the time. But no matter how high we got, we never saw God."

Cal kept his eyes focused on the bare, stripped ground. There were a number of ways to respond to what Tommy just admitted. He had parked so the passenger side faced the sad, rundown church building.

"Hey, man, I'm sorry. I didn't mean no disrespect," Tommy said as he turned to Cal. "You tear'n it down?"

"Not exactly."

Tommy turned and looked at the rundown church, "I get it. You're obviously into fix'n up old things. I'm down with that, but I'm sorry." He turned back to Cal, "That's a waste of time and money."

As a rule, Cal would restrain himself if his first thought might sound a bit over the top. This time he let'r rip, but in a lighthearted tone, "Given your proclivity to wasting time and money, want'a help me waste some?"

Tommy's head wagged his disapproval, "I don't have a clue what proclivity means, but I can assure you I'm not the least bit interested in working on that." Tommy said as he pointed to the dilapidated church.

Cal was undaunted and reached in the back seat to retrieve a roll of drawings, "Your Mom told me you did quite well in carpentry classes at school."

Tommy turned his eyes forward, "Mom needs to spend less time talking and more time minding her own business."

Cal remained silent for a couple of seconds, "For the sake

of time, and to prevent an inevitable argument, I'm going to let that one go." Cal unrolled the drawings and revealed a page to Tommy, "Know what this is?"

Once it became inevitable Cal wasn't going to say anything else, Tommy reluctantly looked. "It's a steeple blueprint," slipped out of Tommy's mouth before he could clam up.

"So you can read a blueprint?"

Tommy nodded but didn't have the slightest interest to hold the blueprints. Then he became offended, and shook his head, "Oh no, you don't! I don't care what you, my Mom and the judge are cooking up, you can't...."

"Hold on there. I'm not cooking anything up with anybody. I haven't even said anything to you about this project for that very reason. If you do anything on this project, it's strictly voluntary. However, it could be an opportunity to explore an honest living."

"There's at least a fifty/fifty chance I might never be able to stand by myself again. So, finding a job ain't real high on my list these days."

"Maybe it should be," Cal suggested as he rolled up the blueprints and tossed them in the back seat.

As if on cue, a white pickup truck crackled gravel as it rolled to a stop behind the Judge.

"I smell a set-up," Tommy accused. "That's who you called before we left the shop."

"You're half-right," Cal readily admitted. "But he and I were already scheduled to meet here at this time this afternoon. I just let him know I wouldn't be alone." There was a moment of intense eye contact between Tommy and Cal before he added, "Keep in mind, you asked me where I go?"

"Well, I changed my mind. I don't wanna know anymore."

"Too late," Cal said as he exited the Judge, then paused, "You can stay in the car for now." Cal informed before he walked to the passenger side of Terry's pickup as he stepped out and closed the door.

Terry extended his hand, "Is he with you now?"

Cal nodded, "He might not be too friendly. He's a work in progress. At this point, I wouldn't stick my hand in the car. He might bite."

## OTIS FARMER

Terry chuckled, "I'll keep that in mind."

Cal walked Terry to the passenger's side of the Judge. He motioned, "Terry, this is Tommy, the young man I told you about a while ago."

Terry glanced at Cal, who tilted his head and raised his eyebrows as if to caution. Nonetheless, Terry extended his hand to the suspicious young man in the passenger's seat, who was very reluctant to respond, but eventually did.

Terry played it off perfectly and turned to face the old church, "Crane will be here around dawn in the morning; and my guys will have the old roof off; the new trusses set; the plywood screwed on; and the tar paper attached before the sun goes down."

"I'm glad we decided to replace the entire roof," Cal nodded.

"Yeah, I spent a lot of time in the attic and there really didn't seem to be a great deal of water damage. I was more concerned about mold spores."

"What about the shingles?"

"They'll be on before the sun goes down the day after tomorrow," Terry promised.

"You're not messing around."

"And we'll deliver the steeple pieces on Friday."

"You still okay with my request?"

Terry nodded, "It's not our S.O.P, but I understand why you requested it that way."

"It had to be just like it was. The steeple was added years after the church was built," Cal recalled, mostly for Tommy's benefit.

"For a non-builder, your idea of how to re-enforce the mounting brackets sounds pretty good. Let's see how it works. I may have to pay you royalties if we use it in the future."

"Oh, I'll be very reasonable. A hundred percent will be enough," Cal quipped as he looked at Tommy, who appeared disinterested. "Betsy and Charlie have some guys lined up to assemble the steeple on Saturday morning. You interested?"

Tommy kept his eyes forward, "Not really. I like sleeping in on Saturdays."

Cal nodded and grinned at Terry, "Think about it. I guarantee none of us know how to read a blueprint. We'll probably need a lot of help."

The more time they spent at the church that afternoon, the more obvious it became why Mutt wanted to stay with Charlie at the shop. He would've only been in the way, a needless distraction in the relationship Tommy, Sheena, and Cal must continue to develop and nurture.

......

Later that evening, Mutt was curled up and asleep on the sofa beside Cal, who was also half asleep. The scuffed, black Bible was opened and face down on the sofa beside Cal.

Numerous questions continued to arise in regard to his past and how those answers related to his future. The direction he should consider as the most logical path forward must be fact and knowledge based. One fact stood out, he knew, or more accurately, could remember so little about the book opened on the sofa beside him. It would take years to replenish the knowledge and memories he'd lost.

It was imperative that he understand why certain people, places, and events had been erased, or blocked from his memory. What was the common denominator, and should he seek to reverse the effects? He had spent a couple of hours in deep thought, until his head ached.

At that moment, Cal had given away to the blissful, foggy daze halfway between conscious thought and sleep. Until his cell phone so rudely jolted him back to consciousness.

Both Cal and Mutt immediately jerked their heads up and looked at the offensive device that dared to disturb them. It rang and vibrated on the cocktail table before them, but had just as well been a thousand miles away.

Cal struggled to lean forward, but smiled when his eyes focused enough to read the name on the screen. He slid his finger across the face of the phone and raised it to his ear, "You just yanked two content beings out of mindless bliss, back into the mean, real world."

"Sorry. But a gal could develop a complex waiting on a fella to call," Betsy's playful humor rang true.

Cal turned and winked at Mutt, who at best was uninterested, and dropped his head back down. He was fast asleep before his head impacted the seat cushion.

"You boys had dinner yet?"

"Mutt, you hungry?"

Mutt's eyes popped open. That was a subject close to his heart. He excitedly wiggled up and leapt in Cal's lap. He licked Cal's face as he snuggled and whined.

A short time later, empty plates sat in front of Cal and Betsy as they sat opposite in his booth. Their eyes communicated more than words could say.

Under the table, Mutt licked the last residue of food off a styrofoam takeout box lid. Content, the little fellow laid across Cal's feet and nodded off.

Betsy smiled, then took a sip of coffee, "Thank you."

"For what? Enjoying that great meal? I should be thanking you," Cal wondered what was next.

"I don't know why, but last night I pulled out Daddy's letter, and read it several times. Today I drove by and parked beside the old church for a few minutes. Wow, it's amazing how much you've accomplished in such a short time. I believe Daddy's smiling down at you from Heaven."

That was the absolute last thing Cal expected to hear. More importantly, nearly the last thing he wanted to talk about at that moment. He hoped that wasn't the reason she invited him to dinner.

"But, that's not why I asked you and Mutt over for dinner," Betsy confessed. "However, there is one more thing I want to say about that, then we'll move on."

Cal nodded and was compelled to share something profound before Betsy continued, "I'll have to admit there's several times I've been in, or at the building by myself. I'll stop, look around and grasp the dramatic transformation taking place. And here's the thing that don't make sense. I feel proud, very proud, but it's far more than for what I've accomplished."

Betsy smiled, "I think deep down, it's more than you are doing it for Daddy. You're just not ready to admit that you might also be doing it for yourself. Especially if it means more than you can accept." She quickly added, "But don't think for a minute I'm questioning anything you're doing. Because, I'm not and never will. I really appreciate everything, and always will."

After that sank in, Cal couldn't think of an adequate reply. What Betsy said made too much sense to a man still at war

# RETURN TO FAITH

with God.

Conversation was light and limited the rest of the meal. Yet Betsy and Cal realized it didn't matter if they talked at all, they just enjoyed each other's company.

......

The moment Tommy accepted Adia was way out of his league was the day he decided to up his game. Not necessarily qualify for a better league, but to earn the respect bestowed on members of the responsible, law-abiding community.

To his credit, since he started the old truck project, every morning Tommy realized the guy who looked back at him from the mirror, looked less and less like "poor white trash." It helped that he no longer acted like it. Socioeconomics had nothing to do with class. In his lifetime, Tommy had come in contact with several individuals who were nothing more than "rich white trash."

The first week of work on the old truck left Tommy totally exhausted and he was in bed by 8:00 PM. The first few days he was asleep as soon as he settled in the bed. Then he started thinking a little more each evening. It was during those quiet moments of self-induced isolation, he was able to really examine his relationship with Megan.

Every day, she wasn't there to tell him what to do and how to do it, led him to believe he was better suited to make the same decisions he always allowed her to manipulate, and control. The odd reality, Tommy was much better without her. He soon detested the man Megan reduced him to be, which put him on the path that would take him much closer to the level Adia existed.

Tommy never considered himself smart enough, or deep enough to understand "class" in terms of socioeconomics, or community groups. He was content to allow those who deemed themselves "better than him" to live in their own minds.

The "class" his poor Mother exhibited every day, and struggled, by example to impart to her wayward son, was worthy and honorable. These kinds of traits a girl like Adia would appreciate, and consider worthwhile. More so than the size of one's bank account and impressive expanse of one's successful stock portfolio.

Then there was Cal, Charlie, and Betsy. Who were these people? Why did they care about him? He knew Betsy and Charlie through Megan, but until she was out of his life, they meant nothing to him.

The most mind-boggling was Cal, the man he could've killed. Now Cal treated him like the son he never had. Ironically, Cal had become the father Tommy never knew. That was the key to Tommy's willingness to take the first steps in the right direction.

Every day Cal said what he meant. He did what he said he would do. More importantly, he lived what he believed was right, and was right about the way he lived.

Tommy was eleven months old when his father abandoned him and his mother. She immediately shifted into protective momma bear mode. She would raise and nurture her cub alone. No man would ever be allowed into her safe zone, her life and her den. While safe and loving, there were important traits a single mother could never impart to her son. A young boy needed to grow up in an environment where the father loved, respected, and treated his wife as the precious gift she was intended.

It wasn't a perfect, fool-proof system, but the odds were in the favor of the next generation, to grow into the man any wife be proud of. A man who knew how to treat a woman like a lady. A prized husband a woman would cherish, both as a mother, and a wife.

Tommy wasn't sure about the status of the relationship between Cal and Betsy. He wished his Mom could find a male companion that would make her smile like Cal did Betsy.

Perhaps, if Tommy could get his life together, and make better choices, both his and his Mom's attitudes would change enough they would appeal to quality men for his mother, and worthwhile young women for Tommy.

That night Tommy would sleep the best and feel the most refreshed the next morning, because of the heart to heart he initiated with his Mom before he called it a night.

It began with a confession that made his Momma cry, "Momma, I'm gonna take your advice about Saturday morning."

......

## 28
## A Change Of Direction Doesn't Mean A Change Of Plans

Day by day, Tommy's legs got stronger and his balance more stable, but he was still very dependent on Sheena. The guys in the shop had noticed and encouraged Tommy to keep working hard, and follow his therapists' advice and instructions. Tommy would happily follow Adia anywhere, for any reason, any time of the day or night.

On that Thursday morning, Charlie, Cal, Tommy, Sheena and Mutt sat in a circle, surrounded by the well organized parts from the disassembled truck.

"Tommy, the dash and door panels look great. Good job!" Charlie bragged.

"Thanks," Tommy was unashamedly proud.

"How long will it take to have the gauges and speedometer refurbished?" Cal asked.

"Supposed to be back in four to six weeks," Charlie shared. "But it could take longer."

"I have an idea," Tommy grinned. "Let's put a wooden bed in the back of the truck."

Charlie and Cal looked at each other, then back at Tommy to allow him to explain.

"I know it'll add time to the build, but a light finished oak plank bed would be really cool. And I know where we can get the lumber, free."

"Free's the best price," Cal nodded.

"We'll have to cut the metal bed out and weld a metal rail structure. You know how to weld?" Charlie asked.

"No, but I'd be glad to learn," Tommy smiled.

Charlie turned to Cal, "This is your build. You make the call. If we're gonna do it, I'd like to cut the bed out today and get started on the rails this evening."

Cal turned to Tommy, "You gonna shape the boards too."

## OTIS FARMER

"Momma's cousin in South Carolina has a cabinet shop. I've already talked to him. He even took the rough sketch I sent him and did a CAD drawing for us," Tommy pointed to his backpack. "Got'm in there."

Cal and Charlie were very impressed. Cal was closest to the backpack and retrieved it for Tommy, who eagerly unzipped the compartment and pulled out the folded drawings. He motioned, "Come over and I'll show you."

Tommy laid the drawings on the floor and explained what he and his cousin had designed.

"Well, you've gone to all this trouble, it'd be a shame to let it go to waste." Cal smiled and turned to Charlie, "Fire up your cutting torch."

Fifteen minutes later, Charlie wore a welding mask and gloves, then clicked the lighter to ignite the flame, "Last chance. Cut? No Cut?"

"Cut."

"Cut."

"And I say, cut," Charlie added.

"It's unanimous," Cal nodded. "Then make it so."

Tommy was surprised and turned to Cal, "Never would'a thought a Preacher would be a Trekkie."

Cal was confused, "A what'ie?"

"You never seen Star Trek? You know, Captain Jean-Luc Picard's famous line, 'Make it so, Number One.'"

"No, don't remember anything like that. Can't say if I've ever seen a Star Trek show or movie."

"Ever heard of it?" Tommy was curious.

"Yeah. I've heard of it. Just never been a fan."

Charlie meticulously, and with a steady hand used the torch to cut the bottom out the bed. In a way their effort to clean up the bed was wasted because they were surprised to discover how solid the bed remained, and there was only limited rust.

A loud clank echoed throughout the shop and startled Sheena and Mutt when the sheet of metal crashed to the floor.

Cal handed Tommy an air grinder with an aggressive grinding disk attached, "Here you go. Smooth up the edges."

They had mounted the bed on four sawbucks and rolled Tommy into the "U" shaped opening on the shop stool.

# RETURN TO FAITH

"Have at it, Young Man," Charlie patted Tommy on the back.

"He also wrote up a list of the metal strips we'll need," Tommy explained. "It's in the same pouch."

Cal retrieved the list and studied it before he handed it to Charlie.

"I'll call a metal supplier in Salisbury to see if they have these pieces in stock. If so, I'll go get'm now."

Tommy wore the respirator and goggles, and created a shower of sparks as he happily ground the bottom of the side panels on the old truck bed.

Cal and Charlie stood nearby with huge smiles on their faces. They watched with tremendous satisfaction as Tommy took ownership of his suggestion.

While Tommy made it rain showers of sparks, Sam called and asked Cal if he could bring Tommy home that evening. She needed to run some errands after she got off work.

Tommy was full of surprises that day, and requested they make a detour by the old church, where they discovered the crane crew had been delayed a few hours by a problem with the engine. They had just set the last truss when the orange Judge arrived. Right behind them was the plywood crew who were ready to screw the plywood to the trusses.

Terry was there as they repaired the crane on site. He met Cal, Tommy, Sheena, and Mutt at the Judge, "As you can see, we had to delay my plywood guys; but they're committed to staying until they get all the wood on the roof, and the tar paper over it. The shingle crew is scheduled to start at daybreak in the morning. You'll be good-to-go for Saturday morning."

Terry led Cal, and Tommy, who held onto Sheena's harness, with Mutt attached to the harness by a leash. They walked around the old church and Cal took photos with his cell phone.

The new trusses extended upward like ribs of a giant creature. The plywood crew had scaled the trusses and started nailing strips to perfectly space them apart. Then they started to lay and screw sheets of plywood to the trusses. The new, raw wood was a dramatic contrast to the weathered and neglected gray boards on the sides of the building.

"It's like a Phoenix, rising from its ashes," Tommy

compared, but immediately seemed embarrassed. "Sorry. That's the only thing I could think of."

"Hey, that's the perfect analogy," Cal reassured with a smile.

Tommy grinned. It dawned on him that he would do himself a huge favor if he would grasp that Cal saw the better side of him; and that's the guy he needed to believe he actually was.

......

Sam sat under a floor lamp, comfortably cuddled on the sofa with a book in hand. She was very familiar with the growl of the Judge's exhaust. She smiled when she heard Tommy's and Sheena's steps on the wooden boards of the porch.

She allowed the front door to open and close before she looked up, "Hey Bud, if I would'a known you were gonna work this late, I could'a come by and picked you up."

Tommy securely held on to Sheena's harness, "I wanted to go by the church and check out how they were com'n along with the roof."

"You're really excited about helping, aren't you?"

Tommy took a few steps, then paused, "Sometimes, you're a lot smarter than I give you credit."

Sam's face beamed with emotion, "I'm so proud of you, Son."

Tommy couldn't remember the last time he'd given his Momma a reason to even think it, let alone say it to his face. At first he couldn't find suitable words, so he just stood there until he felt his eyes welled up as his emotions churned. "I hope to hear that again, real soon," he said as he turned Sheena and they headed toward the hall.

"Did you guys eat dinner already?"

"I'm gonna take a shower now," Tommy said, then paused but didn't look back, "Charlie and Cal are gonna start paying me a little for helping around the shop."

Sam was surprised, "Oh, Honey! That's awesome."

"Actually, today was my first payday," Tommy revealed. It was the perfect time to tell her the rest, but he wanted to see her reaction. He turned to face his Mother, "And this evening I want to take my wonderful Momma out to dinner."

# RETURN TO FAITH

Sam was unable to contain her joy as she tossed the book on the cushion and bolted from the sofa. She explained as she darted across the room, "I know you're too grown up and macho for this silly Momma stuff, but I wanna hug my Baby Boy."

It was more than alright with Sam's "baby boy." He loved the hug as much if not more. Both Momma Bear and Baby Bear clung to each other and cried.

......

Saturday morning was even warmer than predicted and the long sleeve over-shirts would soon be shed. Cal, Charlie and two of Betsy's regulars at the diner, both in their 50's, of average height and weight, sipped coffee from steamy styrofoam cups. They huddled around blueprints of the steeple, spread out on a stack of lumber.

Cal turned around when he heard gravel crunch. He watched Tommy steady himself against the car and ease to the back door. He opened the door and Sheena jumped out. Her tail wagged as if she knew the importance of their visit.

"Okay guys. No more goofing off. The Boss is here," Cal announced.

Sam walked around the back of the car and motioned for Tommy to go on down and join the guys.

"You staying for a while?" Tommy was hopeful.

Sam nodded, "For a bit. Then I'm gonna run over to the diner and help Betsy get you guys' lunch ready." She said as she closed the back door and leaned against the car. Her eyes filled with tears and she wanted so much to hug her son as he began this new adventure. But she knew he wouldn't want his Momma hugging, slobbering and crying all over him in front of "the Guys."

Tommy stepped very cautiously on the thickly packed, gravel pad. He didn't want to let either foot sink too deeply into the loose gravel and cause him to lose his balance.

"Next time I'll park at the end of the gravel," Sam promised.

Tommy held up his hand and waved his approval as he stayed focused on each step. He was in an exceptionally good mood once his feet planted on solid ground, "Thought you guys'd have that steeple together by now." Tommy smiled broadly.

Cal shook Tommy's hand then attached Mutt's leash to Sheena's harness. Mutt was excited to see Sheena, who as usual ignored her son while on duty. Mutt quickly calmed down and appeared ready to follow Sheena's lead.

Charlie introduced Tommy to the diner regulars and after everyone shook hands, they huddled around the blueprints.

"Well, Boss, what should we do first?" Cal spoke up.

Tommy flipped through the blueprints for several seconds, "Let's break into teams. One for the roof, the other to build the base."

Since day one, Cal and Charlie supported and encouraged Tommy to make suggestions. Tommy was amazed how many times the Guys actually approved and followed through, which gave Tommy the confidence to take charge. The steeple project had begun. Tommy gave verbal instructions, pointed fingers, and made head nods as he helped organize the two teams. He assured that each team selected the appropriate tools and tool belts.

"Okay, Boss. Keep us on track," Cal requested.

Terry had sent over several sawbucks and there were enough pieces of plywood to set up two separate workstations. Tommy placed the roof blueprint pages on one workbench and left the base pages on the other.

Tommy and Sheena got a good workout as they were in nearly constant motion back and forth between the two teams. Tommy soon caught on that the Guys often made up questions to call him away from one work table to the other. He didn't mind because he knew they wanted to make him feel important and necessary. He appreciated it. He'd never been important or necessary before.

As the two projects took shape, Tommy had to occasionally sit in one of the chairs Cal and Charlie set up at both work stations. The questions decreased and Tommy didn't mind that either. It was good to sit still for a few minutes.

Fun banter and good-natured joking kept the mood light, but they were very serious about doing quality work. It helped that Terry had paid the guys in his company's working shop to precut the pieces. All Tommy and the teams had to do was identify the pieces, then hammer, screw and glue them together, based on the detailed blueprints.

The base was completed, and the shingled roof attached. Cal stepped up with a paint roller on the end of a pole, a bucket of white paint, and a tray. Tommy reached for the paint roller and Cal gladly obliged.

Before Tommy could dip the roller in the full tray of paint, Betsy, and Sam made a quick delivery of burgers, fries and drinks. After lunch, Tommy sat on a stool and used the roller to paint the steeple base. Cal, Charlie and the rest of the Guys moved over to scrape as much of the chipped paint as possible off the weathered, gray planks on the side of the church. They wanted to accomplish as much as possible while they had access to extra hands.

By early evening Charlie and the Guys had called it quits for the day. Everyone was pleased with the results. The steeple looked great and would be raised to the roof on Monday, if things went well.

Tommy wasn't ready to leave and Cal could tell the young man wanted to talk. So they sat on the side steps and watched the sun sink into the western sky. Sheena's harness lay between them. At the bottom of the steps, Mutt attacked his off duty Momma, and she happily rolled and tussled with him.

Cal decided to remain quiet and not spoil Tommy's train of thought. The young man would start the conversation when he was ready.

Eventually, Tommy took a deep, pensive breath. He was ready, "Here I sit on a Saturday evening, on the steps of a broken down country church I've spent the day working on. And beside me is the renegade preacher who's paying for the remodeling, but has no intentions of ever preaching in the church when it's done."

"So, you feel like you've wasted a Saturday?"

Tommy shook his head, "That's what makes no sense. I actually enjoyed it, and I'm proud of what we accomplished."

Cal nodded, "I'd say that's a good thing. I'm also proud of what we did today, and I'm really proud of how you stepped up and took charge."

"Other than Mom, nobody's ever believed in me."

Cal took a moment before he responded, "I have to be honest, in the beginning, I wasn't so sure I'd made the right decision."

"Me either," Tommy admitted. "After what I did to you, I was surprised you'd even turn your back to me."

"I think the lack of any memory is the key. I know what the law thinks you did; but I don't have a memory of it, so to an extent, it's not real."

"Oh, it's very real to me. I remember it vividly. Especially wrecking your truck. And every time I think about it, I realize I don't deserve the opportunities you're giving me."

Both Cal and Tommy were silent for a few seconds. That was a lot to mentally chew on.

Then Cal shared something he felt Tommy needed to know, "Well you're making up for the truck now, and that means a lot to me. And I don't know if this'll help, but I'm beginning to think the loss of so many memories might be the best thing that's ever happened in my life."

Tommy had to take a moment to absorb that one. Then he turned to Cal, "You mean the worst thing I've ever done in my life might be the best thing that's ever happened in your life?"

"Yep."

Tommy chuckled, "Well, don't ask me to whack you on the head again."

Cal smiled, "I don't think we'll have to worry about that."

That lighthearted moment was the perfect transition Tommy needed to change the subject to what was really on his mind, "Did you have a good relationship with your dad?"

That came out of the blue and caught Cal completely off guard, "I honestly don't remember," Cal turned to face the setting sun. It seemed appropriate, "If I had to guess, I'd say yes."

Tommy drew in a deep breath and his eyes followed Cal's gaze to the amazing, colorful sky, "I can't wrap my head around this whole God thing. To have created such a beautiful world, He sure seems content to allow pain and suffering to ruin it. He let my Dad leave us. Momma has struggled ever since. And she goes to church every Sunday."

"I'm sure in my past life I would've had some words of wisdom, and comfort, probably even quoted a few Bible verses."

"Just like Mom's preacher when I told him I've heard her

crying many nights, worrying how she's gonna pay the bills."

"Your Mom seems like a great person. A strong woman who loves her son very much," He turned to Tommy, "I think it best you look at me for a second."

Tommy slowly, cautiously faced Cal.

"We've come a long way in a very short time."

Tommy nodded, "Yes, we have."

"Then I believe you'll understand why I'm asking, what are you doing to help her?"

Tommy nodded, "Two days ago I would've been very offended if you asked me that. But she's the happiest I've ever seen her since I started working on this church."

Cal nodded, "It's done a lot for me too; but as you said earlier, I still can't wrap my head around this whole God thing."

"And I don't think we're gonna solve it this evening," Tommy concluded as he rose, "Sheena. Let's go so Cal can get home and get some rest. He ain't as young as he used to be."

......

## 29
## When The Time is Right, The Right Things Will Happen

Cal had awakened earlier that Sunday morning, but decided to lay back down and easily drifted back into a restful sleep. That afternoon he stretched out on the sofa and made Mutt the happiest puppy on the planet. He allowed him up on the sofa for a good tussle and tug-of-war with a worn out athletic sock. Until his cell phone rang, and Cal let go of the sock. Mutt rolled backward and was confused that he'd won so easily.

"Sorry, Little Buddy."

Cal retrieved his cell phone and was surprised by the name that appeared on the screen. He tapped the answer icon, "Hello."

"Cal, hope you don't mind me asking, but exactly what happened between you and Tommy, yesterday?"

Cal sat up, "Is he okay?"

Sam paced in her backyard. She was confused, "He didn't say a word all evening. Went to bed without eating. This morning, he shocked my socks off... asked if he could go to church with me."

"Where's he now?"

"He and Sheena are taking a nap. It's really none of my business what you talked about on the porch, but I'd like to know. I could tell a lot was going on his mind when I picked him up."

"I'd rather not say much right now. But I think for the first time in his life, he's doing some serious self-reflection, and truly looking for answers."

"Well, I'm gonna inch out on what I hope isn't a flimsy limb, and thank you from the bottom of my heart. And please take this the way I mean it, but you're turning into the father he always wanted, but never had. But I'm not trying to push him on you."

Cal was rendered speechless. Sam's evaluation landed much closer to his heart than he expected. He went silent.

"Cal, you still there?"

"Uh, yeah."

"I'm sorry. I hope I'm not making you feel uncomfortable, or reluctant to be around Tommy."

"No, actually, you just opened my eyes. I'm going out on my own limb now. Recently I've been wondering if Tommy may be the son I always wanted, but could never have."

"The Lord does work in mysterious ways."

Cal remained silent. He wasn't ready to openly admit that one yet.

As soon as Cal got off the phone with Sam, he called Betsy. Suddenly, he didn't want to be alone.

"Well, hello Cal. Nice to hear from you," Betsy was very pleased to get the call.

"What are you doing after you close this evening?"

"Actually, I'm getting ready to lock up now. It's gonna be a slow afternoon. There's some events going on at the Speedway."

"Mutt and I are bored. You wanna go for a ride?"

"Oh gee. Since you put it that way. How can a girl say, no?"

"Okay, so I'm a little rusty."

"A little rusty? Try cankered."

"Not sure I know what that means."

Betsy giggled, "Let's just say it's worse than rusty."

Of all places on a weekend when there's an event at the Charlotte Motor Speedway, Cal wanted to go to the Bass Pro Shop at Concord Mills. It was only three miles from the track.

"I can't believe you're dragging me here when a bazillion people are in town." Betsy shook her head.

"I don't remember if I've ever had a hobby. I don't know if I ever played golf, tennis, or cards." Cal pointed to the huge bass on the sign about the entrance to the Bass Pro Shop, "Maybe I...."

Betsy chuckled, "I don't see you hunt'n, fish'n, or shoot'n paper targets."

"How do you cook paper targets?"

They stood a few feet from the oversized wooden doors centered in the rustic-themed entrance, and Betsy pointed up at the huge fish on the sign, "You're serious, you actually want to go in there?"

"I think I'm becoming a Dad."

Betsy played it off, "Not by me, you ain't."

"I'm serious."

Betsy's mouth dropped open, "You got someone pregnant?"

"No. He's a beat up chair that's been tossed in the garbage heap. All he needs is some sanding, refinishing and new upholstery."

"Like someone else I know?"

Cal motioned to the new clothes Betsy had picked out for him, "I think you did a great job."

Betsy smiled, "You still need a little more sanding and refinishing."

Cal grinned and placed his hand on the small of Betsy's back. "Come on, let's get started looking for my new hobby."

Betsy stood her ground, "You're talking about Tommy."

Cal nodded, and Betsy flung her arms around him, "That's amazing. Come on, I'll buy you a box of cigars."

The hug was unexpected, but very good, and didn't last nearly long enough before Betsy took hold of his arm. "You're heading in the wrong direction. I can make this very easy."

"Let's not get too excited. I'm not ready to run home and paint a bedroom blue."

"Or, buy a blue commode?"

Cal turned his head to the side like a curious puppy, "I don't know the one in the bathroom at the apartment...."

"Is just fine," Betsy assured, then took hold of Cal's hand and turned him back toward the orange Judge. "Come on. We're in the right neighborhood, just the wrong address."

On the long walk back to the car neither Cal or Betsy wanted to let go of the other's hand. And neither would dare look at the other which might prompt them to get nervous and release the other's hand.

......

A few minutes later Betsy had Cal turn on the service road that looped around the Speedway. The parking lots were packed and people were everywhere. State Patrol officers directed traffic. Even with the windows up the roar of race cars thundered.

"So this is Charlotte Motor Speedway?" Cal was both stunned and amazed.

"Yep," Betsy nodded. "If you want a fast track to Tommy's heart, buy him tickets to the next race."

"Not until October."

"Don't think I want to wait that long."

"Then take him to the NASCAR Hall of Fame."

"Where's that?"

"Close to the Panther's stadium."

Cal looked at Betsy. He didn't have a clue. Betsy shook her head, "You're a lost cause. Do you really want to know?"

"Yeah, let's look it up on my iPad when we get back to the apartment."

"You inviting me over?"

"And I'll fix you dinner."

"Now you're scaring me."

"Take me by the diner to pick up my car first. Oh, and do you have any food at your place?"

"Maybe we need to go back to the Bass Pro Shop so I can buy a gun, or some fishing gear."

"Or, we can stop at the store on the way in."

"Don't worry. I got it covered."

For the entire road trip, Mutt laid quietly in the back seat and appeared to sleep. Cal checked several times but the little pup never moved.

Betsy mused, "Wow your Little Buddy must be worn out."

The one thing neither Betsy nor Cal considered, the little fellow might have played possum so he wouldn't get in their way.

......

Betsy was actually impressed as she watched Cal cut up several fresh veggies. However she became a little concerned when he opened a can of tuna, poured off the water and dumped it in the pan with the veggies, water and vegetable oil. Her mouth twisted into a sour knot when he started adding this spice and that seasoning. She'd never considered mixing that concoction, and wondered if it might be toxic.

"Have you had that "witch's brew" approved by the FDA?"

The unorthodox mixture unexpectedly filled the apartment with an aroma befitting a fine eating establishment. Much to Betsy's surprise her reluctant mouth was treated to an explosion of incredible flavors.

"Okay. I'm officially impressed. I've never eaten tuna and enjoyed it. If you ever want an honest job, come see me at the diner. I'll give you a shot at Chef's Assistant."

"I'll keep that in mind."

Shortly after dinner, Cal looked at his watch, "One of us has a long day tomorrow. May I walk you to your car?"

Betsy wasn't insulted because she realized how important tomorrow would be in the church restoration project.

Before Cal opened Betsy's car door, he initiated a hug that was readily reciprocated, and by mutual consent didn't last too long. They smiled at each other under the bright overhead light.

"Taking it slow will be good for me," Cal spoke first.

"I'm thinking snail," Betsy suggested.

Cal offered his hand and Betsy shook it.

"Snail Speed ahead," Cal confirmed.

......

The next morning, the crane broke down again and delayed the steeple placement until after lunch. Cal, Tommy and Charlie got their burgers to go from the diner, and sat on the tailgate of Charlie's truck. They ate their lunch as the crew completed the repair.

Terry had left to check on an issue at another job site and he parked beside Charlie's truck. "Sorry for the delay," he said as he hopped out of the cab.

"It's ready, Boss," The crane operator called over.

Cal and Charlie hopped down and assisted Tommy off the tailgate. Sheena, with Mutt in tow, moved into position.

As the crane's diesel engine droned in the background, two construction workers, who wore hard hats and safety glasses, attached chains to the steeple. Cal, Charlie, Tommy, Sheena and Mutt stepped around the steeple. They looked at each other.

"Guess one of us should say a prayer," Cal spoke up. It

was the first time he felt a prayer was necessary since he arrived in Faith.

"Would that be you, Preacher?" Tommy grinned.

Cal instinctively reached over and laid his right hand on the steeple. Charlie followed and bowed his head. Cal looked at Tommy, who was hesitant, but finally placed his hand on the steeple. The two Construction Workers removed their hard hats and respectfully bowed their heads. Tommy looked around, then bowed his head but didn't close his eyes. Cal bowed his head and began, but he surely didn't sound like a preacher.

"Well, ah, Lord, here we are, remodeling this old church. We're not exactly sure why; but we're doing it, so I guess we need for you to give us a sign we're doing the right thing. Ah. In Jesus' name. Amen."

Cal turned to Tommy, who was last to look up. The corner of Cal's mouth turned up in a "that wasn't my best prayer" grin.

Cal, Tommy, Charlie and Terry stepped back. They were so proud as they watched the crane slowly hoist the white steeple with black shingles, and a white cross, into position on the rundown church's new roof. Two Construction Workers bolted it securely in place.

The Guys stayed put as Cal stepped closer to the church in the midst of an amazing transformation. The new, freshly painted steeple and new roof were a stark contrast over the weathered, gray plank siding, still speckled with bits of aged, white paint.

The correlation to his own life was so profound to Cal at that moment. He readily recalled his first few nights in Faith, at this very building. In its dilapidated, neglected state, the abandoned church was a physical manifestation of his own shabby and worthless existence. He had become a hollow shell, that few would deem worth the time and effort to rebuild. But by chance, or divine intervention, Cal found the letter left in a broken down desk, in the forgotten church, that was doomed to be burned to the ground. That letter led Cal to this moment.

There was a good chance Cal would never remember the decisions that led him to turn on the road, where Tommy and Megan had set their trap. The question arose, was that random, or ordained? Cal easily recalled a phrase he'd heard several times since they started the church renovation, "The Lord works in mysterious ways."

Mysterious, or convenient, Cal couldn't remember exactly what drove him away from God. But a series of events in and around this abandoned church, in the small country town of Faith, North Carolina, had become significant. He finally had to admit that maybe God had placed him on a most unorthodox path, that could lead him to a possible return to his abandoned Faith.

However, at that moment, the jury was still out. Too many things could still go very wrong.

Tommy was compelled to walk Sheena up beside Cal. Without looking, Cal reached over and put his arm around Tommy's shoulders. The troubled young man smiled. Cal knew Tommy was on a similar journey. There they stood in silent solidarity. The two most unlikely of partners were satisfied and without words, they committed to complete the task before them. Then let the chips fall where they may.

......

Over the next several weeks both physical restoration projects progressed ahead of schedule. The truck and church experienced amazing transformations inside and out. A buzz began to hum around Faith, as does in all small communities when people hear something worth sharing. Of all people, Tommy Forrester had teamed up with the mysterious former preacher. Most of the chatty community supported their gallant attempt to salvage the abandoned church. Others would have preferred the eyesore adjacent the aged "Welcome to Faith" sign would've been burned down and the lot cleared of the mess.

Those in favor of Faith Covenant Church's rebirth pooled their money, and hired a well known sign painter out of Charlotte. She restored the Welcome sign to its original glory.

The freshly painted sign combined with the cleared lot and dramatic progress on the church building had transformed the entrance to Faith into a destination worth a turn off the country road. It was a place to explore, instead of a dying, out of the way city, destined to become a ghost town.

As for Cal and Tommy, the two psychological restorations in progress, each day found them a little more receptive. The next steps on their individual journeys became easier as they inched toward the same destination.

Cal, Tommy and Charlie built a lasting friendship and deep level of trust as they disassembled, cleaned, and in some cases replaced parts, then reassembled and painted the old engine to look brand new.

As the hot summer days lengthened, some of what had been curious passersby started to join Cal, Charlie, Tommy, Sheena, and Mutt after they closed the shop for the day, and moved to the church. It was obvious the Guys needed help to finish the painstakingly slow task of scraping the remaining, stubborn paint from the exterior woodwork. Terry had quoted the job with and without a crew to scrape and repaint. The growing community support and involvement had saved a lot of money. An added bonus was that Terry estimated the community involvement had cut at least a full two months off the projected completion schedule.

As the weeks progressed, Tommy was able to walk longer distances without Sheena's assistance. He was eager to regain his total independence, but in no hurry to be stupid and risk a fall that could put him back in the hospital and cause a serious set back.

The day finally arrived when the truck cab, bed, and frame were returned from the paint shop. Cal and Charlie had kept the delivery day a secret from Tommy.

Unaware of what awaited inside, Tommy entered, as much under control of his own balance as reliant on the support form Sheena. He nonchalantly passed Charlie, who leaned under the hood of a car.

"Morn'n Chuck," Tommy spat out his usual greeting.

"Thomas," Charlie's monotone voice sounded from under the hood.

"Morn'n Cal," Tommy happily chirped as his eyes suddenly focused on the unexpected, incredible sight. His mouth jumped back in gear, "Wow! It looks amazing." Tommy hurried over for a close inspection of the sparkling body parts. He extended his hand to caress the glossy clear coat.

"Don't you dare put your bare, greasy, bacon, egg and cheese biscuit paw on that new paint and clear-coat," Charlie playfully chided.

By the next afternoon, Charlie and Cal had lifted and placed the cab and bed on the frame. Tommy helped eyeball the alignment and leveling of the body parts, so Cal and Charlie could screw, clip and spot-weld them in place. Tommy watched as Cal and Charlie inserted the dashboard.

Every day Tommy had become determined to do more, to stand longer and walk further on his own. But he'd reached a plateau. He was so frustrated and tired of being relegated to a cheerleading spectator on the more involved projects, both on the truck and at the church.

Cal and Charlie devised a plan to help reinforce Tommy's importance to the team. On that morning, Cal was stretched out on a low-profile creeper, and rolled out from under the truck where he'd attached the brake lines to the brake assemblies.

Tommy ambled in and was obviously disheartened by his continued lack of progress with his balance issues. Even though his spirits were low, Mutt and his early morning antics at least made him smile.

Mutt had grown so fast he had already reached three quarters of Sheena's height and weight, but he was still all puppy, and loved him some Tommy.

From the low-profile creeper, Cal pointed to some boxes Tommy had walked past, "Got a little surprise early this morning."

Tommy was less than excited until he stepped over and realized the contents of a brown box on a rack.

That was the perfect surprise to cheer Tommy up, "They're a little late. But cool!" He lifted the round speedometer out of one of the boxes. "Man, it looks great."

Cal rolled off the creeper onto his knees, "You feel up to installing them today?"

Tommy was excited but unsure, "By myself?"

"I gotta spend some time at the church," Cal didn't lie.

"And I have to drive to Charlotte to pick something up," Charlie's excuse was almost a fib, but still wasn't classified a lie.

"You guys trust me?"

# RETURN TO FAITH

"Looks like you're the man," Charlie reassured.

Thirty minutes later, Tommy was stretched across the uncovered floorboard where he attempted to make sense of the clusters of wires. He was baffled by the multi-colored wiring harnesses, but more determined to figure them out.

Over at the church, thanks to generous Spring showers, a thick carpet of bright green grass had covered the brown dirt. The gray, weathered boards were covered by a fresh coat of white paint. New brick steps had been laid, and black railings had been built and installed on the front entrance.

Much to Cal's surprise, that morning Sadie and Ralph Jenkins showed up with several boxes of colorful flowers, that in a million years Cal would've never identified. To be in their late eighties, the Jenkins were still very spry and were on their knees with their gloved hands buried in a mixture of regular dirt and rich potting soil. Their mission was to bring new life and beautiful colors to the newly laid brick flower beds that flanked the front steps. Cal pushed yet another wheelbarrow loaded with forty pound bags of potting soil.

Sadie pointed to the front steps, "Honey, would you be a dear and please spread us four more bags along the base of the steps."

"I think it's gonna take five or six," Ralph countered without so much as a peek behind him.

Sadie stopped and looked over her shoulder to reassess, "You know, for a nearly blind and deaf old man, I believe you're right."

With his head down Ralph didn't miss a beat as he quipped so mildly and humbly, "I might be deaf and nearly blind, but I know how to spread my dirt."

Sadie glanced up and winked at Cal, "That's because the old coot's always spreading his own BS"

"Careful Sadie, I ain't that deaf yet."

Cal prepared to lift the next forty pound bag, "I really appreciate all your help, but you guys are about to work me to death." It wasn't a complaint. It was the embarrassingly ugly truth.

Sadie took Cal's comment in stride, as if all she heard was how much he appreciated their help, "You know, even though you don't remember, we'd never allow you to start up another church, without us helping pretty it up a bit."

"We just don't like being out after dark," Ralph added.

"You can come back anytime. Just keep in mind, I'm not ready to even consider preaching again. I'm getting it ready for the next guy who comes along and wants to step in the pulpit."

Mr. Jenkins held up a gloved-handful of the original brown dirt that had been dumped in the flower beds to be mixed with the potting soil, "Young fella. I can feel it. This is Holy ground. You best be prepared."

Cal was caught off guard, unable to form a response, but was immediately distracted when he heard gravel crackle in the freshly poured parking lot. A white, late-model, E-Class Mercedes rolled to a stop in front of the steps. Steam hissed and billowed from under the hood and below the car.

Todd Fletcher, a handsome man in his forties was extremely upset when he bounded out of the car, "Is there a garage close by?"

Cal called Charlie, who was on his way back from Charlotte. He was ten minutes away.

Sadie and Ralph had loaded up and headed back to Archdale when Charlie rolled into the gravel lot and parked beside the steaming Mercedes.

Todd had opened the hood and was seated behind the steering wheel with the door open. He was in a foul mood and in a heated argument with someone on his cell phone.

Charlie checked under the hood and immediately shook his head. He stepped over to chat with Cal as he waited to speak with Todd, whose bad day was about to get much worse.

"At this point, I don't care anymore. I've tried everything I know to make this work. Nothing I do is right." He finally realized Charlie was there. "The Wrecker Guy's here. I gotta go." Todd listened for a few more seconds. "I don't care what your attorney says, I'm not signing it." He listened even more. "I gotta go." Todd exited the car, tossed the phone in the passenger seat, then met Charlie at the front of the car. "You got here pretty fast."

"My shop's only a couple of miles away."

"You fix cars too?" Charlie nodded. "Is it possible to get it fixed today?" Charlie shook his head but Todd continued before Charlie could explain. "How about tomorrow?" He extended his hand to Charlie. "Sorry. I'm Todd."

"I'm Charlie. And I'm sorry, but you have a blown engine. I've never seen, or even heard of this with a Mercedes." Charlie explained as he pointed to a steaming hole in the block, from which a bent push rod stuck through. "You need a new engine. It looks fairly new, so your warranty should cover it."

Todd looked around and in his state of mind, all he heard was that his car needed a new engine. He was extremely condescending, "Oh, great! I'm stuck in the middle of nowhere, with some red-neck mechanic intending to rip me off." He paused long enough to draw in a deep breath. "Just so we're clear. You're not towing my car to your shop. I don't need this. Not while battling a heartless wife, and her blood-sucking attorney."

Charlie remained calm and professional, "Sir, I never offered to tow your car to my shop. I said you have a blown engine and your warranty should cover it. If you don't have a road-side assistance plan with Triple A, or Mercedes, then I can tow your car to your home, or the nearest dealership."

"I live in South Florida."

"Then the nearest Mercedes dealership's in Charlotte. Thirty minutes away."

Todd spun around and kicked a grapefruit-sized dent in the front quarter panel. He looked Heavenward. He was very angry, "How much more do you want from me?"

Charlie and Cal shared a concerned glance.

Todd took a deep breath before he could face the uneasy strangers, but it only got worse when he realized he'd parked in front of a church. He immediately lowered his eyes. "I'm sorry. I'm not having a good day... or life, for that matter."

Cal was compelled to glance Heavenward, then at Todd as he'd focused his attention on Charlie and his car. There was no doubt in Cal's mind, Todd's mishap was about as much of a coincidence as his encounter with Tommy and Megan, that also brought him to Faith.

"You can call the dealership in Charlotte, but I doubt they can get a truck out here in under two hours. Or, if you'd prefer, I'll tow your car to Charlotte," Charlie offered.

"You hungry, or want a cup of coffee while you think about your options?" Cal asked before he realized what he'd offered.

Charlie was confused at first, until he remembered, Cal was a preacher in his former life. He immediately called Betsy to give her a heads-up.

......

# RETURN TO FAITH

## 30
## Sometimes God Works In Very Overt Ways

Todd and Cal sat at his booth by the window.

"Will you tell your friend how sorry I am? After the way I acted, I'm too embarrassed to ride with him for thirty minutes," Todd was sincere.

"Charlie's a great guy. You would've enjoyed the ride and conversation."

"How long have you been preaching here?"

That wasn't a question Cal was ready to answer, and he was unable to conceal his reluctance to open up to a total stranger. If he were meant to share, then a perfect stranger would be a good warm up, "I'm not a preacher, at least not now. It's kind of a long, twisted story."

Todd looked at his watch, "Well, we've got a while before the wrecker gets here."

Betsy set a steamy plate of food in front of Todd, and a cup of coffee in front of Cal. She winked at him, but he didn't reciprocate. Just in case he'd intentionally, or accidentally slipped back into "preacher mode," she would show him the respect and reverence he deserved. The same went for the stranger seated across from Cal.

Todd bowed his head for a brief, silent blessing.

Cal grinned understandingly when Todd looked up, "Before we get started, may I assume, you're a Christian?"

It was Todd's turn to demonstrate his reluctance to share with a total stranger. Until he opened his mouth and the words flew out, "Used to be. Stopped believing a long time ago."

"Old habits can be hard to break."

Todd's eyebrows raised from genuine curiosity. More importantly, he needed to have a good chat with someone who didn't know him from "Adam's house cat." Fortunately, for his sake, it didn't take long for Todd to feel comfortable with Cal. Comfortable enough to share his current financial crisis, and how it had exacerbated his long-term failure of a marriage.

Cal was amazed at how easily he was able to focus on specific problem areas with Todd's assessment of the way his wife perceived him, which most likely was attributed more to his low self-esteem. Since he wasn't a preacher anymore, he dared not venture into any semblance of a "preacher man." Nor was he a qualified psychologist.

Sooner than expected, but actually right on time, Todd's cell phone interrupted their conversation.

"That was the wrecker driver. He's about ten minutes out."

Twenty minutes later, Todd waved from the passenger seat of a fancy new wreck truck, as it drove him and his car away from the church.

"Really appreciate your time."

Cal waved while Mutt sat patiently beside him.

......

A week later, just before lunch, Cal, Tommy and Charlie pushed a lift with the rebuilt engine into position in front of the sparkling black truck. The chrome wheels had arrived the day before and Tommy had to do a brief, somewhat unstable "I was right dance," once they were bolted on. Especially since Cal and Charlie openly bragged on Tommy's choice and insistence they chrome the wheels.

Charlie pushed a button on a hand held control and the motor whirred and the chains clanked as the engine lowered into place.

Then an unexpected guest stepped in the shop, "Excuse me. May I come in for a minute?" Todd paused rather than continue to invite himself in.

"Having car trouble again?" Charlie looked behind Todd.

"Actually, they let me trade it out for another one the same make and model. It cost me a couple thousand extra. Finished up my business in the Charlotte area and was on my way back to Florida." He eased closer. "You guys need a hand?"

"Aren't you afraid you'll mess up your nice clothes?" Charlie was ready to say, "No," until Cal winked.

Cal nodded to Tommy, "Yeah, help that young fella guide it in."

# RETURN TO FAITH

Working together, the four men carefully positioned the engine in the center of the truck's engine compartment. Charlie stepped away from the lift. "Do you wrestle gators in Florida?"

Todd was confused

Charlie explained, "Grab the front of the engine." He requested as he laid down on the red creeper and rolled under the truck. "Help them line it up with the motor mounts." After a couple of seconds of adjustments Charlie added, " A little to the left."

Cal looked at Tommy and they faced the same direction, which was opposite to Charlie's position under the truck, "Who's left?"

"Your left."

After a few minutes of tweaks and shifts, Charlie was able to securely bolt the engine in place. "Perfect."

Shortly thereafter, Cal, Tommy, Charlie and Todd huddled around the pristine engine compartment, and gazed at the shiny engine.

Todd smiled, "How long you guys been working on this old girl?"

"I've been tinkering with her for over two years. But since these guys came on board, a few months ago, she's really come a long way."

Tommy nodded, "A lot'a long days."

Charlie wiped his hands on a clean rag, "You guys ready to call it a night?"

Tommy reached to shake Todd's hand, "Really appreciate your help."

Cal passed it off as his old occupation that he sensed there was more, but he shouldn't tip his hand and ask Todd what it was. He had to provide him the opportunity to share it on his own terms, "Yeah, thanks. Have a safe trip home."

Todd confirmed Cal's suspicion when his eyes shifted to the floor, "Not really head'n back just yet." He drew in a pensive breath. "Checked into the bed and breakfast across town. Need any help with the old church for a week or so?"

"What about your angry wife?" Cal didn't hesitate.

"She's been angry for a long time."

Todd retrieved his cell phone from his pocket and tapped a few times on the screen, then he held the phone close to his mouth, "Hello, this is, Todd. I'm gonna be on vacation for a couple of weeks. I'll have spotty cell service, and limited email access. Please be patient, I will be in touch."

As they walked out of the garage, Cal asked Todd to meet him at the diner early the next morning.

......

Cal intended to keep the conversation focused on the progress they'd made on the church, and that the interior was in dire need of a good cleaning. The fact that Todd was unfazed by the potential messy work led Cal to believe his intent was genuine. More importantly, Cal sensed something deep inside of Todd had awakened, and he was more than a little curious why he cared about this stranger.

Todd, wearing a tee shirt and comfortable jeans, stood in the front corner of the sanctuary. He leaned on the handle of an industrial push broom .

Cal stepped beside Todd with a regular broom, "Ever ridden one of those?"

Todd cautiously grinned and shook his head.

Cal extended a white dust mask, "You seem like a bright boy. You'll catch on quickly." He pointed, "Start over there."

As with Tommy, Cal knew Todd would have to be comfortable before he could open up, but still on his terms. Tommy had to sand and grind away the destructive layers of rust before the real repairs could begin. With Todd, a "clean slate" was in order, so Cal decided the best way to start was with a big broom.

Cal sensed Todd had to uncover the truth that had been buried under many layers of bad decisions, that were made with good intentions; but for whatever reason, miserably failed. What began as a wonderful relationship that promised a happy and productive life had become coated with resentment. Loud, angry voices and hurtful accusations made matters only worse. That was evident, based on the one phone call Cal overheard, but only from Todd's perspective.

Cal used a regular broom to do a quick sweep of the first two rows of pews. Then Cal handed Todd the regular broom, "Okay, now you understand the process. Take this broom and sweep off the pews, then take the big broom and push it in a long pile on the other side. How you get it up, I'll leave to you."

At first Todd was ticked off that Cal got him started, then left him to do the entire sanctuary by himself. Shortly after Cal walked out, Todd appreciated the solitude. The time to think, while he was able to see the progress he made. At least he was able to accomplish something and feel good about it. He had to admit that the X-preacher might still have a few connections to a higher power. Even if the X-preacher was in denial.

Todd eventually got lost in time and was caught off guard when Cal, Charlie, Tommy and the dogs arrived to pick him up for lunch.

"Where's the piles of dust?" Cal was pleasantly surprised, even impressed when Todd showed him how he'd gotten it off the floor and into the large trash bins recently dropped off behind the church.

Todd worked until 3:30 PM in the hall, offices, and the two classrooms down the short hall. Then he went back to the bed and breakfast, took a shower and slept for a few hours. He couldn't remember a time in his life he'd ever done that much physical work. He was exhausted, but oddly rejuvenated. He opted to stay in for the evening.

......

That evening Cal and Charlie planned a special surprise. It was well earned.

Tommy sat behind the steering wheel in the cab of the old black truck. Cal and Charlie stood on opposite sides of the engine compartment. The hood was up and they looked across at each other.

"All the fluids are full," Charlie confirmed.

"The new battery's attached," Cal nodded.

Tommy chimed in from the cab, "And I have an itchy trigger finger."

Charlie and Cal flashed each other a thumbs up. "Then fire away!" Charlie instructed, "Pump the gas pedal a few times."

Tommy followed his instructions, then turned the key, but nothing happened. Total silence. Not even the click of an electric pulse. Cal and Charlie scanned the engine compartment, then Charlie shook his head and held up an unattached battery cable.

"Oops, forgot I disconnected it when I was checking the spark plug wires."

Charlie reattached the wire, "New battery attached."

Tommy turned the switch and after a few turns of the crankshaft, the engine fired up and idled a little roughly. It took Charlie a few turns on the carburetor set screw to even out the idle.

Cal nodded and wasn't sure if it were based on a memory, or the sheer joy of accomplishment, "She sure does have her own unique sound."

"Give her a few gentle revs," Charlie suggested.

Tommy obliged with a wide smile, until Charlie said, "That's good."

Tommy pumped his fists in the air, "Woo! Whooo!"

"Let's let her idle for a few minutes. Let her warm up and see if we have any leaks," The master mechanic was hopeful.

Cal and Charlie gave each other a high-five as they met in front of the truck. Then Charlie pointed at Cal, who grinned.

After they were satisfied all hoses and pipes were sealed, and there were no leaks, Cal backed the classic truck out of the garage. Tommy was seated in the middle and Charlie was beside the passenger door. Cal turned the truck around and eased forward, "This clutch is more my speed."

"Aren't we take'n the dogs?" Tommy looked behind them.

"They're guard'n the shop," Charlie explained as he leaned forward and smiled at Cal.

Tommy was consumed with being away from Sheena. As they pulled out of the lot, it was way beyond the distance that had been between him and Sheena since Cal and Betsy gave her to him. He was way too concerned to be suspicious.

Cal drove into downtown Faith, a typical small town Main Street, and at that time of evening had few oncoming cars and trucks. By then, Tommy smiled as broadly as Cal and Charlie.

"I'd love to drive this old girl," Tommy gazed ahead.

"What's the doctor saying?" Cal already knew the answer.

"If I can go two weeks without needing Sheena, he'll give me limited, day-time only, driving privileges. Then we'll see how I do."

Cal leaned up and looked at Charlie, who grinned.

Tommy snapped his head in both directions, "What are you guys up to?"

Cal pulled into an empty parking lot. He switched off the ignition, put on the parking brake, opened the door and hopped out. He stepped away, but remained facing away. "Hop out," he invited.

Tommy turned to Charlie, who nodded. Tommy took a deep breath and slid across the seat, then cautiously hung his legs out the door. He was reluctant to exit. He drew in another deep, hesitant breath

Cal refused to turn around, "It's time."

"For what?" Tommy became suspicious, and argumentative. "Are you asking an atheist to take a giant leap of faith?"

Cal shook his head, "This has nothing to do with, God. But it has everything to do with you."

"If I fall, who do I blame, you or your god?"

Charlie felt inclined to encourage, "Tommy, you make a number of steps each day without holding on to Sheena."

"But I can only take so many steps, then I need her."

Cal knew what he was about to say would sound cruel to anyone who hadn't spent as much time with Tommy as he and Charlie, "Are you sure. Do you really need her, or have you grown dependent on her, and afraid to stand on your own?"

Charlie nodded, "If you're afraid, then stay in the truck." Charlie turned and exited the truck. He walked around and stood beside Cal. They both faced away.

Tommy was annoyed, but increasingly defiant, "If I step out, it doesn't mean I believe in your god."

"At some point, you're gonna have to believe in something. A good place to start is believing in yourself," Cal challenged.

Tommy was just about to slide forward and out of the door, then he shook his head and pulled his legs back inside the cab.

Charlie moved to turn around until Cal reached over and touched his arm. They stood their ground.

Cal slowly nodded. It was time for a confession. It remained to be seen if it would affect Tommy, "At this moment, I might not be willing to fully accept that God exists, but I'm not willing to deny that He does. And if He does, He might have a higher purpose for me, and you."

"Oh no! You can't have it both ways, Preacher. You either believe he does, or he don't," Tommy was defiant.

Cal remained stoic, and appeared to ponder his true feelings.

Charlie spoke up, "Tommy, there's one way to prove Cal wrong."

Tommy was insulted, "You want me to fall on my face?"

Cal still refused to face Tommy, "No, we want you to stand on your own two feet, and make something of yourself. Make a better life for you and your Mom."

Tommy snapped, "Leave Momma out of this!"

Cal shook his head, "She's very much a part of your life. Good, or bad. You can't change it. It's up to you."

Charlie had a suggestion, "Use the truck for support."

Cal had one final challenge. Actually it could easily be taken as an insult, "Are you man enough?"

Tommy's eyes narrowed with determination. He swung his legs out the door, and without hesitation, slid out. He stood without holding on to anything.

Cal and Charlie smiled when they heard Tommy take a few tenuous steps.

Tommy grew bolder, more determined. Each step became easier, more fluid. He never wavered as he confidently stepped in front of Cal and Charlie. The determined young man smiled.

Without a word, Cal extended the keys to Tommy, who was reluctant to take them.

"We met with your Mom and your doctor. He said that physically, you've been ready for a couple of weeks. But according to your therapy reports, you were lacking confidence, and that could make you overreact, possibly cause a wreck."

Charlie chimed in, "So don't take the keys, if you're afraid you aren't ready yet."

The young man immediately kicked his ego to the curb, and took the keys from Cal, "Will you guys ride around with me for a while. It's been a long time since I've been behind the wheel."

"As long as we don't end up in the woods," Charlie had to

poke a little fun.

"Come on, Chuck. Cut me some slack."

"Yeah, Chuck, cut the boy some slack," Cal nudged Charlie.

Tommy shook Charlie's hand, "Thank you so much."

"Very proud of you, Tommy."

Tommy shook Cal's hand and held it for a couple of seconds, then hugged him and held on, "I owe you so much."

"No, as of tonight, you're paid in full," Cal had to stop because the lump in his throat was so large.

Charlie patted Tommy on the back as he headed back to the truck, "Come on boy, we're burn'n valuable moonlight."

Then after a quick visit to Betsy's house to show off both Tommy and the truck, the guys headed back to the shop.

The truck rolled back into the shop and stopped almost on the exact spot where they began the odyssey earlier.

Tommy's curiosity got the better of him, "What about Sheena?"

Cal reassured, "She'll be your dog as long as you want her."

The passenger door opened. Cal and Charlie exited and left Tommy behind the wheel with a broad smile etched in his face. He couldn't bring himself to let go of the wheel.

Without looking back, Cal and Charlie walked toward the office, "You gonna sleep in there?" Cal asked and smiled at Charlie, as they entered the office. The door squeaked closed behind them.

A few moments later the door squeaked open. Tommy entered and held the door for the dogs, but Sheena and Mutt sat down outside the door. Tommy entered to be greeted by Cal and Charlie, with Sam who beamed between them. Cal and Charlie were very pleased with themselves. Tommy was confused, "Momma, what are you doing here?"

Cal extended a folded piece of paper to Tommy.

"What's that?"

Cal extended it further, "Guess you'll have to open it."

Tommy cut suspicious eyes at Charlie, who was stoic, but his mother couldn't restrain her ear to ear smile.

Tommy finally accepted and unfolded the paper. His eyes widened with excitement when he realized he held a North Carolina vehicle title, "It's my truck?" His mouth dropped open.

"Charlie and I have already signed it," Cal explained.

"And since it's going on my insurance, I had to sign the title too," Sam struggled not to cry. "But as soon as we can get you a steady job, and you can afford your own insurance; I'm gonna to sign it over to you."

Charlie grinned, "Take care of the old girl."

Tommy's smile faded and in an instant his excitement shifted to sadness as he reluctantly extended the title back to Cal, and said, "I can't afford to pay you for the truck."

Cal smiled, "The deal is you help me rebuild another one, and this one's yours." Cal extended his hand, "Deal?"

Tommy became emotional and wiped tears from his eyes as he stepped past the outstretched hand and hugged Cal really tight.

Through tears of joy, Tommy was able to say, "You three are the only people who ever believed in me."

Cal gently patted Tommy on the back then passed him to Charlie, who after his firm hug, handed him off to Sam. That's when the tears flowed from four happy and proud humans.

When Tommy was finally able to release Sam, he jumped up and down and danced around until he realized he didn't feel the least bit restricted or off balance, "Hey, Momma, wanna go for a ride?"

Sam wiped her eyes, "Well, since Betsy dropped me off, I kinda need a ride back home."

Tommy put his arm around his proud Momma and opened the door. Sheena and Mutt sat patiently and appeared to be as proud of Tommy as the humans.

"Sheena, let's go," Tommy reached down and rubbed his new best friend on her head. "I want to take my two favorite girls for a ride."

Something about that sounded eerily familiar to Cal, and he wasn't sure if it were a good thing, or a bad thing. Nonetheless, Cal, Charlie, and Tommy smiled at each other. They had become a good team, and all three looked forward to the next project.

......

The next morning, Tommy and Charlie arrived at the

shop at the same time from opposite directions. Tommy motioned Charlie into the lot first, then parked the black truck beside Charlie's truck. They got out at the same time.

"You don't have to be here this morning. As far as Cal and the judge are concerned, you're free to do what you want," Charlie explained.

Tommy smiled, "I know. Mom and I talked for a long time last night. She wishes she could find a way to tell both of you how much she appreciates you giving me a chance, and for not kicking me out when you had every right."

"You can thank Cal for that. I was a hard sell, and I think you understand why."

Tommy nodded, and turned his eyes down in shame, "Yeah, and I owe you as much or more because you put aside your justifiable distrust of me."

"You don't necessarily have a clean slate, but you do have an opportunity for a fresh start."

Tommy dared to look up and directly into Charlie's eyes, "I've been looking into going to community college and taking auto mechanics. In a couple of months they're gonna start the next class for beginners. Just wanted to let you know I'm head'n to sign up," Tommy explained as he extended his hand. "Thank you again."

Charlie smiled and nodded as he shook Tommy's hand, "That's great. I'm really proud of you, young man." Charlie pulled Tommy over for a stout, manly hug. Tommy's eyes teared up as he pulled away and turned to leave.

"Hey, you got a job yet? You're gonna need some money to pay for those classes," Charlie asked.

"Gonna start looking after I sign up for class."

"I got a better idea. Come back here, you already have a job wait'n on you."

......

Cal spent the day painting the offices and classroom. Later that day he would meet with Betsy and Charlie to discuss if they were going to sand the wooden floors down and refinish all of them, or put carpet in the offices. The test sections they'd done on the floor so far looked great. The oak boards had held up well over the years.

A late afternoon nap was in order since Todd wanted to

work in the sanctuary that night. He had decided to do a little work and see a few clients during the day.

At 6:00 PM sharp, Cal and Todd started scrubbing the pews with soft brushes dipped in warm soapy water. The beautiful oak grain showed up so dramatically. While wet the pews looked like they would after a light sanding and a new coat of varnish.

To make conversation easier, they worked on parallel rows. Todd was extremely chatty, and unexpectedly candid, "My brothers and sisters are amazingly successful. My oldest brother owns a seventy-foot yacht."

Cal stopped scrubbing and turned to Todd, as he morphed into "Preacher Mode." He felt the urge, but wasn't sure where it would go, and take him with it. But for the moment, it would have to idle in neutral since Todd was on a roll.

"My life's been a tortured roller coaster." He used the brush as an example. "A long, slow, demanding climb up to the edge of success." He tipped the brush. "Only to plunge over the precipice, into utter defeat." He slammed the brush to the floor with a loud thud.

Cal pulled back. Mutt abruptly awakened and looked around.

"Another embarrassing failure, for the family joke."

"You drive a beautiful, expensive car."

"It's leased, and all my credit cards are maxed out. We're way behind on our mortgage."

"It's really none of my business, but what does your wife want in the divorce settlement?"

"Zero responsibility. And ninety percent of the debt is hers."

"Doesn't hardly sound fair," Cal wondered if it were wise to have taken sides. Especially since all he had to go on was Todd's word.

"Fair. That's not a word she ever learned the definition of." Todd shook his head, "I'm going to tell you the truth. My car's engine didn't blow up on its own. That day, I felt my eyes narrow with determination. My teeth clenched. I was ready to end it all on a narrow, winding road near here. I have shift paddles on the steering column, so I downshifted and pushed the accelerator to the floor. The tachometer leapt deep into the red zone. I recklessly raced into sharp turns, barely maintaining control. On a straight stretch, I saw a big truck heading toward me. If I hit it head-on, that would be my instant out. But at the last second, instead of whipping the car into the truck's lane, I chickened out. That's when the warning lights started flashing on the dashboard. Alarms went off and the engine started sputtering. I barely made it to the church. I didn't dare tell the dealer I was over-revving the engine... a split second from suicide." Todd lowered his head in shame. "I'm even a failure at suicide."

Cal was silent until Todd looked at him. Cal was hesitant and Todd continued.

"I've thought a lot about it since that day, and I've decided I was more terrified of facing God as such a failure, than battling my wife and her blood-sucking attorney."

This time Cal nodded to indicate he was still in listen mode, while Todd started to pace as he continued to battle his emotions.

"I'm so angry and confused. I'm so mad at God."

Cal nodded. He felt a gut-punch of familiarity with Todd's fragile emotional and spiritual condition. But a totally unrelated question slipped out of his mouth, "You still love your wife?"

Todd reluctantly nodded, "Since the eighth grade."

"Want to save your marriage?"

"It wasn't my idea to divorce."

"I'm not suggesting this is the answer, but a lot of couples have survived bankruptcies, when their love and commitment to each other were stronger than the problems they face."

Todd seemed to grasp the depth and purpose of Cal's example, "I know how I feel. I just can't get a true read on who and what she's become over the years."

"Please allow me to make a suggestion." Todd appeared willing to listen. "Head over to the diner. Eat a good meal. Tell Betsy to put it on my tab. Go to your room. Take a nice hot shower. Then call your wife and invite her to meet you up here, on neutral turf."

Todd reached to pick up the brush.

"I'll get it. You go on," Cal motioned to the door.

Todd pondered for a moment, "At least I'll know I tried,

one more time." Todd managed a grin, "You might not consider yourself a preacher, but you sure act and sound like a pastor."

That was unexpected. Cal didn't have a response.

Todd smiled, "Gotcha, Preacher man. Didn't I?"

......

# 31
# When The End Is Only The Beginning

Bright headlights from the road revealed Tommy sat in the cab of the old truck, in the driveway. He still couldn't get his head wrapped around the fact that he owned such an amazing vehicle.

Tommy could tell the car slowed down, so he turned his head and was forced to squint, and shield his eyes as the car pulled in the driveway. He was relieved when the bright lights went out. He wondered who would come to visit his Mom at that time of night. A car door opened and closed. He was about to find out.

Tommy wasn't the least bit prepared to see the face that appeared. He froze. He was speechless, as Megan stepped beside the truck. She was far from the beautiful young girl he'd fallen in love with and allowed to take control of his life. Megan was a gaunt shadow of her former beauty. She was so haggard, dirty and trembling. She had gone so far down hill so quickly. Even in the dark Tommy could tell she was ghostly pale and dangerously thin. Her voice was scratchy. She was confused.

"Thought you totaled this truck?"

Tommy was conflicted, "Yeah. You sideswiped me and last thing I remember about that night was sailing off the road. I don't remember anything after the first impact with the ground. They said it flipped several times. I was in a coma for a while."

"I swear, I came back and looked for you, but the brush was so thick."

"Why didn't you call for help?"

Megan started to cry, "I did."

"Then why didn't you stay?"

"I couldn't. I'm so sorry, I just couldn't deal with it. I was terrified I'd end up in jail, for a very long time" Megan shook her head, "Now where did you get this truck? It looks just like the one we stole from that man."

"Rather than have me put in jail, that man asked the judge and prosecutor to let me help him redo another one."

Megan coughed and sniffed as she pulled her greasy hair from in front of her eyes. "I need help. Bad." Megan managed to say before she collapsed into a heap beside the truck.

Tommy immediately sprang into action. He leapt out, knelt and cradled Megan in his arms.

Megan's voice was weak and shaky, "I was so afraid you were going to die. I called the hospital several times and they wouldn't tell me anything. I couldn't handle it. I had to get out of here."

"I coulda died."

Megan's trembling hand gently caressed Tommy's cheek, "I missed you so much."

"I missed you too. I refused to give up on you," Tommy whispered as he pulled Megan close.

．．．．．．

Cal was totally lost to his thoughts as he scrubbed the back of a dirty pew. His cell phone rang and caught him off guard, but he was pleased when he realized who the call was from. He hurriedly dried his hands, then composed himself before he answered, "Cal's pew washing service."

"I'm closing up. Want some help?"

"And some coffee, please."

Cal heard boot steps behind him. He was confused. He hadn't unlocked the front doors in a couple of weeks. The unexpected visitor took a few more steps into the sanctuary. Cal opted not to turn around, "Hold on a sec. I have company." Cal pulled the phone away from his ear, but for some reason he felt it best not to turn around. "Didn't expect you back so soon. What did she say?"

There was no response. Cal's eyes narrowed. His grip tightened on the phone. His head slowly turned and his eyes focused on a chilling surprise. He slowly placed the phone to his ear, "Call you back."

Betsy became alarmed, "What's going on? You okay?" She quickly moved to the window by the door, but she couldn't see the church, just the top of the new street light beside the driveway.

# RETURN TO FAITH

Cal was face to face with the mysterious Biker, dressed in black, who brought him to Faith months ago. The helmet's dark, mirrored visor was down, and reflected Cal's concerned face.

Mutt casually walked over and sat down beside the Biker's black boot, as if they knew each other. Mutt looked up at Cal.

"Is it time for me to go?"

The Biker remained silent, motionless.

"Are you my Guardian Angel?"

The Biker remained silent, motionless.

"Can I see your face, especially your eyes?"

The Biker's male voice was other-worldly, yet calmed him, "Is it really that important?"

Cal nodded.

With a smooth, deliberate motion, the Biker removed his helmet, and revealed long, flowing dark hair and hypnotic, ice blue eyes. His flawless skin emitted a slight glow. He looked to be in his mid 30's, yet something about his countenance assured he possessed eons of wisdom. His face was a mix of the best traits ever painted on a portrait of Jesus, "I realize you have many questions. All are worthy of consideration, but most are unnecessary at the moment."

"Are you going to restore my memory?"

"That will not serve you well."

"Why did you abandon me at the edge of Faith?"

"It was you who abandoned Me, at the edge of your Faith. I simply led you back to where you could find it, and if you so desired, to return."

The Biker removed his leather gloves and turned his palms up to reveal nasty circular scars on each wrist.

Cal grappled to understand the truth he couldn't deny, "Are you...?"

"You know who I am."

Cal was in awe, yet humbled beyond measure as he slowly nodded, "Should I bow? I'm not sure what to do."

"I need you here. There's much to be done."

Cal looked around the sanctuary, then lifted his hands to his waist, "But I don't remember how to preach."

"That's not important right now. It's your journey back that will prepare you to fulfill your destiny."

"How long will that take?"

Jesus smiled understandingly, "No human is perfect, and all are amazing works in progress. It will take as long as it takes."

"You took so many of my wonderful memories."

Jesus slowly shook his head and almost grinned, "I relieved you of the reasons for hating yourself, and blaming Me."

Vehicle lights illuminated the colorful stained glass windows as it slowed and turned into the lot. Gravels popped and crackled as the vehicle pulled around front.

Jesus smiled warmly, "You're about to get very busy," He promised as He slid His helmet on, then without another word He turned and took a couple of steps toward the closed front doors. Mutt rose from his seated position and walked over, then sat down at Cal's feet. Both focused on Jesus as he took another step away.

Cal looked down at Mutt, "Hey?"

Jesus paused but didn't turn around.

"What about Mutt and Sheena?"

Cal would never see the satisfied smile on Jesus' face, "You're welcome. Take great care of these precious animals. They're very special gifts for you and Tommy. If you allow them to, they will help guide you and Tommy to a number of places you're supposed to arrive."

Mutt looked up at Cal and emitted a sound that to Cal meant, "Trust me."

Cal smiled. From the night they met, deep down he knew Mutt and Sheena were special.

"You're right, Cal," Jesus confirmed, "But I'm only a prayer away when you need Me."

"I do have one more question."

Jesus chuckled, "On that country road, if I would've appeared to you as who I really am, and what I really looked like, even with your loss of memory, in your state of mind, you would've rejected me." Jesus said as he vanished into a brilliant flash of warm, loving light. "That's a glimpse of who I AM."

The brilliant light lingered.

"Thank you, Jesus," Cal finally grasped a glimpse of who he was meant to become, in a place he would've never arrived on his own.

# RETURN TO FAITH

"Welcome back, Cal. I missed you." Jesus' voice sent a warm, loving sensation through Cal.

"I missed you, too. And I'm so sorry."

"No worries. All is FORGIVEN."

Cal was forced to shield his eyes. Then as the light faded, the front doors burst open. Tommy stood in the vestibule. Megan's body trembled in his arms.

"She needs help real bad!" Tommy weakened and wobbled.

"Lay her on the first pew," Cal gently, compassionately placed his hand on Megan's dirty face. He retrieved his cell phone.

Megan turned terrified eyes up to Tommy; she could barely whisper, "He's call'n the cops."

"No, an ambulance," Cal reassured.

"He really don't remember?" Megan tried to grin at Tommy.

"I remember all I need to know," Cal confessed.

The loud motorcycle rumbled outside. A headlight came on. Rocks crunched and crackled as the motorcycle loped away.

Tommy turned to the stained-glass windows. He was confused. "Where'd that motorcycle come from? It wasn't outside when I came in."

Cal grinned as his cell phone rang and he answered, "Hello."

The caller's voice was downtrodden, "It's Todd."

"How'd your call go?"

There was a foreboding moment of silence, "Let's just say that she's not interested in meeting with me."

Cal looked at his watch, "Meet me at the church in two hours." He said as a car pulled up out front, and a door opened but didn't close. Someone ran across the loose gravels, and up the front steps.

Betsy dashed in the front door and paused as Cal and Tommy turned to her. She saw dirty female legs extended from the end of a pew, "Is that Megan?" She ran toward the pew, "Megan! Oh, baby girl, Aunt Bet's here." She said as she collapsed to her knees and hugged the grimy girl she would always love as her own.

Cal knelt beside Megan and placed his hand on her

forehead, "Megan, I feel God has a word for you. It's in the book of Isaiah, Chapter Forty-one, Verse Thirteen: 'For I the Lord thy God will hold thy right hand, saying unto thee, Fear not; I will help thee."

Then Cal rose and placed his right hand on Tommy's shoulder, "And for you, Tommy, also in the book of Isaiah, Chapter Forty, Verse Thirty-One: 'But they that wait upon the Lord shall renew their strength; they shall mount up with wings as eagles: they shall run, and not be weary; and they shall walk, and not be faint."

On that night in the sleepy little town of Faith, where an abandoned and neglected church was saved from a fiery end, the man, who was compelled to save it, realized he was destined to experience an amazing Return To Faith, in that little church beside, "Destiny Way."

*It was the End of a New Beginning.*
*It was the Beginning of the End of Calvin Baxter's war against his God.*
*To New Beginnings That God Ordains!*

# RETURN TO FAITH

## ABOUT THE AUTHOR

Otis Farmer was born on the run, the second son to a military family who had three children in four years. The eldest son was born in the Army hospital at Fort Ord, on Monterey Bay, in California. Otis was born, all the way across the country in the Navy hospital in Portsmouth, Virginia. Then halfway back across country his little sister was born in the Army hospital at Ft. Bliss in El Paso, Texas. Six months later the family was living in Germany for four years.

With travel and new adventures so much a part of and influencing his early life, it was only natural when Otis was age thirteen, God would instill deep in his heart an unquenchable thirst for adventure and a strong desire to write about fantastic journeys which would only be possible in a boundless and very active imagination. As an adult, Otis has always sought out new and challenging adventures: hiking, cycling, scuba diving off the island of Maui, flying a high performance glider, and flying into the crater of Mt. St. Helen in a helicopter, to name a few.

However, his greatest adventures still await, those he has yet to boldly launch, in real life and those still inviting, and luring him into amazing worlds he longs to share with eager readers. The best is yet to come.

In January of 2012, due to the "Dedication" of "Merlyn And The Mortal's Curse," Otis was invited to spend three hours a week at The Arc of High Point, North Carolina, where on Friday mornings he taught art lessons to individuals with Autism, Downs Syndrome and a number of other mental and physical developmental issues. It didn't take long for Otis to realize he was the real student being taught unconditional love by the very individuals he was asked to teach. In January of 2013, Otis helped launch a Monday morning pottery program for the same art students at The Arc, which he also assisted with instructing.

## OTIS FARMER

After a couple of years, Otis reluctantly moved on to pursue a more intense and focused effort toward his own creative endeavors. No price can be placed on the joy, the tremendous satisfaction and sense of accomplishment Otis received in the form of precious smiles and the unique humor he shared with his new friends while they completed each work of art and every piece of pottery. In every class new heights of accomplishment were reached in The Creative Arts Studio at The Arc of High Point, North Carolina. It is impossible to put into words the unmatched joy Otis received every second he spent in the studio with such unique and wonderful individuals.

Each November, Otis attends one of his favorite events of the year, when The Arc of High Point holds its annual art auction at the Theatre Art Galleries in High Point. It is an awesome opportunity to visit his dear friends and their families, as well as meet new artists that have joined the program.

It warms Otis' heart to be greeted with bright eyes, genuine smiles and loving hugs, then eagerly escorted to see his friends' most recent works.

Otis considers time one of mankind's most precious commodities. Some of the most important investments creative people will ever make are those precious moments donated to a worthwhile creative cause. Most rewarding will be the time they immerse themselves in a group of human beings with mental and/or physical restrictions. They will soon discover they have entered an amazing world where they can assist, instruct and encourage pure hearts to explore and express their God given talents.

Recently, Otis has assisted a young disabled filmmaker with a couple of his projects. They have developed and built him a website, and they are working toward establishing him a YouTube channel that will enable him to become a motivational speaker.